"WHAT IF RANDOLPH DIDN'T DUMP THE ORDNANCE?" BROGNOLA ASKED

Brooks swallowed hard. The big Fed guessed the general was thinking back, seeing the time in question in a new, disturbing light.

"If Randolph was lying," he said, "then you damn well better worry about that junta."

"Why's that?"

"Because Nixon wasn't entirely bluffing," Brooks stated. "That plane was packed with more than just cluster bombs."

It was the news Brognola had most feared. And yet he was not completely surprised. After all, when the first B-52s came off the Wichita assembly lines in 1955, during the early tempestuous years of the Cold War, they had been designed for one purpose only—to slip through the Iron Curtain and strike key Russian targets, not with conventional bombs, but nuclear warheads. For all their other uses during the ensuing fifty years, to this day, as during the Vietnam War, the Stratofortresses retained the capacity to carry out their original mission.

"A-bombs," Brognola said. "It was carrying A-bombs."

General Brooks shook his head. "Hydrogen," he said. "That B-52 was carrying hydrogen bombs. Eight of them…"

DON PENDLETON'S

STONY

AMERICA'S ULTRA-COVERT INTELLIGENCE AGENCY

MAN®

ROOTS
OF TERROR

A GOLD EAGLE BOOK FROM

WORLDWIDE®

TORONTO • NEW YORK • LONDON
AMSTERDAM • PARIS • SYDNEY • HAMBURG
STOCKHOLM • ATHENS • TOKYO • MILAN
MADRID • WARSAW • BUDAPEST • AUCKLAND

First edition April 2003

ISBN 0-373-61948-0

ROOTS OF TERROR

Special thanks and acknowledgment to
Ron Renauld for his contribution to this work.

Printed in U.S.A.

ROOTS
OF TERROR

PROLOGUE

Mergui Archipelago, Myanmar

Carrie Lamarck fastened the top button of her blouse as she crouched over the short, lean man dozing at the base of a palm tree tilting over the dying campfire. Up this close, she could see Myint Rahn's chest rise and fall in time with his gentle snoring. Clutched in the guide's hand was a nearly empty fifth of Grand Royal whiskey. There were three more bottles, still full, stashed in the guide's knapsack, which he'd used to cushion his lower back. His other hand rested on the butt of a Wilkinson Arms Sherry Auto Pistol tucked inside his belt. To Carrie the gun looked like a toy, but only a few hours ago she'd seen Rahn use it to kill the wild gibbon they'd just eaten for dinner. She remembered the way the guide had looked back at her and her husband after he'd brought down the monkey, not so much with pride at his marksmanship, but more as a subtle gesture of warning.

Myint Rahn was a low-level conscript of Myanmar's State Peace and Development Council, the military-backed junta that, under various guises, had ruled the country once known as Burma for the past forty years. Rahn had been assigned as the Lamarcks' personal guide back in Kawthoung, and for the past two days he'd stuck closer to Carrie and Eric than their own shadows, all but ruining their honeymoon. It was for their own protection, he'd told them, but they'd wearied of his constant presence and had argued that they wanted some time to themselves. After all, they'd explained, that's why they'd come to Mergui Archipelago, one of the least explored corners of the globe. But their guide had been unsympathetic. If they'd wanted to wander about on their own, he'd told them, they should have gone somewhere else. Here they would need an SPDC-sanctioned guide with them at all times. That Eric claimed his father was the U.S. undersecretary of state didn't interest Rahn. He had his orders. Where they went, he went. That wasn't negotiable.

Carrie and Eric had had enough. While the guide was cleaning the monkey and roasting it on a spit over the campfire, Carrie had slipped some antihistamines into the man's whiskey. She had merely hoped to bring on a deep enough sleep to allow her and Eric to make love without Rahn hovering outside their tent. Apparently she'd misjudged the dose, however, because the man was clearly down for the count. When she waved a hand in front of his face and whispered his name, Rahn continued to slumber peacefully, oblivious to the world around him.

Carrie stole back to the tent, smiling triumphantly.

"He's still out!" she whispered giddily to her husband.

Eric Lamarck, a tall, lanky junior partner at the prestigious Boston law firm Marks, Sandberg and Morgan, emerged tentatively from the tent, like a moth wriggling from its cocoon. Like Carrie, he was still a little tipsy from the wine they'd had with dinner. He eyed Rahn, then glanced out at the gently rippling waters of the Andaman Sea. The sun had plunged below the horizon, leaving behind a clouded sky streaked with brilliant ribbons of color. Below the clouds, poking up from the tranquil waterline, was a scattering of the more than eight hundred islands that made up the archipelago. And of course, Eric could also see, extending away from him, the snaking peninsula of this, the island where they'd pitched camp for the night. Rahn had told the newlyweds they were forbidden to venture past the tip of the peninsula. The man's pronouncement, of course, had only made the Lamarcks more intrigued about what might lie beyond the palm-studded spit.

"Maybe he'll sleep through the night," Carrie ventured.

Eric smiled. "Are you thinking what I'm thinking?"

"Right behind you," his wife whispered with a smile.

The newlyweds quietly rounded up a few things—another bottle of wine, a waterproof camera, some cheese, a bedroll and mosquito netting—then eased their kayak into the surf and climbed aboard. Carrie smiled back at her husband.

"Here goes."

The sun dropped quickly as the couple quietly paddled northward, staying close to the shoreline. In the growing darkness, they speculated about what might lie on the other side of the island. Carrie thought maybe the area was a wildlife refuge; after all, the archipelago was said to be the home of countless endangered species, from rare silver-tip sharks and sea crocodiles to Asiatic black bears and monitor lizards, none of which they had yet seen. Eric, however, reminded his wife that Myanmar authorities had recently agreed to let the Outdoorsman channel film a *Survivor*-type cable series on one of the islands. To him, this seemed a perfect locale.

"Maybe we'll wind up on TV," he joked.

"I hope not." Carrie laughed. "My hair's a mess!"

"I think you look great," Eric told her.

"That's just because you're horny," Carrie teased. She slapped her paddle against the water, splashing her husband. "And we better not wind up on TV or your father will go ballistic. My God, if he knew we came here after all the times he warned us not to."

"Yeah," Eric said, "I'm surprised he didn't run a check on our passports to see if we'd applied for visas here."

"How do you know he didn't?"

Eric laughed. "Because if he knew we were coming here, he would've probably pulled some strings and had us arrested or something. 'For our own good.' I tell you, the guy can't get used to the idea I'm not his little Ricky anymore."

"I guess he has a right to be a little concerned."

"You mean all that Four Eights business?" Eric said as they resumed their rowing. "It's no big deal."

"What does Four Eights stand for anyway?" Carrie asked.

"August 8, 1988. The junta clamped down on some street rally and things kind of got out of hand."

"Like Tiananmen Square?"

"Pretty much, only this was a year before that. Nobody heard about it because the press was blacked out."

Between oar strokes Carrie said, "A lot of people were killed?"

"Yeah, a few thousand," Eric admitted. "But don't worry, it's not going to happen again, especially out here in the middle of nowhere."

"I guess not."

"Besides," Eric reminded her, "August 8 is still a few days off. By then we'll be back in Thailand."

"Okay, okay."

"How'd we get talking about this anyway?" Eric said. "Hell, we're supposed to be celebrating. We finally ditched our chaperon, we've got the night to ourselves, and a few minutes from now we'll be making love in the surf like…"

His voice trailed off as a klieg light suddenly blazed to life along the shoreline, blinding him in its harsh glare.

"What the hell?" Eric stopped rowing and held out a hand to block the light. "Who's there?" he called out.

There was no answer. "Are you with that TV show?" Carrie shouted. "Because if you are—"

Carrie's voice was drowned out by a volley of gunfire that streaked toward the kayak, pocking the water like drops of rain. The wine bottle Carrie was holding shattered in her hands as bullets slammed into her chest.

"Carrie!" Eric leaned forward and grabbed his wife. Blood spilled onto his hands and forearms. His wife stared up at him, but the life was already gone from her eyes.

"No! No!"

More rounds chewed at the water. Above their lethal chatter, Eric heard the sputter of an outboard motor.

They were coming after him.

Eric instinctively dived into the water. Bullets chased after him in the dark water like small, lethal fish. His mind raced in a panic. This couldn't be happening. His father was in the State Department. They couldn't do this!

Eric remained underwater until his lungs began to burn. Rising up to the surface, he saw his wife floating lifelessly in the water alongside the kayak. Only a few yards away, silhouetted by the klieg light, was the motorboat. A man was standing in the cockpit, aiming a rifle in his direction.

"Stop!" Eric stood trembling in the shallow water and put his hands above his head. "There's been a mistake!"

The man in the boat pulled the trigger. Eric's knees gave out as the bullets ripped into him. He slipped back into the water. It felt suddenly cold, colder than anything he'd ever felt before.

CHAPTER ONE

Stony Man Farm, Virginia

As near as it was possible for a grizzled Marine veteran to have a look of boyhood wonder, Buck Greene gaped at his new "toys" like a kid on Christmas morning.

"Man, oh, man!" he told Barbara Price, brushing a speck of dust off one of three new, gleaming antiaircraft turrets that had just been installed on the top floor of Stony Man Farm's Annex building. "Are these great or what?"

"They better be," Price teased. "They gobbled up most of your budget for the next six months."

"Worth every damn penny!" Greene enthused.

"Of course, the hope is we never have to use them."

"Yeah, yeah," Greene replied without taking his eyes off the new guns. "But if the shit ever hits the fan around here again, we'll kick some serious ass, no question."

The turrets were modified National Dynamic Y-25 Frog-Tongue air-defense modules, state-of-the-art armament intended primarily for light armored vehicles. The Marines had more than thirty-such AD-equipped LAVs in the field, and the feedback had been so favorable that Greene, Stony Man Farm's longtime chief of security, had lobbied to have the turrets replace the existing antiaircraft guns, installed years back when the covert agency had expanded its facilities on the 250-acre tract of Shenandoah Valley farmland that served as their long-standing headquarters.

Instead of a vehicular chassis, each of the modules had been anchored to the "attic" floor on tracked swivel mounts outfitted with hydraulic lifts. When the overhead roof panels were retracted, the Frog Tongues could rise an additional thirteen feet in the air, allowing more range for each turret's GAU-121U 25 mm Gatling guns, as well as the eight 3-kilo high-explosive warheads packed into its Stinger launch pods. If the Farm were to come under seige again, the building that housed the Y-25s—so meticulously presented to the outside world as a working lumber mill—would quickly transform itself into the equivalent of a land-bound naval destroyer, a structure whose sole purpose was to wage war with deadly efficiency.

As mission controller, Barbara Price held rein on the Farm's purse strings and, much as she thought antiaircraft upgrades verged on overkill, she knew one couldn't put a price on morale, so ultimately she'd decided that showing Greene and his team of blacksuits a little appreciation was a worthy investment. Seeing the spring in Greene's step as he bounded up into the gunner's post of the nearest Y-25, Price felt reassured that she'd made the right call.

"Eighteen hundred shots a minute out of this baby," Greene called out, thumping the barrel of the Gatling gun. "That's nearly twice the output of our old peashooters."

Price smiled indulgently, brushing a hand through her honey-blond hair. "Just don't use the ceiling for target practice."

"And get fragged when the rounds bounce off the plating?" Greene shook his head. "I don't think so."

"I was kidding, Buck," Price said.

"Oh, right."

A pager vibrated on the waistband of Price's designer jeans, which, like the rest of her outfit, gave her the deliberately misleading appearance of a fashion model lounging between catalog shoots. To the other residents of the valley she was just that—a onetime runway diva who'd tired of the New York fashion scene and found a better life for herself running a farm in the mountains. Nothing, of course, could have been further from the truth. Prior to joining the Farm, Price had been a midlevel intelligence analyst with the National Security Agency.

"Briefing in the Computer Room," she told Greene.

Greene wondered aloud, "I wonder where all hell's broken loose this time."

"BURMA," HAL BROGNOLA told the group assembled before him in the Annex Computer Room. Barbara Price stood beside him.

"Burma?" Phoenix Force team leader David McCarter called out. "Don't you mean Myanmar?"

"Only if you insist," Brognola replied. The Farm's longtime White House liaison was in a grim, combative mood. "Personally I have no interest in kowtowing to these thugs by going along with their name changes. And by that I mean in my book they're still the SLORC, not this new, improved SPDC they decided to start calling themselves."

"SLORC?" asked T. J. Hawkins, the youngest of those assembled for the briefing.

"State LAV and Order Restoration Council," Brognola said, "which is a hell of a lot more on the mark than this notion they're into peace development."

McCarter, a onetime British SAS commando, grinned over his shoulder at the other four men in his unit, who were seated haphazardly near the various other computer stations. "Well, lads," he called out, "I've got a feeling we'll be able to leave the kid gloves at home on this one."

"Fine by me," Hawkins drawled. "Hell, we haven't had

a chance to go hog-wild in what, a good three or four days?"

Rafael Encizo and Calvin James were sitting next to the computer station manned by Stony Man's resident cybernetics wizard, Aaron Kurtzman. Both men grabbed wads of paper from the recycling bin and pelted Hawkins, who grabbed one of the wads and threw it back, accidentally hitting Kurtzman.

"Children, children," the burly computer analyst chided.

"Okay, guys, let's stay on task, shall we?" Brognola waited for the room to quiet, then went on. "Burma or Myanmar, call it what you will, we've got a major situation on our hands there."

"The undersecretary's son," Gary Manning ventured.

"Correct," Brognola said. "As I'm sure you all know, Eric Lamarck and his wife were killed off the coast of Burma a little over twenty-four hours ago, their time. The way the junta there is peddling it, they drugged their guide and went off kayaking on their own, only to run afoul of pirates."

"Pirates?" McCarter scoffed. "Not bloody well likely."

"Well, actually, there have been a number of confirmed attacks out that way the past few months," Barbara Price interrupted. "It's been going on since they opened up the Andaman Sea to tourism. Apparently these bandits score enough off money belts and stolen passports to make it worth their while. They've been known to resort to violence, so this fits their MO."

"But we're not buying it," Manning guessed.

Brognola shook his head. "We think the junta's sending the media on a wild-goose chase to throw off suspicion."

"Not a bad strategy," McCarter said. "Hell, you give Fleet Street a choice between headlines about pirates or dictators, they'll raise the Jolly Roger every time."

"Exactly," Brognola said. "And SLORC's worried

enough about how they're going to deal with any demonstrations that come up with this Four Eights anniversary. The last thing they want is a lot of press clamoring around for a story."

"It's not just demonstrators they're worried about, either," Kurtzman added. "According to our intel, a couple of rebel factions to the north—the Shan and Karen—are banking on SLORC having its hands full with crowd control so they can make a move of their own."

"Maybe that wouldn't be such a bad thing," Manning speculated. "I mean, if SLORC and the rebels get caught up in a brawl, maybe they'll cancel out each other and the NLD can move in when the dust settles." Manning was referring to Burma's National League for Democracy, which had swept the popular vote in a 1990 election, only to have the military regime refuse to relinquish the reins of power. Ever since, the NLD had been driven into hiding, with its main leaders, including Nobel Peace Prize–winner Maw Saung Ku-Syi, placed under arrest or, in many instances, executed.

"What you're forgetting," Brognola reminded Manning, "is that any infighting between SLORC and rebel factions would place fifty million innocent civilians in the cross fire. A worst-case scenario could make the Balkans and Middle East look like sandbox squabbles."

"I'm sure you're right," Manning conceded.

"Getting back to the Lamarcks," James said, "what makes us so sure it was the junta that offed them instead of these pirates?"

"Good question."

Brognola turned to Kurtzman. "Can you throw up a map for me, Bear? Just the archipelago."

Kurtzman, paralyzed from the waist down during an attack on Stony Man Farm, powered his wheelchair back a few yards and punched out a command on his computer keyboard. Across the room was a bank of monitors wired both to the Farm's computers and to a sophisticated network of satellite receptors housed outside in a large silo ostensibly used to store wood chips ground out by the lumber mill. Kurtzman cued up a sat intel photo of Southeast Asia on one of the screens and quickly zoomed in on the sprawl of islands just off the southeastern tip of Myanmar. In lieu of a pointer, Brognola used his unlit cigar to indicate areas he was referring to.

"According to the undersecretary, his son and daughter-in-law were going to spend their honeymoon at a resort on Phuket Bay. He warned them to stay in Thailand, but apparently they went behind his back and booked a kayak tour out of Kawthoung—right here at the end of this peninsula that separates the Andaman Sea from the Gulf of Thailand. They were only cleared to visit this handful of islands, which are apparently known for their coral formations, but our understanding is they bribed their guide to let them stray a few miles north here to Guna Island." Brognola pointed to one of the larger islands. "Even then, they were supposed to stay only on the southernmost beachhead."

"Why's that?" Hawkins called out.

"According to SLORC, some of these pirate gangs use the other side of the island as their base. Which, of course, ties into their account of how the couple was killed." Brognola signaled Kurtzman to cue up another visual, then resumed. "The thing is, we've got sat intel picking up activity in that harbor that has nothing to do with pirates."

Indicating a hazy satellite photo of the northern end of Guna Island, the big Fed pointed out eight barges moored in a rectangular formation in the middle of the harbor.

"Salvage operation?" Rafael Encizo speculated.

Brognola eyed the Cuban American. "How'd you figure that?"

"Been there, done that," replied Encizo, a former maritime investigator. "What you've got there is your basic quandrant layout. You stake out a perimeter, then you send divers down to mow it."

"Mow?"

"You know, you follow a straight line for a set length, then move over a few feet, turn around and make your way back," Encizo explained. "Back and forth, back and forth, till you've searched the whole quadrant."

"Mowed the whole yard," Brognola said.

"By George, he's got it," McCarter joked.

"At any rate," Brognola went on, "judging from the blowups, it's pretty clear this is some kind of military operation." He indicated a grainy image Kurtzman had just cued up on another one of the screens. Armed soldiers could be seen standing guard atop one of the barges. "Tatmadaw," he said, "the junta's armed forces."

"Wait, back up," Hawkins interrupted. "By salvage, are we talking sunken ships?"

"Could be," Brognola said. "There's theories about old transport galleons going down there, but it doesn't seem like the kind of thing they'd bring the military in for."

"Maybe they found Atlantis," Encizo suggested.

"I don't think so," Brognola said. "If you rule out a run-in with pirates, my money says the newlyweds stumbled onto whatever the Tatmadaw's up to and paid the price."

There was a brief murmuring among the men, then James called out, "If we've got the junta killing a pair of American citizens, it gives the President a green light to move in and clean house, doesn't it?"

"It would certainly give us more options," Brognola said. "Of course, SLORC is always ranting about the West meddling in their affairs, so we don't want to play into that, especially if we can't disprove this piracy angle."

"Here come the kid gloves again," Hawkins groused.

Brognola shrugged. "What can I say? Sometimes you get to come in with a sledgehammer, other times you have to use a little finesse…at least for starters."

"Finesse is for diplomats," Hawkins countered.

Brognola smiled wanly. "Let me ask you something, T.J. How many times have you gone out on assignment as part of Phoenix Force?"

"I dunno. A couple dozen?"

"Close enough. And of those couple dozen, how many times have you come back without having fired a shot, put your life on the line or, to use your fine vernacular, 'kicked some ass'?"

"Okay, okay," Hawkins conceded.

"If this was just a recon mission, we wouldn't have gotten the call," Brognola insisted. "Trust me, we're not talking a walk in the park here. I can guarantee that, sure as I'm standing here, neither SLORC nor their military will be laying out the red carpet for you."

"And if they do," Kurtzman piped in ominously, "the carpet's likely to be red from somebody's blood."

"Got it," Hawkins said.

"When do we leave?" McCarter asked.

"The crew's prepping the Lockheed as we speak. We're short on pilots at the moment, so you're in the driver's seat, David, if that's all right with you."

"Not a problem," McCarter said. "Always nice to take one of the birds up now and then."

"Are we going it alone?" Manning said.

"Yes and no," the head Fed responded. "Striker's still on assignment in Europe, so I don't see him cutting away to lend a hand." Striker was longtime covert operative Mack Bolan, who'd not only helped found Stony Man but had also handpicked most of the commandos that made up Phoenix Force and its stateside counterpart, Able Team. For a time Bolan had routinely fought alongside both groups, but of late he'd reverted to his infamous lone-wolf mode. It'd been weeks since he'd called in for backup from the Farm on his various handpicked missions.

"Katz and Akira are already out that way, though," Barbara Price interjected, "and a couple of the things they're working on could tie in to this, so we're going to have them fly down. You'll hook up with them in Thailand."

"Decent," Encizo said.

Yakov Katzenelenbogen, Phoenix Force's original team leader, had retired from field duty a few years earlier and now served as the Farm's senior tactical adviser. A week ago, he and Akira Tokaido, one of Kurtzman's ace computer operatives, had flown to Japan looking to bolster the Farm's Pacific Rim intel-gathering resources. However, as Price had just alluded to, the men's attention had been quickly diverted to the situation in Myanmar. Katzenelenbogen had been put on the scent of a missing shipment of LAV-ADs, which ironically had come from the same North American plant as the turret guns presently being installed. The armored vehicles had disappeared while en route to South Korea, and all intel seemed to point a collective finger at China, a longtime supporter of Myanmar's military regime. With Phoenix Force locked into another assignment at the time, it had been left to a U.S. Army Ranger squad—assisted by a Myanmar-born CIA field op Katz had personally recommended—to infiltrate Myanmar and investigate reports that the antiaircraft rigs had been smuggled in from China through the border crossing at Mu-se. Katz had been monitoring the situation when word came in about the killings of Eric and Carrie Lamarck.

Tokaido, on the other hand, had been sniffing around for alternatives to Tokyo for the Farm's comp intel link installation when he'd caught wind of reports that computer hackers had recently made a series of systematic raids on archive files stored at the U-Tapao Royal Thai Navy Airfield, an operating base for the U.S. Strategic Air Command since the early 1960s. The hackers' identities hadn't yet been determined, but there was speculation that the Tatmadaw, which had had several border clashes with Thailand in recent months, might be the culprits.

At this point it was unclear whether either incident had any bearing, direct or otherwise, on the Lamarck killings or the clandestine military activity at Guna Island, but the coincidence factor had been enough to prompt Brognola to have Katz and Tokaido wrap up their business in Tokyo and catch the next plane to Thailand.

"Don't look for them to strap on hardware and march off to battle with you," he advised the commandos, "but they'll be in a position to help out behind the lines."

"What about Able Team?" McCarter asked. "Have they finished teaching some manners to that white-supremacy cult in Denver?"

"As a matter of fact, they have," Brognola said.

"Then how about cutting 'em loose so they can join us?" McCarter suggested. "And spare me the blarney about needing to keep them domestic. With all these angles to cover, we're going to be thinned out in no time."

"You have a point," Brognola said, "but it turns out there've been some developments in Colorado that might tie in to this mess, too. The team's already in the neighborhood, so I've got them following up on it. Once they've checked things out, I'll consider reassignment."

"Well, Able Team might be in Colorado now," Encizo predicted, "but I've got a quarter that says they wind up with us on the road to Mandalay."

CHAPTER TWO

Colorado Springs, Colorado

"They call it Internal Affairs for a reason, pal." Corporal Evan Harris, a twenty-year Air Force veteran, paused to light a Nat Sherman Classic cigarette, then blew smoke in Carl Lyons's face. "This is our business. Our turf."

Harris's "business" concerned the disappearance of fifty-nine-year-old Colonel Christopher Randolph, a long-time chief records officer and data analyst at Pearson AFB who'd left his Colorado Springs condominium two days earlier to buy a pack of cigarettes, never to return. Concern over Randolph's high-level security clearance had prompted AF-IA, under Evan Harris's command, to initiate a full-scale manhunt. The previous afternoon, Randolph's 1998 Lexus had been found abandoned two miles from his condo in a downtown alleyway near an area known as Little Siam. A routine canvas had turned up two eyewitnesses who'd seen a man matching Randolph's description being led into a second vehicle by members of a Thai-based street gang linked to trafficking of heroin and methamphetamines throughout the state. The Asian connection had brought Able Team hustling from Denver to Colorado Springs. Carl Lyons, the Team's field commander, had arranged that afternoon's rendezvous with AF-IA, looking for more specifics. Evan Harris, obviously, wasn't in a sharing mood.

Lyons ignored the smoke Harris had blown in his face and smiled tightly, doing his best to hold his temper in check. He realized Harris wasn't the first anally retentive bureaucrat to get a bug up his ass when told that a special federal task force was stepping in to assist on a sensitive assignment. He, no doubt, wouldn't be the last.

"Orders are orders," Lyons calmly told the other man. "You *do* know what orders are, don't you?"

Harris took another slow drag on his cigarette. He was a ruddy-faced man in his late forties, silvery haired, with mirthless gray eyes. He pursed his chapped lips, sending a trail of smoke rings Lyons's way. "Fuck off."

Lyons's neck reddened. "I tell you what, asshole," he said. "You blow smoke in my face one more time, and you're not going to have any teeth left to clamp around that rolled turd you keep sucking on."

Harris grinned. "Take your best shot."

Lyons weighed the situation. The two men weren't alone. They were seated on the patio outside a coffee shop two blocks from AF-IA headquarters. With Harris was a pair of young, buzz-cut subordinates with holstered pistols tucked inside their snug suit coats. Lyons had brought along his Able Team colleagues. Hermann Schwarz and Rosario Blancanales sat at the next table, nursing foam cups filled with the worst excuse for coffee this side of Aaron Kurtzman's infamous percolator back at the Farm. Schwarz and Blancanales could sense what was going on with their colleague and, if push should come to shove, they were ready to kick some ass. It seemed unlikely the confrontation would escalate to a brawl, however. The coffee shop was located at the edge of a busy downtown strip mall. Other tables were crowded with families, businessmen and a few older couples taking advantage of the seniors' lunch special.

As it turned out, it was someone other than Carl Lyons who took his best shot.

Evan Harris was about to grind out his cigarette on the tabletop when a sniper's bullet bored through his right temple, killing him instantly. Even as Harris was slumping from his seat, Able Team was already in response mode. Lyons dropped to a crouch, kicking his chair out from under him, while Schwarz and Blancanales staked out positions behind the concrete posts holding up the patio overhang. The other two Air Force officers were a little slower, and a second gunshot felled one of them while the other was fumbling for his gun.

Reaching inside his coat for a 9 mm Beretta, Lyons shouted for the terrified citizens to take cover. Some heeded the command, but others, seized with panic, fled, screaming. The squeal of tires tipped off Lyons to a dark 1995 Honda Prelude lurching into traffic from a parking spot across the street. The rear window rolled up as the sniper drew in the barrel of a high-powered Mannlicher hunting rifle. Lyons assumed a firing stance but couldn't get off a shot without jeopardizing bystanders. Lunging past Harris's wounded colleague toward the street, Lyons told Schwarz and Blancanales, "I'm on 'em!"

There was no time to race to the team's rental car, parked tightly between two other vehicles halfway down the block. Instead, Lyons beelined toward a gleaming black Porsche Boxter pulling away from the curb near the coffee shop.

"Out!" he hollered at the driver, a ponytailed man in late thirties with a cell phone pressed to his ear.

The driver stared down the barrel of Lyons's pistol, then calmly shifted into Neutral and told the person he was talking to, "I'll have to get back to you."

"Out!" Lyons repeated.

"I'm trying!" the driver said, opening his door. Lyons helped him along, yanking him out of the car. He dropped his gun in the passenger seat and took over the steering wheel, jamming the Boxter back into gear.

As Lyons sped off in pursuit of the Honda, the Porsche's owner sighed and dialled 911. "That makes twice this month," he muttered to himself. "I'm gonna have to get me a fucking Taurus or something."

AFTER THREE BLOCKS the Honda barreled up the entrance ramp to Interstate I-25. Pedal to the metal, Lyons swerved around traffic and stayed on the other car's trail, slowly closing in. Suddenly the Prelude's rear windshield disintegrated, taken out by the sniper in the back seat, giving him a clearer bead on Lyons. By now he was being whisked along at more than eighty miles per hour, however, and the Honda's stodgy suspension amplified every bump and ripple in the road, thwarting the gunman's aim as much as the constant lane changes. The best he could do was take out one of the Boxter's headlights.

Undaunted, Lyons kept up the pursuit. Glimpsing the dashboard's fuel gauge, he saw that he was needling on empty. If the chase dragged on, he was going to wind up left behind.

"Damn!" Keeping one hand on the wheel, Lyons groped the seat beside him for his pistol. He needed to get as close to the Honda as possible and try to hold the car steady while he got off a shot. Thankfully, if there was any vehicle up to the task, it was the Boxter.

A mile down the highway, traffic began to slow. A blinking sign warned of roadwork up ahead and advised that speeding fines were doubled in construction zones. Lyons ignored the warning and continued to gain on the Honda. The sniper waited for the Porsche to draw closer, then put a hole through Lyons's windshield, missing the man by inches but forcing him to ease off on the accelerator.

"Not bad, asshole," Lyons conceded. "Now it's my turn."

The Honda's driver abruptly cut across two lanes of traffic and passed cars on the right, seeking the nearest exit. Lyons stayed on him, almost rear-ending a panel truck that had slammed on its brakes after being passed by the Honda.

Once off the highway, the Prelude took a hard right, swerving around a makeshift barricade onto an unfinished dirt road leading up to a new housing development nestled in the foothills near the Fort Carson Military Reservation. Lyons stayed close, but the raised wake of dust hampered his visibility. In his favor, the cloud also foiled the sniper's continued attempts to take him out of the chase. Two more shots glanced ineffectually off the sports car's lean chassis.

"Go ahead," Lyons called out. "Piss away your ammo."

As the road wound uphill, the Able Team leader downshifted, redlining the Porsche's tachometer and spitting gravel from beneath its high-performance tires. The fuel gauge lamp flickered on, but Lyons figured he was good for another few miles. Hopefully he could wrap things up by then.

Up ahead, the Honda was having a harder time with the steep grade. Lyons pulled closer. When he saw the sniper taking aim yet again through the shattered rear windshield, he yanked his steering wheel sharply to the left, then the right. The sniper missed him altogether. For the first time, he realized the shooter was Asian. Bringing him in alive for questioning would be nice, but Lyons's foremost concern remained ending the chase before he wound up on the wrong end of one of the sniper's bullets.

"Time for a little Ben-Hur," Lyons murmured.

Once alongside the other vehicle, he veered sharply again, clipping the Honda's rear quarter panel. The other driver panicked and hit the brakes, throwing his car into a skid. As Lyons sped past, the Honda fishtailed, then swerved off the road, coming to a sudden stop as it slammed headlong into a twelve-foot length of concrete sewer pipe.

Lyons brought the Porsche to a stop in the middle of the road and scrambled out, gun in hand. The Honda's horn was blaring. Backtracking, he saw that the Prelude's air bags had failed to deploy. The driver had been flung halfway through the windshield, his face turned into a mangled pulp of blood and ragged flesh. His deadweight lay on the steering wheel, sounding the horn. Beside him, the sniper had toppled into the front seat and lay at a twisted angle, his neck broken. There was no one else in the vehicle.

Lyons took a closer look at the men. As near as he could tell, the driver was Asian, too. On his left forearm was an elaborately sketched tattoo—a reptilian figure with golden scales and teeth as sharp as stilettos. Flames spewed from its mouth and smoke curled from its flared nostrils. The tattoo, however, showed more signs of life than its owner. Lyons checked the man's wrist and was hardly surprised to find no pulse.

"Exit the Dragon," he murmured.

CHAPTER THREE

Insein Prison, Yangon, Myanmar

"Welcome, General."

Lost in thought, it took Bien Phyr a moment to realize the guard was talking to him. The thirty-five-year-old ex-fighter pilot fought back a smile and returned the guard's salute. As his military jeep passed through the moonlit checkpoint and entered Insein Prison, Bien Phyr touched the new, gleaming, gold-plated star on his freshly starched collar. General Phyr. Not bad for a onetime leg breaker for Bangkok loan sharks. Of course, that was years earlier, before he'd risen through the ranks of the Gold Dragons and then enlisted as part of the gang's plan to infiltrate the Myanmar military. Now, through hard work and a few breaks, Phyr was the Dragons' highest-ranked contact within the infamous Tatmadaw.

General Phyr. He liked the sound of it. It was something he could get used to. But not too used to; after all, there was room on his collar for more stars. From here, he would move on to Brigadier General Phyr, then Senior General Phyr, then… Who knew, maybe the head of the entire military, which would make him, in effect, leader of all Myanmar. With the Gold Dragons in his pocket, as well, there was no telling what he could accomplish.

But first things first.

For now, Phyr needed to prove he was deserving of his most recent promotion, which had come about as a result of his computer hacking as a member of the junta's intelligence division. It was Phyr who'd painstakingly roamed cyberspace for the better part of three months, first accessing and then piecing together from various sources the classified information that had prompted the top secret salvage operation in Mergui Archipelago. Although there were concerns about the killing of the American couple that had stumbled onto that venture, Phyr felt confident that the incident could be successfully blamed on emboldened acts by local pirates.

What was left for him now was to show the junta that his years at the computer hadn't softened him; that he still had the fortitude and brutish audacity of his days as a gang enforcer: that he could be more effective—and ruthless—in his new position than his predecessor, General Huevr, whose failings had led to reassignment and the ignominious task of supervising chain gangs laying oil pipeline in the north country while Karen rebels buzzed around them like gnats. If he wasn't killed by guerrillas, the odds were Huevr, like most of the prisoners, would catch dysentery or typhoid and die miles from the nearest hospital. Phyr had no plans to court so grim a fate. For him, laying pipe was something to be done with virgin teenage girls before they were shipped across the border for further ravaging at the Thai bordellos on Patpong Road.

The jeep carried General Phyr past the two brick walls surrounding Insein, the largest—and most notorious—of Myanmar's thirty-six prisons. Located north of the capital, between the Hlaing River and Ywama Railway Station, Insein was an overcrowded caldron of torture and abuse, most of it directed toward political prisoners. As Phyr well knew, there was little, if any, hope of escape from the facility. Not that some hadn't tried. But those few who'd managed to clear the barbed wire topping the inner prison walls had been gunned down by armed snipers stationed in air-conditioned towers that ringed the periphery. Early in his enlistment, before his stint as a fighter pilot, Bien Phyr had been one such sniper, and he could still recall the strange, almost peaceful looks on the faces of those he'd gunned down attempting to scale the prison walls. They'd been put out of their misery quickly, and their deaths usually earned them the admiration of the other political prisoners, who for some reason viewed failed escapes as some noble form of martyrdom rather than acts of cowardice and stupidity. But that was the dissidents for you, Phyr thought, mis-guided to the end.

The jeep finally pulled to a stop before the prison's main entrance. Phyr climbed out of the vehicle and, flanked on either side by an armed guard, passed through the three thick doors leading to the warden's station. Chief Warden Zaw Boesan was waiting for him. Boesan—whose brother-in-law, ailing Senior General Khin Wun, effectively ran the country as head of the Tatmadaw—was an older man, fat and disheveled, with a few long strands of graying hair combed across his balding head. He'd been warden back during Bien Phyr's tour of duty at the prison, but he seemed neither impressed nor bothered by the fact that one of his subordinates now outranked him. He greeted Phyr with a perfunctory nod, then resumed prodding his molars with a toothpick, trying to dislodge a scrap of steak.

"Here to rattle the cages, General?" Boesan asked.

"If that's what it takes," Phyr replied curtly. "Unless, of course, you have some news for me."

Boesan shrugged. "No one's talking…unless you count the complaints about our lack of hospitality."

"I'm not amused," Phyr responded. "We are down to five days until the anniversary of Four Eights."

"I realize that," Boesan said. "I can read a calendar."

In truth, of course, the anniversary wasn't likely to be found printed on any calendar in Myanmar, as the last thing the regime wanted was for the people to recall, much less observe the occasion. It was no secret, however, that NLD sympathizers planned to carry out just such observances. Like the rest of the Tatmadaw and SPDC hierarchy, Phyr was intent on suppressing any dissent, preferably before the Eighth came to pass, so that they could remain focused on the greater threat posed by Karen and Shan rebels to the north. The military was on high alert, with all leaves and furloughs suspended through the end of the month. Further, spies were out in full force throughout the country, trying to intercept the word on the street as to the nature of any planned demonstrations. While these measures were being taken, General Phyr had come to Insein to deal directly with the NLD's imprisoned leaders, who were, he felt, the key to nipping any civil unrest in the bud.

"Surely Ku-Syi and the others know what their underlings are up to," Phyr insisted. "Times, locations, who will be speaking…we need details."

"Ku-Syi and the others have been incarcerated here for months," Boesan reminded the general. "How do you expect them to know what their people on the outside are up to?"

"I'm sure they have their ways," Phyr said.

"You give them too much credit. I run a tight ship here, as you remember. We screen all mail, coming and going. There is no visitation for political prisoners, no access to outsiders. They couldn't tell you anything of what's going on outside these walls even if they wanted to."

"Perhaps we should give them some outside access," Phyr suggested. "Let them speak to their sorry minions."

Boesan frowned. "You can't be serious."

"I'm thinking of a broadcast message. We can have Ku-

Syi and her leaders go on camera and tell their followers to forego any demonstrations."

Boesan flicked away his toothpick. He laughed mockingly. "What a brilliant plan! Why didn't I think of it?"

"A good question," Phyr retorted.

"I was being sarcastic," Boesan told Phyr. "I *have* thought of such a plan. I've tried to get these fools to go along, but they won't hear of it. They refuse to cooperate."

"Perhaps you need to be a little more insistent."

Boesan sighed. "You were always so full of yourself, Bien Phyr, even as a young recruit."

"It's called confidence."

"If you say so." The warden made a grandiose, sweeping gesture toward the doorway. "Be my guest, General," he said. "Ku-Syi's aides are down the hall, in the dog cells. See if you can bend their will with that supreme confidence of yours."

Phyr ignored the contempt in the warden's voice. "What of Ku-Syi herself?" he asked calmly.

Boesan shrugged. "We have her in one of the house units. She is being self-righteous and uncooperative as always. Ask her anything and she responds with slogans. 'Remember the Four Eights.' 'Reconvene Parliament.' 'Honor the will of the electorate.' The usual blather."

Phyr grinned savagely at his former superior. "I think tonight Maw Saung Ku-Syi will sing a different tune."

THEY CALLED THEM the dog cells because, years ago, the small enclosures had been used as kennels for the prison's German shepherds and rottweilers. But in 1988, the same year as the military crackdown on public discord, there had been an uprising at Insein. Inmates, enraged at mistreatment and a diet that consisted of little more than fish paste and water, had gone on a rampage. By the time order had been restored, the dogs had all been killed; some had been eaten.

There had been reforms, but they were not long lasting. Zaw Boesan had been brought in as new chief warden, and Insein soon reclaimed its unsavory reputation. Boesan hadn't bothered reintroducing dogs to the prison. Instead, he'd set aside the cells—less than half the size of those housing hardened criminals—for the incarceration of political prisoners.

Soe Paing was one such prisoner. A fifty-five-year-old university professor with two grown children, his crime had been meeting with students outside class to discuss the Four Eights massacres, as well as SLORC's refusal to honor the 1990 elections that would have spelled democracy for the long-oppressed country. Branded a seditionist, Paing had been sentenced to thirty years. This was his fifth year at Insein, and it showed. Thin, stooped, his frail body scarred from constant beatings, Paing looked at first glimpse as if he were teetering at death's door. But his dark, gleaming eyes told another story. They were eyes filled with strength and cunning, patience and resolve—the resolve of a man who'd vowed to himself that he would survive, not only Insein, but also the brutality of the junta and its military goons. He endured his imprisonment with the thought that, one day, he and children would walk free again among his fellow Burmese. And that same day, he would salute Maw Saung Ku-Syi as she claimed her due as the nation's rightfully elected leader.

Such were Paing's thoughts as he and six other of his fellow prisoners began their second hour of squatting on their haunches, hands placed above their heads, in the squalid hall outside their cramped cells. They'd been rousted from sleep and ordered to assume their positions by a handful of guards who, as was customary, refused to give a reason for the exercise. Paing knew an explanation would be eventually forthcoming. The guards might wait until one of them keeled over, either from exhaustion or leg cramps, or until they tired of having to stand watch. Then would come the usual rhetoric about how the junta wouldn't tolerate disloyalty, how the prisoners were fools to think their high-minded ways would have any influence on the other prisoners, much less anyone outside the cell walls. Perhaps someone would be singled out for a beating, either with a rubber hose or thick length of bamboo, but ultimately the guards would have no choice but to send the men back to their cells, frustrated that they'd failed, once again, to break their spirit.

The guards were taunting Paing and the others when the door at the end of the hall swung open. In walked two soldiers, followed by a lean, stern-faced man in a crisply pressed uniform. Paing had never seen the officer before. He noticed the star on the man's collar. A general. So this was merely a late-night inspection, a little performance for the Tatmadaw brass, showing them that the political prisoners of Insein were being properly abused.

"Good evening, gentlemen," General Bien Phyr called out, offering a smile that held no trace of warmth. "I can see that you are busy, so I will make this quick and simple. I'm looking for a volunteer. A man who would like his freedom."

"At what cost?"

Paing glanced to his right. The prisoner who had responded, U Hla Pyin, was one of Ku-Syi's top advisers and easily the most respected of the political inmates. He stared at the general with a look of calm contempt.

"You need only help us to prevent any civil disruption on the anniversary of the Four Eights," Phyr explained. "A simple speech to the masses, renouncing the NLD and calling off any plans for demonstrations, here in Yangon and elsewhere in the country. Help us keep the peace and you can walk out of here a free man."

U Hla Pyin glared at the general. "As long as the Tatmadaw and SPDC hold power, there is no such thing as a free man in this country."

Phyr said nothing. Still smiling, he strode past Soe Paing and hovered next to U Hla Pyin. Then, without warning, he calmly unholstered a Glock G-36 pistol, pressed the barrel to the prisoner's head and pulled the trigger. A .45-caliber slug ripped through Pyin's skull and lodged in the thigh of the man crouched next to him. As Maw crumpled lifelessly to the floor, Phyr nonchalantly wiped the Glock's barrel on the leg of his pants, then slid it back into his holster.

Stunned, Paing watched the general step over the body of U Hla Pyin and approach the wounded man, who'd fallen on his side, clutching at his bleeding leg. With the deliberateness of a soccer player taking a shot on goal, Phyr forcefully laid into the prisoner's head with the steel-reinforced toe of his combat boot. The prisoner's neck snapped under the force of the blow. He sprawled limply across the floor, blood seeping from his shattered nose and mouth.

Phyr looked over the remaining prisoners. "Now, then," he said, "let me ask you again. Do I have a volunteer?"

Soe Paing slowly drew in a deep breath and forced himself to look away from his fallen comrades. He blinked a few times to hold back the tears of rage welling in his eyes. His body trembled, but he did his best to maintain his crouched stance. Staring straight ahead, he tried to clear his mind of the horrific exhibition he'd just witnessed. He knew, however, that the images—like those dating back to the brutalities of the Four Eights—would never leave his mind.

Behind Soe Paing, there was a faint murmuring among the other prisoners. But no one spoke up. No one volunteered.

"Very impressive," the general intoned, pacing alongside Paing and the others. "Very impressive indeed."

Phyr circled in front of Paing, then dropped to a crouch, meeting the professor's gaze. "It's a bit warm in here, don't you think?" When Paing said nothing, the general patted him gently on the cheek. "What do you say we all go for a little walk? It's warm outside, but the air is fresh. Perhaps it will help you come to your senses. If not, I have another little surprise for you."

CHAPTER FOUR

Bang Thao Beach, Thailand

The Banyan Tree Phuket was by far the most indulgent of the five luxury resorts that had sprung up over the past fifteen years along beachland on Ko Phuket's western coast. Built on the site of a former high-yield tin mine, the Banyan's private, teak-floored bungalows were set apart from one another by dense vegetation, providing guests with far more privacy than the other more traditionally designed hotels. Not surprisingly it was a popular honeymoon resort. As Yakov Katzenelenbogen had learned soon after arriving at the Banyan Tree, the weekend of their stay Eric and Carrie Lamarck had been but one of eleven couples registered as newlyweds. They'd chosen one of the pricier villas, which had its own small pool and private garden. Unfortunately two other sets of guests had made use of the bungalow since the Lamarcks had checked out, and Katz came up empty-handed searching the quarters for clues as to what, if anything, the couple had had in mind for their ill-fated excursion to Guna Island.

Katz had arrived with Akira Tokaido at Bangkok's Don Muang International Airport, 150 miles north of Phuket, earlier in the day. At the terminal, Tokaido had transferred to a military helicopter, and by now Katz assumed the computer wizard was already looking into the reported hacking incidents at the Strategic Air Command's U-Tapao AFB headquarters. Katz, meanwhile, had taken a connecting flight to the Banyan Tree, hoping to retrace the Lamarcks' steps prior to their departure to Kawthoung. While investigatory work would never replace the adrenaline rush the former Mossad agent recalled feeling in the thick of battle, for him it was a nice respite from his usual advise duties back in Virginia. He never brought it up with Hal Brognola or Barbara Price, but there were times when he felt on the verge of going stir-crazy holed up at the Farm playing armchair general. Assignments like this were a tonic for him.

Although his sweep of the honeymoon suite had proved a bust, Katz had better luck when he returned to the main building and met with the hotel concierge, a petite woman in her twenties who spoke fluent English. After presenting credentials identifying him as a special agent with the State Department, Katz had asked if the woman recalled anything out of the ordinary in her dealings with the Lamarcks.

The woman, whose name was Salai, first expressed sadness over the news of the couple's death. Then, with some hesitation, she told Katz, "Right after check-in, they asked me to arrange a ride to Ranong on the day they'd be leaving. I'd seen them bring some scuba gear with them, so I assumed they'd be ferrying on to Kawthoung to go diving. When I mentioned a tour we offered to the archipelago, Mr. Lamarck took me aside and said they wanted their plans kept secret. He said he was concerned that his father not find out they were planning a side trip to Myanmar."

"Did he give a reason?" Katz asked.

Salai shook her head. "He just said it was personal. I didn't want to pry beyond that."

"Of course not." From the briefing papers he'd read on the flight from Tokyo, Katz had gotten the sense of some ongoing animosity between Undersecretary Lamarck and his son. It was only a theory, but Katz suspected Eric's decision to go to Myanmar was as much an act of defiance as anything else. If that was the case, it seemed unlikely he or his wife had had any knowledge of military activity at Guna harbor. More and more, it looked as if Hal Brognola was right about the couple innocently winding up in the wrong place at the wrong time. Still, Katz wanted to follow through on any possible lead.

"Would it be possible for me to talk to the driver who took them to Rangon?" he asked.

"Of course," Salai said. "He has a pickup here in an hour, but he usually comes by early for dinner at the bar."

"That works out perfectly," Katz said. "I'm expecting someone else around then, so I'll just wait in the bar."

"If you'd like," Salai said, "I'll keep an eye open for your guest and send him over when he shows up."

"That would be great," Katz said. "His name is U Pag Ti. He's Burmese, around five foot five—"

"And so handsome that women are always falling all over him."

Katz glanced over his shoulder. The CIA operative had just entered the lobby and was standing directly behind him at the concierge's station. He looked fatigued, but managed a smile as he winked at Salai.

"He's also shameless," Yakov told the woman before offering the man his left hand. Katzenelenbogen had lost most of his right arm a lifetime ago during the Six-Day War. In its place he wore a prosthesis, his manufactured hand concealed by a glove. After exchanging an awkward handshake, the two men excused themselves and headed to the bar.

U Pag Ti was the CIA operative Katz had recommended the Army Rangers take with them on their recon mission near the border at Mu-se. The match-up hadn't panned out, and when Pag Ti had bowed out of the mission at the last minute, Katz had made quick arrangements to have the

Burmese agent flown down to Phuket Bay and brought into the Stony Man fold.

"Rangers weren't your cup of tea, I take it," Katz told Pag Ti after they'd both placed orders for Bell's Scotch whiskey, just one of the shared passions that had forged a fast friendship between the men during their brief association in Tokyo.

Pag Ti shrugged. "Don't get me wrong," he explained quickly. Like the concierge, his English was flawless. "The Rangers are good men, but they want to do everything for themselves. I have better things to do than waste my time playing fifth wheel."

The bartender brought their drinks. Katz paid for them, then chinked his glass against Pag Ti's and told him, "Well, we're damn glad to have you aboard."

"Are you speaking for everyone in your group?" Pag Ti asked warily. "Or just yourself?"

"Granted, our men are like the Rangers when it comes to being stubborn and self-reliant," Katz admitted, "but they're savvy enough to know when a mission needs support. And as far as this one goes, you're hands down the best man for the job."

Katzenelenbogen wasn't exaggerating. If he'd asked Aaron Kurtzman back at the Farm to scan every available database for ideal candidates to round out Phoenix Force's mission in the Mergui Archipelago, the Burmese operative would have been at the top of the short list. Yangon born, Pag Ti had as a child spent countless springs and summers vacationing in the archipelago with his father, an acquisitions official for Kandawgyi Lake's National Aquarium. Straight out of high school, he'd enlisted in the Myanmar militia, serving as part of their naval air force in the Andaman Sea up until the fateful month of August 1988. Then, like many of his naval counterparts, he'd been sent ashore to help put down growing dissent in the streets of his hometown.

On the infamous day of the Four Eights, when ordered to fire on demonstrators, Pag Ti, who'd become increasingly disillusioned by the Tatmadaw's strong-arm tactics, had instead deserted. Shedding his uniform, he'd helped a handful of student dissidents slip past government checkpoints and escape across the Myawaddy border into Thailand. From the refugee camps, he'd made his way to Bangkok, where his background drew the attention of CIA agents monitoring the junta's reign of terror. Recruited soon after, Pag Ti, now thirty-two, had been on the Company payroll for more than thirteen years. He spent most of his time at the Thai refugee camps, interviewing the endless procession of fellow Burmese fleeing SPDC oppression and passing along any worthwhile information to agency superiors in Bangkok. On several occasions, he'd flown back across the border to run interference with Tatmadaw forces giving chase to refugees. With credentials like these, there was no question in Katz's mind but that U Pag Ti could play a key role in helping Phoenix Force try to unearth the secret behind the military activity at Guna Island.

Before they could begin to discuss the mission in detail, Katz's cell phone rang. He excused himself and crossed the room briefly, then returned, slipping the phone back in his pocket.

"Just an update on your Ranger friends," he told Pag Ti. "They're pretty sure the LAVs had passed through Muse."

Pag Ti nodded as he took a sip of his whiskey. "Care of the Chinese?" he asked.

Katz nodded. "We still don't know how they managed it, but along with the LAVs, they stole the cargo container the Y-25s were shipped in. The Rangers have five witnesses claiming they saw the container pass through the border checkpoint this morning on a flatbed 18-wheeler.''

"Bribes," Pag Ti guessed. "So where's the container now?"

"Don't know. So far the Rangers have only traced it as far as Myinykina.''

"That means they transferred it to a barge or something so they could float it down the Irrawaddy," Pag Ti said.

"Bound for Yangon?''

Pag Ti shrugged. "Maybe some of them will wind up there, but I think the Tatmadaw wants the guns to use on the Shan and Karen rebels. If that's the case, at some point down the river, they'll probably put them back on flatbeds and haul them east again.''

"To Manerplaw and Ho Mong?'' Katz guessed.

"There, and maybe near Taunggyi, too. The Shan there are packing SAM-7s, so you have to figure the Tatmadaw want to level the playing field. Especially if the Four Eights demonstrations get out of hand.''

"Do you think that will happen?'' Katz asked.

"Depends on how well and fast the junta can quell things," Pag Ti ventured. "If they can keep things quiet without having to expend manpower, the rebels aren't going to go on the offensive. But if the people come out in droves and refuse to back down, who knows? It'd be like the rebels to make their move when the Tatmadaw has its back turned.''

"So the protestors are in a no-win situation," Katz said. "If they don't protest, they're stuck with the junta. If they do, they could trigger a civil war and wind up even worse off.''

Pag Ti nodded again and stared gloomily into his drink. "Life can be a bitch sometimes.''

CHAPTER FIVE

Nyaung-U, Myanmar

Daw Bodta Paing stood atop the ruins of Kondawgyi Temple, which itself rested upon a mound overlooking a sluggish, moonlit bend in the Irrawaddy River four miles north of Bagan. Through a pair of high-powered binoculars, she stared down at a powered barge making its way downriver. The barge sat low in the brown current, weighed down by its cargo, a large rectangular container the size of a railroad car. Daw Bodta had no idea what was being transported, but it was clearly something important to the military. Six armed soldiers roamed the deck, and she suspected more were posted on the other side of the container. Her guess was that the barge was bound south for Magwe or Pyay, where the Tatmadaw had military bases close to the river.

She was wrong, however.

As Daw Bodta continued to observe the barge, it began to shift course, making its way toward a small jetty near the town of Nyaung-U. On shore, a military jeep rolled to a stop near the end of the docks. Four soldiers piled out of the vehicle. One ignited a flare and waved it like a baton, signaling the barge. The other soldiers stationed themselves near the mooring gear. To Daw Bodta, the implication was clear—the barge would soon be docking, no doubt to unload its cargo.

A chilling wave of paranoia passed through the young woman. Lowering the field glasses, she shuddered. Had they found out about her and the others?

With some difficulty, Daw Bodta moved away from the temple's domelike stupa and made her way down to the ground, using eroded crevices in the brickwork for hand- and footholds. She knew it was blasphemous to desecrate a place of worship—no matter how many centuries it had stood abandoned—but she hoped Buddha would sympathize with her plight and that of her fellow members of the National League for Democracy.

Daw Bodta had left her mountain bike propped against the base of an acacia tree ten yards from the temple. Hiking up her ankle-length *longyi,* she began pedaling eastward. Unlike the vast, level plain upon which nearly two thousand ancient stone monuments rested in nearby Bagan, the terrain here was rugged, slashed by ravines and studded with bare outcroppings. Daw Bodta had been pulling sentry duty for nearly a week now, however, and she'd memorized the landscape. Following a barely discernible path, she pedaled furiously past scattered stands of acacias and other small trees.

In her haste, she failed to spot a small boulder that had tumbled onto the path from a nearby slope. Losing control of the bike, she flew over the handlebars and landed roughly on the hard ground, bruising her shoulder. Tears of pain came to her eyes, but there was no time to dwell on the injury. She had to warn the others. Grimacing, she retrieved her bike from the brush. She was inspecting the frame and tires when she heard a noise off to her right. Someone was moving through the brush toward her. Terrified, she eased the bike back down to the ground and reached for a small .22-caliber handgun tucked behind her in the waistband of her *longyi.* It was a puny weapon, she knew, but it was all she had. Her shoulder throbbed as she aimed in the direction of her unseen pursuer. Her hands trembled around the gun. She'd never fired it before.

After an interminable silence, there was a snapping of twigs in the brush less than ten yards away. In the moonlight, she thought she could see the outline of a figure crouched alongside a bush near where she'd fallen from her bike.

Daw Bodta eased her finger against the trigger of the .22. She was about to fire when someone called out to her.

"Daw Bodta?" he whispered. "Is that you?"

She slowly lowered the gun, gasping with relief. "Aung?"

Soe Paing's eldest son emerged from the brush. Like his sister, he was armed, though with a more potent 9 mm Uzi submachine gun. Like her, too, his *longyi* was emerald-green, a color symbollic among the Burmese as a show of support for liberation from decades of military occupation.

"Did you hurt yourself?" he asked his sister.

"My shoulder," she answered quickly. "What are you doing out here?"

By way of response, Aung signaled behind him. One by one, another six men and two women emerged from the thickets, each carrying provisions in bags slung over their backs.

"They're from Myingyam," Aung told his sister. "They've come to join us."

Daw Bodta greeted the others with a faint smile, then quickly told her brother about the military barge docking at port just north of Nyaung-U. Aung shared her alarm.

"This is not good." He deliberated a moment, then handed Daw Bodta the Uzi, taking in its place the woman's handgun. "Take them to the temple," he told her, "and have everyone prepare to evacuate. If the Tatmadaw have found us out, we'll have a better chance out in the open."

"What about you?" Daw Bodta asked.

Aung took his sister's bike and turned it around, then settled onto the seat. "I'm going to take a closer look."

"Be careful."

"You, too."

Daw Bodta watched her brother pedal back toward Nyaung-U, then stared down at the submachine in her small hands. Was there a safety? She had no idea. She could only hope she wouldn't have to use the weapon.

"Follow me," she told the others.

On foot, the group stole quietly through the foliage. Soon they came to the edge of a cliff. Instead of a drop-off, however, the villagers from Myingyam saw before them the uppermost terrace of another temple—far larger than Kondawgyi—that had been built a thousand years before flush against the precipice. Overgrown with weeds and vegetation, the temple seemed untouched by time, save for the small spire of stupa centered over the main entrance. The stupa had been whitewashed with limestone, a ghostlike contrast to the dark brickwork around it.

"Kyaukgu Umin," Daw Bodta told them. "This is where you'll be staying until the day of the rally."

The daughter of Soe Paing led the group around the periphery of the terrace to a staircase that extended to the base of the ravine. The climb was steep, without a handrail, so they made their way down slowly. On the way a woman beside Daw Bodta asked her, "Are you and your brother with the NLD?"

"Yes," Daw Bodta responded. She explained that their father was one of the party leaders.

"Will he be speaking at the rally?" the other woman asked.

Daw Bodta shook her head sadly. "My father is in Insein." There was no need for further explanation. A sadness welled up inside her. It had been more than five years since her father had been dragged off to prison. She'd sent him letters at first—dozens of them, but there had never been replies. Her brother told her it was a waste of time for her to write, that all mail was routinely burned after being read by prison officials. She continued to write nonetheless, but now she kept the correspondence. If her father was ever released from Insein, she would give him the letters, so that he could have a glimpse at what her life had been like during his imprisonment.

At the base of the temple the new arrivals were met by two young men who quickly escorted them through a large archway leading into the temple. As with most of the other shrines in Bagan and Nyaung-U, Kyaukgu Umin contained a likeness of the Buddha, in this case an image carved in stone depicting him seated on a lotus throne. Other carved reliefs adorned the temple's inner walls, as well as the two massive pillars that rose in the center of the large central chamber.

The villagers weren't alone. Dozens of other NLD loyalists lay sleeping on blankets and bedrolls spread out upon the dirt floor. Other supporters were awake and they stared at the new guests.

"How many of us are there here?" one of the villagers asked as Daw Botha helped her with unload her provisions.

"So far, at least five hundred," Daw Bodta said. "They've been coming in small groups for a week now, so as to not draw attention. Once the main hall fills, there are tunnels behind the pillars that lead back into the hillside. Years ago, the monks here used them for meditation. All in all, we figure we can fit maybe a thousand people in here."

"My cousin said you have people gathering in some of the other temples, too."

Daw Bodta nodded, nursing her shoulder. "Some near the airport at Thamiwhet and Hmyatha, others at some of the more isolated sites in Bagan. Anywhere we can fit people where they can stay out of sight until the day of Four Eights. Then we'll all come out together and rally for freedom."

"Just here in Bagan?"

Daw Bodta shook her head. "We have other groups gathering in other small towns. Ye U, Monywa, Yamethin... Altogether there will be tens of thousands of us."

"Why just small towns?" the other woman asked. "Why not in Yangon or Mandalay?"

"Because the Tatmadaw expects us to show up in the cities, not here. Out here, we will have time to rally before they can respond. Once they're on the way, everyone will scatter. We won't allow another massacre."

"I heard you talking to your brother," the other woman said. "You said something about the military showing up here in Nyaung-U. What if they've discovered your plan?"

"Let's just hope they haven't," Daw Bodta said. "Let's just hope and pray."

THE MILITARY BARGE had already docked at the jetty by the time Aung Paing reached Nyaung-U. Though it was late, a small group of villagers had gathered along the shoreline to watch the unloading. Aung parked his sister's bike behind a market stall, then quickly turned his *longyi* inside out. The inner fabric was more blue than green and would be less likely to draw notice from the soldiers.

Aung joined the villagers and watched as soldiers extended a ramp from the docks up to the barge's loading platform. Once the ramp was in place, other soldiers unlocked the cargo container's side door, which creaked open on steel rollers, and several men slipped inside. On shore, there was a murmuring among the villagers. Some thought perhaps the military was bringing in equipment to repair the huge pumps that provided Nyaung-U and Bagan with water. The others were more skeptical, however, suspecting that the Tatmadaw had come, not to help out the villagers, but rather to bring them more grief, be it through yet another supply of propaganda leaflets or new metal detectors to replace the broken ones at the bus terminal.

Aung Paing, of course, feared an even more sinister delivery, and when he heard the amplified roar of engines snarling to life inside the container, his heart sank. If the Tatmadaw had brought jeeps or some other all-terrain vehicles to Nyaung-U, it could mean only one thing: that they'd learned of the NLD's plans and had come to hunt down the demonstrators.

Aung's apprehension turned to despair when he saw the first vehicle emerge and begin to descend the ramp. It looked something like a tank, only smaller, and instead of cleats, it rolled along on eight massive tires. The villagers around him gasped as a second, identical vehicle appeared, followed by yet another.

"They've come to kill us all!" one of them groaned miserably, voicing Aung Paing's worst fears.

However, by the time a fourth vehicle had joined the procession down the docks, the young man's panic began to subside. However formidable looking, these mobile units were a poor choice for tackling the ravines where most of the NLD followers were gathering; they seemed too large and unwieldy. Even more encouraging—at least in terms of the young man's most immediate concerns—mounted on the rear of each vehicle was a bulky, rectangular launch system. Surface-to-air missiles, Aung thought. He knew that the Shan rebels had similar weapons in their arsenal, and from what he'd read, they were intended primarily as a defense against air strikes. True, they could probably be fired at ground targets, too, but for all its faults, the Tatmadaw had been steadfast over the years in refusing to interfere with the nation's worship of Buddha. It seemed unlikely they would resort to blasting away at shrines and temples when there were other, less destructive ways to dispose of the dissidents cloistering inside the ancient buildings.

Any of Aung Paing's last remaining fears were dispelled when he heard the drone of the LAVs answered by the even louder engines of a large freight truck lumbering into view on the access road that lead to the docks. Once the truck reached the jetty, the armored vehicles slowly circled behind it and idled in place. The truck's driver left his cab and, with the help of the soldiers, threw open its rear doors and lowered a ramp to the ground. Clearly the LAVs were going to be loaded and shipped elsewhere.

They don't know, Aung Paing thought to himself. The preparations for the rally could continue.

One after the other, the LAVs were guided up the ramp into the rear of the truck. By the time three of the vehicles had been loaded, however, Aung Paing saw that the truck was full. The soldiers moved around the fourth LAV, drawing up the ramp and closing the truck's doors. The driver got back in the cab. Shifting into gear, he pulled away from the parking lot, leaving behind the last armored vehicle. The young man's spirits sank yet again and he was filled once more with paranoia.

A number of the other villagers were equally disheartened. Some were even so bold as to call out to the soldiers, demanding to know why one of the LAVs had been left behind. Others picked up the cry, and soon the crowd began to swell, encircling the vehicle and the soldiers stationed around it. The officer in charge shouted for everyone to disperse, but he was drowned out by the chanting. Aung Paing was surprised by the crowd's sudden furor, but alarmed, as well. He watched on with dread as the soldiers, equally taken aback by the spontaneous demonstration, unslung their assault rifles and formed a human barrier around the Y-25. Inside the vehicle itself, an unseen gunner slowly pivoted the turret gun, giving the demonstrators a glimpse down its deadly barrel. It seemed clear to Aung Paing that any further provocation by the crowd would trigger a bloodbath.

Several tense seconds passed, then the officer in charge pointed his handgun in the air and fired a single shot. It served its purpose, giving the crowd immediate pause. As their chanting flagged, the officer shouted that the villagers were rushing to false conclusions. The Tatmadaw had no intention of using the LAV against the citizens of Nyaung-U, he insisted. Rather, it had been brought here to help defend the local airfield, as well as the temples of Bagan, against rumored air strikes by Shan and Karen rebels.

"The rebels are the warmongers, not the Tatmadaw," he shouted to the demonstrators. "They are the ones you should fear, not us. We are here to keep the peace."

Aung Paing stared past the officer at the armed soldiers, who looked like anything but peacekeepers. They still seemed more than willing to empty their rifles into the crowd.

A handful of demonstrators began to heckle and taunt the soldiers, but the others refused to join in. Aung Paing wasn't sure whether they believed the officer's assurances or had merely shaken off the hysteria that had gripped them only moments before. In any event, when the officer reiterated that the villagers' fears were unfounded and that they should disperse, the gathering quickly broke up. Following the villagers back toward town, Aung Paing listened sympathetically to the grumbling of those who felt the crowd had backed down too easily, but he was secretly relieved. If the incident had gotten out of hand, not only would there have been a massacre, but also more troops would likely have been brought in, quashing any hopes of carrying out the forthcoming Four Eights observance rally in Bagan.

And the rally, far more than some futile demonstration, would offer a better chance of leading the way to freedom for the citizens of Nyaung-U and all of Burma.

Once he reached his bicycle, Aung Paing pedaled to the town's central market square. The stalls were all closed for the night. He stopped alongside a large fountain with a view of the bus terminal, a modest one-story structure located at the edge of the market. One of Aung Paing's contacts in Yangon had sent word earlier that he would be arriving with five demonstrators on the last bus.

The bus arrived ten minutes later. More than two dozen passengers disembarked. Most were tourists bound for local hotels. Four men and two women, however, discreetly made their way across the market square to the fountain. Aung Paing greeted his colleague, a young man named Mi-Che Dwe, then told the others that as a precaution they would split into two groups and approach the distant temple from different directions.

Mi-Che Dwe led a man and a woman back across the plaza. Aung Paing, meanwhile, directed his charges—a young couple and a man in his early twenties wearing the flowing orange robes of a monk—to follow him the other way. At the edge of the market square, he flagged down a passing horse cart.

While Paing tethered his sister's bike to the back of the cart, the monk waited for the couple to board, then took a seat on a bench directly across from them. In Burma, monk-hood wasn't always a lifelong commitment; as a rite of passage young men would don the robes and lifestyle for several months, then return to their normal lives. For the noviate in the cart, it appeared his time of service couldn't end soon enough. He was perspiring heavily, clearly uncomfortable with the way the billowy fabric of his robe clung to his skin.

"You should have done like my husband and performed your service during the cooler months," the woman teased.

"Perhaps so," the monk replied.

As the woman drew her husband's attention to one of the nearby temples, the monk reached down to loosen his sandals. His sleeve caught on the handrail and rode up his forearm, revealing a fist-sized tattoo of a dragon's head. Quickly the man pulled the sleeve back down, glancing around to see if the others had noticed. Aung Paing was just then climbing up into the seating area.

"Is everything all right?" he asked.

The monk nodded. "Fine," he said. "I'm just a little stiff from the bus ride."

"Well, be prepared," Aung joked as he took a seat next to the monk. "You'll find the bus was comfortable compared to this horse cart. Fortunately, it's only a short ride."

The other man smiled. "Thank Buddha for small favors."

The driver climbed up to his perch and jostled the reins. As the horse began to clop away from the square, Aung Paing leaned close to the monk and asked, "Are you looking forward to the rally?"

"Yes," said the man with the Gold Dragon tattoo. "I'm anxious to hear all the details."

CHAPTER SIX

Colorado Springs, Colorado

"Apparently they were part of this gang called the Gold Dragons," Blancanales told Lyons after clicking off his cell phone.

Two hours had passed since the shooting of AF-IA Agent Evan Harris. After dealing with the police, Blancanales and Schwarz had returned to their hotel room at a Holiday Inn three miles from Pearson Air Force Base. Lyons had shown up a short while later. Stony Man pilot Jack Grimaldi, who'd flown Able Team to Colorado Springs from Denver, had slept through their arrival and could still be heard snoring off in one of the bedrooms.

Blancanales passed along the rest of the information Aaron Kurtzman had given him on the band of renegades who'd shot Harris and led Lyons on the protracted car chase.

"Their roots go back to Thailand," Blancanales explained, "but they have a lot of Myanmar in their ranks, too, mostly refugees looking for a quick hand up in the world. Back in Asia they're into loan sharking, gambling and prostitution, but they've gone global in terms of running smack and speed out of the Golden Triangle. They ship to the States by way of L.A., then parcel out to distribution spots along the coast and a few places inland."

"Like Colorado," Lyons said.

"Exactly."

"Okay, that all makes sense to me," Lyons replied. "Where it gets fuzzy for me is when these punks suddenly kidnap an AFB officer, then whack the lead guy looking into the kidnapping. I mean, if they're strictly a drug outfit here in the States, it'd be the DEA they'd have a bone to pick with, not the Air Force."

"Maybe they're worried we'll start bombing their poppy fields again," Schwarz called out from across the room, where he was crouched over a laptop.

"Actually, that's not a bad idea," Blancanales said, "but I don't think this is about drugs."

"You never know," Lyons countered. "Maybe somebody inside the Air Force or SAC was diverting planes to the Golden Triangle for drug shipments."

"Like all that drugs-for-arms Contras shit the CIA pulled in the eighties?" Schwarz said.

"Yeah," Lyons told him. "Maybe Harris was close to blowing the lid off something. It sure as hell would explain his being so goddamn tight-lipped. He could've been worried we were gonna swoop in and steal the limelight."

"If that's the case, then where does this Randolph guy fit in?" Blancanales countered.

Lyons shrugged. "How should I know? There hasn't been a ransom note, though, so you gotta figure these Dragon guys wanted him for information."

"The guy's a desk jockey, Carl," Blancanales said. "He shuffles papers for a living."

"Yeah, but given his security clearance, you can bet your ass some of those papers he shuffled were classified," Lyons reasoned. "Come on, Pol, you've run a business before. You know how it goes. The clerks and secretaries know more about what's going on than the guys with the nameplates."

"Okay, you got me there," Blancanales conceded. "Any way we stack it up, though, the bottom line is Randolph's still missing. And if the Gold Dragons are still holding him, I'd hate to be in his shoes once they find out it cost them two of their guys to take out Evan Harris."

"In other words, we better find the poor shit, but quick," Lyons said. "Any ideas? Other than going door-to-door through Little Siam?"

"Actually," Gadgets called out, glancing up from his computer, "we might have better luck in Durango."

"Durango?" Lyons was puzzled. "That's clear across the state."

"Six hours by car," Schwarz reported. "I ran a plates check on that Honda you chased down after the shooting. It's down for a couple parking tickets in Durango. First was the day before Randolph disappeared. Second was the day after."

"Ladies and gentlemen," Lyons said, clapping his hands, "the original Inspector Gadgets!"

"Hell, I'm not even finished," Gadgets said. He toggled his mouse, switching files on the laptop's screen. "The Honda's originally from California. It was stolen last week from a neighborhood two blocks from the harbor at Long Beach. If the Gold Dragons are running their smack and speed out of L.A., they've gotta have some kind of operation down there."

"Now we're getting somewhere." Lyons resumed his pacing, thinking out loud. "So, from the sounds of it, these guys must've drove out here from Durango, nabbed Randolph and then hauled him back, probably for interrogation. Whatever he coughed up, it sent them back here gunning for Harris."

The men were interrupted as Grimaldi wandered out of the bedroom, yawning. "What's with all the racket?"

"Fire that bird back up, flyboy!" Lyons told him. "We need a lift to Durango."

CHAPTER SEVEN

Insein Prison, Yangon, Myanmar

To keep their sanity, those enduring long terms of captivity often resort to various rituals. Most common is visualization, eyes closed, a prisoner will conjure up a better world than the one he or she has become trapped in. Maw Saung Ku-Syi was no different. Thirteen weeks into this, her most recent incarceration at the hands of the SPDC regime, the woman's moments of private fantasy were becoming more frequent. Usually she looked ahead to the future, envisioning her country on the road to recovery from years of military domination. She saw the universities reopened and filled with students eager to gain the knowledge and skills that would allow them to help Burma—she never thought of her land as Myanmar—modernize without losing the purity of its ancestral heritage. She saw a healthy economy, freed of graft and corruption, where any of the land's seventy million citizens could have the means by which to pursue their dreams. She saw an end to the ravages of disease and a flourishing of the arts. She saw the entire country opened up, not only to tourists, but also to the international press, giving the world a chance to see firsthand the wonder of the land and its people.

But there were also times, like this night, when the future seemed too bleak, too painful to contemplate, and at these times Ku-Syi's thoughts would instead take her back in time, to her childhood, before the coming of the regime, when both she and Burma still enjoyed a sense of innocence. She would recall playing with her father, one of the country's most beloved and respected leaders, the man who, before his death, had led the quest for a return to the short-lived independence Burma had experienced shortly after World War II.

In these moments of pained recollection, Ku-Syi would also recall the voice of her mother and the lilac smell of her freshly washed hair as they sat, side by side, patiently hammering gold into thin-layered sheets that villagers would then use to adorn the countless Buddhas enshrined throughout her hometown of Mandalay. One sheet of gold was a thing of beauty unto itself, Vahd Ku-Syi often told her daughter, but put together many sheets and you can beautify an entire statue. The simple allegory echoed her husband's democratic yearnings, but then that was her way, and from her mother Maw Saung Ku-Syi had learned that people could be swayed as much by polite reason as by inflamed rhetoric.

For all the pleasure they brought, such memories came at a price, for they came coupled with the painful recollection of her parents' death before a firing squad after they'd been charged with "treason" in the aftermath of the country's 1962 military coup. To this day, the mere pop of a firecracker or backfiring of an automobile would be enough to make Ku-Syi's pulse race. But if, by some miracle, she could suppress her sense of horror and focus wholly on those happier times before the coup, Ku-Syi would find herself transported to a warm, loving place where, however tenuously, she was at peace. In this relaxed state, sleep would finally come to her.

Maw Saung Ku-Syi had just managed to drift off into one such restful slumber when she was awakened by a strange sound just outside the door of her one-room "cottage" adjacent to the main facilities at Insein prison. Startled, Ku-Syi, a tall, thin, elegant-looking woman in her late fifties, sat upright on her cot. Though it was the middle of the night, a harsh, bright light forced its way through the flimsy shades of her front window, illuminating her Spartan quarters. Besides the cot, there was a rough-hewn table, a rickety stool and a bedpan. Compared to most of the other cells, these were lavish accommodations. Not that Ku-Syi had asked for special treatment. When taken into custody, she'd asked to be placed in the dog cells with the other political prisoners. The warden had refused, however, no doubt hoping that being isolated from her inner circle might more readily weaken her will to stand up to the SPDC.

"What is it?" she called out.

There was no answer. Moments later, however, there was a knock on her door, loud and persistent.

Ku-Syi hurriedly pulled on her drab prison garb. Denied a clock, she had no idea of the time other than the fact that several hours had passed since lights-out. Was it midnight? Later? She couldn't be sure. Whatever the case, she'd never been summoned at such a time. And, save for during a few ill-fated jail breaks, she'd never seen the tower searchlights trained on the grounds outside her cell. What was the reason for it?

When she opened the door, Ku-Syi was momentarily blinded by the searchlights. She waited for her eyes to adjust, then looked around, puzzled. No one was standing outside the doorway. She sensed a presence at her feet, however, and glanced down. An involuntary gasp leaped from her throat and she took a step backward, recoiling in horror.

Lying in a crumpled heap on the wooden planks that served as her front stoop, Ku-Syi saw U Hla Pyin. Half of his face obliterated by gunfire, her longtime friend and colleague had been haphazardly dumped at her doorstep as if he were no more than a bundle of unwashed laundry.

"Greetings, Maw Saung Ku-Syi."

The voice, coming from somewhere out in the brightly lit clearing beyond her cell steps, was unfamiliar. Ku-Syi, trembling, tore her gaze from the body of U Hla Pyin. When she looked out into the clearing, her heart, already akilter, pounded even more frantically inside her chest. Before her, lined up against the taller of the prison's two walls, were four more of her most loyal followers—Kyaw Myo Oo, Zaw Myat, Soe Paing and Annuw Win. Standing twenty yards away from them, rifles raised in firing position, were seven prison guards. Beside them stood the man who'd addressed her. She didn't recognize him, but judging from his uniform she took him for a high-ranking member of the Tatmadaw.

"You fancy yourself a savior, yes?" General Phyr called out to her. "Here is your chance to do some saving."

"Who are you?" Maw Saung Ku-Syi demanded, her voice quavering with emotion.

Phyr ignored the question. "I have a broadcast crew at my disposal," he told her instead. "They can be here within the hour. Go on the air with a message advising your people not to observe the anniversary of the Four Eights, and these men will be spared the fate of your friend lying there before you."

Ku-Syi stared past the general and eyed the prisoners. All but Soe Paing were staring at the ground, ashen-faced. Paing, however, met her gaze and shook his head defiantly.

"Don't give in to them!" the professor called out.

Ku-Syi closed her eyes a moment. How could they do this? What had become of this world that animals like this could engage in such brutality without fear of consequence?

"You have ten seconds to decide," General Phyr told

her. Beside him, the guards peered through their sights at the prisoners. "Ten…nine…eight—"

"Stop!" Ku-Syi called out. "Leave those men alone!"

"You will cooperate?" Phyr asked her calmly.

"This is barbarism!" Ku-Syi shouted. "Have you no decency?"

Phyr sighed and resumed his countdown. "Seven…six… five…four…"

"Shoot *me!*" Ku-Syi cried out. "Shoot me if you want, but leave them be!"

"Wrong answer," the general countered. He raised his right arm out at his side. "Three…two…one!"

General Phyr dropped his arm. Seven Ruger No. 1H Tropical rifles fired in unison. All seven shots slammed into Kyaw Myo Oo, the youngest of the prisoners. He pitched forward, even as the other three men cried out reflexively, certain they'd been marked for execution, as well. Phyr stared at the fallen prisoner, then looked back at Ku-Syi.

"Perhaps you need to sleep on this matter," he suggested. "I'll ask you again in the morning."

The guards stepped past the executed man and gruffly led away the remaining prisoners. The searchlight snapped off and the clearing was consumed by a sudden darkness.

"Pleasant dreams," Phyr called out from the shadows.

Maw Saung Ku-Syi stood in the doorway, shaken to her core. She stared past the body of U Hla Pyin to that of Kyaw Myo Oo. Kyaw had been her driver the fateful afternoon three months ago when the junta had stopped her car as she attempted to leave Yangon in hopes of rallying followers outside the capital to observe the anniversary of the Four Eights with nationwide demonstrations. Kyaw had joined the NLD only a few weeks before, inspired by Ku-Syi's long-standing call for freedom in Burma. He'd told her he'd just celebrated his first wedding anniversary and that his wife was expecting. If it was a daughter, they were going to name her Maw Saung, as a tribute to Ku-Syi. Ku-Syi had felt honored, flattered. Even more, in Kyaw Myo Oo she'd seen a new generation willing to make sacrifices in the name of freedom. It had filled her with hope for her country. But now Kyaw was dead. He would never see his daughter. What would that little girl think when she grew up and learned she'd been named after a woman whose silence had cost his father his life?

A single tear fell down Ku-Syi's cheek as she stared once more at the dead men lying before her. "What have I done?" she whispered. "What have I done...?"

CHAPTER EIGHT

U-Tapao Royal Thai Navy Airfield, Thailand

Huddled beside Akira Tokaido in the restricted-access comp-intel room at the Air Force's U-Tapao base head-quarters, Yakov Katzenelenbogen glanced at his watch and realized the two of them had just spent three hours straight staring at various computer screens. He rubbed his eyes. No wonder he had a splitting headache. Of course, he realized, it might also have had something to do Tokaido's relentless gum smacking and the muted blaring of rock-and-roll music seeping from the headphones flattening the young Japanese American's disheveled hair. Katz couldn't believe Akira could listen to such loud music and go through so many packs of gum without his jaws and ear-drums giving out. Even more amazing, the cyber-wiz had been at it for another four hours before Katz had flown up to the base after sleeping off his drinking session with U Pag Ti at the Phuket Banyan Tree resort. Pag Ti would be rendezvousing with Phoenix Force in Kawthoung later this morning, after Katz had briefed them at U-Tapao.

"The boys should be landing any minute," Katz said, rising from his chair as Tokaido paused to change CDs. "I know you like flying solo when you're on a roll, anyway."

"Tell them howdy for me," Tokaido said.

After leaving the room, Katz stopped by the PX for some

aspirin and washed a tablet down with a bottle of mineral water as he headed for the airfield. The sun was just coming up, but it was already eighty-five degrees outside. Heat waves rippled up from the black tarmac of the eleven-thousand-foot runway, giving the illusion that the landing strip was puddled with water.

This wasn't Katz's first trip to U-Tapao. He'd been there a few times thirty years earlier, when, as a guest of the State Department, he'd come to monitor the waning stages of America's involvement in the Vietnam War. U-Tapao, home of the 307th Wing of the Strategic Air Command, had, since its opening in 1966, been a primary staging area for B-52 bombers making forays against the Vietcong, not only in Nam but also Cambodia and Laos. Though at the time Katz had had misgivings about certain aspects of the bombing program, he'd been impressed by the clocklike efficiency with which the monstrous Stratofortresses had taken off down the runway, one after the other, destined to return, hours later, with equal precision, having dropped their ordnance on strategic Vietcong positions. He still found the eight-engine monoliths—first brought into service fifty years earlier yet still the largest bomber ever to come off the assembly line—a wonder to behold.

There was a handful of the planes out on the airfield, along with several smaller KC-135 Stratotankers and a sprinkling of fighter jets. To this day, U-Tapao remained a key USAF installation. In addition to overseeing the B-52s, the facility, backed by seven thousand U.S. personnel, lent its might, on an as-needed basis, to other American military units in the area. Should matters get out of hand in Myanmar, U-Tapao would play a key role in any retaliatory action taken against the SPDC regime.

Katz hoped such a course wouldn't become necessary, but from what Brognola had told him during their morning conference call, back home there were sabres aplenty rattling in Congress. The President was still trying to remind everyone that there was not as yet any solid proof that the Tatmadaw had had a hand in the killings of Eric and Carrie Lamarck, but his words were falling on deaf ears. Brognola had reported that one senator, an elderly hawk from South Carolina, had gone so far as to hold up a wedding photo in Senate chambers and bellow, "Remember the Lamarcks!" Thankfully no one had yet cobbled together a conspiracy theory linking the Lamarcks' killing with that of Evan Harris, much less the missing LAVS or the incidents of computer hacking at U-Tapao. But it was only a matter of time, Katz knew, before the connections would be made and picked up by the media. He just hoped the headline frenzy could be stalled until Phoenix Force had a chance to access what the Myanmar military had been up to at Guna Island. Their mission would be difficult enough without the junta bolstering its defenses against so-called "American interventionists."

Access to the airfield was restricted, so when he reached the checkpoint, Katz presented the attending guards with the same ID he'd shown the concierge at the Banyan Tree.

"State Department, eh?" one of the guards said. "You here to see the undersecretary?"

Katz remembered Brognola mentioning that Darryl Lamarck would be flying into U-Tapao to oversee the loading of his son's body, as well as that of his daughter-in-law, onto a plane bound for the States. On impulse, he nodded. The guard waved him through the checkpoint, gesturing across the airfield. "Last hangar on the right. You can't miss it."

The guard was right. The closer Katz got to the hangar, the tighter the security and the more frenetic the activity. A hearse was parked at the mouth of the service bay, and eight uniformed Air Force officers were transferring two gurney-supported, flag-draped coffins to a nearby C-130 cargo plane. Overseeing the grim ritual was the base commander, an honor guard composed of twelve rifle-toting marksmen, and Undersecretary Lamarck, a tall, distinguished-looking man in a black suit. The man was ashen-faced and clearly fatigued from the long ordeal of the past forty-eight hours.

On the commander's signal, the pallbearers stepped aside momentarily, allowing Lamarck a moment alone before the two caskets. Katz felt for the man; less than a week earlier the undersecretary had presided over a festive wedding ceremony for his only son at St. Patrick's Cathedral in downtown Boston. Now he was seeing to it that Eric and his murdered wife would be safely transported back to the States, where, instead of crossing the threshhold to their newly purchased town home in Martha's Vineyard, they would be laid to rest, side by side, at the Lamarck family plot in Norristown, Pennsylvania.

Katz watched Lamarck place a hand on his daughter-in-law's coffin, then lean forward and kiss the flag draped across his son's encased remains. Taking a deep breath, Lamarck then took a step back, signaling the pallbearers to resume the task at hand. When he saw Katz, Lamarck offered a bleak nod of recognition. The two men had met several times at the White House, and though the undersecretary wasn't privy to Katz's role with Stony Man Farm, he knew the man's presence meant that the President, despite his public restraint, had decided to leave no stone unturned in getting to the truth behind his son's murder.

The two men stood silently until the coffins were loaded and the transport plane had lumbered off down the runway, gaining speed and then rising up into the hazy morning skies over the Gulf of Thailand. The honor guard marked the departure by lofting their rifles and offering a twenty-one-gun salute. Eric Lamarck, after all, had been one of them, having served with distinction in the Persian Gulf prior to passing the bar.

The sound of gunfire still hung in the air when Darryl Lamarck walked over and joined Katz. The two men shook hands, then Katz offered his condolences.

"He was always reckless, my boy," the undersecretary said, his voice strained. "Reckless and headstrong. Growing up, you have no idea how many nights my wife and I stayed up worrying about him."

Katz nodded empathetically. Years ago, he'd endured many a sleepless night thanks to a similar high-spiritedness on the part of his own son, who, like Eric Lamarck, had gone to an early grave, a victim of the same Six-Day War that had cost Katz his arm.

"They were too young to die," Lamarck murmured, watching the cargo plane shrink from view. "Too young."

"It's hard," Katz said. "I know. It's a loss you never get over."

The hearse pulled away and normal activity resumed as the two men headed from the airfield. Lamarck seemed lost in his thoughts, so Katz walked alongside him silently, now and then scanning the runway for incoming planes. A limo with a uniformed driver was waiting for Lamarck just beyond the checkpoint. The undersecretary lingered a moment with Katz. He clearly had something specific on his mind but was having trouble putting it into words. Finally he blurted it out.

"I don't care what it takes," he said determinedly. "I want justice. Not revenge, mind you. Justice."

"We'll do everything we can."

"And you think you can do it without dragging the whole country into it?"

"If it's possible," Katz promised. "You have my word."

"Thank you," Lamarck said, his features relaxing. "I

need to get back to my wife. She's at the hotel. Still in shock.''

"My condolences to her." Katz gestured at the limo. "Go ahead. We'll take it from here."

Lamarck nodded. He edged past the driver holding the door open and slid into the back seat of the vehicle. As the door was closing, Katz saw the undersecretary's jaw begin to quake. Poor bastard, Katz thought. His life would never be the same.

As the limo pulled away, Katz backtracked through the checkpoint and sought out a bench in the shade. There he went over the notes he'd culled since the beginning of the whole Myanmar intrigue. He was still at it twenty minutes later, when he was interrupted by the arrival of an Air Force AC-130H Spectre gunship. The four-engine plane, appreciably smaller than the B-52s and the KC-135s elsewhere on the tarmac, was primarily a recon craft and had been summoned from Anderson AFB in Guam to assist in surveillance over Myanmar during the coming days. Prior to takeoff, the gunship had additionally taken on five passengers who'd arrived from the States via a Lockheed C-141 Starlifter. Striding briskly across the concourse, Katz caught up with the plane as its passengers were disembarking.

"Mornin', Yakor." T. J. Hawkins, the first man down the steps, snapped a salute at the former commander of Phoenix Force. Behind him, the other members of the team made their way to the ground, each lugging a canvas tote stocked with gear and weaponry rationed out from the Stony Man armory.

"I'm glad to see you boys came prepared," Katz said. "We've got our work cut out for us."

CHAPTER NINE

Durango, Colorado

It was the weekend of Durango's first annual Summerfest, a spin-off of its popular Snowdown celebration, held each January in the small Colorado town perhaps best known for its narrow-gauge railway, which did a steady business shuttling tourists on a scenic trek through the San Juan Mountains to nearby Silverton and back. The festivities had kicked off the previous day with beer-tasting at several local microbreweries, followed by a parade down Main Street and party action until the wee hours at most of the city's bars and nightclubs. Later this day there would be a rodeo and a much anticipated outdoor concert featuring Roachclip, a sixties cult group reuniting for their first public performance in more than thirty-five years.

This morning, while most of the town slept in, a few dozen hearty souls assembled in the parking lot at Durango High School. Carefully they laid out long, brightly colored cloths of stitched silk that, once filled with hot air, would swell into large balloons attached to wicker carriages that would carry their pilots and selected riders up into the brisk mountain air for a lazy airborne run along the Animas River, which flanked the west edge of the city. Altogether more than two dozen balloons would be going up, affording breathtaking views for those in the baskets, not to mention an equally dazzling sight for those down on the ground.

For Able Team warriors Carl Lyons, Rosario Blancanales and Hermann Schwarz, the balloon rally served another purpose: it would hopefully provide a much needed distraction as they attempted to raid an isolated log cabin in the mountainous backcountry just east of town, near the Ute Indian reservation in Ignacio. The three men would be making use of a balloon themselves, but their liftoff preparation took place a few miles from the high school, atop a remote mountain bluff still scarred from the raging fire that, three years earlier, had decimated much of Mesa Verde National Park.

"And here I thought I'd run out of ways to schlepp you guys around," Jack Grimaldi said as he closed his fingers around a propane valve and prepared to fire up the carriage burners.

"A guy full of hot air like you, you had to figure you'd wind up doing this sooner or later," Schwarz taunted.

During his years of service as Stony Man's ace pilot, Grimaldi had flown everything from Nam-era Chinooks and Hueys to state-of-the-art stealth planes and a space shuttle. This, however, would be the first time during the course of duty that he'd manned the controls of a balloon. It'd been years since he'd even flown one on the contraptions recreationally, but compared to staying on top of things while pushing a B-1A to Mach 3, he figured this for a walk—or flight—in the park.

While Schwarz and Lyons held the balloon's mouth open by its skirt band, thirty yards away Blancanales clutched the drag rope, ready to keep the balloon stable as it filled out.

"All set!" Blancanales called.

Grimaldi cranked open both of the carriage burners. With a dragonlike roar, two gouts of flame spewed forth, racing past Lyons and Schwarz through the large loop of the skirt band. Immediately the balloon began to stir to life, swelling with hot, gaseous air. The name of a fictitious real estate firm—Colo-Real—soon appeared, emblazoned in large letters on the balloon's side panels. The sign would give the desired impression that this was but another of the sponsored entries in the balloon rally.

There was, of course, a reason for the commandos slipping away from the other aerialists. Once their balloon had taken shape and began to right its carriage, Lyons retreated briefly to a late-model Land Rover parked ten yards distant. When he returned, he was carrying two M-16 assault rifles, a pair of high-powered field glasses and a web sling bulging with German-manufactured Dibke-10A smoke grenades. He handed the weapons to Grimaldi, then joined the pilot inside the basket. Grimaldi checked his watch. He'd already monitored wind conditions in the valley—there was a 10 mph breeze blowing west to east—and surveyed a topographical map of the area, calculating the time it'd take to reach their target.

"Forty minutes," he told Blancanales and Schwarz, who would approach the cabin by ground, using the SUV.

"Got it," Schwarz said. He and Blancanales unhitched four of the ten small sandbags clinging to the sides of the carriage, then stepped back and unfastened the mooring rope that tethered the balloon to the ground.

As they drifted skyward, Grimaldi told Lyons, "Don't worry, Dorothy, I'll get you back to Kansas."

Lyons watched Blancanales and Schwarz get into the Land Rover and head down the dirt road leading back to town. Once Grimaldi had guided them up over a stand of pine trees, the Able Team leader caught his first glimpse of the other balloons, rising colorfully up into the morning air like so many inverted teardrops. The city of Durango, which retained much of the small-town charm dating back to its inception as a mining center back in the nineteenth century, lay before them, dwarfed by the jagged peaks of the surrounding San Juan Mountains.

"It's like we're in some damn John Denver video," Lyons mused, taking in the scenery. "Who the hell'd think there was some Asian gang on the prowl around a place like this?"

"It's all that new money," Grimaldi said, filling the balloon with another blast from the propane tanks. "I mean, check out those new homes going up down there."

The Stony Man pilot pointed at the ridgeline they were passing. More than a dozen new homes, under various stages of construction, saddled the crest, rising up from patches of land carved out of the pines. While only a couple of the estates could be called mansions, all the homes were multileveled and easily in the million-dollar price range.

"I see what you mean," Lyons said. "Boomers with this much money to throw around wind up getting pricey with their substance abuse. Get enough morons hungry for speed and heroin and, bingo, you've got Gold Dragons up from L.A. aiming to corner the market."

"Capitalism on parade."

"Maybe so," Lyons said, "but this is one parade that's about to get rained on."

As it turned out, Able Team wasn't the only government entity besides the Air Force with the Gold Dragons in its sights. When following up on the license-plate check Schwarz had run on the Honda used by Evan Harris's killers, the men learned that the Colorado arm of the Drug Enforcement Administration had had the Durango branch of the Gold Dragons under surveillance for the past five weeks. Though unaware of the gang's involvement in any Air Force intrigue, the DEA had the goods on their drug-dealing throughout the region. Earlier in the week they'd finally pinpointed the remote mountain cabin being used as the gang's base of operations. Preparations were under way for a raid on the site when Able Team showed up with orders giving them priority in the matter. Like AF-IA's Evan Harris, the local DEA honchos groused at the arrangement. However, unlike Harris—and, no doubt, in light of his murder—the agency quickly fell in line after Hal Brognola played the "national security" card during a middle-of-the-night phone call to the DEA's Durango field office. It was the DEA that had supplied Able Team with a hot-air balloon, not to mention the Land Rover currently on its way to the mountain hideaway where, it was hoped, they would find and free Air Force officer Christopher Randolph. The agency was also providing backup for the raid. In fact, one of the other balloons that had taken off from the high school, a twin burner with the name of a nonexistent insurance company stenciled on its side, was manned by two DEA undercover officers armed with concealed 9 mm H&K P-9 S pistols.

Once he picked out the DEA's balloon from the others, Lyons tracked its course over the river. The drug agents stayed low, less than a hundred feet above the water, until they'd passed downtown Durango. Then they brought up their balloon, catching the breeze and drifting away from the pack. By now Grimaldi and Lyons had fallen in with the other entries, but they, too, cut away and veered eastward toward the mountain range where the cabin was located. The plan was to make it appear as if the wind had swept them off their designated course along the river. The ruse wasn't all that far-fetched. Once in the air, pilots of conventional hot-air balloons were largely at the mercy of wind currents. To change directions they were, for the most part, limited to giving the balloon more or less gas until they reached an altitude where the breeze came into play. On the chance the Gold Dragons weren't duped by the balloon ploy, the DEA also had a six-man strike force waiting standby in a refurbished Huey tucked inside a cattle barn two miles from the cabin. They would respond only if all hell broke loose and there seemed little likelihood of Able Team freeing the kidnapped officer on its own.

As Grimaldi followed the DEA balloon's errant course, Lyons saw several of the other pilots staring their way with disbelief. Several of them gestured wildly at Grimaldi, and one went so far as to shout through a megaphone that they were heading off course and were apt to rile the good people of Durango, who in the past had protested being awakened by the belching of the carriage burners over their rooftops.

"Something tells me we're not gonna get invited to next year's rally," Lyons quipped.

"Let's just hope they don't get the idea they're supposed to follow us," Grimaldi stated. "They don't want to crash the party we're going to."

"No shit," Lyons said, setting his M-16 on full automatic.

Durango soon fell away from view. Grimaldi and Lyons found themselves passing over a few scattered farms and thick sprawls of green-leaved aspens. Down in a clearing near the edge of a small lake, they saw a herd of several dozen elk grazing in an open field.

Once past the lake, the land began to pitch upward, giving way to mountainsides thick with pines. Grimaldi took out his topo map and checked it against the landscape below. Once he had his bearings, he peered out through the field glasses. Atop the nearest mountain, less than a quarter mile away, he spotted a chimney poking up through the forest canopy. As they drew closer, he saw the roof of a two-story cabin. Standing on a small balcony just off one of the top-floor bedrooms was a bare-chested man smoking a cigarette, a bath towel wrapped around his waist. Even from this distance, Grimaldi could see that the man was

Asian, probably Thai. From the expression on his face, the gangster didn't appear unduly alarmed by the sight of the two balloons heading his way.

Grimaldi lowered the field glasses and turned to Lyons. "Looks like we're in business."

THE SOUPED-UP Land Rover was being tested to its limits as it tackled the back side of Ludaeti Mountain. There was no sign of a path, and the rise was steep and pocked with boulders, as well as dense thickets. Even with their shoulder restraints firmly secured, Gadgets Schwarz and Pol Blancanales bounced about inside the cab like a pair of Mexican jumping beans.

"Don't try this at home, kids," Schwarz mused as he guided the Rover around the blackened, lightning-shattered trunk of a lodgepole pine.

"You got that right," his partner said, clutching the armrest and dashboard to steady himself. "My teeth are starting to feel like a cheap pair of castanets."

Schwarz carved a switchback out of the foliage and zigzagged another ten yards up the mountainside. Somehow, over the grinding of gears and tires, he and Blancanales managed to hear Lyons calling in over the two-way radio clipped to the dash. "Oz to Rover, out."

Blancanales grabbed the transceiver. "Rover here," he said, adding, "You guys don't know how good you've got it up there."

"Yeah, we see you trailblazing away down there," Lyons responded. "Another twenty yards and you might want to park, though, and do the rest on foot."

Blancanales peered up through the pines and caught a partial glimpse of the DEA's balloon passing overhead. The one carrying Lyons and Grimaldi was trailing by a good half mile. "How close are we to the cabin?" he asked.

"A hundred yards max," Lyons reported. "We see only one sentry, and it looks like he just got out of bed."

"He's about to get a jolt from something besides his morning coffee," Pol said.

Lyons chuckled on the other end, then said, "Your best approach is to head straight up, then dogleg to your right."

"Got it."

"Just don't make your move until we're overhead."

"Sounds like a plan." Blancanales signed off as Schwarz sought out the next patch of level ground and eased the Rover to a stop under the cover of a tall aspen. The men quickly shed their bulky jackets, revealing camou fatigues beneath which they wore armored Kevlar vests.

"Ready?" Schwarz asked.

Blancanales nodded. The two men piled out of the SUV, each carrying an M-16. Additionally packed in each man's web holster was a 9 mm pistol; Schwarz had a Beretta, Blancanales a Colt. They still couldn't see the cabin, but given the coordinates Lyons had passed along, they had a clear enough bead on its position.

"I'll take them head-on," Blancanales said. "You wanna swing around to the right?"

"No prob."

Crouched over, Schwarz advanced through an untrampled maze of pines. A carpet of dead needles crackled dully under his feet. He maneuvered deftly around low-hanging branches, making his way uphill wherever the topography allowed. Overhead there was a chattering in the trees—two squirrels playing tag in the upper branches. Beyond them, up through a break in the trees, Schwarz saw a hawk flying in lazy circles on the same air current propelling the two balloons.

After another thirty yards, Schwarz dropped to a crouch, spotting a man's footprint in the soft soil directly before him. As he shifted his weight, leaning forward for a closer look, his boot snagged on something in the brush. On instinct, Schwarz dived forward just as a catapult-like device sprang up out of the nearby ferns. Schwarz's reflexes had saved him from being impaled by the trap's swing arm, which bore evenly spaced rows of sharpened bamboo spikes. The contraption, which looked to Schwarz like an oversize meat tenderizer, set off a cowbell rigged high in a nearby tree. The clanging was short-lived but clearly loud enough to carry all the way to the cabin.

"Shit!"

Staying low to the ground, Schwarz grabbed the two-way radio from his belt and sounded a warning to Blancanales.

"They've got the perimeter booby-trapped!" he whispered.

"So I hear," Blancanales replied over the transceiver. "Are you all—?"

Blancanales's voice was abruptly cut off. In the distance, Schwarz heard another bell clang. Moments later, there were cries from the unseen cabin. Within seconds, the once tranquil mountainside rocked with the sound of gunfire.

"Pol!" Schwarz grated into his radio. "Are you there?"

There was no response. Schwarz was clipping the transceiver back on his belt when he heard thrashing in the brush. Someone was heading his way. He stayed prone and assumed a firing position. Soon he could make out two men advancing toward him, using the thick-trunked pines for cover. Once they were in his sights, Schwarz fired. The M-16 kicked against his shoulder as it spit out a brief volley. Two of the three shots struck home, burrowing into the neck and chest of his nearest foe. The man sprawled to the forest floor and lay still. His colleague, several yards behind, ducked behind the nearest tree, leaning out just far enough to return fire. Bullets ripped through the foliage around Schwarz.

The Able Team commando had to make a decision. Already he could hear more men rushing his way. Trying to advance on them would be suicide; if they didn't catch him in a cross fire, there was always the chance he'd stumble across another booby trap. Staying put wasn't an option, either; the gangsters would quickly have him surrounded.

After firing another round to hold his foes at bay, Schwarz scrambled to his feet and retraced his steps to the Land Rover. It was time to find out just how well the DEA'S mechanics had prepared the vehicle for all-out war.

CHAPTER TEN

U-Tapao Royal Thai Navy Airfield, Thailand

The comp-intel room at the U-Tapao AFB was even smaller than the original quarters where, for several years, Aaron Kurtzman's cybernetic crew had conducted business. There was a rec room next door, however, with a tennis table large enough for the men from Phoenix Force to gather around while Yakov Katzenelenbogen spelled out the latest developments relevant to their mission in Southeast Asia. At the last minute, Katz, however, had been called away for a conference call with Hal Brognola and Barbara Price. In his absence, Akira Tokaido briefed the others on the incidents of computer hacking at the Thai air base.

"For starters," the Japanese American began, "to make sure you're paying attention, let me say up front there's some sort of connection between the hacking and the military activity at Guna Island you're going to be checking out."

"You sound a little defensive there, Akira," Calvin James teased. "Are you suggesting we can't field a little cyber-talk without our eyes glazing over?"

"In a word, yes," Tokaido said with a grin. "T.J., I know you'll have no trouble following this, so I'll be counting on you to translate for these Neanderthals."

"My pleasure," Hawkins replied.

"Let's just get on with it, shall we?" David McCarter groused. "And if you'll spit out your gum and dish everything out in layman's terms, I'm sure we Neanderthals will keep up."

"Rough flight, David?" Tokaido asked.

McCarter smiled tightly. "How'd you guess."

Tokaido tossed his gum in the trash, then began, "The hacking took place here over a three-day period. On a hunch, I cross-referenced the dates with the sat-com surveillance footage that turned up the first signs of military activity at Guna Island. Turns out the activity got under way the day after the last hack-tap."

Hawkins piped in, "'Hack-tap' is shorthand for—"

"—I know what it stands for," McCarter said. He turned to Tokaido. "In other words, whatever the hackers found, it led to the military activity."

Tokaido nodded. "Which means, too, of course, that the junta was behind the taps. That or somebody working for them. I managed to backtrack some of the encryption trails, and it looks like they were made through two different trunklines."

"Say what?" James called out.

Hawkins told him, "See, here in Thailand they use elephants to carry e-mails to—"

"T.J., shut up," McCarter said. "Go on, Akira. Remember, keep it simple."

"Okay, no gory details," Tokaido said. "The bottom line is, near as I can tell, the hacking was carried out from two sites, one in Myanmar—Yangon most likely—and the other in Bangkok. You guys know about the Gold Dragons, right?"

Gary Manning nodded. "They're based out of Bangkok."

"Exactly," Tokaido went on. "I don't have maps, but

their main turf is the south side, a few blocks from Patpong Road.''

"The flesh strip," Manning said.

"Yeah, and I'm sure they have a hand in that somehow. Anyway, while you guys were in the air, I spent half the morning doing some hack work of my own. Thai intelligence has files on the Dragons, so I pulled out their listing of all known addresses for gang operations, then cross-checked with utility records from Bangkok Water & Power and every phone carrier within a fifty-mile radius. I got three addresses with extra phone lines and spiked meter readings.''

"Hackers use that much electricity?" Manning asked.

"Not all of them," Tokaido said, "but you have to consider the amount of equipment it takes to bust through to a military site. We're talking at least two, maybe even three mainframes, each going around the clock trying to log on and then do the whole eenie-meenie thing with passwords and access codes.''

Rafael Encizo spoke up for the first time. "I got the eenie-meenie part. As for the rest, I'm with David. Can we cut to the chase?''

"Okay," Tokaido said, "but you guys better watch it next time you yank out your guns and start yapping about windage and Parabellum.''

McCarter laughed and stroked the air with his index finger. "Score one for the kid.''

The door behind the men opened. Katz rejoined them, his face expressionless. He sat down, motioning for Tokaido to continue. "I'll catch up," he said.

Tokaido went on. "Now, of the three addresses, two are apartment complexes. The third is an electronics store the Dragons apparently use as a front for their drug operations.''

"I'll take door number 3," Hawkins said.

"Wait, wait," McCarter said. "You're talking like this Bangkok gig is ours. What happened to Guna Island?"

"You guys are going to have to split up," Katz interjected. "Mission-wise, both Bangkok and Guna are top priority now."

"Now?" James queried.

"We just found out the Army Ranger unit looking into those stolen Y-25s had its cover blown by one of the witnesses they interviewed in Mu-se. They just made it back across the border, a step ahead of the Tatmadaw."

"Great," McCarter said. "That means they'll be even more on their guard when we come snooping around."

"Afraid so," Katz said. "Which is another reason for splitting you up. Rafe and Cal, you're our underwater guys, so we'll send you two down to Kawthoung. I'll draw up a cover so that when you hook up with Pag Ti, it won't draw suspicion."

"Fine by me," James said.

"Ditto," Encizo added.

Katz turned to Hawkins, Manning and McCarter. "You three will go to Bangkok and look into this electronics store. What we're looking for, of course, is some kind of hard evidence the President can hold up for the cameras when he's countering whatever interventionist rhetoric the junta cooks up over this whole Rangers thing. If we've got solid proof their military tapped into the computers here and then turned around and rushed off to Guna Island, their story about pirates killing the Lamarcks is shot. The junta will be on the defensive, and that's where we want them."

"Let's do it, then," McCarter said.

"Before we do, though," Manning interrupted, turning back to Tokaido, "you still haven't told us what these hackers were looking for here, besides something about Guna Island."

"Actually, the files they tapped weren't strictly about

Guna, or even Myanmar for that matter," Tokaido said. "They were archive files on U.S. operations at U-Tapao during the 1960s."

"Can you be more specific?"

"I wish I could, but when they accessed the file they used a variant of the FBI's old Carnivore computer-surveillance program. Once it bypassed the firewalls and got into the hard drives, it was like a looter in a supermarket. It ran down the aisles and grabbed everything it could get its hands on, then got the hell out of there. I ran a search through the files they raided, but there's no reference to Guna Island or the archipelago."

"Well, I guess Rafe and I will just have to get our sorry asses over there and find some answers," James said.

"And we'll do the same in Bangkok with these Gold Dragon chaps," McCarter added. "Speaking of which, how did Able Team fare with that batch holed up in Durango?"

"No word yet," Katz said, glancing at his watch, "but my guess is they're right in the thick of things about now."

Durango, Colorado

WHILE BOOBY-TRAPPING the perimeter around their mountain cabin headquarters, the Gold Dragons had opted for variety. When Blancanales tripped a device while conferring with Schwarz on his radio, he was spared having to duck clear of bamboo spikes. Unfortunately he'd set into motion the dropping of a half-ton branch serving as the counterweight for a noose buried under the pine needles at his feet. Before he could react, the noose had tightened around his ankle and, the next thing he knew, he was being jerked up into the air as if he were a trout being yanked from the Animas River by an overzealous fisherman. His assault rifle flew from his grasp, and a stabbing pain shot through his leg as he found himself dangling upside down from a fifteen-foot-high aspen. A cowbell, like the one that had betrayed Schwarz's position, clanged noisily in his ear.

Blood rushing to his head, Blancanales cursed, furious with himself. There was little time for self-reproachment, however. Less than fifty yards away, he saw a handful of men pouring out of the cabin. Two of them headed toward where the first bell had sounded. Another three spotted Blancanales and drew their guns as they fanned out and moved in on him.

Gunfire streamed past as Blancanales torqued his body, trying to at least make himself a moving target. He drew his pistol from his web holster and thumbed off the safety, then did his best to take aim at the men gunning for him. It was hard enough being upside down. To be bobbing to and fro at the end of the rope with his skull feeling as if it were about to burst didn't help matters. Amazingly he still managed to clip one of the Asians, slowing him with a slug to the right hip. The other two men continued to advance, however, using boulders and a parked Dodge Ram for cover.

During a lull between gunshots, Blancanales bent at the waist and stretched upward, hoping to grab hold of the rope and right himself. He could barely reach his calf, however, and, curled up, he'd made himself a wider target. More gunfire stormed his way, and he winced as two rounds plowed into his side. The Kevlar blunted their impact, but the bullets still packed enough whallop to knock the wind from his lungs. Blancanales unfolded, barely conscious enough to keep a grip on his Colt.

Emboldened, the two gunmen moved from cover and assumed steady firing positions. It was clear that they'd wised up to his vest and would next be going for killshots to the head.

Before either man could fire, however, there was a sudden thundering from overhead. One of the Asians dropped, never knowing what hit him. The other at least managed an upward glance before a blast from Carl Lyons's M-16 took him out.

"COME ON, CAN'T YOU take this thing down any faster?" Lyons roared as he jammed another clip into his assault rifle.

"This isn't a chopper, Ironman," Grimaldi said, easing off on the burners. "I'm dropping it as fast as I can!"

Grimaldi, in fact, had begun lowering the balloon the moment they'd heard the first bursts of gunfire. He was hampered by the fact that they'd yet to reach any clearing large enough to accommodate a landing. Setting down in the trees wasn't going to help their cause any. A quarter mile to the east, he could see that the DEA was having the same problem. Their balloon skimmed above the treetops, unable as yet to set down.

Lyons fired at two more gunners who'd appeared on the second-floor balcony of the cabin, driving them back inside. He then turned his attention back to the tree where Blancanales still hung suspended like a human piñata. He was moving, clearly alert, but unable to free himself from the noose choking the circulation to his right ankle.

"Here goes nothing." Lyons took aim, drew in a breath and fired.

A series of 3-shot bursts buzzed around the taut rope trailing up from Blancanales ankle. Several bullets chafed the rope enough to weaken it; Blancanales's weight and gravity did the rest. He dropped to the ground like an over-ripe piece of fruit, tucking his body inward just enough to avoid landing on his head. His shoulders and right forearm absorbed most of the impact, dazing him momentarily.

"Nice shot," Grimaldi told Lyons. Their balloon was now sweeping down toward the twin dirt ruts that served as the cabin's driveway. Grimaldi yanked open the balloon's rip panel, hastening their descent. One of the Asian gunmen, huddled near the parked Dodge, raised a Remington LT-20 autoloader and blasted away. Buckshot whizzed past Lyons and Grimaldi, clanging off the burners and ripping a large hole in the balloon's hoop skirt. Deflating unevenly, the balloon pitched to one side, landing at an angle on the rough terrain. Grimaldi was thrown from the carriage and tumbled headlong into a boulder, knocking himself out. Lyons managed a clumsy somersault, then sprawled low in the dirt. He'd lost his rifle but still had his pistol.

Peering under the Dodge, he spotted the shotgunner's legs and fired. The gangster howled in agony as a 9 mm Parabellum round shattered his left shin just above the ankle. Lyons quickly sprang to his feet and finished the job, firing through the vehicle's windows until the other man dropped. He was lowering his weapon when a spray of gunfire clipped him from behind. As with Blancanales, Lyons's Kevlar vest neutralized the slugs to his chest, but one of the rounds creased his shoulder, drawing blood. Whirling, Lyons returned fire, dropping the shooter, a barefoot Asian wearing only his trousers.

"That'll teach you to shoot a guy in the back," he fumed.

Grimaldi was slowly coming to. Lyons rushed to his side and led him to cover behind the Dodge.

"Baby, did that smart," Grimaldi groaned, dabbing an egg-sized bump the boulder had dealt to his forehead.

"Stay put," Lyons told the pilot. Moments later, Blancanales hobbled over, clutching his retrieved M-16.

"You okay?" Lyons asked him.

"A little embarrassed, but yeah. I'll live. What about you? Looks like you took one in the shoulder."

"Flesh wound," Lyons said. "Look, you two stay put. I'm gonna hit the cabin."

Before Lyons could break cover, however, more gunmen

appeared on the second-floor deck and drove him back with rounds from what looked to be a pair of top-loading Owen submachine guns. Down on the ground floor, more gunfire poured from one of the front cabin windows, pinning Able Team behind the Dodge. Blancanales swung his M-16 into play, wounding one of the deck snipers. Another man quickly appeared from the bedroom and took his place.

"Christ, how many of them are there?" Blancanales cursed.

"More than there are of us, that's for damn sure," Lyons said. "We need to level the playing field."

"DEA should be on the way," Blancanales reminded him.

"That's assuming they got in a smoother landing than we did," Grimaldi said, slowly rising to a crouch. Another volley of gunfire pounded the Dodge, forcing him back. "And that Huey of theirs is going to have an even rougher time of it."

"Then we better not sit around waiting for them," Lyons said. He glanced back at the fallen balloon, which had quickly deflated and draped itself across the ground. The smoke grenades, still in their web pouch, had been thrown from the carriage and lay in one of the driveway ruts. Lyons handed his gun to Grimaldi, telling him and Blancanales, "Keep them busy for me."

Blancanales and Grimaldi obliged, directing a few well-placed shots at the cabin. As the return fire danced about them, Lyons sprang from cover long enough to snatch the Dibke-10As. Bullets chased him back to the Ram.

"Okay," he said, emptying the grenades out onto the ground, "let's close down the shooting gallery."

Ignoring the pain in his shoulder, Lyons lobbed one of the projectiles in front of the truck. Grimaldi and Blancanales followed suit, aiming closer to the cabin. The Dibkes went off with a flash, throwing up a quick smoke screen.

There was hardly any breeze at this elevation, allowing the makeshift clouds to rise directly upward, obscuring the Asians' aim. On the downside, the smoke screen also kept Able Team from being able to draw a bead on the enemy. Worse yet, someone up on the cabin deck started flinging some grenades of his own, not smokers but rather frag-packed Mills bombs. Hurtling shrapnel kept Lyons and the others pinned behind the Dodge, which rocked from the impact of one of the charges.

"So much for that plan," Lyons muttered.

IF HE GOT THROUGH this debacle alive, Gadgets Schwarz was going to have to congratulate the DEA on the way they'd tricked up their Land Rover. Besides the bulletproof glass and Kevlar-reinforced siding—which handily repelled the gunfire that assailed Schwarz as he drove back into the fray—the underside of the vehicle had been outfitted with two-inch-thick armored plating. One booby trap after another, including two half-buried Claymore mines, took their best shot at the Rover, without significant effect. True, a bamboo shaft had managed to embed itself in one of the front tires, but the slow leak did little to slow Schwarz's steadfast advance on the cabin. When one of the Gold Dragons suddenly stepped in his path and drew aim with an H&K MP-5 A-5, Schwarz kept the accelerator to the floor, clipping the gangster with a thick, steel-bar "deer catcher" affixed to the front grille. The Asian fell beneath the Rover's wheels and was crushed to death.

"Sorry about that," Schwarz murmured.

The clearing around the Dragons' mountain compound was still engulfed with smoke when Schwarz finally burst through a last bit of foliage. He was promptly assailed by a grenade flung from the second-story deck. The charge went off five yards to the Rover's right, peppering it with shrapnel and briefly raising the front wheels several inches off the ground. Schwarz kept the vehicle under control, however, and continued to drive headlong toward the cabin. Passing into the smoke screen, he briefly lost visibility, then, coming through the other side, he spotted two men up on the deck. Both were preparing to lob more grenades, not at Schwarz, but in the direction of the ravaged Dodge he'd spotted moments before. He guessed his teammates were holed up near the truck; he wasn't about to risk having them taken out by the bombs.

The cabin was old, a onetime hunting lodge built in the 1940s with little concern for building codes. Schwarz saw that the front deck was supported largely by two columns made of lashed 4×4s. He took aim at the closest upright and floored the accelerator. As the Rover raced forward, Schwarz veered sharply, striking one of the uprights at an angle. The Rover's steel foregrille snapped the timbers as if they were made of balsa. The balcony collapsed, throwing the grenade lobbers over the railing to the ground. Schwarz slammed on the brakes, threw his door open and came out firing. One of the fallen Asians crumpled, blood seeping through a bullet hole in his chest. The other scrambled about on all fours, trying to grab hold of his dropped grenade. He was reaching for it when the charge detonated, killing him instantly and further weakening the cabin. With an eerie groan, the structure listed faintly to one side, threatening to collapse on itself.

"All clear!" Schwarz shouted to his teammates behind the Dodge. Without waiting for their response, he bounded up the front porch and dived into the cabin, rolling across the hardwood floor. Gunshots whistled over his head. He gauged where the shots had come from and whipped around his M-16, firing point-blank at a charging Thai gunman. The Asian got off one last, errant shot before dropping to the floor less than two feet away. The cabin groaned a few seconds longer, then fell silent, apparently determined to remain standing.

Schwarz sprang to his feet and glanced around. Aside from the dead man, there was no one else in the large main room. Off in one corner he saw a card table topped with a scale, several glass beakers filled with white powder and a stack—two piles wide and four bags high—of heroin packed into plastic bags. Schwarz was heading up the staircase to the second floor when he heard someone coming up the front steps. He whirled and crouched low, carbine at the ready.

"It's me!" Lyons called out.

Schwarz held his fire. Lyons strode into the cabin, his M-16 aimed at the dead man on the floor.

"I think we got them all," Schwarz called out. "I want to check upstairs for Randolph."

"Wait up." Lyons stepped over the body and started up the steps. When the cabin began to tremble again, he stopped and stared at Schwarz. "I don't know about you, but I got a feeling the upstairs is gonna come down to us."

Clearing the staircase, both men barreled out the front door. Behind them, the cabin began to topple. They barely managed to scramble clear before the entire west wall slammed to the ground, scattering what was left of the smoke screen.

"That was close," Schwarz groaned as he rose to his feet and helped Lyons up. Blancanales and Grimaldi joined them, and all four men quickly surveyed the fallen structure for signs of life.

"If Randolph's in that mess somewhere," Blancanales observed grimly, "he's a goner."

Able Team had just begun to sift through the debris when the DEA balloon crew arrived on foot. They were followed in short order by the Huey carrying the agency's backup force. As Grimaldi had predicted, the pilot was having trouble finding a place to set down the chopper.

"Shove that Dodge out of the way," he called out.

The two DEA agents put the Ram into neutral and pushed it downhill, freeing up room for the Huey to land. Six heavily armed men barreled out of the chopper.

"Sorry, guys," Lyons told them. "We tried to save a few of them for you, but they wouldn't have it."

"What the hell happened?" demanded Howard Boddicker, the agent in charge of the DEA commandos.

"Apparently your surveillance guys were out for coffee break when the Dragons booby-trapped this place." Lyons went on to explain how the cowbell alarms had blown any chance of using the balloons to catch the gang off guard. "After that," he concluded, "well, you can see for yourself."

Boddicker took in the scattered remains of the fallen cabin and muttered, "Talk about search and destroy."

"Well, actually we're not done with the search part," Lyons said. "Our hostage hasn't turned up yet."

Boddicker sized up the situation, then ordered half of his men to help Able Team scour the wreckage for Christopher Randolph. He and the others, meanwhile, scoured the perimeter on the chance there were surviving gang members in the surrounding woods.

Lyons tried to ignore his shoulder wound, but after a few minutes of heaving aside sections of the fallen cabin, he'd lost so much blood he was getting light-headed.

"Hit the sidelines, Ironman," Blancanales advised him. "We can wrap this up."

Lyons grudgingly retreated to the DEA's chopper. The pilot took one look at Lyons and told him to take off his shirt and vest while he grabbed a medkit from the cockpit. In addition to the bullet wound, Lyons had bruises the size of silver dollars where he'd been struck in the chest by gunfire.

"That Kevlar saved your ass," the pilot said as he swabbed Lyons's shoulder with disinfectant.

"Yeah, I guess so." Lyons winced as the pilot slapped a wallet-sized bandage over the cleansed wound.

"This might do the trick if you keep pressure on it," the pilot said, "but you're gonna need stitches."

"What, and ruin a good scar?" Lyons wisecracked.

There was a sudden clamor near the ruins of the cabin. Lyons quickly thanked the medic, then strode over in time to hear one of the commandos telling Boddicker, "We gotta clear out and leave this for hazmat."

"What's going on?" Lyons asked.

"We stumbled on a cellar," the commando responded. "Fucking place looks like Frankenstein's laboratory!"

Lyons frowned. "They had a smack setup on the ground floor."

"Well, whatever they were cooking downstairs," the commando said, "it wasn't smack. You should see all the chem containers stashed down there. I'm talking phosphorous trichloride, acetonitrile, sodium flouride...."

"Hazard materials is right," interjected Schwarz, who'd wandered over in time to overhear the exchange. "Whip that shit up with some isopropyl and a few more goodies and we're talking poison gas."

"That's what I'm trying to tell you," the commando said. "A lot of stuff got knocked around down there. If the right shit mixes together, we're gonna start dropping like flies!"

"Listen up!" Boddicker shouted. He passed along the news, telling his men to get ready to evacuate. "There's room for you guys, too," he told Lyons.

"We'll stick with the Rover," Lyons responded.

Boddicker nodded. "Just don't get any ideas about going

back in there," he warned, gesturing at the fallen cabin. "I don't think your guy's in there, anyway."

"I think you're right," Lyons said.

As the DEA agents clambered back aboard the Huey, Able Team piled into the Land Rover and headed down the trail Schwarz had blazed earlier.

"Shit," Lyons cursed, his shoulder throbbing anew each time they careened over the rough terrain. "First drug dealing, then kidnapping and assassination, and now we've got these goddamn Gold Dragons in the biochem-war business! What next?"

CHAPTER ELEVEN

Bangkok, Thailand

"Pretty soon they'll be calling you just plain Fear."
Swarng Bancha chuckled over the phone with General
Phyr. Phyr had just related his brutal ploy to convince Maw
Saung Ku-Syi to call off demonstrations during the upcoming anniversary of the Four Eights. Impressed, Bancha also
felt a twinge of pride. After all, he was the one who, years
earlier, had first recruited Phyr into the Gold Dragons,
plucking him from a Thai refugee camp across the Moei
River from Kaw Moo Rah. Phyr had killed a fellow refugee
with his bare hands in a dispute over rations, demonstrating
just the sort of unblinking savagery Bancha wanted in a
loan enforcer. The headstrong brute had proved his worth
and served loyally for several years with the organization
in Bangkok, and when Bancha had floated the idea of having Phyr cross back into Myanmar and infiltrate the Tatmadaw, Phyr had jumped at the opportunity. And now here
he was, risen through the ranks, a general's stars on his
shoulders, playing head games with none other than Ku-
Syi herself.

"And what of you?" Phyr asked Bancha. "Are you
making progress?"

"Everything is going smoothly," Bancha assured the

general. "I'll be arranging a rendezous within the hour. Once I have results, I'll call you."

"Very good. Remember, we are under a very tight schedule."

"Yes, yes, I know," Bancha said. "The anniversary of the Four Eights is nearly here. Trust me, I will hold up my end."

The two men exchanged a few parting words, then Swarng Bancha placed the phone back on the nightstand, taking in its place a cigar from a small glass humidor. He rose from his disheveled bed and paused to admire his reflection in a teak-framed mirror on the wall. Bancha was a balding, handsome man whose fortieth birthday this coming November would coincide with Loi Krathoung, the full-moon atonement festival wherein Thais placed lit candles on lotus-shaped floats made of banana leaves and set them in the nearest sea or river, imploring water spirits to absolve them of the past year's transgressions.

Bancha found the coincidence amusing. His only observance of Loi Krathoung had been during his early years with the Gold Dragons, when he and his friends used to burglarize homes while families were off tending to their banana boats. When his mother had found out, she'd whipped him with a cane, telling him he would need an ocean liner to carry away the sins he'd committed. That same night, Bancha had packed his things and run away. Ever since, his home had been with the Gold Dragons.

Of course, over the years, Bancha, like his protégé, Bien Phyr, had risen through the ranks, as had his tastes in living environments. The rank and file of Bangkok's Gold Dragons still dwelled in the gang's original spawning grounds, the run-down tenements south of Lumphini Park, but Bancha had long ago bailed out of that hellhole. He now had two homes in suburban Bangkok and another out in the country. He spent most of his time, however, here at the

Royal Peacock, a small, three-star hotel within walking distance of the high-priced retail shops on Charoen Krung Road. There were nine renovated luxury suites on the middle two floors that went for a rate comparable to that of the Oriental, regarded by many as the best lodging in Bangkok, if not all of Thailand. Of course, the Oriental catered primarily to high-end tourists and businessmen. The Peacock, purchased ten years ago from Gold Dragon heroin profits, hosted another clientele entirely. The rooms here came equipped with not only state-of-the-art amenities, but also with one's choice of bedmates. The Peacock was a rich man's bordello, the sort of place preferred by those who felt it was beneath them to haunt the infamous sex parlors of Patpong Road.

As part of the Gold Dragon's hierarchy, Bancha had a hand in various mob activities, but prostitution was his forte. In addition to the Peacock, he oversaw a handful of other similar "hotels," in the process lording over an ever-changing pool of more than one hundred desirable young women, some of them native Thais, others—usually virgins—imported for service from the northern provinces of Myanmar. He, of course, assigned himself the honor of breaking in new girls, and as he continued to stare at his reflection, he smiled, recalling the fourteen-year-old he'd deflowered shortly before speaking with General Phyr. She'd been a spirited one; there were scratches on his arms and chest from the fight she'd put up before yielding to his will. She would be more readily compliant when she received her first client. By then her black eye and bruised cheek would be healed, too, and her resewn hymen would restore the appearance of virginity, allowing Bancha to charge top dollar for those who wanted a piece of her.

The ganglord's reverie was interrupted by a knock on his door. "Who is it?" he called out, lighting his cigar.

"Semba Hru," came a sultry, languorous voice from the other side of the door.

"Ah…"

Bancha grabbed a *longyi* from the foot of the bed and knotted it around his waist as he crossed the room. When he opened the door, in walked a woman in her late thirties with faintly Amerasian features, wearing a flowing red silk kimono. Her short, dark hair was piled atop her head, held in place by clips made of whittled ivory. She smiled at Bancha, little trace of innocence in her large brown eyes. Semba Hru was an anomaly among the concubines at the Peacock. She'd been working there almost nine years, more than three times longer than any other woman. She rarely bedded strangers. She was too much in demand by her regular customers, some who traveled more than a thousand miles several times a year to engage in her favors. Beyond her sexual prowess, borne of years of experience, the woman was popular for another reason: her uncanny resemblance to Maw Saung Ku-Syi. In the flesh trade there were always those aroused by the thought of carnal trysts with celebrities, and in Bancha's stable there were high-paid look-alikes for everyone ranging from Marilyn Monroe to Suzie Wong and *Charlie's Angel* star Lucy Liu. And yet, none of them were as popular as Semba Hru. Bancha figured it was for the same reason as his success peddling would-be virgins: some men liked the idea of foisting their lust upon the innocent and virtuous. And who better embodied such traits than the imprisoned Nobel laureate?

Semba Hru kissed Bancha lightly on the cheek.

"Entai Lette is ready to see you," she said.

"Excellent," Bancha said. He stroked the woman's cheek. "He's in the bar?"

Semba Hru nodded. "With a smile on his face."

Bancha laughed. "I would imagine so."

The gangster wandered to the bathroom, grabbing a

money clip from the sink counter. Returning, he peeled off several large-denomination bills and reached inside Semba Hru's kimono, brushing the back of his hand across her breasts and the taut, smooth skin of her stomach before slipping the payoff inside the sash around her waist. "Buy yourself that necklace you were telling me about."

Semba Hru clasped her fingers around Bancha's wrist and directed his hand lower, past her waistline, until it was between her legs. She gently squeezed her thighs together while staring intently into the man's dark eyes.

"You're so good to me," she murmured.

Bancha grinned. "You tell that to all your men, yes?"

"Yes," she admitted, rubbing herself against his hand. "But when I say it to you I mean it."

Bancha's smile widened. "I almost believe you."

For the first time, Semba Hru noticed the scratches on Bancha's body. "From the virgin?" she asked.

Bancha nodded. "I need to have her declawed. You know how much men hate having to explain scratches to their wives."

"Fortunately, you have no wife…yet." Semba Hru leaned forward and tenderly kissed the scratches, then asked him, "Does that feel any better?"

"Much," Bancha said. "Only I just remembered, she scratched me down here, too."

Semba stared down at the bulge in Bancha's *longyi* and laughed. "Naughty boy." She gave him a playful shove, then pointed to the bed. "You need to be punished."

Semba moved across the room to where Bancha's motorcycle leathers lay strewed across an ottoman. She reached for the jacket, then began to slip one arm free of her kimono.

"I need to meet with Entai Lette first," Bancha told her. He opened a closet, revealing a number of the tailored suits most of his clients preferred to see him in—some Westerners in particular were still put off by the sight of men wearing the equivalent of a long kilt. "Maybe later, my pet."

Semba stiffened. Her mood changed abruptly. She threw Bancha's jacket across the room to get his attention. "You know I don't like it when you call me that," she told him, all trace of playfulness gone from her face. "I'm not your pet."

Bancha sighed. "Not this again."

"The other whores here are your pets, not me." Semba threw down the money Bancha had given her and stormed toward the door, calling over her shoulder, "Never forget that!"

Bancha rolled his eyes as Semba slammed the door behind her. She'd be back later; he knew it. She'd fall all over herself apologizing for making such a fool of herself, then she'd take him to bed and show him just how much she wanted to be forgiven. And, of course, she would inquire about the money she'd "left" behind.

"Women," Bancha muttered.

But, as he'd said, Semba Hru would have to wait. For now, he had business with Entai Lette, the man who held the key to making the best of the precious cargo Bien Phyr's men had pulled two days ago from the depths of Guna Island.

Stony Man Farm, Virginia

"AND SO THE GOOD NEWS is we knocked out the Asian drug flow into Durango."

"Good for us." Hal Brognola smiled halfheartedly at Barbara Price, who'd just passed along word about the skirmish in Colorado. "It's a small crumb compared to what we were after, though."

"If you have a moment," Hunt Wethers said as the pair

entered the Computer Room, "I'm just finishing up something you'll want to take a look at."

"No problem," Brognola told him. He and Price had brought a sandwich and coffee with them. "We'll just grab a quick bite over here." They sat at a worktable next to Wethers's station. As they ate, they discussed how to best utilize Able Team in the aftermath of the seige in Durango.

"I don't like the sounds of this poison-gas lab they turned up," Brognola said. "In my head, I had these Gold Dragon pegged as your basic street goons, but now they're starting to sound more and more like full-fledged terrorists."

"I agree," Price said. "It definitely ups the stakes as far as this kidnapping goes."

Brognola nodded. "I also would've bet the house they were holding Randolph at that cabin. Now, who knows where the hell we're supposed to look? They could've taken him anywhere. That is, if he's not lying in a shallow grave someplace."

"If he's still alive, it might be that the Dragons took him to L.A. Bigger haystack to hide him in."

"Makes sense," Brognola admitted. "We'll have to wait on a report from the hazmat crew, but I doubt those chemicals they had stashed in that laboratory came from Durango. L.A.'s a better bet."

"Actually," Wethers called out from his station, "instead of L.A., I think we might want to have Able Team head back to Colorado Springs."

"Why's that?" Brognola asked, moving over to Wethers's station.

Wethers said, "Remember how you got the Air Force to send us a back-feed from all their Colorado surveillance cameras?"

Brognola nodded. That had been one of his more spirited phone conversations in the past few months. The Air Force

Internal Affairs chief, all but blaming Able Team outright for the death of Evan Harris, had stonewalled Brognola's request for taped surveillance footage from all Air Force installations throughout the state. Brognola had patiently heard the man out, then sympathized with his situation, claiming that if the shoe was on the other foot he'd probably feel the same. When push came to shove, however, Brognola had reminded the AF honcho that his request carried the weight of a directive from the President, who, as commander in chief of the Armed Forces, would soon be reviewing the proposed Air Force budget for the next fiscal year. Needless to say, the cyber-skids were quickly greased, and requested footage had been filtering into the Stony Man database since late the previous night.

"I've only gone through half the feed so far." Wethers cleared his screen and called up another software program. "I got bogged down with this one piece here. Take a look."

Wethers loaded streaming footage of what looked to be some kind of guard station, the kind set up at entrances to high-security facilities. The camera, as near as Brognola could tell, had been mounted under the cubicle's eaves, focused on the front windshield of vehicles approaching the main entrance. In this instance, the footage revealed an armed guard checking the credentials of someone driving a late-model Lexus coupe.

"This is the Air Force's contaminant-disposal site in Colorado Springs," Wethers explained. "They run it under EPA supervision. Mostly they handle fuel wastes, but they also take in shipments of obsolete weapons and armament. Anything that can be salvaged gets stripped away and sent to a recycling facility. The rest gets stored according to FFA guidelines."

"I'm sorry," Brognola interrupted, "but these weapons and armament...some of them involve G-agents, right? Mustard gas, napalm, things of that sort?"

Wethers nodded. He knew what Brognola was getting at and added, "I checked the preliminary report on what they found at that cabin in Durango. All of it could've come from CDS."

"And where in Colorado Springs is this site?" Price asked.

"A ten-minute drive from Christopher Randolph's condominium," Wethers responded.

"When was this surveillance-camera footage taken?" Brognola asked.

"The night before he disappeared."

Brognola leaned in for a closer look at the computer screen. As with most security cameras, the images were black-and-white, laid down on cheap video film that had already been recorded over several times before. Despite the grainy results, there could be no mistaking the two men in the front seat of the Lexus.

"Christopher Randolph and Evan Harris," he said.

"Correct." Wethers pointed his cursor at the timeprint on the upper right corner of the video image. "It's 10:46 p.m., assuming their camera was set right."

"Nice catch, Hunt," Brognola said. "This puts a whole new wrinkle on things."

"My thinking exactly," Wethers concurred. "According to the brief I read, the night before he disappeared, Randolph told a neighbor he was going to a movie."

Brognola finished Wethers's thought. "But now we've got him joined at the hip with the lead guy who winds up investigating his disappearance."

"A tad fishy."

Brognola nodded, eyes still on the screen. "Whatever they're doing here, you have to figure it has something to do with all those biochems that turned up in Durango."

"We need to find out who they'd come there to see," Price said. "The guard station must have a logbook."

"They do," Wethers said, "but I skipped the middle-man."

"What do you mean?" Brognola asked.

"Give me a minute." Wethers split the computer screen's viewing and called up yet another software program. "I think you'll enjoy this."

Before Wethers could implement the second program, a woman's voice carried loudly across the room. "Hang on there!"

Price and the two men glanced up at Carmen Delahunt, a petite, red-haired woman in her early fifties. She strode toward them, wiping her brow with a hand towel. She was dressed in jogging sweats, having come to work straight from the Farm's on-site gymnasium. "I hope you weren't planning on unveiling our baby behind my back, Hunt."

"Your baby?" Brognola said.

"Guilty as charged," Wethers told Delahunt. "But something came up that couldn't wait."

"Yeah, I'll bet." She rolled up her hand towel and snapped it, squarely striking the back of Wethers's chair with a sound like gunfire. Wethers flinched in his seat, startled.

"Sorry," Delahunt told him, "I thought I saw a fly."

Wethers exchanged a look with Price and Brognola. "Feisty, isn't she?"

"Next time it'll be your earlobe." The woman was smiling, but Wethers doubted that she was entirely joking. Like Barbara Price, Delahunt had proved time and again that she could hold her own in the largely male environment of Stony Man Farm.

"All right, all right," Brognola intervened. He gestured back at Wethers's computer screen. "What do we have here? It looks like some kind of enhancing software."

Price told Brognola, "You're going to love this, Hal."

"You know about this, too?"

"I had to approve funding," she told him. "Otherwise I'm sure they would've kept me in the dark, too."

"Well, it's nice to be finally brought into the loop," Brognola said. "I only run things around here."

"We know how much you like surprises," Delahunt said. "Come on, don't be a sorehead. Check this out."

Wethers had filled his computer screen with a grainy freeze-frame of Evan Harris conferring with the security guard. As the others watched, Wethers used his cursor to highlight Harris's mouth, then switched from freeze-frame to stop-action playback. Over the computer's speakers, Brognola was surprised to hear Harris "speaking." It wasn't the man's real voice, however, but rather a synthesized one, like the one most people heard when they called the operator for the current time.

"I'm…here…to…see. Sergeant. Lacy," Harris seemed to be saying.

"A software program that reads lips," Brognola guessed.

"Bingo," Delahunt said. "Pretty nifty, eh? We retroengineered one of our voice-recognition programs so that it could key off visuals instead of just audio."

"We ran some tests and it's ninety-five-percent accurate," Wethers added. "There're a couple dipthongs it has trouble with, but we'll fix that soon enough."

"Very impressive," Brognola conceded.

Onscreen, the security guard stepped back and Harris drove past, Christopher Randolph in the passenger seat beside him. Wethers switched off the program and looked up at Brognola.

"Unless I'm mistaken," he said, "outside of Evan Harris, this Sergeant Lacy is the last person we know of who had a conversation with Randolph before he disappeared."

Price frowned, trying to make sense of it all. "I might have missed something, but I don't recall coming across anything about Harris going to this CDS site."

"You didn't," Wethers said. "I checked the records on all of Harris's briefings after the disappearance. No mention."

"What do you make of it, Hal?" Delahunt asked Brognola.

"I'm not sure, but something's definitely not right." Brognola turned to Price. "Hunt's right. Let's get Able Team back to Colorado Springs, pronto."

"I'll get right on it."

As Price headed off to make the call, Wethers told Brognola, "Whatever went on in that meeting, it seems a pretty safe bet it triggered Randolph's kidnapping."

"Maybe," Brognola said.

"You don't sound convinced," Wethers said.

"I'm not. How deep is our background dossier on Randolph?"

"Not too deep," Delahunt interjected. She'd taken a seat at her computer station, located directly behind Wethers. "Most of what we have comes straight from AF files. You want me to call it up?"

"Sure," Brognola said, "but how about a quick run-through while you're doing it?"

"Hunt, you pulled in that info, right?" Delahunt said. "I haven't had a chance to look at it myself."

Wethers took his cue and told Brognola that Randolph was a lifer at Pearson AFB with high security clearance as chief records officer. "Apparently he never got into any kind of trouble," Wethers went on, "but he also never earned any commendations. You know the type—they punch the time clock and ride seniority through the ranks till their pension's in order, then they retire. End of story."

"There's got to be a lot more to him than that," Brognola said. "Who wrote up the report, anyway? Was it Harris?"

"I got it over here," Delahunt called out. She drew

Brognola's attention to a scanned copy of the official AF-IA documentation on Randolph. Sure enough, the report—every bit as sketchy as Wethers had made it out to be—had been authored by the late Evan Harris.

"Bingo," Wethers said. "Good call, Hal."

Brognola shrugged off the compliment. "Obviously there's some kind of cover-up going on here."

"You want us to dig a little deeper?" Delahunt asked.

"Absolutely. And don't stop with Randolph. Find out all you can about Evan Harris and this Sergeant Lacy. Whatever they and Randolph were up to has *conspiracy* written all over it. And if that's the case, as far as Randolph's disappearance goes, I'm starting to wonder if it's really a kidnapping we're dealing with."

CHAPTER TWELVE

Bangkok, Thailand

Entai Lette anxiously drummed his pudgy fingers on the bartop as he waited for his martini. The Peacock Bar was a large, tastefully designed room set on stilts out over the Chao Phraya River. The place was busy, especially for a weekday morning. Most of the clientele were men, either bracing themselves with drink before their sexual trysts upstairs or else winding down, having already sated themselves with one of Swarng Bancha's women. Lette was among the latter. He hadn't bothered to shower after his time with Semba Hru, and the oscillating fan behind the bar stirred up her scent on him each time it blew his way. What a woman she was! He'd chosen her every time he came to the Peacock during his trips to Bangkok and he had yet to be disappointed. She always had something new to show him, a new way to bring him to climax. And for a man his age, such things were important.

Lette was in his late sixties. Years ago, in the first years after the coup in Myanmar, he'd been a procurement officer for the new regime's air force. Aviation was still his trade, but these days he called his own shots as proprietor of the Mandalay Aero-Circus, a touring extravaganza that was part air show, part barnstorming troupe and part roving recruitment aid for future Tatmadaw air cadets. Six months a year, from early spring until the onset of monsoon season, Entai Lette traveled throughout Southeast Asia with a caravan of flyers that performed twice daily before ever dwindling crowds of peasants, tourists and curious onlookers from Yangon to Ho Chi Minh City and back. Most of his planes were long-obsolete fighter jets rescued from the scrap heap, and the not-so-daring feats their pilots put them through were, for the most part, pale imitations of more daring maneuvers routinely displayed back in the States by the likes of the Thunderbirds and Blue Angels.

Though the novelty had obviously long worn out, Lette persisted in putting the show through its yearly paces. Amazingly, despite declining revenues, the man lived extravagantly. He owned even more real estate than Swarng Bancha, including expensive homes in Bangkok and Mandalay, as well as maintained condos in Cambodia, Laos and Vietnam. He also boasted a small fleet of vintage automobiles, including a cherry-red 1953 Astin Martin parked in the valet lot outside the Peacock. When questioned about his wealth, Lette made vague allusions to a long-ago inheritance and a shrewd sense for the Tokyo stock market.

Anyone seeking a more plausible explanation, however, had only to compare the aero-circus's annual itinerary with distribution routes for heroin being trafficked out of the so-called Golden Triangle. The similarities were more than mere coincidence, for Entai Lette was, beneath his entreprenurial facade, first and foremost a drug smuggler. His planes, which routinely avoided inspection as they traveled from country to country, just as routinely carried in their holds millions upon millions of dollars' worth of U.S.-bound heroin. Most of the shipments were on behalf of the Gold Dragons and, as such, Lette's trips to the Royal Peacock were as much a matter of business as pleasure. In fact, just prior to his much anticipated rendezvous with Semba Hru, Lette had met in the Peacock's dining room with Gui

Rahb, a Thai-born Dragon who oversaw most of the gang's Asian drug operations. They'd finalized arrangements for Lette to smuggle in the season's largest opium harvest during his aero-circus's upcoming two-day stopover in Bangkok. After the meal, Rahb had mentioned that Swarng Bancha had an interesting proposition for him. Lette knew Bancha from his countless visits to the Peacock, but the two men had never exchanged anything more than small talk.

Now, as he waited for Bancha to show up, Lette sipped his martini and gazed back out at the lounge. Off in the corner, a middle-aged man with an absurdly black pompadour played "The Look of Love" on an upright Steinway, flanked by two young women wearing heavy makeup and tight cocktail dresses. At first glance they both seemed to be in their late twenties, but as they crossed the room to present themselves to potential customers, Lette saw that they were teenagers. It occurred to him that perhaps Bancha wanted to meet with him about smuggling in girls from Myanmar's northern provinces. The notion sickened Lette. He had granddaughters the age of these girls, and he shuddered at the idea of them being forced to solicit men for sex. It was another reason he was so fond of Semba Hru. She was old enough, he figured, to have determined her own fate.

The more he watched the girls and thought of Bancha's likely proposition, the more agitated Entai Lette became. Finally he swilled the rest of his drink and told the bartender to inform Bancha that he'd been called away on some last-minute business and would have to cancel their meeting.

"You can tell him yourself," the waiter responded, gesturing over Lette's shoulder.

Lette turned and saw the gangster saunter into the bar, wearing a tailored suit offset by a small gold cross dangling from his right earlobe. He patted the piano player on the back and chatted briefly with a few of the patrons before taking a seat next to Lette at the bar.

"Thank you for agreeing to see me." Bancha signaled the bartender. "Another drink for my friend. On the house."

Lette smiled flatly. Now that Bancha was here, he felt obliged to at least hear out the man.

The two men exchanged pleasantries, and when the subject of the aero-circus came up, as usual neither man discussed Gui Rahb or any ulterior motives behind the show's annual tour. Lette, impatient for Bancha to get to the point, was terse with his end of the conversation. Finally, after his second martini arrived, he told the gangster, "I understand you have a proposition for me."

Bancha nodded. "It has to do with your planes," he said. "I know some people who might be interested in some of them."

Here it comes, Lette thought to himself.

"The F-105s in particular," Bancha added.

Lette was startled. "My fighter jets?"

Bancha nodded again. "You have several of them, yes?"

"Yes," Lette said, on his guard. "Four, in fact."

"I thought so."

"These people you mentioned," Lette said. "What do they want F-105s for?"

"These people," Bancha told Lette, "are with the SPDC."

Lette stared at Bancha, confused. "Myanmar has newer jets," he said. "What would they want with F-105s?"

Bancha shrugged. "I don't know the specifics. I'm acting only as a middleman."

"I hadn't planned on selling the jets," Lette confessed. "They're useful to me, as you well know."

"Of course." Bancha paused to light the cigar he'd

brought from upstairs, then said, "Perhaps it would be best if you spoke directly to my contact."

As if on cue, another man appeared at Lette's side. Lette had seen him earlier, lingering in the bar. Now he was more confused than ever, because the man wasn't Burmese, or even Asian. And though he addressed Lette in Thai, there could be no mistaking the fact that he was American.

"Hello, Mr. Lette," the man said, extending a hand. "My name is Christopher Randolph...."

Kawthoung, Myanmar

ALTHOUGH THE SPDC WAS still regulating access to the Andaman Sea, preparations were well under way to milk the tourist potential of the small coastal towns along the tip of the narrow peninsula separating Myanmar waters from the Gulf of Thailand. To the north, in Dawei and Myeik, newly completed rail connections had already spawned a development boom. Now it appeared that Kawthoung would be the regime's next fledgling cash cow. Entering town, Calvin James and Rafael Encizo had seen a huge, gaudy sign proudly informing visitors that they had just arrived at the gateway to the Mergui Archipelago. The sign contained architectural renderings of what the town might look like five years down the road—luxury resorts, fine restaurants and a proposed zoo featuring all of the exotic animals Eric and Carrie Lamarck had failed to cast eyes upon before their untimely deaths. At present, however, Kawthoung was little more than a sleepy hamlet best known for turning out some of the nation's best kickboxers. There were only a few small run-down hotels and food stalls. The drab market square had yet to be inundated with souvenir trinkets and offered mostly staples for the local population. The only industry of note was a modest two-story building where nests made from the spittle of sea swallows were packaged for delivery to the Chinese, who considered the nests a delicacy.

Striding past the building down a narrow two-lane street that ran through the heart of town, James and Encizo—both dressed in expensive-looking linen suits and alligator-skin sandals—drew ambivalent gazes.

"Must not be used to ugly Americans yet," James remarked.

"We're way past ugly," Encizo said. "We look like a couple pimps."

"I don't think they know what a pimp is," U Pag Ti told them. Walking alongside the men, whom he'd met up with earlier outside Kawthoung Motel, Pag Ti was more conventionally dressed in a *longyi* and T-shirt. He smiled to the locals in a way that suggested that he, too, found the Americans a bit outlandish.

"Well," James said, "once the tourist boom hits they'll lose their innocence faster than you can say Starbucks."

"Perhaps," Pag Ti said, "but I think the Tatmadaw has already stripped our country of its innocence."

Pag Ti had already asked around, and the few villagers who recalled seeing Eric and Carrie Lamarck before they'd set out for Guna Island had echoed the sentiments of the man who'd driven them up from Phuket Bay. As far as anyone knew, the honeymooners had come to Kawthoung with nothing in mind other than a quick tour of the archipelago. To find answers, Pag Ti and the men from Phoenix Force were going to have to carry out their plan to retrace the couple's itinerary to Guna Island.

At the end of the main street was the government post where the Lamarcks had received clearance to venture out into the archipelago. The old, dilapidated building, white and blue paint flaking from its wooden siding, was manned by a handful of junta soldiers, two of whom stood posted outside the main doorway, armed with assault rifles. A newly posted sign a few yards to their right announced that due to recent pirate activity, the archipelago had been declared off-limits to all but military personnel. One of the customs officials, in fact, was in the process of turning away two Americans weighed down with scuba gear they'd hoped to take to the islands.

"This has all been arranged!" the taller man bellowed with a thick Texan accent, thrusting some paperwork in the official's face. "We got our confirmation two weeks ago!"

The customs agent, a silver-haired man with two gold teeth, ignored the papers and shook his head. Gesturing at the sign, he stated, "Change in plans."

The Texan scanned the sign. "Pirates, my ass!" he fumed.

The customs official glanced at the soldiers. They quickly stepped forward, flanking the scuba divers, making a point to noisily thumb off the safeties on their AK-47s.

"Answer is no," the customs agent insisted. "You go now."

The Texan eyed the soldiers, then told his partner, "Shit, Tony, looks like we'll have to go over this asshole's head."

Tony, clearly the more intimidated of the two, motioned for his cohort to calm down. "C'mon, Rick, let's just go," he said. "We can do Phuket Bay."

"You mean Fuck-it Bay," the Texan snapped. "Hell, up there you can't swim three feet without bumping into some other goddamn schmuck with a snorkel. Screw that shit. We came here to do Guna. We're gonna do Guna."

"Guna closed to tourists," the customs official repeated.

Rick glared at the man. "I'm calling our embassy, pal. You're gonna end up pushing pencils in a back room somewhere."

"You go now," the official repeated, adding, "Or maybe you like a day in jail. Maybe you wind up with prisoners who want to push their pencils into *your* back room."

Rick's face reddened. The soldiers around him chuckled.

"Let's get out of here," he told his partner. As they filed past, he advised James and Encizo, "You're wasting your time on these chumps."

James and Encizo shrugged.

"I'll handle this," Pag Ti assured them.

As the Myanmar operative stepped forward to speak with the gray-haired man, Encizo told James, "I still think we should've just grabbed ourselves a submarine and snuck in the back way."

"The junta has a radar installation in Myeik," James reminded him. "They'd see us coming and take us out before we got anywhere near the island."

"I know, I know," Encizo said impatiently. "I just hate having to play 'Mother May I' with these scumbags."

"That's why we've got Pag Ti," James said. "All we have to do is stand around and look like we're made of money." Indeed, along with their suits and gator-skin sandals, the men had come accessorized with faux Rolex watches and gold-plated necklaces designed to look like the real thing. As far as the Myanmar customs officials were concerned, James and Encizo were front men for a Panamanian cruise line operating out of the South China Sea. The way Pag Ti was peddling it, they knew of Myanmar's plans to build a casino as part of Kawthoung's redevelopment and wanted to use the town as a port of call for highrollers looking to gamble somewhere besides the boat. Of course, Pag Ti explained, such an arrangement would involve regular payments of a "discretionary fee" that the local agents could keep or pass along to the junta as they saw fit. The implication was clear; with James and Encizo obviously trying to avoid having to deal with the SPDC, the customs official could pocket the bribes without anyone being the wiser.

After glancing over the group's papers—all forged back

in U-Tapao—the gray-haired man eyed James and Encizo. To avoid suspicion that they were here looking into the deaths of the Lamarcks, both men's passports listed them as native Panamanians. James smiled amiably back at the official. Encizo did the same while muttering out the side of his mouth, "He's gonna ask for something up front."

Sure enough, the customs official turned back to Pag Ti, his face masked with concern. He spoke in a low voice, indicating the soldiers around him. Pag Ti nodded, unperturbed, and withdrew an envelope tucked into his *longyi.* The official peered inside the envelope, then slipped it into his own pocket and excused himself. He disappeared briefly inside the customs house, then returned, handing the stamped passports to Pag Ti. The two men exchanged a few more words, then Pag Ti rejoined James and Encizo.

"We're all set," Pag Ti told them.

Encizo said, "Nothing like a little graft to grease the ol' skids."

"We have twenty-four hours," Pag Ti said.

"Should be plenty of time," Encizo replied.

As they headed away from the customs house, James asked Pag Ti, "How much did you have to give him?"

"Enough to convince him not to send along someone to keep an eye on us like they wanted."

"Way to go," James said.

"Obviously I didn't mention Guna Island," the Myanmar operative went on. "As far as they're concerned, we're just scouting out things at Thahtay Kyun and Salon Island." Both islands were located only a few miles out to sea from Kawthoung.

On the way back through town, the men took another route, closer to the shore. Encizo noticed a flurry of activity in a clearing adjacent to a large, half-erected structure neither he nor James had noticed earlier. More than a hundred laborers—half of them women and children—were hacking at a sprawl of ground cover, piling their cuttings into large wheelbarrows. Watching over the workers was a handful of armed soldiers.

"Railway station," Pag Ti explained. "They're extending the train line down from Myeik. Part of the redevelopment."

"What's with the soldiers?" James asked.

"Forced labor," Pag Ti said. "Or, as the government calls it, 'civil works program.'"

As they watched, an elderly man collapsed under the weight of the clippings he was carrying. Two soldiers quickly moved in, kicking the man and then dragging him to his feet. When he collapsed again, they started clubbing him with their rifle stocks. Some of the other laborers looked up; the soldiers shouted for them to get back to work.

"It's like this all across the country," Pag Ti told him. "SPDC tells the outside world they've stopped using forced labor, but it goes on."

"No wonder people want to hold demonstrations," James said.

"Demonstrations won't help," Pag Ti told him, recalling his own experience. "It only leads to more brutality."

"What about this anniversary of the Four Eights coming up?" Encizo asked. "Aren't there supposed to be rallies all across the country?"

"That is the plan," Pag Ti said. "The government won't stand for it, though. There will probably be even more bloodshed than before."

"And they think they can get away with it?"

"The military has been in charge here for forty years," Pag Ti told Encizo bitterly. "They think they can get away with anything."

James watched some children crying as they brought

their meager handfuls of weeds to the wheelbarrows. "It's like Siberia without the snow," he commented.

Pag Ti nodded. "We'd best move on. If they see us watching, there will be a scene."

Once they reached the port, the men stopped by a bait shack with lockers where they'd stashed their gear. They weren't traveling light. Each man headed down the docks toting two bulky, waterproof gearbags. The small inlet around them was crowded with small long-tail boats and a handful of trimarans. Pag Ti apparently hadn't been tapped out by the customs officials. He produced a second wad of currency, using it to rent the hardiest looking of the boats, a fifteen footer moored at the end of the docks. It had a thatch roof and a 350-horsepower aft-mounted outboard motor.

"This should get us there and back in one piece," he told James and Encizo.

As the men were transferring their gear to the craft, two familiar figures headed down the docks toward them—the two Americans who'd been turned away at the customs house.

"Going somewhere, gents?" Rick the Texan called out.

"Looks that way," Encizo said.

"How'd you wrangle past customs?"

"We said, 'Please,'" he told the diver.

The Texan moved close to Encizo and eyed the boat. "Looks like you got room for a couple more passengers there."

"Sorry," Encizo told the man.

The Texan glanced around to make sure no one was looking their way, then nodded to his partner. Both men suddenly produced 9 mm pistols. The Texan pointed his at Encizo's chest while the other took aim at James and Pag Ti, who were already in the boat. The Texan grinned. "Please," he said.

STIJEL RASS, the man who'd rented the boat to Pag Ti, whistled to himself as he entered his rickety cabin at the foot of the docks. Plopping into a chair, he counted the money Pag Ti had given him—five thousand bhats, more than he'd made all week so far. He was contemplating how to spend the windfall when the cabin door suddenly burst open. In strode three young men. Two remained in the doorway as the third approached Rass, training an Iver Supershot 9 revolver on the man's face. Rass tried to discreetly slip the money inside his *longyi,* but the other man shook his head and held out his other hand. Rass had no choice but to hand over the money. As he did so, he noticed a tattoo on the man's forearm—a dragon's head.

The gunman pocketed the money, asking Rass, "The men in the suits. Rich, yes?"

Rass nodded bleakly. "I think so. They had gold jewelry."

The gunman turned and led his cohorts out of the cabin. Trembling, Rass fumbled through his desk for a bottle of cheap gin. As he took a long drink, he stared out the cabin window. The Gold Dragons were heading to the end of the docks. Out in the harbor, a high-powered speedboat had droned into view. Rass figured it must have been lying in wait around the bend.

"Damn pirates," he muttered.

CHAPTER THIRTEEN

Bagan and Nyaung-U, Myanmar

The SPDC was building a casino in Bagan, as well. Just inland from the jetty near the Ayar Hotel, workers were nearing completion of a twelve-hundred-room facility with more than twenty-two thousand square feet of gaming area. Daw Bodta and Aung Paing watched the construction with contempt. Both had fond memories of roaming this part of the old city as children. They would play for hours on end with the sons and daughters of local villagers who earned a modest living off visitors who'd come to view the city's famed sprawl of temples. All that had changed in 1990, shortly before the national elections, when the junta had unceremoniously driven all four thousand villagers, including the family of Soe Paing, from the city, forcing them to relocate in Bagan Myothit, a dusty no-man's-land miles to the south. The junta had considered the townspeople like the Paings to be an eyesore, a troublesome distraction tourists shouldn't have to be bothered with. Despite the mass evictions, however, tourism had failed to meet expectations during the ensuing years. Soe Paing, like many other dissidents, had claimed travelers were shunning Bagan and the rest of the country in protest of the junta's totalitarian rule, but the regime had been of the opinion that tourists merely needed some additional incentive, a more provocative lure than mere scenic wonders. And what better lure for vacationing capitalists than the get-rich-quick offerings of a casino?

"Bad enough they corrupt people with their games of chance," Daw Bodta complained, watching the faux temple rising on the site of the former market bazaar. "But to blaspheme Buddha in the process? It's unforgiveable."

She was referring to the resort's architectural motif, modeled after Bupaya Pagoda, a whitewashed, golden-spired temple that had been rebuilt after crumbling into the Irrawaddy River during the earthquakes of 1975. When completed, Casino Bagan would be three times the size of its coastal counterpart, located less than a mile away.

"You watch," Daw Bodta continued. "There will be slot machines where you win a jackpot for lining up three Buddhas."

"You're probably right," Aung told his sister. "But enough about that. We have business to attend to."

The Paings hadn't come down to Bagan to watch the construction, but rather to await the arrival of more supporters. As they walked past the old brick walls that had once bordered the ancient city, Aung and Daw Bodta saw a touring barge round the bend and make its way toward the jetty. They reached the shore just as people were filing out of the vessel. A handful of soldiers milled about, but, as usual, none of them bothered to search the new arrivals. Aung scanned the crowd, then offered a wave to another young man carrying a duffel bag in addition to the knapsack slung across his back.

"Do you have it?" Aung asked the man, whose name was Lon Mar.

The man nodded, patting his duffle bag. "And you? You have the relay antennas?"

"Yes, yes, of course," Aung said excitedly. "They came in the day before yesterday."

"Excellent."

The threesome boarded a bus parked just inland from the jetty. Heading north toward Nyaung-U, they passed the temples of Upali Thein and Htilominlo. Hills rose to the south of the road, and atop the highest peak Lon Mar noticed the Y-25 armored vehicle that had arrived in Nyaung-U the day before. When he asked about it, Aung leaned close and told him how the LAV's arrival had triggered a confrontation between villagers and the military.

"It would have been 1988 all over again," Aung whispered. "A massacre swept under a rug."

Lon Mar nodded, then asked why the antiaircraft vehicle had been stationed in such a remote area. Aung told him of the military's insistence that the LAV was there to protect the area against rebel air strikes, adding, "from that hill they can probably see both the airfield and the temples."

"Up that high, too," Daw Bodta guessed, "it's probably easier for them to defend themselves against ground attack."

Lon Mar eyed the LAV warily. "I'd feel better about our rally without that thing looking down at us."

"They'd never fire at us like that," Daw Bodta said. "Not with the temples all around us."

"I hope you're right," Lon Mar said.

When the bus stopped at the small town of Wetkyi-in, the three dissidents got off. Aung and Daw Bodta led Lon Mar to a waiting horse cart, which would take them circuitously back to their base camp at Kyaukgu Umin. On the way, Lon Mar finally opened his duffel bag, showing the Paings a digital camcorder he'd secured from an NLD sympathizer in Magwe. The device was attached by cables to a laptop, as was an Erikkson Wireless PC modem card. The bundled equipment was far smaller than either Aung or Daw Bodta had expected.

"This will allow us to transmit the rally overseas?" Aung asked dubiously.

"If everything is in order with our routers and relay antennas, yes," Lon Mar responded. "And not just television. We'll be able to send stream feeds out on the Internet."

"As things happen?" Bodta asked.

Lon Mar nodded. "Yes, a live broadcast. Can you imagine?"

Aung smiled faintly as the cart continued to carry them along a dirt road leading from Nyaung-U. Perhaps the military had been able to carry out the massacre of the Four Eights without anyone outside the country's borders being any the wiser, but that would not be the case this time. This time—not only here in Bagan, but at the other rally sites, as well—trained cameramen would be filming the demonstrations, as well as any response by the Tatmadaw. And though the Paings and others now carried weapons with them, come the day of the demonstrations, they would be unarmed. If there was to be violence, it would be prompted solely by the military, and their show of force would be documented for all to see. Those in the West who had been lulled by the junta's rhetoric about peace development and embracing the world community would see these tyrants for what they really were. Aung Paing, for one, would not be afraid to lay down his life if he knew that his death might spur the world into finally taking action against his country's oppressors. It would be a small price to pay.

"Nothing can stop us," he murmured hopefully.

BARI TU, the Gold Dragon whose tattoos lay concealed beneath the folds of his monk's robe, appeared contrite as he was led deeper into the cliffside tunnels at Kyaukgu Umin.

"I am sorry to impose," he told the man who walked alongside him, lighting their way with a torch that threw an eerie, flickering light upon the scalloped walls of the tunnel. "I know that by now I should be able to meditate anywhere, but I find that unless I have complete privacy—"

"No need to explain," said U Lir Gon, an elder among the NLD sympathizers gathered at the remote temple. "I used to have the same problem, as did our ancestors. That was the reason these tunnels and caves were first carved out—so men of prayer could shut themselves off from the temporal world."

The two men had earlier passed several other caves, but in each case demonstrators had already set up accommodations.

"How are preparations for the rally coming?" Bari Tu asked casually, trying to draw information out of the older man.

"All goes well," Lir Gon responded. "We're taking care to avoid the mistakes from before. Those of us who survived the Four Eights are older now, and wiser."

"I hear that we will be broadcasting," Bari Tu said.

"True." Before he could elaborate, they reached a bend in the tunnel. U Lir Gon gestured for Bari Tu to halt, then bent to a crouch, bidding the monk to do the same.

"Bats," he whispered.

Once Bari Tu had dropped to one knee, Lir Gon extended the torch around the corner, waving it back and forth. Soon there were high-pitched shrieks and a mad rustle of wings as hundreds of small bats hurtled past, mere inches above the men's heads. Once the creatures had fled, Lir Gon rose and led Bari Tu around the bend to a small, vacant cavern, unadorned save for a lone stone bench. The enclosure, like the tunnel, was cool and the walls were moist with condensation.

"This should do," Lir Gon said, handing Bari Tu the

torch. "If not, there are more caves still farther down the tunnels."

"Thank you." Bari Tu knew that he couldn't broach the subject of the rally again without drawing suspicion, so he bowed slightly to the older man, then returned the torch. "I have a flashlight."

"Very well." Lir Gon retreated to the mouth of the cavern, then glanced back. "I will see that you are not disturbed."

"I appreciate it, Lir Gon."

Bari Tu unslung the shoulder bag he'd brought with him from Yangon. He withdrew a prayer mat, unfolded it and set it on the ground, then sat on it, cross-legged, eyes closed, trying not so much to meditate as to make sure he could hear U Lir Gon's footsteps retreating back the way they'd come. Once satisfied that he was indeed alone, the man opened his eyes. He'd expected to find the cave engulfed in darkness, but a faint beam of light shone down from an air shaft carved out of the rock ceiling, illuminating the area. Bari Tu unfolded his legs and reached for the tote bag. Ignoring his flashlight, shaving kit and other toiletries, he clawed at the base of the bag, prying open a false bottom. Hidden in the recess was a cell phone and a palm-sized 5-shot Grodon semiauto pistol. He slipped the gun inside the folds of his robe, then activated the cell phone and stared at the display screen. An icon soon flashed telling him he was too far from range of the nearest antenna to make any calls.

Bari Tu cursed. He was already an hour late in reporting back to military intelligence. He knew that there was some allowance for extenuating circumstances, but he didn't want to start off the first assignment since his promotion by making excuses. He wanted to be able to report his success in taking the place of the Yangon monk who—before dying from wounds inflicted during his inquisition—

had divulged only that he'd planned the previous day to ride a bus north from Yangon to assist with the NLD's planned observance of the Four Eights. Already Bari Tu had learned that Bagan was but one of several sites chosen for rallies, and that these rallies would be somehow broadcast to the world. Now he wanted to learn the details. The more information he could pass on, the more credit he could take once the demonstrators' plans were thwarted.

Rising to his feet, Bari Tu moved to the wall and peered upward. He could see sky through the air shaft, which was easily wide enough for him to climb up through. Even better, there were rungs chiselled into cave wall.

"Yes," he murmured.

Bari Tu was wearing shorts and a T-shirt beneath his robe, but much as he wanted to strip down before tackling the orifice, he fought off the temptation. Instead, he tucked his cell phone inside his shorts, next to the pistol. Then, robe and all, he started up the rungs. It was a tight squeeze, and at one point he slightly tore one sleeve on the jagged rock of the air shaft, but finally he reached the top and crawled out into the open. He found himself surrounded on all sides by small shrubs and other vegetation. Looking back in the direction of the temple, however, he could make out the tip of the whitewashed spire rising up from the main entrance. Nearby was another vertical structure, narrower and made of metal, wavering oddly from side to side. Curious, Bari Tu inched quietly through the brush for a better look. After a painstaking twenty yards, he finally realized what he was looking at.

An antenna! Someone was installing an antenna!

Bari Tu kept an eye on the activity near the spire as he withdrew his cell phone and activated it. Several moments later, a faint bleep notified him that he was within signal range of the nearest Tatmadaw transmitter. Bari Tu was about to dial when a voice suddenly carried across the clifftop.

"Who's there?"

Bari Tu glanced up. There was a man standing next to the antenna looking his way. Bari Tu shut off his cell phone and concealed it back inside his robe, then strode forward, apologizing for giving the other man a start.

"I needed some fresh air," he explained. "The caves are stuffy." As he drew closer, Bari Tu saw that, sure enough, the other man was setting up some sort of portable relay antenna.

"You're just in time," the man said. He was Bari Tu's age, bare chested and slightly overweight, folds of flesh hanging over his *longyi*. "I could use an extra hand."

"I am happy to help," Bari Tu said. He reached out and held the antenna steady as the worker dropped to a crouch, tightening it to a base plate the size of a manhole cover. "This isn't a very big antenna," he remarked.

"Big enough," the worker explained. "It just needs to be in line of sight with another one we'll set up near Tetthe. That one will pick up a camcorder feed from Bagan."

"Where does the signal go from here?" Bari Tu wondered.

"More relays," the worker said, "all the way to Thailand. There we have connections with a television broadcaster, as well as someone who can send streaming images onto the Internet—"

The man suddenly fell silent and rose to his feet, eyes clouding with rage. It was only then that Bari Tu realized that while holding the antenna he'd let the sleeve of his robe slide up his arm, revealing the dragon tattoo above his wrist.

"Spy!" the worker hissed. He took a swipe at Bari Tu with the large wrench he was holding.

Bari Tu leaned away from the blow, at the same time

torquing his body and kicking outward with his right leg. The folds of his robe blunted the full impact, but the worker still staggered backward, off balance. Bari Tu, trained in kickboxing since his childhood in Kawthoung, bounded forward, driving his feet into the worker several more times, knocking the wind from his lungs and doubling him over. A blow to the back of the head rendered the man unconscious.

Standing over the fallen worker, Bari Tu looked around. No one else was about. To keep his cover from being blown, however, he needed to kill the worker, but in a way that wouldn't draw suspicion. Surveying the area around the relay antenna, Bari Tu noticed that large sections of the terrace railing had crumbled and fallen over the years. There remained, however, a few lengths wide enough to sit on.

Bari Tu dragged the unconscious worker to the terrace. Then, with great difficulty, he hoisted the man up against the railing, then began kicking at the brickwork until it began to give way. As he was doing so, he heard the worker sputtering back to consciousness. The moment the man opened his eyes, Bari Tu let go and gave him a hard shove. The railing gave way beneath him. With a startled groan, the man plunged backward over the edge of the cliff. He flailed his arms and legs as he plummeted down the steep face of the temple, landing with a sickening thud on the ground below.

Hearing screams down near the temple entrance, Bari Tu raced from the terrace, backtracking through the brush, then lowering himself down the air shaft. The cave was as he'd left it. He quickly reassumed a lotus position on the prayer mat, then wiped the sweat from his brow and drew in a deep breath and let it out slowly, trying to slow the jack-hammering of his heart. When the others came rushing to tell him there'd been a terrible accident, he wanted them to find a man deep into his meditation.

CHAPTER FOURTEEN

Stony Man Farm, Virginia

Hal Brognola had been on the gymnasium treadmill a little over thirty minutes. Without breaking stride, he checked his pulse. Right in the target range. That was good. Now, if his cholesterol levels would just follow suit, maybe he could get his doctor to knock off the talk about cutting back on his workload. Not that he wanted to give up his new exercise regimen. It'd taken a while, but Stony Man's director had finally reached a point where he could abide by the slogan posted in the men's locker room: When The Going Gets Tough, The Tough Go For The Burn. And it wasn't just a matter of managing stress. Brognola had discovered that his daily workouts also gave him time to sort through all the angles and complexities that came with orchestrating the efforts of his action teams. And, too, there was the matter of his increased vitality. These days he could work longer hours without feeling overly fatigued and still fall asleep within minutes after hitting the pillow at night, assured that he would have this workout time the following day to dwell on the things that used to keep him up, often for hours on end.

This afternoon, Brognola's focus was trained on the ever widening agenda of the Gold Dragons. He found it troublesome enough that criminal syndicates ruled the world's vice rackets; having them expand their influence into the spheres of politics and espionage was a recipe for disaster. The Farm already had its hands full putting out repeated fires in Russia and its sister nations, where mob chieftains—capitalizing on the chaos of decentralization—had brashly come to the fore and turned the former Soviet Union into a powder keg even more volatile than it had been during the height of the cold war. At least with the USSR, there had only been one leader with access to the button that could unleash Armageddon; now, any nickel-dime mob boss worth his salt had some weapon of mass destruction at his disposal. As for the Gold Dragons, it was clear they were already tinkering with G-agents—thanks no doubt to Air Force turncoat Christopher Randolph. From there it was only a short leap to going nuclear.

And what had they been planning with their Durango stockpile? A strike somewhere in the U.S.? Or had they planned to ship the G-agents back home for use in Myanmar or Thailand? The latter scenario seemed most likely, but that didn't mean America would be off the hook. Brognola had never given much credence to the domino theory, but if Thailand, a longtime U.S. ally, were to somehow fall under totalitarian rule—especially one in collusion with gangsters and the Myanmar junta—ASEAN, Southeast Asia's answer to NATO and the closest thing to a calming influence in the region, would be in danger of collapse. Factor in the uncertain loyalties of other neighboring countries like India, China, and North Korea—who all had a vested interest in supporting the SPDC—and America could well find itself steeped in a quagmire every bit as difficult to escape as 1960s Vietnam.

"Earth to Brognola."

The big Fed snapped out of his reverie and realized he was racing along at nearly twice his normal pace on the treadmill. As he slowed, he nodded a greeting to Buck Greene, who'd just climbed onto the adjacent machine.

"Hells bells, chief," Greene told him, "you were going at that thing like a lab rat chasing the cheese."

"Chasing after rats is more like it," Brognola said. "How goes it with you? You happy with the new antiaircraft guns?"

"And how," Greene replied. "Little bastards are up and running. Now we just have to keep them free of cobwebs. I hear we've tracked down their cousins down Myanmar way."

"We're definitely on the scent," Brognola said. He passed along the latest on the search for the stolen LAVs, including the news that the Army Ranger team had been forced to retreat to Thailand.

"Gonna be tougher now for Phoenix Force," Greene said. "These SLORC goons'll be itching to fire at anything that moves."

"On the bright side, they've cut back operations at Guna," Brognola said. "From the looks of the latest sat intel, they might have even pulled out altogether."

"Probably because they know we've got the eye in the sky trained on them," Greene said.

"That or maybe they got their hands on what they were looking for," Brognola countered. "In any event, Calvin and Rafe won't be going up against a full-scale operation. It's a small break in our favor, but we'll take it."

Greene was about to ask why only two members of Phoenix Force were tackling the Guna assignment when Brognola held up a hand to quiet him. Greene followed his boss's gaze to a large ceiling-mounted television suspended in front of the treadmills. Onscreen was a CNN story on funeral services for Carrie and Eric Lamarck. Brognola turned up the sound. There was a clip of the undersecretary's eulogy, after which the news anchor reported that the

U.S. government was looking into the circumstances behind the couple's deaths in the waters off Myanmar. Thankfully there was no mention of specifics, but Brognola's relief was short-lived.

"When we come back," the anchorman intoned gravely, "news of a possible link between the Lamarck killings and the recent kidnapping of an Air Force officer in Colorado Springs. Has a notorious Asian cult declared war on the U.S.? Stay tuned...."

"Cult?" Greene muttered. "They're gangsters, for crying out loud!"

Brognola muted the sound as the newscast broke away for commercials. "Somebody must've leaked word about the hazmat findings," he told Greene. "They're leaping to the conclusion it's Aum Shinrikyo."

"Those idiots who gassed the subways in Tokyo?"

Brognola nodded. "Happens every time these people race each other for a scoop," he muttered. "They get it all wrong."

Without breaking stride on the treadmill, Greene toweled his forehead and asked, "What have you guys come up with on this Randolph guy?"

Brognola told Greene the Farm was now working on a theory that Randolph hadn't been kidnapped. "We're getting new information that points toward espionage."

"Whoa!" Greene said. "Randolph's a spy?"

"It's looking that way," Brognola said. "I had a conference call an hour ago with some of his colleagues back at Pearson AFB in Colorado. Seems Randolph wasn't exactly a happy camper there the past few months."

"What, he wasn't getting enough paper clips?" Greene said.

"More like he'd had his fill of paper clips altogether," Brognola said. "He wanted reassignment overseas."

"Wait. I'd heard the guy spent thirty years glued to same desk and was happy as a clam about it."

"Like I said, this was left out of Randolph's dossier," Brognola said. "Deliberately, no doubt, when you consider Evan Harris was the one who left it out."

"Let me guess," Greene stated. "This overseas gig Randolph wanted was in Myanmar."

"Actually he'd kept it broad," Brognola said. "He just wanted to be stationed somewhere in Southeast Asia."

"He give a reason?"

"Apparently he took his vacations there every year and felt that made him some sort of expert," Brognola said. "And, get this—he wanted out of records. He was looking to do intelligence work."

Greene had to laugh. "Based on what qualifications?"

"That we know of? None," Brognola said. "I'm sure he handled his share of sensitive papers, but you don't go from that to spy work, especially when you're as close as he was to retirement. They told him as much when they turned him down."

"And so he got pissed and switched sides?" Greene asked. "Just like that?"

Brognola shook his head. "No, we're thinking this was all a long time coming. All those vacations he took out that way? It would've given him plenty of opportunities to get acquainted with the Gold Dragons. Hell, for all we know, he's been in their fold for years, passing along info every time he got his two weeks off."

"Regular Jekyll and Hyde, huh?" Greene mused. "Plays mild-mannered desk jockey, then turns around and passes state secrets to the enemy."

"It's a theory at this point," Brognola said. "For better or worse, when you think it through, things start to fit."

Brognola finally got off the treadmill. Greene did the same and both men headed for the locker room. On the way Greene muttered, ''You're right. If you figure Randolph for a spy, all this shit makes sense in a screwy sort of way.''

''Exactly,'' Brognola said. ''And if we're right about this, Randolph's the first U.S. spy SLORC's managed to bring in under their wing. Quite a coup for them.''

''Which means, wherever he is, they're probably treating him like royalty.''

''If that's the case, he better enjoy it while he can,'' Brognola said, stopping by the water cooler. He took a sip, then went on. ''Now that he's cut loose, there's only so much more intel he can turn over before he's tapped out. After that, he's going to find out SLORC's idea of a retirement home is a little more severe than ours.''

CHAPTER FIFTEEN

Yangon, Myanmar

Soe Paing woke with a start. As always, his first sensation was the rank smell from his bedpan. It was set in the opposite corner from where he'd fallen asleep, but in the dog cells that was only a few feet away. The stench churned his stomach, stifling the pangs of hunger that had awakened him. Slowly he sat up. He was stiff and his body ached from lying on the hard concrete floor. He had no idea how long he'd slept but it couldn't have been more than a few hours. Stretching as best he could in his cramped confines, Paing thought back to the horrors of the previous night and was overcome with despair. Why bother trying to keep his strength up? Any minute he was likely to be hauled back out before the firing squad. If he wasn't gunned down this time, he'd have only a short reprieve before it happened all over again.

Paing slumped back down onto the concrete. Shortly, an armed soldier appeared at the barred door to his cell. Saying nothing, he crouched over and slid a wooden tray through a small gap between the door and the concrete. In the bleak light, Soe Paing saw two plates on the tray. One contained a cupful of tepid, rust-colored water, the other a dollop of fish paste floating in some broth the same color as the water. For the political prisoners of Insein, this was breakfast.

Of course, Soe Paing knew there was a way to earn himself a more substantial meal. Not only that, but also a hot shower and fresh clothes. Maybe even a chance, after five long years, to see his children and lead the sort of life most took for granted. He could put an end to this constant state of degradation that had become his life. All he had to do was agree to become a mouthpiece for the SPDC. Stand before some camera and tell his fellow countrymen not to observe the anniversary of the Four Eights, tell them to forget how the Tatmadaw had butchered the innocent fifteen years ago when they dared to stand up and raise a cry for freedom. He could follow the general's advice and couch his words with nobility, saying his only concern was to prevent unnecessary bloodshed and keep the peace. It could sound like a public-service announcement.

"No," he told himself. Never. If Maw Saung Ku-Syi could maintain her resolve, then so could he.

Soe Paing stared across the cell at his breakfast. Soon he heard, above the pained growling of his stomach, a faint wriggling sound. Something brushed past him along the floor. Paing recoiled. A large rat scurried over to the breakfast tray and sniffed the fish paste, then began to nibble at it.

Soe Paing stared at the rodent with revulsion. Then, in a sudden fit of temper, he lashed out with one leg and kicked the tray. The rat fled as the plates—both made of cheap plastic—clattered noisily across the concrete, spilling their contents. Paing crawled forward and devoured what was left of the fish paste, then licked his fingers, laughing maniacally as he glanced around the cell, hoping to taunt the rat. The creature was nowhere to be seen, however. Paing's laughter faded as quickly as it had erupted. He regarded the mess he'd made, then slowly shrank back in the corner.

Footsteps echoed down the hallway and soon the guard reappeared, drawn by the disturbance.

"Plates!" he barked.

Paing stared at the door but did not answer.

"Your plates!" the guard repeated. "Slide them back under the door! Now!"

Paing's jaw trembled, then the words tumbled out. "I'll do it," he said.

The guard peered at the old man quizzically. "Do what?"

"Anything," Paing sobbed, his voice trembling. "Tell the general I'll do anything he wants."

Dwiti Military Base, Myanmar

BIEN PHYR STOOD to one side as the other generals swarmed around the three newly arrived LAVs being displayed outside the armory at the Tatmadaw's military base twenty-five miles north of Yangon. Nestled in a remote mountain valley between Bago and Tharrawaddy, the Dwiti installation was far and away the largest and—due to its proximity to Yangon—the most strategic of the country's eleven bases. The Y-25s would help bolster the facility's defense against aerial attack.

"The others will soon be in place near key rebel stations to the north," boasted General Dy Lii, the officer responsible for securing the weapons from his contacts with the Chinese military. "They will go a long ways toward repelling any offensive by the Shan or Karen."

Bien Phyr wasn't impressed. Not only had the LAVs come at the price of further indebtedness to the Chinese, but their acquisition had also clearly raised the hackles of the U.S. military. Already one team of American commandos had been reported within Myanmar's borders. Who was to say there weren't more, giving the Tatmadaw yet one more headache to contend with as the anniversary of the Four Eights approached? Besides, what were a few antiaircraft guns compared to his recent contributions to the junta? It grated him to see Dii bending over backward to curry favor with the other generals. But that was Dii's way; kiss up and hoard the spotlight. Phyr despised the man. He wanted to put him back in his place.

"How goes it with your spies?" Phyr asked Lii once the other generals had finished fawning over the contraband weapons. "Have they learned any more about the NLD's plans?"

Lii shrugged. "Not yet, but they are close."

"They were close yesterday, too, yes?" Phyr said.

Lii's eyes narrowed as he glared at Phyr. Two years older than Phyr, Lii had been a general for more than a year. With the military's upper ranks getting on in years, many within the Tatmadaw had come to view the young officer as a prospective successor to Senior General Khin Wun. Now, out of nowhere, Bien Phyr was being mentioned as a candidate in the same breath as Dy Lii. It was not a rivalry Dy Lii cared for. He thought Phyr was an upstart, an opportunist who would still be working behind a computer at intelligence headquarters if he hadn't stumbled upon the secret of Guna Island.

"We are still within the timetable," Lii responded coolly. "These things take time...as, perhaps, you have noticed with your efforts at Insein."

Several of the older generals chuckled, amused by the sparring. Senior General Lon Kyth, however, was in no mood for internal bickering. True, he had personally championed Bien Phyr's recent promotion, but as ranking officer among those gathered outside the armory, he felt it his duty to keep the others focused on more pressing matters.

"If you'll all take your seats," he said, gesturing at a

table set beneath a nearby canopy, "we have much to discuss."

Bien Phyr and Dy Lii took seats at opposite ends of the table. As an obvious gesture of neutrality, Lon Kyth situated himself directly between them. Ample servings of food had been set out. Most of the generals began to eat immediately, attacking their plates as if they were battlefields. Though he said nothing, Phyr found their voraciousness obscene. He made a quick vow to himself that he would never end up looking like them, so fat their uniforms seemed ready to burst at the seams and send their medals flying from their chests like so much shrapnel.

Lon Kyth began the briefing, arguing against making an issue of the U.S. Army Rangers who'd been reported near Mu-se. "They have obviously slipped back into Thailand and we have no proof other than hearsay that they were here," he explained. "Of course, if we find other evidence of infiltration, it will be another matter."

"I think restraint is wise," Dy Lii agreed, "not just because of the killings in Mergui, but also because of what has happened back in America with the Gold Dragons."

Phyr bristled. Of course Dy Lii would have to bring up the Colorado business. According to intelligence that had just come in prior to the meeting, things hadn't gone well there the past two days, and, worse yet for Phyr, the events all cast the Gold Dragons in a highly unfavorable light. He felt compelled to defend his fellow gangsters and quickly pointed out that the SPDC's primary objectives in Colorado had been carried out. The American spy Christopher Randolph had made it safely to Thailand and would soon be joining them here at Dwiti to attend to the items salvaged from Guna harbor. With him, he'd also brought along a promised shipment of G-agents.

"All in all," Phyr concluded, "despite the loss of a few men, we are far ahead of the game."

There were murmurings of agreement around the table. Dy Lii, predictably, refrained. Lon Kyth was beginning to discuss troop movements to coincide with the anniversary of the Four Eights when an aide emerged from the armory and made his way to Bien Phyr's side, carrying a cell phone.

"For you, sir," the aide said. "It's from Insein."

Phyr eyed his fellow generals, then took the receiver. The conversation was brief, and when it was over, a smile broke across the young general's face.

"Ku-Syi has capitulated," he announced, sending the aide away. "So has one of her advisers."

Cries of triumph broke out around the table. Beaming, the general closest to Phyr slapped him repeatedly on the back.

"Was that Ku-Syi on the phone?" Lon Kyth asked once the commotion had settled down.

Phyr shook his head. "It was the warden," he explained. "Apparently Ku-Syi wants to see me personally."

"Well, on your way, then, General," Lon Kyth called out, snapping off a salute without leaving his seat. "You've done us proud, Bien Phyr."

Phyr returned the salute and said he would call back shortly with more details. As he rose from the table, Phyr stole a glance Dy Lii's way, relishing his rival's look of unmitigated envy. Leaving the gathering, Phyr's spirits continued to rise. He felt as if destiny were on his side, guiding him along the path to his dreams.

"Life is good," he told himself as he strode toward the military jeep waiting to take him to Insein.

IN DAYLIGHT, the open courtyard between the prison's two walls looked far less ominous than it had the previous night. Two prison trustees were scrubbing blood off the front steps leading to Ku-Syi's cottage. As Bien Phyr and the warden approached, the men on the steps looked up, then slowly moved aside, staring all the while at the general. Phyr pretended not to notice the attention. Like all good generals, he knew that one had to choose carefully when to respond to awe and adulation. The rest of the time, it was better to merely go about one's business, as if the demands of one's position allowed no time for flattery.

"Perhaps we should bring out Soe Paing and wait for a cameraman," Phyr suggested. "We can tape their remarks and have them broadcast by the end of the day."

"We can deal with Soe Paing later," Boesan told Phyr. "As for a camera, I'm not sure that's a good idea."

"Why not?"

"See for yourself, General."

With that, the warden opened the front door and ushered Phyr into the small cabin. Phyr knew at once something was amiss. His attention was drawn to a shadow stretching across the floorboards in front of him. The shadow swayed slightly, back and forth. Slowly Phyr raised his gaze upward. A gasp sprang involuntarily from his throat.

Before him, Maw Saung Ku-Syi, the noose from a knotted bedsheet wrapped tight around her neck, dangled lifelessly from the rafters.

"Congratulations," Warden Boesan told Phyr. "You definitely have a way with the women."

CHAPTER SIXTEEN

Andaman Sea, Southern coast of Myanmar

A half hour had passed since Pag Ti, at gunpoint, had guided the hijacked longboat out of Kwathoung Harbor into the tranquil waters of the Andaman Sea. The mainland had just dropped from view below the horizon, and for the first time, there were no other boats in sight. Or land, either, for that matter. Thathay Kyun and Salon Island, the resort isles Pag Ti had told the customs officials they would be visiting, were miles south of the course Calvin James and Rafael Encizo found themselves now taking.

"Nice place to dump a few bodies without anyone being the wiser," James whispered ruefully to Encizo, sitting across from him on a bench in the holding bay of the long-boat.

"The question is, whose bodies is it gonna be," Rafael whispered back.

"No yappin'," Rick the Texan snapped. He crouched nearby, shaded by the boat's thatched roof, holding both his gun and the 9 mm pistol he'd taken from James. Behind him, Tony was similarly armed, standing guard over Pag Ti, who was under orders to take the boat to Guna Island.

James and Encizo knew they could have easily overpowered their captors back in Kwathoung, but doing so would have drawn the militia to the docks, which, in turn, would have led to a search of their weapon-laden gear bags, scuttling the mission and placing themselves at the junta's mercy. Now that they were out on the open sea, however, they could feel freer about taking matters into their own hands. The gear bags, which the hijackers had yet to inspect, lay within easy reach at James's and Encizo's feet. What the men needed was a distraction.

"What's so important to you about Guna Island?" James asked Rick, hoping to lull him with a little conversation.

"I thought I just told you to shut up," Rick said.

James persisted. "Some great snorkeling?" he asked. "Hardly seems like something worth hijacking over."

"Kinda depends what you're snorkeling for," Rick said.

James played dumb. "Coral formations? Shark schools?"

"Oh, quit trying to be coy, you asshole," Rick told him. "You're after the treasure, too, and we both know it."

"Treasure?" James laughed, sticking to the script that went with his passport identity. "We've got gambling on our cruise ships, ace. If we want loot, we just open the casinos and the chumps hand it over as fast as they can get it out of their pockets." He quickly embellished his and Encizo's cover story, explaining how they'd hoped to establish Kwathoung as a port of call. "Hell, we're just looking for a way to ease the sting once everybody's tapped out their ATM cards."

"Yeah," Encizo said, playing along. "You send the losers snorkeling, nobody has to listen to them complain."

Rick frowned. "You're bullshitting me, right?"

Encizo shook his head. "I don't know what this treasure is you're talking about, but why bother diving for it when you can rake it in without getting wet?"

"Maybe because we're talking millions of dollars," Rick said. "We're talking sunken ships, hundreds of years old, stuffed with gold bullion and who knows what else."

"And you think that's why the junta's closed off Guna Island?"

"Damn right," Rick said. "We've heard the rumors. That couple was killed because they caught the junta pulling up gold bars. And if they've found one galleon, there's gotta be more nearby. We'll just stay clear of the military and sniff around till we find our own ship. One quick haul and we'll be rich!"

Encizo recalled the talk back at Stony Man about long-sunken galleons. He'd been skeptical, but maybe there was something to it after all. He was about to prod the Texan for more info when Tony called out from the rear of the boat.

"Looks like we got company, Rick!"

Rick glanced away from Encizo and James and peered out across the water. A boat had just broached the horizon and was headed their way, cutting a wake in its path.

"It's a hell of a lot faster than we are," Tony said.

Concerned, Rick tucked James's pistol in the waistband of his slacks and fumbled through his own gear bag for some binoculars. In the process he took his eyes off James and Encizo for a fleeting second. It was the break they were looking for. James, already crouched forward on the bench, suddenly sprang forward. He broadsided the Texan, lashing out with his right hand and knocking the man's gun from his hand. Caught off balance, Rick toppled backward. James's momentum carried them both over the side of the boat into the water.

Tony stood up in the rear of the boat and whirled. He was still trying to figure out what had happened when Pag Ti spun away from the motor and struck him sharply just below the knees. Tony fired an errant shot through the thatch roof as he stumbled into the boat's hold. Encizo quickly sprang forward and disarmed him, then used the

butt of his reclaimed Beretta to knock the hijacker unconscious.

In the water, meanwhile, James made equally quick work
of the Texan with a judo chop to the back of the head.

"What a couple of stooges," Encizo said. "My mother
could've put up a better fight than that."

Pag Ti left the engine running and helped Encizo haul
Rick back aboard. Meanwhile, off in the distance, the
speedboat continued to draw closer. A few men were standing up in the back of the vessel, looking their way.

"Whoever they are, we owe them some thanks," Pag Ti
said.

Encizo grabbed Rick's fallen binoculars and took a
closer look at the other boat. One of the men had just
propped a grenade launcher on his shoulder. Encizo told
Pag Ti, "I think they're looking for something besides
thanks."

FOR ALL the fanciful images they conjured up in the public
imagination, the pirates of the Andaman Sea were, on the
whole, pale imitations of their swashbuckling forefathers.
Their Gold Dragon tattoos were equally misleading, as
none of the men had any current affiliation with the
Bangkok-based gang. At one point or another they'd all
been ostracized, usually on grounds of stupidity or insub-
ordination. Having blown their chance at big money on the
mainland, these exiled hooligans—as Barbara Price had
mentioned back at the Farm—were forced to subsist on the
meager plunder of tourist robberies. The high murder rate
associated with their crimes, consequently, had as much to
do with exasperation as the men's inherent brutality.

Ki Var Mayt's crew was no exception. Over the past two
months, they'd staged thirteen attacks on tourist vessels,
leaving eight dead while raking in less "booty" than
Swarng Bancha made off his women on a good weekend

at the Royal Peacock. After splitting shares, there'd barely been enough money left over to repair Var Mayt's ten-year-old Chris-Craft boat, which doubled as the group's sorry excuse for a pirate ship. And now, to make matters worse, their turf was being cordoned off due to some recent killings for which, ironically, they were being blamed. It wasn't fair. But what could he do about it? Life had dealt him a shit hand; all he could do was play it out as best he could.

"Go ahead," Var Mayt called out to his cronies as he opened the throttle, closing in on the longboat.

The man beside him nodded and fired his M-79 grenade launcher. He'd aimed wide, intending to deliver nothing more than a warning shot, but his trajectory was off and the 40 mm projectile exploded directly alongside the craft. Var Mayt cursed as he watched the longboat's prow rise up out of the water, then pitch sharply to one side, tossing some of its passengers into the water before beginning to take in water.

"Idiot!" Var Mayt took a hand off the controls and shoved the other man. "How can we rob the ship if it sinks!"

The other man glared back at Var Mayt, waving the M-79 in his face. "Don't blame me! Blame this! I told you the sights were off, but you never listen!"

Var Mayt was about to say something but checked himself. The rest of the crew—men armed with cheap pistols and assault rifles—was eyeing him with weariness and disgust; the last thing he needed was a mutiny on his hands.

"All right," he said tiredly, "Let's get this over with."

RAFAEL ENCIZO SURFACED in the warm water, dazed, his ears still ringing from the explosion. A charcoal-sized piece of shrapnel had embedded itself in his shoulder. He grimaced as he yanked the shard free and felt the sting of salt water on the wound. He would have to tend to the bleeding later. Brushing away a floating section of the longboat's thatch roof, he swam over to Pag Ti, who was a few yards away, dragging one of the hijackers up onto the hull of the overturned boat. It was Rick the Texan; he was either dead or unconscious. His partner was missing, as was Calvin James.

"Here." Pag Ti took Encizo's gun from Rick's waistband and held it out to him. "They're coming in for the kill."

Encizo peered over the hull. The speedboat was less than fifty yards away and rapidly closing in. On deck, the pirates were preparing to fire. Encizo drew a bead on the man with the grenade launcher. The waves threw off his aim, however, and his shot flew wide. The little Cuban was about to fire again when someone surfaced off to his right, gasping loudly. It was Calvin James. He was treading water with one hand while he used the other to haul one of the gear bags onto the hull. "The other one slipped away before I could get to it," he sputtered.

Before Encizo could respond, bullets strafed their way. Both he and James dropped low behind the bobbing hull to avoid being hit. Rick the Texan, however, took three shots to the torso and rolled limply back into the sea, never having regained consciousness. Encizo let the body sink past him, then fired on the speedboat, emptying his clip in a sweeping arc that sent one pirate over the side and dropped another onto the deck beside Var Mayt. The other pirates quickly ducked for cover. Realizing they were in for a fight, Var Mayt, crouching low behind the speedboat's controls, let up on the throttle and began to circle the capsized longboat.

James, meanwhile, tugged the gear bag's zipper open. Inside, along with his and Encizo's scuba gear and other underwater paraphernalia, was a handful of M-26 A-1 fragmentation grenades.

"So much for keeping their boat in one piece." He passed grenades to Pag Ti and Encizo, whispering, "On three."

They counted down, then tossed the bombs in unison. Encizo's and Pag Ti's grenades detonated side by side off the front of the speedboat, ripping a gash in the hull. James had even better luck. His M-26 landed on deck and went off as one of the pirates was reaching for it. The man's arm disintegrated, splattering those around him. There were screams of agony as the boat took on water and began to sink. The deck caught fire and within seconds flames reached a ruptured fuel line, setting off an explosion louder than the first three combined. The boat split in two and, within a matter of seconds, sank from view, leaving behind flames to feed on a fuel slick and scattered bits of debris. There was no sign of survivors.

Encizo, James and Pag Ti silently stared past the bobbing remnants of the pirate boat. An uninterrupted blue horizon stretched away from them in all directions. They may have cheated death for the moment, but with few provisions and not one of the archipelago's eight hundred islands within view, it seemed only a matter of time before they would be joining the band of renegades at the bottom of the sea. Encizo finally voiced the men's despair.

"This really sucks," he said.

CHAPTER SEVENTEEN

Bangkok, Thailand

While tension hung darkly over Myanmar's pending ob-servance of the Four Eights, the mood in Bangkok was festive, as this time of year marked the birthday of Thailand's Queen Sirikit. There would be a somber religious ceremony at Chitlada Palace on August 12, but afterward the city would erupt with several days' worth of boisterous, Mardis Gras-like revelry. Already city work crews were out in full force stringing lights up and down the streets and avenues.

"'It's beginning to look a lot like Christmas,'" T. J. Hawkins sang from the back seat as David McCarter ne-gotiated their rental car through the slow crawl of traffic along Rama 1 Road. Gary Manning, riding up front with McCarter in the late-model Nissan, glanced back at Hawkins. "Keep it down, would you?"

"Killjoy," Hawkins said.

At the next intersection, the three men found themselves waiting for a red light alongside an open-topped bus filled with English-speaking tourists. A guide with a cheap mega-phone was directing everyone's attention down the nearby lane. There, she intoned, was the house of Jim Thompson, the infamous onetime OSS agent who made a fortune re-viving the Thai silk industry before mysteriously vanishing off the face of the earth during a 1967 trip to the Malaysian highlands. Most theories linked his disappearance to the same kind of espionage-tinged intrigue now surrounding missing USAF officer Christopher Randolph.

"Hey, maybe we should check it out," Hawkins said. "Who knows, maybe Randolph and Thompson have hooked up."

McCarter eyed Hawkins in the rearview mirror. "Exactly how much sugar did you have with your cereal this morning, T.J.?"

"Just trying to stay loose, guys. Cut me a little slack."

The light changed. As McCarter continued down the road, Manning's cell phone bleated. He took the call, his features darkening as he listened.

"Got it," he said. Hanging up, he glanced at Hawkins and McCarter. "That was Katz. He just got off the horn with Stony Man. Seems the Gold Dragons might have a little something at their base here besides comp gear and a smack lab."

"Tea and crackers?" McCarter said.

"You wish," Manning said. "Try an arsenal of G-agents." He quickly told the men about Able Team's firefight in Durango and the subsequent discovery of a biochemical stockpile. "No one's sure if any of the stuff made it overseas," he added, "but Katz doesn't want us taking any chances."

"We're supposed to hold off on the raid until he can arrange some hazmat backup. He also wants to see if the Thais have some kind of SWAT crew they can send along."

"Forget that shit," Hawkins said. "Hell, if Able Team can kick ass with just three guys, so can we. I say we go for it."

McCarter thought it over, then asked Manning, "How did Katz put it? Is this an order?"

Manning shook his head. "Sounded more to me like a strong recommendation. Definitely not an order."

"So, if we showed up and were forced into action…"

"I'm sure he'd understand," Manning said with a grin.

"Hell, yes," Hawkins agreed. "Happens all the time."

"Fair enough, lads." McCarter turned onto Wireless Road. "Let's get those bastards."

After passing the American Embassy and the eastern periphery of Lumphini Park, the men crossed Rama 4 Road and found themselves in what seemed to be a whole other world. Gone were the tourist-friendly sights—the Bangkok of quaint spirit houses, gilded wats and roving, orange-robed monks. In their place, the men from Phoenix Force found themselves surrounded by a charmless squalor where the city's poor were packed into cramped, poorly constructed tenements that seemed on the verge of toppling into the refuse-strewn streets. There was hunger on the gaunt faces of thousands who teemed along cracked sidewalks, and when traffic slowed to yet another stop, children dressed in rags flocked around the Nissan, pounding on the windows and holding out their hands for alms.

"Hardly seems like the kind of place to open an electronics store," Hawkins mused grimly.

Indeed, two blocks later, when McCarter drove by their target destination, the store in question had a rusty, padlocked gate drawn across its front doors. Grimy, half its windows broken and replaced by plywood boards covered with flyers for Patpong Road sex clubs, the two-story building looked as if it hadn't been open for business in years. The adjacent storefronts were equally desolate, and, like the electronics store, their front doorways weren't only gated, but also heaped with what appeared to be a month's worth of accumulated trash and litter. Understandably there was only a trickle of pedestrian traffic compared to what Phoenix Force had encountered only moments earlier. And yet, despite the dreariness of the neighborhood—or perhaps because of it—a crew of five city workers in white coveralls was diligently stringing lights along the sidewalk. Even the poor, it seemed, would have their chance to go crazy over the queen's birthday.

"Are you sure this is the right place?" Manning asked. "This whole block looks like it's ready for the wrecking ball."

"Take a closer look." Hawkins drew Manning's attention to the rooftop of the electronics store. "They've got more antennas than a bushel load of grasshoppers up there, and my money says they're not just trying to get better reception on the weather channel."

"The antennas look newer than the rest of the building, too," Manning remarked.

"'More antennas than a bushel load of grasshoppers'?" McCarter repeated. "You steal that one from Dan Rather, T.J.?"

"Har-har," Hawkins said. "Actually it was my aunt Denise. Used to dip those little bastards in chocolate and sell them at the roadside stand along with the okra and summer squash."

McCarter made a face. "I'd bloody well hate to see what that woman does with the Christmas turkey."

Half a block past the electronics store, McCarter wedged the Nissan into a curbside parking space. Getting out of the car, the men noticed two chain-smoking teenage boys eyeing the car's hubcaps. McCarter approached them, smiling, using hand signals to ask if the boys would like to earn some money keeping an eye on the car. The boys quickly conferred with each other, then flashed fingers, indicating how much they expected to be paid. McCarter wasn't about to squabble with them. As he reached for his money, however, he made sure both youths got a good look at his Beretta.

"That should keep them honest," McCarter reflected as he led Manning and Hawkins down the nearest alleyway.

"That or they'll make sure they have us outgunned when we come back," Hawkins said.

"Take a lot to outgun us, now, wouldn't it?" McCarter said, patting his duffel bag, which contained an MP-5 subgun, extra ammo and an assortment of grenades. Hawkins and Manning carried similar bundles. All three men were dressed in loose cotton, the better to conceal their Kevlar vests.

Coming up behind the electronics store, the men crouched behind a row of trash bins and paused to evaluate the situation. The store's rear-loading platform was sealed off by a segmented, retractable gate. Several yards to the right of the gate was a door. Both were made of steel and secured by high-security locks that looked as new as the rooftop antennae.

"Something tells me the windows are reinforced with something besides just plywood," Manning stated.

"I'm sure you're right," Hawkins said. "They've got to have lookouts posted inside somewhere, too. What do we do?"

McCarter shifted his attention from the building to the work crew stringing lights between two power poles across the street. He watched them briefly, then turned to Hawkins and Manning. "How would you lads feel about doing a little charity work for the fine folks of Bangkok?"

"YOUR BELOVED General Phyr called while you were out riding your Suzuki," Gui Rahb told Swarng Bancha. "He wants to see Semba Hru. Immediately."

The two Gold Dragon members were huddled by Rahb's computers in a storage room above the onetime electronics store. Despite the room's stultifying heat, Bancha hadn't bothered taking off his motorcycle leathers. Gui Rahb, by contrast, wore only a *longyi,* sandals and a sleeveless T-shirt. Two other men were in the storeroom, both dressed like Rahb but armed with Uzi submachine guns. One was posted at the doorway leading downstairs; the other peered out at the street through a narrow slot in one of the boarded windows. Although the Gold Dragons had operated out of the storefront for years without incident, Gui Rahb remained a stickler about security, especially when the gang's renegade chemists were downstairs cooking up a million dollars' worth of fresh methamphetamines.

"Why does he want to see her?" Bancha asked.

"He didn't say," Gui Rahb responded, "He just said to have her put on the next available flight to Yangon. Oh, there was one more thing—he said she needn't bother packing."

Swarng Bancha didn't like the sound of it. Much as he was still annoyed with Semba Hru after her little snit, he was hesitant to turn her over to Phyr. The last time he'd come by the Peacock—several weeks ago, just before the beginning of salvage operations at Guna Island—Phyr had asked for Semba Hru, but, knowing the general's reputation for rough sex surpassed even Bancha's, she'd refused. Phyr, of course, had taken offense. Bancha had smoothed things over, allowing the general two girls in the presidential suite for a night, but he knew Phyr had a long memory, especially when it came to being slighted. It was just like him to summon Semba Hru the way he had. Now she would have an entire flight during which to agonize over what he might have in store for her.

"How did Phyr sound on the phone?" Bancha asked.

"The way he always sounds," Rahb responded bitterly. "Like he had hemorrhoids that I was somehow to blame for."

"I see you're still upset he came by and borrowed your computers for a few days last month," Bancha said.

"If he'd have asked, I wouldn't have minded," Rahb said. "But, no, instead he raises a hoop and expects everyone to jump through it, just because he is the mighty general."

"I'll make sure to tell him that's what you think of him," Bancha threatened, only half joking. He crossed the room and placed a quick call to the military base in Dwiti. He wanted to speak with Phyr, not about Gui Rahb, but rather Semba Hru. He wanted to know what the general had in mind for her. Phyr, however, was unavailable. Bancha didn't leave a message. He hesitated a moment, then made a second call, this time to the Peacock. There was only one way to handle this. Once he had Semba Hru on the line, Swarng Bancha mustered humility into his voice as he apologized for his part in their earlier argument. "I want to make it up to you," he told her.

There was a lull on the line, then the woman responded tentatively, "What did you have in mind?"

"I want to take you somewhere," Bancha offered.

"Where?"

"I want it to be a surprise," Bancha said. He checked his watch. "Just put on something nice and meet me at the airfield. I'll have the private jet waiting."

"The Lear? Now I'm really curious."

"Be there as soon as you can, my p— My precious."

"That's more like it." There was now a ring of playful laughter in Semba Hru's voice.

Once off the phone with her, Bancha called the airfield and arranged to have his jet fueled and readied for departure to Yangon. He would go with Semba Hru. It was the only way.

Rahb was still at his computer when Bancha rejoined him. "We're in good shape." Rahb directed Bancha's gaze to the screen, which displayed communication briefs between Thailand's Drug Interdiction Force and a dozen other law-enforcement agencies operating between Bangkok and the Golden Triangle. He'd just run a broad-scale search, and by all accounts, no one suspected the barnstormer of planning to use his aeroshow to smuggle the Dragon's latest opium haul into Bangkok. Nor, of course, was there any indication the authorities knew that Lette, at this very moment, was in Chiang Mai showing off his two F-105 Thunderchiefs to an American by the name of Christopher Randolph.

"It's amazing what you get those computers to do for you," Bancha told Rahb. "Someday you'll have to show me how this hacking business works."

"General Phyr is the great hacker. Ask him."

Before Bancha could respond, the watchman stationed before the boarded window called out to Rahb. "Come take a look."

Rahb saved the computer file he was working on, then walked with Bancha to the window. There was room enough for both men to peer through the surveillance slot. They saw that there was some kind of activity in the street.

"City workers preparing for the queen's birthday," Rahb remarked, noticing the work crew stringing lights out front. "They're working their way up the block. What of it?"

"Look closer at the man on the ladder," the guard said. "His uniform is several sizes too small. He's not Thai."

Bancha took a closer look, alarmed. "He's white."

Rahb, suddenly on his guard, crossed over to the guard posted by the doorway. "Have some of the men downstairs check on those workers," he said. "I don't like the way…"

His voice trailed off as he sniffed the air wafting up the stairwell. He was used to the smell of chemicals being used to process methamphetamines in the downstairs laboratory; this odor was different.

"What the hell is that?" he said, stepping out onto the landing. "It smells like burning trash."

Another gang member suddenly appeared at the foot of the stairwell. "There's a fire in the front doorway," he called up to Rahb. "Some idiot must've tossed a cigarette through the gate and lit something—"

"No!" Rahb cried out. "It's a trick!"

As if to confirm his suspicions, the building suddenly went dark. The power had gone out. Rahb cursed his way back to the computers. The CPUs, linked to a backup power supply, were still up and running, but Rahb was worried the system might crash. He sat down and began clattering away at the keyboard. Bancha, meanwhile, took charge, ordering both guards to yank the plywood from the window facing the street. Daylight flooded into the room as all three men inched forward, guns at the ready, and peered out into the street.

"Looks like some kind of accident with the city workers," Bancha observed. "They must've nicked a power line while they were stringing up lights."

"It's a trick!" Rahb repeated without taking his eyes off the computers.

With a loud crash, the exposed pane of glass suddenly shattered inward, driving back Bancha and the two guards. Glancing down at his feet, Bancha saw a tear-gas grenade and kicked it across the floor. But already a noxious cloud was beginning to envelop the room.

"Out!" His eyes burned as he lurched toward the doorway. "Everybody out!"

"Bastards!" Rahb shouted. The computers were shutting down, but now he was faced with a hard—and quick—decision. If they lost control of the building, the computers, along with the files, would wind up in somebody else's hands—most likely the authorities. The Gold Dragons' entire drug-running operations could be compromised indefinitely. That couldn't be allowed to happen. And taking the computers with him was out of the question. They were too heavy, and there was no time to lug them from the storeroom. As it was, he figured he only had a few more seconds to flee before the tear gas incapacitated him entirely.

Rahb dropped to his knees. Months ago, he'd rigged a timed C-4 plastic-explosive charge under the table after local police, haggling over bribes, had made vague threats about raiding the electronics store. The matter had blown over, but, like the reinforced locks on the exterior doors, the bomb had remained in place, its two-minute timer ready to be activated by the mere entry of a four-digit code.

With a curse, Rahb entered the code, then rushed for the stairs.

CHAPTER EIGHTEEN

U-Tapao Royal Navy Airfield, Thailand

Yakov Katzenelenbogen entered the AFB communications room carrying a paper sack filled with takeout.

"How are we doing?"

Akira Tokaido had his headphones on and didn't hear Katz, but the wafting aroma of *mee krob* and duck salad drew his attention away from the computers.

"All right," he called out, pushing away from his workstation. "I'm starved."

"Any word from Cal or Rafe yet?" Katz asked as he took containers from the sack, handing two of them to Tokaido.

The young man shook his head as he pried open the *mee krob* and fingered some of the sweet, sticky noodles into his mouth. "No, but I'm sure we'll hear from them soon."

"I hope so," Katz said. "Hackers made any moves yet?"

"Afraid not," Tokaido reported. "I've been running word searches through those raided archive files, but I'm still drawing blanks on Guna Island. Mergui came up once, but only as part of a weather forecast."

"Keep at it." Katz raided the take-out sack for some chopsticks, then started picking at the bits of duck in his salad. "They had to be looking for something in those files.

And next time you run a search, throw Christopher Randolph's name in the hopper and see what you come up with.''

"That kidnapped guy? Why?"

Katz, who'd placed a call to the Farm while waiting for the take-out order, quickly briefed Tokaido on Brognola's theory that Randolph hadn't been kidnapped, but rather had orchestrated his disappearance in collusion with Evan Harris, the AF-IA investigator subsequently gunned down by the Gold Dragons in Colorado Springs. "Able Team's on their way to check on this guy Harris and Randolph met with the night before everything started to go down," he concluded.

"Man, is this turning into a can of worms or what?" Tokaido said. "If the chief's right, Randolph's gotta be in cahoots with the Gold Dragons somehow, right?"

"Not only that," Yakov reported, "Hunt's been digging into Randolph's military record and it turns out the guy did a tour of duty in Nam back in the 1960s. Same time frame as those raided archives."

"Was he stationed here in Thailand?" Tokaido asked.

"We don't know that yet," Katz said. "We're having trouble accessing his records back that far."

"If he's gone bad, he probably jimmied the records," Tokaido speculated, "which means there was something worth covering up."

"I'm sure you're right," Katz said. "Bear has Hunt and Carmen going at it full tilt from every direction."

"Good," Tokaido said, "but help me out here. Are we saying now that the Gold Dragons tracked down Randolph based on what they hacked out of the archives?"

"That or the other way around," Katz said. He quickly told Tokaido about Randolph's annual vacations to Southeast Asia, adding, "He was last out two months ago. According to State Department records, he was in Thailand the whole time, which means he could've been the one who orchestrated the hacking in the first place.''

''If that's the case and Able Team hasn't tracked him down in Colorado,'' Tokaido said, ''I say Randolph's come back to see things through.''

''Whatever those 'things' are,'' Katz said. ''Bear's already running a cyber-check on all international flights out of Denver and Colorado Springs. If Randolph hopped a plane he probably used an alias, but he had to go through customs and security, so maybe he'll turn up on the surveillance cameras.''

''Let's hope so.''

The men ate silently for a moment, only to be interrupted by the ringing of the phone near Tokaido's workstation. Hooked up to a security scrambler, the phone only rang through prioritized calls with proper clearance.

''Must be Cal and Rafe.'' Katz reached past Tokaido and took the call. His expression clouded as he exchanged a few words with the caller, then slammed down the receiver.

''They make it to Guna yet?'' Tokaido asked.

''It wasn't them,'' Katz said. ''It was our contacts in Bangkok. Seems McCarter's crew went incommunicado and hit the electronics store without backup.''

''Maybe they didn't have a choice,'' Tokaido suggested.

''Right,'' Katz groused. ''And maybe the world's flat.''

Bangkok, Thailand

ONCE HE'D TRIPPED the electronics store's circuit breakers, T. J. Hawkins moved from the rooftop control box and took cover behind the rusting hulk of a rooftop air-conditioning condenser. Behind him, an acrid-smelling cloud drifted up past the roofline, trailing from the store's front entryway where David McCarter had set off a smoke grenade. Peering down, Hawkins saw that McCarter, dressed as a city worker, was now playing possum on the curb near the crew's panel truck. Behind the truck, Gary Manning was reloading the AGS-17 grenade launcher he'd used to fire tear gas into the building. A few shots hailed his way from the second story, then the gunfire ceased; T.J. figured the tear gas had forced the gunmen to flee. There were only three ways for them to go: out the front or rear entrances or up onto the roof. Hawkins, hoping, for the latter, turned his attention to a locked trapdoor twenty yards away. He didn't have long to wait.

Soon he heard the sound of a sliding bolt, followed by the creaking of the trapdoor's hinges. One of the storeroom guards climbed up onto the roof, quickly followed by two others. All three men carried Uzis, but they were, at least for the moment, still suffering the effects of the tear gas, gagging and rubbing at their eyes. Hawkins made sure no one else was coming up to join them, then grabbed a stray metal bracket lying at the base of the condenser and flung it over the men's heads. When the bracket clanged off one of the antennae, two of the gunmen whirled and fired blindly. The third man, however, had spied Hawkins's throwing motion out of the corner of his eye. He shouted to the others as he leveled his rifle and fired Hawkins's way, rattling his shots harmlessly off the condenser. The Phoenix Force commando returned fire, strafing the man's chest. In short order, he took out the other two men, as well, dropping them before they could bring their weapons into play. He paused to reload, then jogged past the corpses to the trapdoor. Tear gas clouded up through the opening. Hawkins slipped on the gas mask he'd brought with him, then cautiously started down the ladder.

MOMENTS AFTER GUNFIRE sounded on the roof, David McCarter heard the steel door swing open in the front entryway. He pushed himself up off the sidewalk, and not a moment too soon. Bullets chipped at the space where he'd been lying. Whirling, he fired his MP-5 through the smoke-choked entryway, dropping one of the gunmen charging out of the electronics store. Another gangster was right behind him, however, and McCarter was nearly pegged twice as he hurried to join Manning behind the panel truck. The undersized uniform he'd thrown on over his fatigues ripped free at the seams with every step.

Manning fired a tear-gas round into the front entryway, then switched to his assault rifle and began trading shots with the enemy gunmen. "I've got them under control," he told McCarter. "Go ahead and check around back."

McCarter nodded. Cradling his MP-5 close to his chest, he broke from cover and circled to the rear of the building. No one had yet tried to escape out the back way, but a loud rumbling behind the retractable gate tipped him off that something was in the offing. Ducking behind the trash bins, he waited for the Gold Dragons to make the next move.

Moments later, the side door swung open and out charged two gunmen. They glanced around wildly, then shouted at each other over the blare emanating from inside the building. McCarter rose from cover and fired, aiming high on the chance that, like him, the men were wearing body armor. One of the Dragons took a shot to the skull and toppled headlong from the loading dock. His cohort, struck in the neck and shoulder, staggered to cover behind the opened door.

McCarter was about to move in for the kill when, in quick succession, two Suzuki motorcycles barreled out of the building, launching off the dock toward him. They were street bikes and took the jump clumsily, but Swarng Bancha and Gui Rahb were both in control when they landed. Opening their throttles, they raced past the trash bins toward the street and, hopefully, a getaway.

McCarter sprang atop the nearest garbage bin and leaped

outward as the bikes roared past. Bancha was too far ahead of him, but he managed to grab hold of Rahb. The Suzuki lurched out from underneath them as both men toppled to the asphalt. McCarter lost hold of his weapon, and it clattered across the ground away from him. Rahb rolled toward the gun and had his hand on the stock when McCarter swung around on the ground, kicking the gun clear. Cursing, Rahb rolled the other way, yanking an autopistol from the waistband of his *longyi.*

A bullet sang past McCarter's ear as he dived toward his opponent. He grabbed the gun's barrel before Rahb could get off a second shot. Rahb drove his knee toward McCarter's groin, but the Briton twisted to one side, taking the blow in the hip without losing his grip on his adversary's weapon. As they wrestled for control of the pistol, Rahb managed to get his finger back on the trigger. It was a fatal blunder, however, because at the same time McCarter twisted Rahb's wrist, tilting the barrel upward so that when a shot discharged, it cored up through the underside of the drug dealer's chin and plowed into his brain. His hand shrank from the gun and he went limp.

McCarter shoved the dead man off him and was struggling to his feet when a bullet slammed into his side, deflecting off his vest. Wincing at the impact, he traced the shot to Swarng Bancha, who had idled his Suzuki in the alleyway while he fired. McCarter dodged the next shot and made his way to the other motorcycle, which had stalled out ten yards from where he'd tackled Rahb to the ground. The muffler was bent and its tank was scraped, but otherwise the bike seemed operable. The Phoenix Force leader hauled it upright and climbed aboard. Kick-starting the engine, he opened the throttle and roared after Swarng Bancha. The chase was on.

T. J. HAWKINS ADVANCED cautiously through the low-hanging cloud of tear gas in the darkened upstairs hallway.

He had yet to encounter any other gunmen, but he wasn't taking any chances. Nearing the doorway that led to the storage room, he unclipped a stun grenade from his belt and tossed it through the opening. He plugged his ears, waiting out the flash and bang, then charged in. The room was deserted. Through the dying smoke he spotted a bank of computers lining the far wall. Surprised to see some of the LED lights still glowing, he checked under the table, spotting the ancillary power pack…and a timing device linked to a slab of plastic explosives.

O:06…

0:05…

''Holy shit!''

Hawkins was rushing from the table when a gas-masked figure appeared in the doorway, rifle in hand. Manning.

''There's a bomb!'' Hawkins shouted. ''Out the window! Now!''

Manning followed his teammate across the room toward the broken window through which Manning had fired the tear-gas grenade. They dived through the opening just as the explosive charge went off. The blast propelled them past the jagged glass and sent them hurtling toward the street below. Fortunately, directly below them was an old abandoned newsstand. Hawkins hit the sloped roof shoulder first and tumbled to the sidewalk. Manning was right behind him. Debris rained down on them as they lay, stunned, on the concrete. Hawkins winced as a slab of plywood glanced off his hip. He whipped off his gas mask and staggered to his feet, offering a hand to Manning.

''You okay, man?''

Manning nodded, tugging off his mask, as well. Both men stared up at the second floor of the building. Smoke and flames poured out of the ravaged windows. Behind them, the terrified city workers peered out from inside the panel truck. Elsewhere on the street, a crowd was beginning to gather, drawn by the commotion. Sirens howled in the distance.

"Our backup's a little late," Hawkins said.

"Let's get the hell out of here."

The two members of Phoenix Force fled toward the back alley leading to their rental car. On the way they passed three slain Dragons, including Gui Rahb.

"Where's McCarter?" Hawkins asked.

"Rounding up a stray," Manning said. "He's on his own."

HUNCHED LOW astride his commandeered Suzuki, Mc-Carter raced along the side streets of Bangkok's south side, his eyes riveted on the tailpipe of Swarng Bancha's motorcycle. The Briton was an accomplished rider, but so, apparently, was Bancha. The Thai gangster also had the advantage of knowing the streets and could power his way more readily through the growing congestion.

McCarter, forced to ride more defensively, began to lose ground. At one point, Bancha slipped from view, cutting a corner sharply and veering off South Sathorn road into a back alley. To keep pace, McCarter had to veer around a garbage truck, leaning the bike sharply to one side to keep from colliding with the vehicle's massive hoist arms. Any miscalculation would have sent the bike into a roll, but McCarter persevered. Once through the alley, he righted the bike and kept the throttle open until Bancha was back in view.

At the intersection of Sathorn and Rama 4 Road, both bikers sped through a red light, nearly colliding with a Thai patrol car en route to investigate the explosions at the electronics store. The officer pulled a quick U-turn and sounded his siren as he followed McCarter and Bancha through the entranceway into Lumphini Park.

The largest tract of parkland in the entire city, Lumphini was a popular getaway spot for locals and tourists alike. Along with sprawling foliage, topiary displays and playground areas for children, the park featured a large manmade lake that encircled the grounds like a wide moat. Families were out on rental pontoons and paddleboats, and a handful of young boys frolicked near the lake's edge, trying to skip stones across the water. The tranquil tableau was shattered when Bancha burst into view, throttling his motorcycle across a wooden pedestrian bridge. McCarter was right behind, but the bridge was too narrow for the patrol car. The officer hit the brakes, then called for backup before bounding out, gun in hand, shouting for everyone to take cover and get out of his way.

Once he'd passed over the bridge, Bancha rounded a corner and bore down on a tourist group strolling up a dirt footpath leading away from the lake. When an elderly woman was slow in getting out of his way, Bancha clipped her with the cycle, knocking her to the ground. Enraged, the other tourists shouted at Bancha, then turned their fury on McCarter, pelting him with rocks and stones as he sped past. The Briton grimaced as one of the projectiles glanced off his knuckles, almost forcing him to lose control of the bike.

Bancha stayed on the path another fifty yards, then veered off into a heavily wooded area. McCarter stayed with him, bike whining beneath him as he weaved through the tightly clustered trees. Anxious to end the pursuit, he forged right and blazed his own trail, riding parallel to Bancha while looking for a point at which to converge. Coming up on a gently pitched knoll, he let up briefly on the gas, reopening the throttle once he hit the incline. The burst of momentum sent him airborne through the uppermost branches of a thicket. He came down hard, rear end first, on a wet patch of grass. Tapping his brakes, he sent the bike into a short skid and then changed directions, putting himself back on Bancha's trail. The maneuver had brought him to within thirty yards of the fleeing gangster.

Startled, Bancha doglegged to his left and raced toward the center of the park, finally bursting out of the woods to a clearing. Before him, stretched out on a long, raised platform, was a forty-foot-long reclining Buddha the color of porcelain. Still hounded by the roar of McCarter's Suzuki, the gangster powered his bike up a handicapped ramp leading to the platform. The huge Buddha stared down at him with a look of beatific understanding. At the last possible second, Bancha yanked up on his handlebars, hoping to coax the bike over the statue's shoulder. He mistimed the jump, though, and his front tire struck the figurine, upending the Suzuki and launching him over the handlebars.

Seeing Bancha's fall, McCarter bypassed the ramp and circled around the viewing platform. He was forced to brake when he saw that, behind the Buddha, the ground pitched steeply downward into a terraced floral garden. The other Suzuki lay half-buried in a cluster of lush pansies. Thrown clear, Bancha was already halfway down the incline, tumbling through the flowers toward the lake and a docking area where an assortment of rental boats idled in the shallow water.

With no path in sight, McCarter braced himself and eased his motorcycle down the terraced incline. He was stopped less than twenty yards later when he came up against a retaining wall rising several feet out of flower beds. Abandoning the bike, he bounded over the wall and unholstered his pistol.

Bancha, meanwhile, had already reached the docks. His motorcycle leathers dotted with flower petals, he shoved his way through the throng of people waiting to rent boats. At the rental booth, he strong-armed the woman behind the counter, demanding the keys to the only boat with a motor.

Bancha had reached the boat and was starting the engine by the time McCarter reached the docks. The Briton cursed. There were too many bystanders in the way for him to get off a shot. He could barely even see Bancha through the crowd. He started elbowing his way through, hoping to reach the edge of the docks and get a shot at Bancha as he powered his way out into the lake. The crowd had other ideas, however. Most of them recoiled at the sight of McCarter's gun, but two men decided to play hero and tackled the Briton. When he tried to fight them off, all three of them toppled into the shallow water.

McCarter was quickly back on his feet. Amazingly he'd managed to keep hold of his pistol. He waved it at the other two men and motioned for them to keep their distance, then glanced over his shoulder. Out on the lake, Bancha guided his motorboat around the bend and vanished from view. He'd gotten away.

Disgruntled, McCarter glared at the men who'd derailed him from the chase. They glared back at him, equally furious.

"Freeze!" someone called from the docks.

McCarter looked up. The patrol officer, huffing for breath, stood before the angry crowd and repeated the warning he'd obviously learned from some cable rerun of an American cop show.

"Freeze!"

Resigned, McCarter grudgingly tossed his gun ashore, then raised his hands into the air.

CHAPTER NINETEEN

Andaman Sea, South Coast of Myanmar

The afternoon sun bore down heavily on Calvin James and Rafael Encizo as they bailed water from the disabled longboat. With Pag Ti's help, they'd managed to right the craft, but the grenade blast had left it riddled with leaks and it was taking in water nearly as fast as they could scoop it out. The outboard motor, like the communications gear stored in one of the gear bags, had taken a drenching, as well. Pag Ti had already opened the housing and drained out the seawater, but he wouldn't be able to test the engine until the spark plug and other internal components had dried out. On the bright side, they were alive, which was more than could be said of their hijackers or the pirates who had left them in their present predicament.

Encizo's shrapnel wound had bled out, and he'd patched it with a strip of his shirt. The dressing kept riding up his shoulder, though, and, as he had a dozen times already, he finally took a quick break to pull it back into place.

"You holding up okay, there, Rafe?" James asked.

"Yeah, I'm fine," Encizo said. "I got a feeling I'll be bailing water in my sleep for the next ten years, though."

"Hey, guys," Pag Ti called out, "take a look eastward."

James and Encizo looked up from their bailing. A hundred yards off, another craft was quietly headed their way.

"Friend or foe?" Encizo wondered.

"Dunno," James said. "They're being awful damn quiet, though." He freed one hand and reached for his Beretta.

"It's another longboat," Pag Ti said as the other craft drew closer. "Pirates never use them."

"What about the military?" James asked.

Pag Ti shook his head. "Not that I know of."

"Who the hell else would be out here in the middle of nowhere?" Encizo said.

"Moken," Pag Ti told him. "Water people."

The Myanmar operative stood up and waved to the other craft, calling out a greeting. His call was returned and the people on board the other thatch-roofed vessel waved back. As they drew closer, James and Encizo saw a family aboard: three men, two women and four young children.

"They're aboriginals," Pag Ti explained. "They've lived off the sea here for centuries. They're totally nonviolent."

"That's a relief," James said. "They're Good Samaritans, too, I hope."

Soon the Moken had pulled up alongside the crippled longboat. They stared with particular wonder at James.

"I take it they don't get a lot of brothers around here," he told Encizo as he smiled at the Moken. They smiled back.

Pag Ti exchanged a few words with one of the older men, then told James and Encizo, "He says we're welcome aboard. They'll take us wherever we want."

"Just like that?"

"They're good people," Pag Ti said. "Even the junta leaves them alone."

"Is that so?" James traded a look with Encizo, then eyed the other boat's hold. Beneath the thatched roof were stacked heaps of loose clothing and large woven baskets, some filled with foodstuffs, others with odds and ends. There were also a few folded blankets, easily large enough for three men to hide under. James turned back to Pag Ti. ''Would they have any objections to smuggling us to Guna Island?''

''I wouldn't put it that way,'' Pag Ti said, ''but I'll see.''

While Pag Ti conversed with the men on the other boat, the women and children helped James and Encizo transfer their scuba gear and a few other things from the leaking boat, which had begun to drop below the waterline. By the time they finished and moved to the other craft, Pag Ti had finished negotiating.

''They may keep to themselves,'' he said with a grin, ''but they can horse-trade as well as anyone.''

''Meaning…''

''Meaning they'll take us to Guna…for a price. They want our motor….''

Stony Man Farm, Virginia

THE STRAWBERRIES were ripe in the fields at Stony Man Farm. Barbara Price, out for a welcome breath of fresh air after six hours in the windowless confines of her office, crouched and plucked one of the berries, then slowly bit into it, savoring its sweet flavor. Nearby, some of the blacksuits—jeans and light cotton shirts concealing their body armor and guns—were gathering the harvest into small baskets. Over the weekend, the berries, along with other fresh produce, would be peddled at the local farmers' market along with offerings from the other area farms. Price usually put in an appearance at such gatherings, but she had a feeling this time she would have to beg off. Too much was happening.

Her break over, Price strode purposefully down the dirt path leading past the fields to the main house. Though it looked much like a typical country manor, behind the facade Stony Man's headquarters, like its companion Annex on the other side of the property, was a veritable fortress of reinforced steel and concrete. Price had to pass through two separate security checkpoints just to retrieve the notes she'd left in her room, and there was yet a third screening on the way to the basement, where she got behind the controls of a powerized railcar for the short underground drive to the Annex.

Halfway along the subterranenean tunnel connecting the two facilities, Price brought the tram to a stop. Buck Greene was helping two blacksuits install new gridwork for computer lines in the tunnel wall. Less than ten yards away, another crew was carving out a room-sized cavity in the wall. As with the computers, it was a precautionary move. In the event of an underground fire or other calamity within the tunnel, anyone en route between the main house and the Annex would now have a safe haven to duck into.

"How's it coming?" Price called out.

"Moving right along," Greene told her. "Should be operational by the end of September."

"Good," Price said.

"Mind if I thumb a ride?" Greene said. "I need to see Carmen at the Annex."

"Hop in," she told him.

Once they reached the Annex, Price and Greene proceeded directly to the Computer Room. Buck quickly pigeonholed Carmen Delahunt to go over specs for a relay system that would link the new tunnel facility with the Farm's main computers. Price, meanwhile, joined Aaron Kurtzman and Huntington Wethers, who were, as usual, hunched over their computers. Kurtzman glanced up from his work long enough to update on the status on James and Encizo.

"Still no word," he said. "I'm trying to pull in a satellite feed to see if there's any trace of them."

"Good," Price said. "What about Able Team? Have they caught up with this Sergeant Lacy yet?"

"Negative," Kurtzman said. "He called in sick at work."

"Why don't I believe that?"

"Lyons didn't buy it, either," Kurtzman said. "They're going to drop in on him and take his temperature, so to speak."

"When they get to him," Wethers piped in, "we've got a few things they might want to run past him."

"Like what?" Price asked.

"You might want to sit down for this," Kurtzman interjected.

"Oh, please," Price said. "I don't do 'faint of heart.' You know that."

"I don't think that's what he meant," Wethers said. "It's just that we've come up with a lot in the past hour."

Price pulled up a chair. "Okay, let's have it."

"For starters," Wethers began, "the latest update from the hazmat crew in Durango just came in, and it's looking like the lab there was set up primarily to manufacture sarin gas."

"Sarin," Price repeated, her voice tinged with dread. "The stuff used in those subway attacks in Tokyo."

"That's right," Wethers confirmed, "only in Tokyo, the gas was released by poking canisters with umbrellas. Not very effective, which is why the death toll was so low."

"The Dragons were working on another way to release it?" Price asked.

Wethers nodded. "Bombs."

"Bombs." Price closed her eyes a moment, then reopened them. "How far along were they?"

"Well, here's where it gets a little complicated," Wethers said. "From what hazmat is telling us, it looks like the Dragons already had their hands on a bomb and were trying to retroengineer it so they could make more."

"Where'd they get hold of a sarin bomb?" Price wanted to know. Even as the words were spilling from her lips, however, she realized she knew the answer. "Rocky Mountain Arsenal?"

Wethers nodded.

"The serial numbers on the bomb's housing match up with the RMA inventory from that whole fiasco a couple years back," Kurtzman told Price.

"This isn't good," Price said, thinking back to the scandal that had flared up three years ago at Rocky Mountain Arsenal, a seventeen-thousand-acre wilderness parcel ten miles northeast of Denver. The Air Force had used the land during World War II as a manufacturing site for mustard gas, white phosphorus and other so-called G-agents, but the entire stockpile—little of it ever used—had supposedly been removed by the mid-1960s. Then, in the early fall of 2000, nearly a dozen sarin bombs, all dating back to the cold war, had turned up during a routine grounds inspection by EPA Superfund officials overseeing the site's transformation into, of all things, a national park.

Price remembered the incident because Able Team had been nearly called in after a discrepancy had arisen regarding the number of the bombs that had been properly disposed of after removal from the site. Of the eleven grapefruit-sized explosives, only two had been officially verified as having been detonated in specially designed Donovan chambers. There were log entries on destruction of the other nine devices, but the actual detonations hadn't been witnessed, as mandated, by federal overseers. Even more suspicious, the entire three-man crew that had signed off on the unsupervised disposals had been killed that same night in a mountain car accident shortly after finishing their shift. The concern had been that terrorists had somehow infiltrated the disposal facility and stolen the bombs, then falsified records and killed the workers as part of a coverup. Thousands of investigatory man-hours later, however, both the Army Material Command and Soldier Biological Chemical Command had concluded there had been no foul play involved. According to their final report, the crew in charge of the sarin disposal had indeed destroyed the nine bombs, bypassing protocol only because EPA overseers had been waylaid on another assignment. However suspicious, their subsequent deaths in the car accident remained on the books as purely coincidental.

Now, thanks to the hazmat findings in Durango, it seemed clear the final reports had been in error.

"Those bombs weren't destroyed after all," Price surmised.

"At least one of them wasn't," Kurtzman said.

"Come off it, Bear!" Price countered. "Why would they have gone to all the trouble of doctoring the log books for just one bomb? Face it, the other eight have to be out there somewhere! And if these gangsters have figured out how to make more of them, God help us all."

"Hold on, hold on," Kurtzman said. "First off, hazmat is pretty sure the Dragons hadn't gotten very far with the retroengineering. So the odds of there being more than eight bombs out there is slim. I know that's not much of a consolation."

"Lacy!" Price interrupted. It was starting to make sense to her. "This contaminant-disposal site he works at…it's the same place the RMA bombs were taken to."

"Lacy was on staff then," Kurtzman said.

"Not disposal, though, right?" Price said. "I don't remember anyone surviving the car crash."

"No, Lacy worked storage and inventory," Wethers said, referring to data pulled up on his monitor. "A whole different building. He went through routine questioning like everyone else there, but he was never a suspect. Said he didn't even know they were handling sarin until all hell broke loose.''

"Who did the questioning?'' Price asked. "Evan Harris?''

"We don't have that yet, but I wouldn't be surprised if Harris's name showed up.''

"And Randolph's, too, for that matter,'' Price added. "There's one thing I don't understand, though.''

"Only one?'' Wethers grinned. "Then you're way ahead of me.''

"The bombs disappeared from the CDS three years ago,'' Price went on, "but we're saying the Gold Dragons just got their hands on them recently. Where were they the rest of the time?''

"As a matter of fact,'' Kurtzman interjected, "that's what we were working on when you got here. Hunt, you ant to bring her up to speed?''

Wethers went back to his computer keyboard, telling Price, "We went deep on Lacy's background and collared something. Have a look.''

Price looked over Wethers's shoulder. He'd called up a file listing all known fringe political groups within a five-hundred-mile radius of the contaminant-disposal site. It was a large file, including the white supremacist group Able Team had just shut down in Denver, as well as a mixed bag of skinheads, student radicals and even the Boulder affiliate of the Daughters of the American Revolution. Wethers highlighted Mark Lacy's name, showing him as a dues-paying members in a sect known as the Rocky Mountain Patriots. "They're a survivalist group based out of Colorado Springs,'' Wethers explained. "Pretty standard, from what we've been able to come up with. They peddle foodstuffs and provisions on the Internet and have a newsletter full of the usual doomsday prattle, but so far they've managed to keep out of trouble.''

"Which isn't the same as saying they've kept their noses clean," Price guessed. "You think they stole the bombs?"

"With Lacy working the inside," Kurtzman said, "they sure as hell had opportunity on their side."

"What about motive?"

Kurtzman shrugged. "They probably figured the bombs could bring top dollar if the right buyer came along."

"So we're saying they stole the bombs, then stashed them somewhere like Krugerrands until somebody met their price, is that it?" Price said.

"That somebody being the Gold Dragons," Wethers said. "In which case, we have to figure Randolph as the middleman."

"Because of that surveillance camera footage of him and Harris showing up to see Lacy at work," Price said. "Okay, I get it."

"They were probably brokering the deal," Kurtzman said, "only somewhere along the line something must've gone wrong, because the next thing we know, Harris is dead and Randolph's taken a powder."

"Has Hal been briefed on any of this yet?" Price asked.

Kurtzman nodded. "I just got off the phone with him. He's going to run it all past the President before the Joint Chiefs of Staff meeting."

"And I better run this all past Able Team like you said," Price told Wethers. "Provided they can find this Lacy fellow, it'll be good for them to have an ace or two up their sleeves."

CHAPTER TWENTY

Insein Prison, Yangon, Myanmar

Soe Paing didn't want to get out of the shower. The hot, near scalding water had not only stripped away months of grime, but it also helped soothe the long-standing aches that racked his body. Enveloped in steam, he felt as if he'd been transported, for one imprisoned without shower privileges as long as he'd been, this was almost nirvana.

"Hurry up!" a voice called out, echoing off the walls of the shower stall. "We don't have all day!"

"Yes, yes," Paing murmured. He turned off the water but remained in the stall until the steam began to settle around him. Then, wrapping a towel around his waist, he stepped out into the locker room used by the prison guards. An armed soldier glared at him, gesturing at a white cotton shirt and crisp new *longyi* laid across one of the benches. "You have ten minutes to shave and get dressed!"

The elderly dissident nodded and moved to the sink. The guard turned away from him as Paing removed the towel and patted himself dry, then donned the *longyi*. There was an electric razor set out for him, along with a comb and toothbrush. The Tatmadaw wanted him to look presentable for his broadcast to the masses. As he groomed himself, Paing tried to convince himself that he was doing the right thing. He tried to convince himself that he would, in fact, be saving lives by giving his little speech. What point was there in having people take to the streets on the anniversary of the Four Eights? It would only be 1988 all over again. Futile cries answered by gunfire and increased repression. More of his country's finest young men and women would be sent to prison. All for a lost cause. Better that he tried to reason with the people. Yes, he would tell them, they could observe the Four Eights, but they should do so quietly, in the privacy of their homes. It was important to keep the peace.

As he dragged the razor across his cheeks, Soe Paing stared hard at his reflection and was overcome with shame and disgust. Who was he kidding? Supporting the cause of peace? Ha! His was no noble gesture; far from it. He was acting out of cowardice, a pathetic grasp at self-preservation. Anyone watching the broadcast would see that. He would be disgraced in the eyes of the whole country. Former students who'd once looked up to him would sneer with contempt at his facile pleas. And what of his children? What would Aung and Daw Bodta think when they saw their father parroting the rhetoric of the SPDC?

"Two minutes!" the guard barked.

Paing's face flushed with anger as he finished shaving, then set down the razor and slowly donned the white shirt over his *longyi*. The shirt was several sizes too large. In it he looked like a child playing dress-up.

The soldier snorted with contempt and lit a cigarette, then flicked the match at Soe Paing. "Some sight you'll be for your sorry followers!"

Something inside Soe Paing snapped. In one swift movement, he grabbed the electric razor and hurled it, striking the soldier in the face. The guard howled as Paing attacked him, flailing madly with his small fists. The old man had no more chance against the soldier than the citizens of Myanmar would have against the four hundred thousand troops of the Tatmadaw. The guard, two inches taller than Paing and fifty pounds heavier, fended off the professor's feeble punches, then shoved him into the lockers. Enraged, he then raised his service revolver and fired a single .357 round into the older man's face.

Soe Paing collapsed to the floor. Blood trailed from his body across the cold tiles to a drain, where it spilled down and joined the water-borne wastes of Insein Prison. From the prison, his blood would be carried to the Irrawaddy River and flushed into the waters of the Andaman Sea.

Kyaukgu Umin Temple, Nyaung-U, Myanmar

DAW BODTA PAING was brushing her hair in the main chamber of the temple when she suddenly stopped and shuddered.

"What is it?" her brother asked.

"I'm not sure. I was just thinking about how Father... how proud he'd be of us, when I felt this...chill."

"The wind," Aung suggested. "It's been picking up the past few hours."

"Maybe so."

Bodta put away her comb. She and her brother moved away from the corner of the temple they were sharing with a dozen others. The main chamber was crowded. The hundreds hiding out in Kyaukgu Umin had gathered around a makeshift stretcher, upon which lay Hahrn-Li Jym, the volunteer who'd plunged to his death while rigging up the relay tower atop the entrance to the temple. The man had been draped in a pair of dark green *longyis,* and once Aung had made his way to the stretcher, he eulogized the worker, praising the sacrifice he'd made in the cause of freedom for his fellow Burmese.

"There is a recess within one of the first caves behind the pillars," Aung told the mourners. "We will lay Hahrn-Li Jym to rest there and seal off the wall. And once we have won our freedom, this temple will be rededicated in his honor.''

There were murmurs of assent among the congregation. Daw Bodta felt a stirring in her heart as she looked out at the sea of faces. What an inspiration! She'd wanted the services broadcast. What better way to test the makeshift network they'd patched together, she'd told her brother. Anyone hesitant about partaking in rallies to mark the Four Eights would surely be moved after seeing those gathered here in the temple. Aung had applauded his sister's intentions, but he and the others were concerned the Tatmadaw might intercept a broadcast and learn of the dissidents' plans. The risk was too great, he'd said. They couldn't allow the military to thwart the rallies before they even began. Bodta knew that her brother was right; still, she wished that others could have shared in this moment.

TWENTY YARDS AWAY, Bari Tu, shrouded in his monk's robes, stood at the rear of the crowd massed around the fallen dissenter. He wore a look of sadness, but inwardly he was overjoyed that everyone had been so quick to rule Hahrn-Li Jym's death an accident. It made his job that much easier.

While one of the dead man's friends stepped forward to continue the eulogy, Bari Tu took a step back from the throng. Once he was sure no one was watching, he slipped around one of the huge columns and retreated back into the darkness of the tunnels. Reaching the cave he'd been led to earlier, he quickly climbed back up through the air shaft. Once atop the cliff, took out his cell phone and dialed. Less than twenty seconds later, he was in touch with his contact in Meiktila. The voice on the other end came through clearly.

"We were wondering what became of you."

Bari Tu told the other man, "The news I have will have been worth the wait."

CHAPTER TWENTY-ONE

Colorado Springs

Air Force Sergeant Mark Lacy powered his Jeep Wrangler up Gold Camp Trail, a precarious, winding dirt road that snaked along the eastern perimeter of Pike National Forest. He was less than five miles from downtown Colorado Springs, but as he rounded yet another hairpin turn, all views of the city were choked out by yet another thick stand of tall, hearty pines. The vehicle's tires bit into the loose gravel as he muscled the Jeep up the steep incline leading to the Gold Camp Outdoorsman's Retreat. Pulling up to the gated entrance, he left the engine idling and raided the glove compartment for his gun, a Bernardelli Model PO-18 with fourteen 9 mm rounds packed into its magazine. The double-action semiautomatic pistol was a nice piece to have in a firefight. Lacy hoped it wouldn't come to that, but if worse came to worst, he was damn well going to be prepared.

Earlier that morning, Lacy had received a call from Stan Raines, leader of the Rocky Mountain Patriots, advising him to call in sick so that he could attend an emergency group meeting. The meeting was supposedly to settle yet another discrepancy in the Patriots' labyrinthian set of by-laws, but Raines had sounded hinky on the phone and Lacy was suspicious of the timing for the rendezvous. His gut instincts told him that it more likely had to do with the recent shooting of Evan Harris and the disappearance of Christopher Randolph. If that was the case, things didn't bode well for him. After all, he'd never told the Patriots of his dealings with the two other men. What if they had found out somehow?

Gun at his side, finger ready on the trigger, Lacy got out of the Jeep and scrutinized the grounds as he approached the entrance. The retreat was normally open daily to hikers, gun enthusiasts and ATV riders, but today the gates were chained closed. Next to the padlock securing the chains was a sign that read Closed For Private Gathering. As if to emphasize that the gathering in question was something other than Junior's birthday party or some paintball war game for weekend warriors, a handwritten warning had been scrawled beneath the printout. Trespassers Will Be Shot.

Four years ago, Lacy would have had a good chuckle over the latter message. When he'd first met the Patriots, he'd taken them for the usual doomsayers who talked a good game but were essentially harmless blowhards who vented their angst blasting soda cans off rocks with their beloved side arms. He'd milked the group's love of guns, turning a nice profit for himself by funneling them the occasional obsolete weapons—usually handguns or rifles—that passed through the contaminant disposal site where he worked. After the discovery of the sarin bombs at Rocky Mountain Arsenal, however, the Patriots had surprised Lacy, asking him to help get their hands on the explosives. When Lacy balked, Raines assured him they only wanted the bombs for defensive purposes. If Armageddon came, they figured a sarin bomb or two would discourage anyone knocking at their bunker door in search of handouts. The Patriots also knew a few affiliates across the state who wanted to similarly arm themselves.

Ultimately Lacy relented and made arrangements to doctor the log books and have the bombs smuggled out. When the three coworkers in on the ruse subsequently turned up dead in a car crash, Lacy, for the first time, realized what a devil's pact he'd gotten himself into. By then, however, it was too late for him to back out. In fact, shortly after the incident, Raines "suggested" it would be in Lacy's best interests to join the Patriots. Lacy knew it was Raines's way of keeping tabs on him and making sure he didn't spill to the authorities. The Patriots decided to sit on the bombs and lie low until the investigations were over. Their caution paid off, and Lacy was relieved when the final reports came out with all their botched conclusions. A couple years passed, and there even came a point when Lacy stopped thinking about the matter. Then, last week, out of nowhere, he was paid a visit by Christopher Randolph and Evan Harris of Air Force Internal Affairs. Harris had apparently been conducting his own private investigation over the years and had pieced together what had really happened. The reason for his secrecy became apparent when he told Lacy that he and Randolph now wanted the bombs for themselves. That same night, backed into a corner, Lacy secretly took both men here to the Outdoorsman's Retreat and showed them the bunker where the bombs were being kept. Tentative arrangements were made for delivery the next afternoon, but Lacy never received a follow-up call with instructions on where to make the drop. He tried to contact Randolph, only to learn the man had mysteriously disappeared. Harris, in turn, refused to return Lacy's phone calls, and the next thing Lacy knew, Harris was dead, gunned down while talking to some federal agents looking into Randolph's disappearance. Now, returning to the compound for the first time since he'd shown the men the bombs, Lacy was understandably concerned that he might be next to join the ranks of the dead or missing.

Lacy unlocked the gate, then resecured it after he'd

driven onto the property. All the while, he kept an eye out for any sign that he was stumbling into an ambush. As he'd anticipated, the main building, a one-story cinder-block structure set back a hundred yards from the main entrance, was deserted. Driving past the building, he heard the staccato rattle of gunshots a quarter mile downhill at the compound's shooting range. Lacy relaxed slightly as he guided his Jeep down the rugged trail leading away from the parking lot. He took it for a good sign that the men were out taking target practice. Maybe he was wrong about this whole situation after all.

Downshifting, Lacy negotiated the Jeep around a cluster of stepping-stones that rose from a shallow stream. Watching out for the stones, he took his eyes briefly off his rearview mirror, missing his chance to catch a glimpse of a man in camou fatigues who briefly rose into view behind a cluster of boulders, then just as quickly dropped back out of view.

SPEAKING INTO HIS headset mike, Gadgets Schwarz whispered, "Yeah, it's him, all right."

"Good," came the response from Carl Lyons, who was positioned a hundred yards away atop a bluff overlooking the shooting range. "Ring Jack, then let Pol catch up with you and circle around to your positions. I'll give the signal."

"Got it," Schwarz responded.

Able Team had broached the grounds an hour earlier. Along with news of Lacy's ties with the Rocky Mountain Patriots, Barbara Price had told the men that Patriots founder Stan Raines was listed on the county tax rolls as co-owner of the Outdoorsman's Retreat. When they hadn't found Lacy at home, they'd come here hoping to find him. The gamble had paid off. Pol Blancanales, hiding in the brush near the front entrance, had spotted Lacy's arrival.

CHAPTER TWENTY-TWO

Dwiti Military Base, Myanmar

General Bien Phyr dragged on a cigarette as he flipped through a handful of computer printouts that had just been sent to him via messenger from the intelligence division. Along with listings of all confirmed fighter jets currently in use by the Indian and Chinese military, there were several full-color pages profiling some of the aircraft from various angles. Taking a pen from his pocket, Phyr circled several of the pictures, then handed them to an aide.

"Work with these," Phyr said. "I want everything to be exact. Decals, coloring, insignias…everything."

"When should I have it all ready?" the aide asked.

"The other jets should be here by the end of the day. Be ready by then and have crews ready to work around the clock until the job is done. Understood?"

As the aide saluted and strode off with the circled pages, Phyr was joined by Senior General Lon Kyth. The elder officer looked concerned. "The TV people think you've gone mad," he told Phyr. "I told them you know what you're doing, but they don't seem convinced."

"Let's see what the problem is."

The two generals moved across the hangar, one of the largest at the airfield. Two Russian-made MiG-29 Fulcrums were undergoing maintenance side by side in the service bay, while a third sat idle nearby.

"I have to tell you," Lon Kyth told Phyr. "After this debacle with Ku-Syi, some of the other generals are clamoring for your head."

"That's understandable," Phyr conceded.

"They say you've risen too quickly in the ranks," Lon Kyth went on. "That your decisions reflect a lack of experience."

Phyr scoffed. "That's not what they were saying a few days ago. A few days ago, they praised my daring. They said I was the kind of new blood they were looking for."

Lon Kyth smiled sadly. "That is how it is with generals. Fortunes can change in the blink of an eye."

"I will rectify things," Phyr promised. "Have faith."

"My faith will only take you so far," Lon Kyth advised his protégé. "Just like you, I am subject to the other generals' whims. If I fall out of favor, you will be on your own."

"That won't happen," Phyr said.

The generals suspended their conversation once they reached the far side of the hangar. There, a mobile television crew was busily preparing for a remote broadcast on Myanmar's state-run network. Three banks of stage lights glared harshly down on a wooden podium draped with blue cloth. Behind the table, workers were propping up a crudely painted mural in which a peasant family was flanked by a pair of noble-faced Tatmadaw soldiers. The family members beamed contentedly, as if nothing could please the citizens of Myanmar more than to remain enslaved to a military dictatorship. Two bulky television cameras were aimed at the tableau. A lean man in his mid-twenties stood behind one of the cameras, shaking his head as he peered through the viewfinder. When he spotted Phyr and Lon

Kyth, he strode over to them, stepping over the snarl of cords and cables snaking across the floor.

"This is all wrong!" the director protested to Phyr. "The lighting is terrible and the acoustics are even worse!"

"We're broadcasting a news conference," Phyr reminded the man, "not an art film."

The director went on as if Phyr hadn't spoken. "We can't even send out a clear picture! There's too much interference!"

"Khar Mon—" Phyr addressed the director by name to make sure he had the man's attention "—when you broadcast, will the people be able to see and hear what is going on?"

"Yes," the director confessed, "but as I said, nothing will be clear. There will be echoes, distortion, glitches on the screen. We have a studio only three miles from here. Why don't we just reschedule and—?"

"I have no problem with echoes or distortion. And the more glitches, the better," Phyr interrupted.

The director stared at Phyr, dumbfounded, then turned his gaze to Lon Kyth. "Did I hear him correctly?"

The senior general seemed equally perplexed, but backed Phyr, saying, "Perhaps for your next assignment you would like to report on guerrilla skirmishes in Taunggyi."

Khar Mon paled, then returned to the makeshift stage, muttering. Lon Kyth watched him, then looked back at Phyr.

"I trust there is some method to this madness," he said.

Phyr nodded, adding, "I've already arranged it so that our regular programming is experiencing similar glitches and distortion. We'll blame it later on the weather or some problem with transmission towers. 'Technical difficulties.'"

"Now you have completely lost me," Lon Kyth said. His eyes narrowed angrily. "I give you thirty seconds. Convince me you haven't lost your mind or you'll be relieved of your command immediately.''

Bien Phyr sighed. "It all has to do with the matter of Maw Saung Ku-Syi," he began.

"Oh, I see," Lon Kyth responded sarcastically. "You plan to prop her up at the podium and hope the distortion will keep people from figuring out she's dead."

"If you will just hear me out," Phyr said.

Before Phyr could go on, Khar Mon rejoined them, even more agitated than before. He was waving a cell phone. "That's it. Now we have no choice but to call off the broadcast."

"Why is that?" Lon Kyth asked.

"There is no one to give a speech," Khar Mon said, indicating the cell phone. "I just heard from Insein. Soe Paing is dead. He tried to overpower a guard and was shot."

Lon Kyth cursed.

General Phyr was silent a moment, then he said, "Actually this will work out better."

"Better?" Lon Kyth exclaimed.

"Continue with the preparations," Phyr told Khar Mon. "We will broadcast as scheduled."

"Broadcast what?" the director wanted to know. "There was no mention of any other prisoners coming forward to speak."

"We don't need another prisoner," Phyr said calmly, smiling as he stared past Lon Kyth and the director. "We have something better."

The other two men turned. Simultaneously they both gasped in astonishment. Walking through a side door, unassisted and filled with vitality for someone who had supposedly just hung herself, was Maw Saung Ku-Syi.

SWARNG BANCHA FOLLOWED the woman into the hangar. He'd bruised his right femur on the Buddha's shoulder back during the motorcycle chase at Lumphini Park and favored the leg as he walked over to join Bien Phyr and a still incredulous Senior General Lon Kyth.

"I can't believe what I'm seeing!" Lon Kyth said.

"She *is* a dead ringer, isn't she?" Bancha replied, watching Semba Hru make her way to the podium. "It's amazing what a little hair dye and makeup can do."

Finally Lon Kyth understood. "The woman from Bangkok I've heard so much about. The queen of the Royal Peacock."

Bien Phyr nodded. "She is no stranger to this role," he said. "Only this time it is for another purpose."

Lon Kyth quickly regained his wits and regarded the man in the motorcycle leathers. "Then you must be Swarng Bancha," he said. "Bien Phyr's *other* mentor."

"The same."

Phyr made the introductions official, then Bancha quickly related what he knew of the raid on Gui Rahb's electronics store, concluding, "I abandoned the motorboat in a canal near Rajadanmri Road, then hailed a taxi to the airfield. My jet was waiting, along with Semba Hru."

"And you're sure Gui Rahb was killed?" Phyr asked.

"Almost positive," Bancha said. "In any event, we will have to reroute the heroin shipment away from Bangkok."

"That is an easy fix," Phyr said. "Have Entai Lette change the itinerary of his air circus. I'd like those jets of his inside our borders as soon as possible anyway."

Bancha thought it over briefly, then said, "The quickest way would be to have him cross near Pansauwng, then make for Taungoo. You have rail connections there, yes?"

Phyr nodded, then gestured at the two fighter jets in the service bay. "We'll give him these two MiGs for the F-105s."

Bancha eyed the jets. "Are these ones you flew as a pilot?"

"The one on the right is, I think," Phyr said. "But I'm not attached to it, if that's what you're asking. I like to look forward, not back."

"What about the heroin?" Bancha asked.

Phyr told Bancha to give him a moment, then took Lon Kyth aside momentarily. The men spoke briefly, then Phyr deferred to the senior general, letting him negotiate with Bancha.

"We'll pay you market value," Lon Kyth bartered, "then handle the distribution ourselves."

Bancha chuckled. "I thought the SPDC had declared war on the heroin trade."

Lon Kyth shrugged again. "We have more than our share of enemies at the moment," he said. "The war on drugs will have to wait for another day."

Bancha responded, "Even if Gui Rahb is dead, it's not my place to make such a decision. I'll have to make some calls."

"Fair enough," Lon Kyth said.

"I'll wait until after Semba Hru has spoken," Bancha stated. "I want to see how she handles herself."

"Of course," Lon Kyth replied.

The three men directed their attention back to the preparations for the telecast. Lon Kyth clearly wasn't the only one who'd been taken in by Semba Hru's close resemblance to Maw Saung Ku-Syi. No one on the television crew had been told of Ku-Syi's suicide. They thought they were dealing with the NLD leader herself and, despite their allegiance to the SPDC, they were in awe of the woman at the podium. Prison had been kind to her, they thought. She seemed not only stoic and composed, but also far healthier than in her recent photos. Once recovered from his shock, Khar Mon stepped forward and bowed slightly, then snapped his fingers, telling the crew to adjust the lights beaming down on Semba Hru.

For her part, Semba Hru did her best to ignore the stares and attention. She did insist, however, that there be no close-ups. And she told Khar Mon she would like it if they could put some kind of filter over the camera lens to soften her features. "I'm being vain, I know," she said modestly.

"I'll see to it." The director moved off. Semba Hru stared down at the speech that had been given to her earlier while she was undergoing her transformation into the one person most able to help the Myanmar junta stave off demonstrations during the forthcoming observance of the Four Eights.

Bien Phyr had written the speech, and as he watched the crew complete a sound check on the podium microphone, he nudged Lon Kyth and said, "Now do you understand why we are broadcasting here instead of at one of the station facilities?"

Lon Kyth nodded. "Of course. The poorer the broadcast quality, the less likely people will realize they are watching an impostor. Though I have to say, unless this woman's voice is dramatically different from Ku-Syi's, I'm not sure you needed to go to so much trouble."

"The echo will help mask her voice," Bien Phyr said, his own voice reverberating in the cavernous hangar."

"A gamble, but a shrewd one," Lon Kyth responded.

General Phyr saw that Khar Mon was ready to begin the telecast. "Now we roll the dice," he said.

From her place behind the podium, Semba Hru stared outward. When her gaze met Bancha's, the gang lord beamed. Semba Hru stayed in character, however, and her own features remained expressionless. Once she saw the red light flash on atop one of the cameras, she cleared her throat, trying to recall the sound of Maw Saung Ku-Syi's voice. "Greetings, my fellow citizens," she intoned. "I have agreed to speak to you today out of concern that we as a people do not repeat the mistakes of the Four Eights. I am here to impress on every one of you the importance of keeping the peace...."

Kyaukgu Umin Temple, Nyaung U, Myanmar

"...AND SO, in the coming days, I implore you once again, fellow citizens, to be swayed by reason and not emotion. Let us keep order and remember the Buddha's commandment that we look first for peace from within. Thank you."

At the conclusion of Semba Hru's remarks, there was a stunned silence within the great hall of Kyaukgu Umin temple. Only a few of the dissenters had been able to actually view the telecast on Aung Paing's small, battery-powered television, but during the course of the speech, the message had been passed along in disbelieving whispers, until finally everyone was aware that their spiritual leader and inspiration for their planned demonstrations was now urging them to let the anniversary of the Four Eights come and go as if it were no more than any other day on the calendar. Already saddened by the burial services for Hahrn-Li Jym—who now lay entombed behind a wall of stone in the first cavern behind the temple—the throng was now numb and demoralized.

As Senior General Lon Kyth took the podium and began to reiterate the call for restraint, Aung Paing reached forward and turned off the small set.

"This can't be happening," he murmured. "They must have drugged her or something."

"She did not seem drugged," his sister said.

"Then she was coerced somehow," Aung insisted. "Have us just sit on our hands and ignore the SPDC's tyranny? Ku-Syi would never advocate that if she were speaking freely."

"Perhaps she was speaking in some sort of code," Lon Mar suggested. "I've heard such things are done when prisoners of war try to get a message back to their country."

"But who would know the code?" Aung countered. "I've spoken with other leaders within the NLD. There has never been any mention of codes. No, there has to be another explanation."

Slowly the others began to speak. Some shared Aung's belief that Ku-Syi's remarks had been forced out of her. Others, feeling an ebb in their resolve, called for the group to disperse from the temple. The majority, however, merely tried to voice their uncertainty. Bari Tu had rejoined the group in time to hear the speech and, like the others, he was convinced that it had been Ku-Syi who'd spoken. He was as surprised as anyone to hear the woman so readily play into the hands of her captors. Hoping to capitalize on the situation while there was still a mood of despair, he called out, "Perhaps we should vote on whether or not to rally."

"I vote no!" someone cried out. "If it is Ku-Syi's will that we avoid confrontation, then we must call the rally off!"

"And I say Ku-Syi wasn't speaking of her own free will!" another charged. "The rally is a call for democracy! We owe it to ourselves to carry on as scheduled!"

The argument quickly escalated, and the cavern echoed loudly with a hundred competing voices. Aung stood on a stone bench and shouted for quiet. It took a while, but finally the cacophony subsided. "It would be a mistake for us to make any decisions in the heat of the moment," he asserted. "We need time to think matters through and, as Ku-Syi said, to look into our hearts."

After another heated exchange, it was agreed that the congregants would put off a vote for another hour. Meanwhile, Aung suggested that everyone—as much as was possible in the confines of the temple—seek solitude. Murmuring, the throng dispersed. Some retreated to the tunnels, while others remained in the chamber but separated into smaller groups.

Daw Bodta remained with her brother. Together they stared at blank screen of the television set. "No matter how the vote turns out," Aung muttered bleakly, "we have been undone. We had strength in unity. Now?" He shook his head.

Daw Bodta put a hand on his shoulder. "We must have faith that things will work out," she told him. "That's what Father would say if he was here with us. We must never lose faith."

"I wish he *were* here."

Insein Prison, Burma

JUST OUTSIDE the prison walls at Insein was a large field, overgrown with weeds. Thousands of slightly raised mounds marked the graves of those who'd died during their incarceration. Two fresh holes had been dug in the ground, neither more than a few feet deep. Setting aside their shovels, the grave diggers ventured over to a horse cart, where the bodies of Maw Saung Ku-Syi and Soe Paing lay side by side, each swathed in a moth-eaten blanket. The diggers hauled Soe Paing's corpse from the cart first and carried it back to one of the graves. Without ceremony, they let the body tumble from the blanket into the shallow hole.

"Okay, let's get the other one and be done with this before the vultures come," one of the diggers said.

They returned to the cart, carrying Soe Paing's shroud with them. Worn as it was, the blanket was still sturdy enough to be reused, and if the two men had learned one thing during their months of tending to the burial field, it was that there would always be more bodies....

CHAPTER TWENTY-THREE

Colorado Springs, Colorado

Mark Lacy felt he was a good judge of character, and when he looked Stan Raines in the eye while the two men shook hands, he saw no sign of ambivalence or betrayal. The Patriots' ringleader, as always, had a look of straightforwardness.

"Good to see you," he told Lacy, giving him a light slap on the back. "How's the wife?"

"Clueless and beautiful," Lacy responded with a grin. "Just the way we like 'em."

"From your lips to God's ears."

"I see you brought your piece," Raines said, staring down at the Bernardelli pistol clutched in Lacy's right fist.

"Figured I'd blast a few rounds while I'm here," Lacy responded, making no move to holster the weapon. He glanced past Raines and called out a greeting to the other Patriots. Three of the men were firing rounds into human-silhouette targets at the opposite end of the range. Another two were crouched over a nearby picnic table staring at a large, unfolded sheet of paper.

"They're going over the bylaws, I take it," Lacy said.

"Not exactly. That malarkey was just a cover in case the phones were tapped."

Lacy forced a smile. "I kinda figured."

"We have more important things to deal with," Raines said.

Lacy cringed inwardly as the older man turned and called out to the Patriots at the shooting range. "Okay, guys, let's get down to business!"

"Lemme get a bull's-eye first," one of the men yelled back.

"Christ, Ventura, if you haven't hit a bull's-eye yet, you're fucking hopeless. C'mon!"

Bob Ventura, a beer-bellied plumber in his early fifties, took a last few shots, then made a face as he glared at his target, which had sustained only hits to the wrist and knee-cap.

One of the other shooters laughed. "We're gonna have to let you move up closer, Bob."

"Yeah, step up to the women's tee, Bobbo," another joked.

Ventura waved his .44 Magnum pistol at his taunters and snapped, "Tell you what, assholes. Up this close, I don't miss."

"Put it away, Bob, before somebody gets hurt," Raines called out.

Lacy was relieved by the levity. He doubted there'd have been as much of it if he were truly in the hot seat. Relaxing, he holstered his gun. Raines led him to the picnic table, saying, "I'm sure you heard about what happened to the ARC chapter up in Denver a few days back."

"Sure did," Lacy said. "Feds shut them down, big time."

"That they did," Raines said. "Forced them to leave behind a lot of unfinished business, too."

Lacy nodded. He'd heard about the raid on the Aryan Right Coalition's headquarters while at work the night he was visited by Evan Harris and Christopher Randolph. The ARC bordered on psychotic, and Lacy'd thought, years back, that the white-supremacy group was probably on the shortlist of people most likely to put in a bid for the stolen sarin bombs. As far as Lacy knew, however, such a bid had never materialized. Which wasn't to say the group had gone soft. As Raines proceeded to explain, the ARC had apparently come under federal scrutiny two months ago after being linked to a home-invasion robbery during which the wife of Democratic State Senator Kurt Bollster was shot twice.

The incident had taken place less than three weeks before a key vote on a Bollster-sponsored gun-control measure. According to what Raines was told by his ARC contacts, two of their members had carried out the robbery hoping it'd give Bollster second thoughts about his bill. As it turned out, the ploy backfired. After his wife came through surgery with a good prognosis, Bollster went back to the Senate determined to add even tougher language to his measure. The upcoming vote was expected to be close, with Bollster himself being the potential swing vote in the event of a deadlock. As such, the ARC had apparently decided on even more drastic intervention. An intricate assassination plan—targeting Bollster during groundbreaking ceremonies for a new prison facility in Idaho Springs—was less than twelve hours away from being carried out when the ARC headquarters was raided by federal agents.

"Now, of course, everyone's breathing a little easier," Raines concluded, "and this Commie-ass Bollster's milking the whole situation for all it's worth. Hell, there's even talk of him turning this whole thing into a bid for President."

"There's a nightmare for you," Lacy said.

"Amen," Raines said. "Something's gotta be done."

Thus far, Lacy had been playing along with Raines, thankful to have the conversation focused on something other than himself or Evan Harris and Christopher Randolph. Now, however, he was suddenly struck with a grim realization that was confirmed when he glanced at the diagram on the table. It was a sketch of the Focus on the Family Welcome Center, located off the interstate seven miles north of town. Lacy knew from the morning paper that Senator Bollster would be making a speech at the tourist haunt later in the week as he stumped through Colorado Springs drumming up last-minute support for this bill. There could be no mistaking the penciled markings on the diagrams—the Patriots were planning to kill Bollster.

"We're picking up where the ARC left off?" Lacy said, trying to conceal his shock. "We're going to take him out?"

"The torch has been passed, bro," replied Al Hart, a beefy man with thick, short-cropped hair and handlebar moustache. He stabbed the sketched drawing of a speaker's podium with his pudgy forefinger. "That son of a bitch needs to be shut up once and for all."

Lacy nodded, more out of reflex than conviction. His head was reeling. After all these months of lying low, the Patriots were picking up where they'd left off with the sarin heist. Only now, instead of trafficking in G-agents, they were out to assassinate a U.S. senator, no doubt using firearms that could be tracked back to his place of work. Lacy was no lawyer, but he knew he was probably already an accessory, even though he'd known nothing of the plan until this moment.

"You okay, Lace?" Raines asked him.

"Yeah, of course," Lacy said.

"You sure? You look a bit pasty-faced all of a sudden."

Lacy thought fast. "I rushed through lunch on the way over," he said. "I guess it's sitting a little heavy is all."

"It'll pass," Raines said.

"Yeah. I'll be fine."

"Good, good. That's what we like to hear. 'Cause we

were kind of thinking that when it comes time to take care of the good senator, you should get the honors.''

"Honors?" Lacy felt the hairs on his neck rise.

"We took a vote while we were waiting for you to show up," Al Hart piped in. "Seeing as you're such a hotshot here at the range, we chose you to be the triggerman."

"Congratulations." Raines patted Lacy on the back.

Lacy stared down at the diagram. Hart had penciled in a sniper post some sixty yards uphill from the outdoor podium where Bollster would be speaking. From the looks of it, Lacy would have a clear shot—provided, of course, that he wasn't sniffed out by security. That's my out, he thought to himself. If security was too tight, no one would blame him for having to scrap the mission at the last second. They'd understand.

When he glanced up from the diagram, Lacy realized the others had closed ranks around Lacy, hemming in him. Their expressions had changed, too. Gone was any sense of jocularity. The other men eyed him with coldness and hatred.

Lacy laughed uneasily. "What's the deal, guys?"

"What do you mean?" Raines asked innocently.

"The way you're all looking at me. Look, I got no problem with this. I'll just case the place out and when the time comes, I'll do it. No problem. Piece of cake."

"Of course, if there *were* problems," Raines said, "we should probably have a backup plan. Right, guys?"

"Yeah," Hart said. "Say it was raining and they moved inside. We might want to go with something besides a shooter."

"I know!" Bob Ventura said. "We could use one of the sarin bombs!"

Lacy blanched. He felt his stomach drop. They knew.

"You remember those bombs, don't you, Lace?" Raines asked.

"Of course I remember them," Lacy said. "They're still out in the bunker, right? Unless you guys already peddled them."

"Us guys?" Raines laughed. "That's rich, Lace. Funny."

"Look, what are you getting at?" Lacy demanded, letting his right hand fall loosely to his side. As the others had already conceded, he was a better shot than anyone else in the group. If he could somehow get the drop on them...

Raines suddenly lashed out with his fist, catching Lacy in the stomach. Lacy doubled over, the wind knocked out of him. It was all he could do to stay on his feet. Raines and Hart grabbed him by either arm while Ventura quickly relieved him of his gun. Wheezing for breath, Lacy trembled with fear. He was as good as dead; he knew it.

"The bombs, Lacy," Raines said. "Where are they?"

"What are you talking about?" Lacy groaned.

Raines let go of him, then took another swing. Lacy reeled backward onto the table. The other men grabbed him and hauled him back onto his feet. Raines glared at him.

"Last week you came here with two strangers and gave them a little tour of the facilities," Raines said. "You showed them the bombs. Now the bombs are missing. And guess what? Those two men? Christopher Randolph and Evan Harris. Harris is dead. Randolph's missing, along with the bombs. You wanna add that up for us, shithead?"

Lacy was stunned. He'd thought he'd made sure all the surveillance cameras were off the night he'd brought Harris and Randolph to inspect the sarin arsenal. They'd left bombs behind, yet now Raines was saying they were missing. It made no sense. "Look," he protested, "I don't know what happened, but I can explain."

"Oh, you'll explain, all right," Raines said. "But how about if we make sure you're telling the truth?"

On Raines's signal, the other Patriots dragged Lacy to the far end of the shooting range. There, Ventura produced a length of rope. With Al Hart's help, he tied Lacy to a stake supporting one of the silhouette targets.

"Well, Al, next to Lace here, you're the best shooter we got. Guess you better brush up on your aim before you go gunning for Bollster."

"Good idea," Hart said, stepping away from Lacy and unholstering an M-9 semiautomatic pistol.

Lacy's knees quaked as he watched Hart stride back to the firing line, then calmly turn, raising his gun. "Ready," he called out.

"Give us just a second," Raines yelled back at Hart. He motioned for the other men to step clear, leaving him alone with Lacy. "Now, then, either you come clean with the truth or Al's gonna use you for target practice."

"I THINK WE'VE SEEN enough," Carl Lyons barked into his headset. Rising from cover, he took quick aim with his M-4 A-1 and fired a warning shot at Al Hart's feet. Startled, Hart lowered his gun and looked around, as did the other Patriots.

"Party's over, gang," Lyons called out. "Federal agents!"

Schwarz materialized into view on the other side of the target range, giving the survivalists a clear view of his assault rifle. "Guns on the ground, hands in the air!"

Most of the Patriots, taken aback by the sudden turn of events, were quick to comply. Stan Raines, however, took cover behind the post Mark Lacy had been tethered to, unholstering his .357 Magnum gun and placing the barrel to Lacy's skull.

"Back off or he's hamburger!" Raines snarled.

"Knock, knock," came a whispered voice directly behind Raines. As he turned, Rosario Blancanales—who'd leaped out from the rocks behind the target range—clipped the Patriots leader's skull with the stock of his Heckler & Koch 9 mm MP-5 A-5 submachine gun. Knocked senseless, Raines pitched forward to the ground. Blancanales stepped around him, shielding Lacy.

"Who are you?" Lacy blubbered.

"Even assholes have guardian angels," Blancanales said. "Now shut up and stay put."

Recovering his wits, Hart dodged behind the nearest boulder and sent Lyons ducking for cover with a burst from his semiautomatic pistol. Ventura blasted away with his .44, too, but in his panic he fired wildly, missing Schwarz by a good ten yards. The Able Team commando returned fire, nailing the Patriot in the shoulder. Howling, Ventura clutched at the wound. Blood seeped through his fingers.

"Next one's to the brainpan," Gadgets warned.

Ventura dropped his weapon. "Okay, okay," he sputtered.

Hart and two of the other Patriots, meanwhile, decided to buck the odds and traded shots with Lyons and Blancanales as they backtracked to the picnic table. Schwarz jogged to his right, triangulating the perimeter around the gunmen. His carbine chattered in unison with Lyons's, nailing Hart in a cross fire. When Grimaldi appeared moments later, strafing the grounds with machine-gun fire from the underbelly of the Apache assault chopper, the skirmish was over as quickly as it started. The two resisting Patriots cast aside their handguns and stepped out into the open, hands above their heads.

Hart, near death's door with five slugs in his upper torso, fumbled with a cigarette lighter. He was about to set fire to the assassination diagram when Lyons finished him off with a shot to the head. As Schwarz and Blancanales rounded up the other survivors, Lyons sprinted over to the picnic table, wresting the diagram from beneath Hart's body. The plans had been bloodied, but Lyons could make out enough details to realize what the Patriots had been plotting.

"That friggin' senator again," he muttered. "Christ, how many times do we gotta pull his fat from the frying pan?"

Grimaldi set the Apache down in the middle of the firing range, then climbed out to help wrap things up. Lyons, meanwhile, carried the bloodstained diagram over to where Blancanales was untying Lacy. Raines began to stir on the ground. Lyons jerked him to his feet. "Party's over."

Raines ignored Lyons and glared at Lacy.

"Traitor!" he spit vehemently. "Turncoat!"

"Save the gab for your lawyer," Lyons said, prodding Raines with his carbine. Schwarz came over and hauled away the ringleader, leaving Lyons and Blancanales with Lacy.

Once he was untied, Lacy rubbed his chafed wrists and stared at the assassination plans Lyons was holding. "I didn't know about that," he insisted. "You gotta believe me."

"Hold that thought," Lyons told him. "You've got a few other things to explain first."

CHAPTER TWENTY-FOUR

U-Tapao Royal Thai Navy Airfield, Thailand

"Sorry, no sarin or anything else even close," David McCarter told Yakov Katzenelenbogen. "The Dragons might have been multitasking in Durango, but their Bangkok operation was strictly drugs."

"And a little computer espionage," T. J. Hawkins reminded the Phoenix Force leader.

"Oh, right," McCarter said. "That, too."

The three men were huddled in one corner of the AFB communications room. They spoke quietly so as to not disturb the staff officer working at one of the mainframes. Gary Manning, who'd arrived from Bangkok with McCarter and Hawkins a few minutes earlier, was off tracking down Akira Tokaido at the base library, where he was doing some research through some older AFB records.

Katz turned to Hawkins. "And you're pretty certain their computers could have been used to tap into the archives here?"

"Yeah," Hawkins said. "Mind you, with a time bomb ticking down, I was a little rushed, but it was a sophisticated setup."

"I don't suppose there's any chance some of their hard drives survived the explosion," Katz said.

Hawkins laughed. "No way. Those drives are toast, man."

The AF staff worker eyed the men coldly, then stormed out of the room. McCarter watched the man, then turned to Katz. "I guess we've worn out our welcome, eh?"

Katz smiled. "Heaven forbid that national security should take precedence over some geek's need to surf the Internet."

Changing subjects, McCarter asked, "How long since Cal and Rafe checked in?"

Katz checked his watch. "Going on seven hours."

"That long?" Hawkins leaned forward in his seat, incredulous. "Why didn't you say that before? Shit, we need to get our asses over there and find out what's going on."

Katz nodded. "They're going over options back at the Farm. We'll have a plan of attack soon enough."

"I should hope so."

"What's with Able Team?" McCarter wondered.

"They've been busy," Katz reported. "They had to stomp on some cockroaches that crawled out from under one of the rocks they turned over looking for Christopher Randolph." He was still briefing the other men on the thwarted assassination plot by the Rocky Mountain Patriots when Akira Tokaido strode into the room, a look of disgust on his face.

"Tell me I'm an idiot," he said, plopping down in a seat before one of the computers.

"Good to see you, too, Akira," McCarter said.

Tokaido ignored the Briton and told Katz again, "Go ahead, tell me I'm an idiot."

"What's this about, Akira?" Katz asked.

"I should have figured it the first day we were here!" Tokaido fumed as he pecked away at the keyboard. "Idiot!"

McCarter and Hawkins exchanged glances with Katz,

who then told Tokaido, "I'm not sure about the idiot part, but we're beginning to worry about your sanity."

As he called up the Nam-era archives that had been hacked into prior to the salvage activity at Guna Island, Tokaido tossed Katz a thin book with glossy, yellowing pages. It was an old map atlas of Southeast Asia. Obviously Tokaido had come across it at the base library.

"Think fast and tell me the first thing that comes to your mind when I say Rangoon," Tokaido said without taking his eyes off the screen.

"I'm really not in the mood for games, Akira," Katz said.

"Rangoon?" McCarter said, playing along. "Yangon?"

Tokaido nodded. "Burma and Pagan."

"Myanmar and Bagan," McCarter said.

"Exactly," Tokaido said. "Hell, everybody knows these clowns in the junta like to change the name of everything they come across, right? But did I think of that when I was searching the archives? No, of course not. I'm an idiot!"

"Okay, okay, you're an idiot!" Hawkins said. "And I must be one, too, because I don't have a clue what the hell you're talking about."

Katz, like McCarter, was finally on Tokaido's wavelength, and as he glanced through the atlas, looking for one of the old maps depicting the area where Calvin James and Rafael Encizo were missing in action, he called out, "Mergui Archipelago."

"Burma Banks," Tokaido said, typing the words into the archives search program. "Back during the war, that part of the sea was called the Burma Banks. Not Mergui."

"Ah!" Hawkins said. "Got it."

"And Guna Island was known as Hadj Atoll," Katz murmured, locating the isle on the old map. "No wonder you kept coming up empty on those searches."

"I'm an idiot," Tokaido repeated.

"We got that part," Hawkins said. "Say, you didn't happen to cross paths with Manning on the way back here, did you?"

Tokaido shook his head. He stared at the screen, clicking his cursor to narrow down his search through the raided archives. The other three men moved over and stared over his shoulder as he zeroed in on the answer as to what the Myanmar junta had been salvaging for in Guna harbor.

"Well, grill my goddamn goose and serve it up for Sunday dinner," Hawkins uttered with astonishment.

Katz couldn't match Hawkins's flair for Southern aphorisms. The best he could manage was, "I don't believe it."

Guna Island, Mergui Archipelago, Myanmar

LEANING OVER the prow of the Moken longboat, Rafael Encizo used his forearm to measure the length of anchor line he was feeding into the still waters of Guna harbor. His shoulder had stiffened on the way to the island, and pain radiated from the shrapnel wound whenever he moved. He'd replaced his makeshift dressing with a poultice made by one of the aboriginals, but the wound still bled enough to serve as a possible magnet for underwater predators. According to Pag Ti, most of the sharks infesting the archipelago were harmless, but it would take only one maneater to jeopardize the mission. As such, much as he wanted to be in on the discovery of whatever it was the Tatmadaw had been salvaging for in the harbor, Encizo had reluctantly decided to remain on the boat. In his place, Pag Ti, an accomplished diver in his own right, had agreed to go down with Calvin James. Both men had already charged their regulators, donned steel doubles and clipped aluminum 80s to their sides. Once they'd fastened crotch straps over their weight belts, the men slipped on their German-made LAR V Draeger scuba gear. Equipped with carbon-dioxide scrubbers, the closed-circuit rigs would allow James and Pag Ti to rebreathe their own air without expelling bubbles. Once they'd tested the transceivers built into their full face masks, the men donned their fins and were ready to dive. By then Encizo had finished dropping anchor.

"Ninety feet, give or take a few yards," he called out. "Take your time coming up and the bends won't be a problem."

James grinned. "That's good, seeing as we didn't have room to pack a decompression chamber."

Pag Ti fished through the gear bag for a pair of high-powered flashlights, along with two strap-sheathed SEAL Ka-bar knives. "Should we take these?" he asked, also removing a pair of waterproof Heckler & Koch MP-5 A-5s.

"They won't do us much good down there," James said, strapping on one of the submachine guns, "but what the hell."

"You should be good for twenty minutes," Encizo told them. "While you're down there, I'll keep working on the comm gear. It's practically dry." The gear, which included a global positioning module, as well as a long-distance radio transceiver, was laid out in the sunlight at the rear of the boat, being watched over by the Moken boatman who'd dressed Encizo's wound earlier. The other aboriginals, who'd been dropped off earlier on the island, stood watching from the shoreline, and when one of the children waved and shouted, the Moken aboard the ship grinned and waved back.

"Are we ready?" Pag Ti asked, securing his flippers.

James donned his mask, then nodded. In unison, the two men dropped over the side, taking care to avoid a wide, clotted bed of floating kelp. It became quickly clear why the archipelago was fast becoming a target destination for scuba divers. The crystalline waters just below the surface thrived with sea life. Pale blue surgeonfish, giant groupers and schools of homely puffers swam past the men, feeding off luminous clouds of plankton.

"Man, it's like we're in a freaking aquarium," James told Pag Ti as they flippered their way downward.

"Just wait—it gets better," Pag Ti said.

Working their jaws to equalize the pressure in their ears, the men eased farther into the depths of the harbor. Soon they were able to make out the shadowy outline of a vast coral ledge directly below them. The jagged shelf was festooned with wrasses and multicolored nudibranchs, among which the men spotted lobsters, sea anemones and sharp-toothed moray eels.

"It's a pretty eyeful," James said into his condenser mike, "but I don't see any sign of a salvage operation."

"We probably have to go a little deeper." Pag Ti pointed out the anchor line, which trailed past them from behind a stag coral formation that rose from the ledge like an underwater forest. "It looks like there's a drop-off up ahead there."

James checked his depth gauge. "Okay, but we're only good for another twenty yards, tops," he said.

Pag Ti nodded, then led James around the coral. They were within sight of the drop-off when something darted up from the unseen depths and headed toward them. James was reaching for his knife when he realized it was a stingray, roughly the size of a bathtub mat. The creature, equally startled by the two divers, veered to one side and glided past them.

"Sucker had me going there for a minute," James said.

"He was just the advance scout," Pag Ti said as they neared the edge of the shelf. "Look out there."

James didn't need the warning. He already saw them, a school of sharks swimming toward them in a loose formation. They were medium-sized, none of them longer than a few feet.

"Gray reefers," Pag Ti said. "They're just curious."

"I don't like the looks of those teeth," James said.

"They won't attack if they aren't provoked," Pag Ti assured James. "Just ignore them unless they drop their fins and arch their backs."

"And if they do that…?"

"Then give them a wide berth and— Whoa!"

"What?" James glanced over at Pag Ti. The Myanmar operative didn't respond. He was no longer concerned with the sharks. Instead, he was looking downward, into the murky depths that lay just beyond the ledge. James followed the man's gaze and let out an exclamation of his own.

"I'll be damned."

Stretched out before the men on the ocean floor, barely visible in the dark water, was not some ancient Spanish galleon, but rather the hulking, shadowy outline of a sunken B-52 Stratofortress.

White House, Washington, D.C.

ON DAYS when the President met with the Joint Chiefs of Staff, it wasn't uncommon for Hal Brognola to meet beforehand with the chief executive. Together in the Oval Office, they would go over a compilation of the most pertinent—and highly confidential—intel churned out in recent days by the CIA, NSA and any other well-placed sources with a finger on the pulse of global hotspots. Usually the men spoke purely in terms of which items should be brought up with the Joint Chiefs and which should be designated for covert handling by the Farm's commandos. However, the President would occasionally pick Brognola's brain on other matters, and there were times when Stony

Man's liaison officer felt as if he were secretary of defense and national security adviser rolled into one. The head Fed indeed.

This day was such a day. From the time they shook hands upon Brognola's arrival to the moment the President's personal secretary reminded him that he was ten minutes late for his meeting with the Joint Chiefs, the two men focused on one solitary matter: how to best deal with Akira Tokaido's discovery of what the Tatmadaw military had been looking for in the remote harbor waters of Guna Island.

Now, having advised the President on how to handle the matter with the Joint Chiefs, Brognola paced the White House's first-floor cross hall, awaiting the arrival of a car that would whisk him five blocks to another meeting every bit as significant—if not more so—as the one he'd just gotten out of. Brognola had with him the President's personal copy of a book both men had referred to during their meeting. The book, dog-eared from countless readings, was *Won if by Air*, a Vietnam memoir by retired SAC General David Brooks, who, like his mentor, Air Force General Curtis Lemay, contended that America had doomed its war effort during a fateful strategy conference held in Honolulu the summer of 1964, when it was decided that the Air Force would play second banana to the Army in a ground-based conflict commanded by Army General William Westmoreland. Brognola had already read the book years earlier, and he still had a copy of his own, but there was a key chapter he wanted to review before his upcoming meeting, which was to be with none other than the book's author, General Brooks himself.

In the chapter entitled "Madman across the Water," Brooks had recounted one of SAC's higher-profile missions, Operation Maximum Fear. Launched October 1, 1969, MaxFear was the belated implementation of the so-called secret plan to end the war Richard Nixon had suckered American voters with the year before. The Strategic Air Command had been placed on DefCon 1 for the first time since the Cuban missile crisis, and over the next few weeks, wave after wave of B-52s—most of them flying out of U-Tapao under Brooks's jurisdiction—had conducted clandestine bombing raids in Laos and Cambodia, as well as against the VC targets in Vietnam itself.

But Nixon hadn't stopped there. He'd told the CIA he wanted to give both Russia and China the impression that he'd cracked under the pressures of his first year in office, so much so that he was ready to resort to drastic measures, including tactical nuclear strikes north of the DMZ, to bring the Vietcong to its knees and bring the war to a quick end. Despite its reservations, the CIA saw to it that the disinformation was "intercepted" by Russian and Chinese intelligence agencies. Meanwhile, B-52 forays into the skies over Indochina were stepped up dramatically. Only a fraction of the flights were actual bombing runs. The rest were meant to give the appearance that Nixon had indeed gone off the deep end and might, at any second, lose patience with the enemy and give the signal to—as many hawks had been long advocating for—bomb North Vietnam back into the Stone Age.

The ploy, for all its screwball ingenuity, hadn't paid off. Neither Russia nor China had risen to the bait. They'd called Nixon's bluff, continuing to lend support to the North Vietnamese, who themselves showed no signs of being intimidated by the increased bombings. By October 15, when more than a quarter million Americans swarmed to Washington calling for an end to the bombing, it was clear that Nixon's gambit had failed. DefCon 1 remained in effect for another two weeks, but finally, on October 29, the operation was brought to an abrupt halt. The official reason given was that SAC was concerned about wear and tear on the Stratofortresses, which were logging increased flight hours at the expense of normally scheduled maintenance. Nowhere in Brooks's book was there any mention that one of the bombers had in fact gone down a mere two days before the sudden end of Operation Maximum Fear. Brooks had to have known about the incident, Brognola thought. The downed plane, after all, had been one of his own U-Tapao-based bombers. So why, then, had he deliberately misled not only his readers, but also the rest of the military chain of command? Brognola was determined to find out the answer.

"DAVE, WE NEED to talk about Operation Maximum Fear," Brognola said to General Brooks twenty minutes later, standing at the foot of the large bed where the withered airman now spent most of his days.

There had been a time, years earlier, when General David Brooks was an imposing figure with the dashing good looks of a matinee idol. As a protégé of the Strategic Air Command's first two leaders, George Kenney and Curtis Lemay, he'd helped see SAC through its formative years following World War II. By the height of America's involvement in the Vietnam War in the midsixties, Brooks had been promoted through the ranks and put in charge of B-52 operations at U.S. air bases at Don Muang, Takhli and, most significantly, U-Tapao, then known as Satahip. He'd served with distinction, his proudest claim being that none of his bombers had been brought down by enemy fire until the waning stages of the Linebacker I air offensive in 1972, a streak of more than five years during which his pilots had flown more than fifty thousand sorties into enemy territory.

After the war, Brooks was tapped by both the Ford and Reagan administrations to serve as an adviser with the Defense Department. He and Brognola crossed paths a number of times at the White House, forging a casual friendship based as much on a shared passion for Havana blunts and the Washington Redskins as on their political ideologies. The men fell out of touch, however, after a 1987 heart attack prompted Brooks to retire to Los Angeles. There, between several exasperating stints as technical consultant for a handful of Vietnam-based war movies, he spent five years writing *Won If By Air*. Work on a second memoir ground to a stop several years earlier when Brooks was diagnosed with spinal cancer. He moved back to Washington and fought the disease into a brief remission, but now it was back, spreading through his system with slow but fatal certainty, in the process robbing him of both his vitality and good looks.

Brognola, who hadn't seen Brooks in years, was stunned when he was ushered into the bedroom at the general's Pennsylvania Avenue condominium. The older man had lost his hair to chemotherapy and shriveled to half his normal weight. He looked almost cadaverous, pallid skin clinging to his once robust frame. Only his steely gray eyes seemed familiar, and even they were dull and unfocused. For a moment, when Brooks failed to respond to his question regarding Operation Maximum Fear, Brognola feared the general might have died right in front of him.

"General?"

Brooks shifted his gaze, narrowing his eyes as he took Brognola in. "How about those Redskins?" he wheezed. "Think they have a chance this year?"

"Dave, please," Brognola said. The two men had already exchanged small talk and caught up on each other's doings. It was time to get down to business. "I know this isn't a good time for you, but—"

"I'm a dying man, Hal," Brooks replied. "There's no such thing as a good time for me...unless you count those enemas I get from that cute little Puerto Rican nurse of mine."

"General," Brognola said, "this is important."

"All right. What do you want to know?"

"In your book," Brognola said, "you wrote that Maximum Fear was called off because SAC didn't want to start losing planes to engine fatigue."

"That was one of the reasons," Brooks said. "You know the others. The Commies didn't blink when Nixon played madman, and then there was that damn march on Washington."

"Yes, I know all that," Brognola replied. "But let's stick with the main reason. Had you already lost a plane when the operation was suspended?"

"Nonsense," Brooks scoffed. "Charlie didn't get to us until '72."

"I'm not talking about enemy fire," Brognola said. "I'm talking about a plane going down due to lack of maintenance."

A flash of anger spread across Brooks's face. He stared hard at Brognola and demanded, "Don't cat-and-mouse with me, you bastard! If you've got something to say, say it!"

"Fair enough," Brognola said. "We have information that a B-52 went down off the coast of Burma two days before Operation Maximum Fear was officially brought to a halt."

Brooks's jaw clenched. He turned away from Brognola and stared out the window, which offered a view of the Washington Monument rising up past the rooftops of neighboring town houses. The general remained silent for some time, then, without taking his eyes off the view, he said, his voice a cracked whisper, "It wasn't lack of maintenance."

"The pilot called in reporting an electrical fire in the cockpit," Brognola said, passing along the sketchy information Akira Tokaido had managed to cull from the archives at U-Tapao. "That would seem to suggest—"

"I don't care what it suggests!" Brooks interrupted. "It wasn't lack of maintenance, at least not on our end. That bird was coming in fresh off a carrier in the Indian Ocean. We never even got a chance to lay eyes on it in U-Tapao."

Brognola frowned. "Is that true?"

"You're damn right it's true!" the general shot back. "What's this all about, anyway? Here I am, trying to die in peace, and you come along wanting to rewrite the history books. I thought we were friends!"

"I'm sorry, Dave," Brognola said, "but this goes past friendship."

"Spit it out, then!"

Brognola sighed. He was beginning to remember what a bullying pain in the ass Brooks could be when cornered. "We're concerned," he explained, "because the Myanmar military just completed a salvage operation near where that B-52 went down."

"What's to be concerned about?" Brooks countered. "Hell, even if they do find the plane, what good's it going to do them? There's not going to be anything left of it but a heap of scrap metal."

"What about cargo?" Brognola asked. "Ordnance."

"Gone," the general said. "The pilot jettisoned everything before he and the crew bailed. I thought you said you had the information."

"We have scraps," Brognola stated. "The rest came up classified. We've tried to fill in the blanks but we're coming up empty."

"Nice to know somebody can keep a secret," Brooks said.

"That's why I'm here. We don't have time to go door-to-door with everyone in the chain of command trying to get answers."

"Then I guess you'd better humor me, eh?" Brooks said. "What's going on? Besides this salvage mission?"

Brognola hesitated. His information on the situation in Myanmar was every bit as classified as whatever it was Brooks was sitting on. Normally there'd be no way Brognola would bring somebody like the general into the loop regarding the Farm's affairs. But Brognola needed answers, fast. And by Brooks's own admission, he was dying; he hardly posed a security risk. And maybe the man would open up more if he felt he was being given one last chance to have his voice heard in the corridors of power. It was worth a shot.

"Okay," Brognola finally responded. As succinctly as possible, he laid out the situation, not only with regards to the activity at Guna Island, but also the theft of the Y-25 LAVs and the role of the Gold Dragons in the shooting death of Evan Harris and the disappearance of Christopher Randolph.

Brooks stiffened. "Jesus, Mary, Joseph."

"You know Randolph?" Brognola asked.

"I know his background. The stuff you haven't been able to get at." Brooks stared intently at Brognola. "He was the pilot of that B-52 that went down."

It was Brognola's turn to be taken aback. "Go on," he managed to say.

"It's a long story," Brooks said. "Before we get into it, tell me, exactly how sure are you that he's a double agent?"

"I'd bet the farm on it," Brognola said.

"Going back how long?" Brooks asked.

"We haven't pinpointed that," Brognola confessed.

"Shit."

Brognola guessed at the reason for Brooks's consternation.

"When that fire broke out," he asked, "was there any

verification that he followed orders and dumped his ordnance?''

Brooks grimly shook his head. ''We flew recon over the islands and got an image reading where the plane went under, but, no, we didn't go down to check on things.''

''Why not?''

''Because nobody else was going to spot it,'' Brooks said. ''That harbor was so remote it might've well as been Mars as far as anyone was concerned. We wanted to keep it that way, so we took Randolph at his word and made like it never happened.''

''You swept it under the rug.''

''More or less, yeah, that's exactly what we did,'' Brooks said. ''Without the ordnance, that plane had no use except as proof to the enemy that the Strats weren't invincible.''

''What if Randolph was lying?'' Brognola suggested. ''What if he didn't dump the ordnance?''

Brooks swallowed hard. For a moment his eyes glazed over with a faraway look. Brognola guessed the general was thinking back, seeing the time in question in a new, disturbing light. It was clear that Brooks didn't like what he saw. When he glanced back at Brognola, he seemed shame-faced, his gaunt features pinched into an expression of self-recrimination.

''If Randolph was lying,'' he said, ''then you damn well better worry about that junta.''

''Why's that?''

''Because Nixon wasn't entirely bluffing,'' Brooks said. ''That plane was packed with more than just cluster bombs.''

It was the news Brognola had most feared. And yet he wasn't completely surprised. After all, when the first B-52s came off the Witchita assembly lines in 1955, during the tempestuous years of the cold war, they had been designed for one purpose and one purpose alone—to slip through the iron curtain and strike key Russian targets, not with conventional bombs, but nuclear warheads. For all their other uses during the ensuing fifty years, to this day, as during the Vietnam War, the Stratofortresses retained the capacity to carry out their original mission.

"A-bombs," Brognola said. "It was carrying A-bombs."

General shook his head. "Hydrogen. That B-52 was carrying hydrogen bombs. Eight of them."

Guna Island, Mergui Archipelago, Myanmar

THE STRATOFORTRESS entombed in the dark waters of Guna harbor was a B-52D. Redesigned specifically for the Vietnam air war, the plane's engineers had straddled the fuselage with a pair of wing-mounted Hound Dog stand-off missiles, the better to fend off fighter jets and acquisition hard-to-hit ground targets. When he and Pag Ti lowered themselves from the coral shelf to inspect the plane, Calvin James wasn't surprised to find the latter weapons missing. They were, after all, to his knowledge the aircraft's most potent armament and therefore the likeliest target for the Tatmadaw's salvage divers. He was puzzled, however, when he flashed his underwater light on the underwing mountings. Like the eight Pratt & Whitney turbofans that had powered the B-52, the missile mounts were encrusted with several decades' worth of mineral deposits, as well as coral and sponge formations like those up at the higher elevation. "Those Hound Dogs were long gone before the Tatamdaw got here," James told Pag Ti.

"They probably didn't know that until they came down."

"Must've pissed them off," James said. He flashed his light elsewhere along the surface of the plane, looking for other signs of recent tampering. There didn't seem to be any. For that matter, from what they'd seen of the aircraft, there didn't seem to be any sign of external damage. "I wonder what brought this sucker down?" he wondered.

The men got their answer when they swam to the nose of the B-52 and shone their lights in the cockpit. Even years of deterioration couldn't hide the fact that most of the cabin had been ravaged by fire. "Must've been a nasty one, from the looks of it," James observed.

Pag Ti checked his watch. "We should be heading up soon."

James nodded. "Okay," he said, "but first let's take a quick look downstairs."

Pag Ti followed James to the underside of the B-52, waving aside a trail of cuttlefish attracted by his flashlight.

"Hey, hey," James called out, directing his beam to the ocean floor, where there were clear signs of recent activity, especially near the bomber's wheel wells. "Looks like they dragged something out from under the plane."

Pag Ti flashed his light along the underside of the plane. "They raided the bomb bay," he called out through the mike in his face mask. The two men swam forward twenty yards to where the bay doors lay on the ocean floor like discarded planks. They'd been cut away from aircraft with underwater torches, and the outer perimeter of the bay itself still gleamed where the torches had laid bare the plane's metallic skin.

"Let's check it out," James said, pulling himself up through the opening.

Along with exterior Hound Dogs, most of the B-52Ds had seen their war-making potential increased by an expansion of the original bomb bays, upping their load capacity from twenty-seven thousand to eighty thousand pounds of convential ordnance. As such, there was plenty of room for James and Pag Ti to both squeeze their way into the cavity. James flashed a light on the bay riggings and cursed, "This son of a bitch wasn't carrying cluster bombs."

"What do you mean?" Pag Ti asked.

The Phoenix Force commando took a closer look at the riggings, which showed the same scorch marks as those left when the bay doors had been torched open. This was what he'd expected to find on the Hound Dog's mounts: proof that the Tatmadaw had cut the missiles loose and taken them to the surface in hopes they could be rendered serviceable. The missiles here in the bomb bay, however, hadn't been Hound Dogs; James was sure of it. What was more, they'd been far better sealed off from the elements than anything out on the wings. The odds of them being operational were good—damn good.

James told Pag Ti, "Let me put it this way—if we'd brought down a Geiger counter, about now it'd probably sound like we were making popcorn."

"Nukes?"

"Nukes." James quickly counted the number of torched mounts. "Eight of them, from the looks of it."

"We need to get back."

James nodded. The two men swam out of the hold, then began their slow ascent to the surface, following the anchor rope leading up to the Moken longboat. On the way, James speculated as to what kind of bombs the B-52 had been carrying. "If I remember rightly," he told Pag Ti, "they were probably Mark 28s. Thermonuclears."

"Smart bombs?" Pag Ti asked.

James shook his head. "No. They were freefallers, but I think they could be rigged for airbursts, too. I know there was talk of using them in Nam, but I never thought…"

James's voice suddenly trailed off. The anchor rope had suddenly gone limp and was collapsing on itself, curling like some elongated sea snake. "What the hell?"

The two divers instinctively glanced up. They were fifty

feet from the surface, and the sunlight penetrated deep enough for them to make out not only the underside of the longboat, but also that of a second, larger vessel that had apparently pulled up alongside it.

"I don't like it," Pag Ti said, reaching behind his back for his strapped MP-5. James did the same but motioned for the Myanmar operative keep their ascent slow and steady.

"We get the bends, we're done for," he reminded Pag Ti.

As they drew closer to the surface, they saw a body tumble from the longboat and begin to drift toward them, trailing a streak of blood. It was the Moken who'd stayed aboard with the longboat with Rafael Encizo.

James cursed and swam clear of the severed anchor line. He pointed to one of the larger kelp beds floating twenty yards from the two boats and told Pag Ti, "Let's come up over there and hope we'll have some cover."

Pag Ti followed James, averting his gaze from the eerie sight of the sinking aboriginal. They were halfway to the kelp bed when James detected movement off to his right. Less than twenty feet away, an eight-foot-long gray shark was bearing down on them. The MP-5 wasn't going to be of any use underwater, so James grappled at his weight belt, unsheathing his Ka-bar knife. "Jaws at ten o'clock," he warned Pag Ti.

The Myanmar diver had seen the shark, too. He already had his knife out. But the predator wasn't interested in either him or James. With a forceful wag of its tail, it propelled itself past them and tore into the body of the slain Moken, turning the water around it red.

James and Pag Ti watched the feeding frenzy for a horrified moment, then resumed their ascent. Thanks to their rebreathers, there was no trail of bubbles to betray their position. They surfaced on the far side of the kelp bed just as the second boat began to drift away from the aboriginal's craft, which had been set afire. There were soldiers aboard the other vessel, a powerboat three times the size of the one that had carried the pirates James and Pag Ti had battled earlier.

"Tatmadaw," Pag Ti confirmed.

Encizo was aboard the ship, as well. One of the soldiers aimed an assault rifle at the Phoenix Force commando's head while another bound his hands behind his back.

"They want him alive for questioning," Pag Ti guessed.

He and James were too far away for their MP-5s to be of much use. All they could do was watch and listen. The two soldiers' voices carried across the water as they shouted at Encizo. When he refused to answer, one of the men elbowed him in the ribs, doubling him over. The other was about to strike him with his rifle stock when a third man appeared and told them to stop. He spit out a few orders, then signaled the boat's driver to fire up the engines. A throaty roar cut through the air, followed by the churning of the boat's wake as it headed out to sea, away from James and Pag Ti.

"Did you make out anything they said?" James asked.

"I'm not positive," Pag Ti replied, "but I think they're taking him to Insein."

CHAPTER TWENTY-FIVE

Nyaung-U, Myanmar

Aung Paing stood alongside his sister, watching the others file back into the main chamber of Kyaukgu Umin Temple. He'd sent out word that it was time to decide whether the gathered followers of Maw Saung Ku-Syi would demonstrate on the anniversary of the Four Eights. At least two dozen more people had arrived since the broadcast, and now there was barely room in the cavernous enclosure to hold everyone. Searching the faces of those gathered before them, both Aung and Daw Bodta felt disillusioned.

"They're going to vote not to rally," Daw Bodta said.

"It's not an all-or-nothing vote," Aung said. "Those who decide to leave will leave. The rest of us will go ahead. And don't forget, there are hundreds more of us in the other temples and elsewhere across the country."

"And I'm sure they're as divided as we are," Daw Bodta said.

"Well, I'm going to demonstrate even if I have to do it alone," Aung said determinedly.

"I think there's a way to bring everyone around," called out the man who'd brought the camcorder from Magwe. He was several yards away, crouched over his laptop. "We can tell them it wasn't Ku-Syi who made that speech."

"Don't be ridiculous," Aung Paing said. "They'd see

through us. They'd know we were lying out of desperation.''

''That's the thing!'' Lon Mar said. ''We wouldn't be lying!''

''What are you talking about?'' Daw Bodta asked.

''Come, look, I'll show you.''

The two siblings knelt beside Lon Mar and stared at his computer. He'd split the screen vertically. One side displayed a grainy still frame of the woman who'd just made the telecast message arguing against rallies in observance of the Four Eights. The other screen was filled with a scanned newspaper image of Maw Saung Ku-Syi, taken several years ago.

''Take a close look,'' Lon Mar told the brother and sister, pointing at the screens. ''Ku-Syi has a mole high up here on her right cheekbone. The other woman's mole is lower, halfway down her cheek. And the cheekbones themselves...look close, they're completely different.''

''Neither of these photos is very clear,'' Aung said cautiously, trying not to get his hopes up.

''They're clear enough,'' Lon Mar replied. ''What's more, I played back the telecast, and this other woman is clearly left-handed.''

''Ku-Syi is right-handed?'' Bodta guessed.

''Yes! And if you're still not convinced, look closer at the eyes. Ku-Syi's are wider apart. And their chins. This other woman's is squarer, with a slight dimple.''

''This is incredible!'' Aung said. ''How did they think they could get away with such a thing?''

''Because they think we're all fools,'' Lon Mar said. ''The SPDC thinks we are all sheep, easily led around by the nose.''

As Aung and Daw Bodta contemplated Lon Mar's discovery, they were joined by Bari Tu. The Gold Dragon's contacts in Meiktila were obviously anxious to know the outcome of the vote regarding demonstrations. Bari Tu had been eavesdropping on the others gathered in the temple, and his sense was that most would decide not to rally. He wanted to make sure a vote was taken before the mood changed.

"Is there a problem?" Bari Tu asked Aung innocently. "The others are waiting to—"

"In a moment!" Aung snapped irritably. He waved the man away, then looked back at his sister. "What do you think we should do?"

Daw Bodta eyed the two images on Lon Mar's computer screen, then told her brother, "You know what we have to do."

Aung nodded, drew in a deep breath, then stood on the stone bench near one of the pillars and waved for quiet. "Before we vote," he called out, looking past Bari Tu at the other congregants, "there is something you all need to know."

Colorado Springs, Colorado

LESS THAN AN HOUR after the abbreviated shootout at the Outdoorsman's Retreat, a contingent of FBI agents and county sheriff officers had arrived to tend to the dead and take the surviving Patriots into custody. Gadgets Schwarz and Jack Grimaldi were still at the scene. The Stony Man pilot was in the Apache, conferencing by phone with Hal Brognola and Barbara Price on the latest developments. Schwarz, meanwhile, handled the authorities, telling them what they needed to know to mop things up and nothing more. When grilled for more details, he threw up the usual stonewall. He was part of a special federal task force and the overall scope of their assignment was classified on grounds of national security. If somebody didn't like it,

Justice Department verification was a phone call away, end of story.

The spiel sounded familiar to Bureau Agent Pierce Mullreck. He grinned maliciously at Schwarz. "Let me guess. You're the same guys who ruffled the feathers of that AF-IA honcho who wound up with his brains scrambled."

Schwarz nodded. "Not that we did the scrambling."

"All the same," the agent said, "I take it if we haul you guys in for questioning, we'll wind up regretting it."

Schwarz shrugged. "You said it, not me."

A scowl crossed the Mullreck's face as he glanced over his shoulder and saw Carl Lyons and Rosario Blancanales leading Mark Lacy down a mountain trail behind the shooting range. Lacy had taken them up to the mountain bunker where the Patriots had stored the sarin bombs along with other weapons and enough provisions to wait out a year's worth of nuclear fallout.

"More of your guys?" Mullreck said.

"Yep," Schwarz said. "I guess I forgot to mention them."

Cursing under his breath, Mullreck strode off to confront Lyons and Blancanales. There was a brief exchange between the three men, during which Schwarz saw the agent point several times at a small rectangular object Blancanales was carrying. The Able Team commando clearly wasn't about to turn over the item. Finally Mullreck gave up and took out his frustrations on Lacy, shoving the prisoner toward one of the Bureau's sedans.

"What an idiot," Lyons said as he and Blancanales rejoined Schwarz. "We hand over some guys looking to take out a senator and he calls *us* the vigilantes."

"Rogue vigilantes at that," Blancanales added, smirking. "As if J. Edgar Hoover never took the law into his own hands."

"What'd you find out?" Schwarz asked Lyons as the

men headed back to the Apache. Grimaldi was in the cockpit, still on the phone, though with someone besides the Farm.

"The sarin bombs are gone," Lyons reported. While the men boarded the chopper, he quickly passed along Lacy's tale of how he'd been forced to join the Patriots after helping them get their hands on the explosives, only to have Christopher Randolph and Evan Harris show up out of the blue three years later wanting the bombs for themselves.

"Lacy says he brought them here for a look-see, but Randolph disappeared and Harris wound up dead before they could finish the transaction," Lyons went on. "At some point, though, Randolph doubled back and swiped the bombs, leaving Lacy in the hot seat when they turned up missing."

"Which is why they were about to vent him at the shooting range," Schwarz guessed.

Lyons nodded. "Einstein that he is, Lacy jammed two of the bunker surveillance cameras but missed a third."

Blancanales showed Schwarz the videotape he'd removed from one of the cameras. "We already played it back. Not only do we have Lacy giving Harris and Randolph the tour, but we've also got Randolph coming back for the bombs four hours later."

"With Harris?" Schwarz asked.

"Nope. With the same two Gold Dragons Ironman ran off the road after they cooked Harris's noodle."

"Randolph double-crossed both guys?" Schwarz said.

"Sure looks that way," Blancanales said. "And if that's the case, he was probably worried Harris might spill to us and had him taken out."

"Of course the only thing he spilled was his brains," Lyons said. "But enough about all that. After all this shit, we've still got a cache of sarin bombs to track down. I don't know about you guys, but I think the Dragons have already schlepped them back overseas."

"Maybe not," Grimaldi called out, hanging up the chopper's comm-phone.

"Maybe not what?" Lyons said.

"That was Air Force IA," Grimaldi said. "They've been sweeping Randolph's P.O. box, and today he got a billing statement from some storage facility a mile up the road from his condo. They checked it out, and the guy's got a garage-sized cubicle there."

"I'm liking the sound of this," Lyons said. "Go on…"

"The place is open 24/7," Grimaldi reported, "but the folks that run it say Randolph only showed up at odd hours, when nobody was around."

"What about the night the bombs were swiped?" Blancanales asked. "He show up then?"

Grimaldi nodded. "Hazmat's already on their way there," he said, firing up the Apache. "I thought maybe we ought to have a peek ourselves."

"You thought right," Lyons said. "Let's go!"

Dwiti Military Base, Myanmar

LIKE NERVOUS FATHERS peering into a hospital maternity ward, Senior General Lon Kyth stood with rival underlings Bien Phyr and Dy Lii before the thick protective glass affording a glimpse into Laboratory B at the research and development facility at Dwiti Military Base. Inside the lab, resting within their insulated "cribs," were five globular sarin bombs, untouched since arriving the day before yesterday after a long, clandestine journey from Colorado Springs. A sixth bomb had been moved to a stainless steel workbench near the window. Delicately pried open, the crude device was surrounded by a trio of pneumatically powered robotic arms and a tray stocked with sophisticated precision tools. The bomb was being worked on by a technician sealed off inside an adjacent chamber, his hands and forearms sheathed within a pair of tentacle-like reticulated conduits built into the wall to prevent contact with the gas should it, for whatever reason, begin to leak from the bomb's housing. The precautions were understandable. Sarin had twenty times the lethal potency of cyanide gas. Even fleeting exposure to trace amounts would throw the technician into simultaneous respiratory and cardiopulmonary arrest, killing him in a matter of seconds.

On the table next to the bomb was a 3 kg high-explosive warhead taken from one of the Stinger missiles that would arm the two stolen LAVs now posted near the outer walls of the military compound. The technician was trying to determine whether a sarin charge could be "piggy-backed" onto the warhead. If so, several Stingers would be doctored with the nerve agent and sent north for use on Karen and Shan rebels should they attempt an offensive while the Tatmadaw was preoccupied with the anniversary of the Four Eights.

"What is the verdict?" Phyr asked a fourth man accompanying the generals on their tour of the facility.

"I'm sorry, but we don't have an answer yet," responded Dr. Gat Makirt, a onetime Yangon University physics professor. "Please realize we have to work slowly on this. An accident could be catastrophic." He addressed his remarks less to Phyr than Lon Kyth, a man with whom he had a better rapport.

"We understand," Phyr responded. He knew all too well the calamitous potential of the arms stored here in the R&D wing—not just the Stinger warhead and sarin arsenal, but also the eight salvaged Mk-28 hydrogen bombs being meticulously cleaned and examined next door in Laboratory A. He'd be glad once all the weapons were out of the laboratory and loaded for use.

"Take your time," Lon Kyth told the physicist, "only remember we need results in two days. Do you understand? We want them at our disposal on the eve of the seventh."

"May I be frank, General Kyth?" the physicist asked.

"You have a concern," Lon Kyth guessed.

Makirt nodded. "Even if we succeed ahead of schedule, I'm not sure this is the best use of the sarin."

"Why's that?" Phyr interjected.

"When the warhead explodes, yes, the nerve agent will be spread over a wide area," the physicist said, "but it will also begin to dissipate almost immediately. At most, you'll kill a few additional people. No more."

"We realize that," Phyr responded. "But if the rebels see their men dying, not just from the explosion but also from poisoning, it will give them pause. It will make them more cautious, less likely to take the sort of measures that could get them past our defenses."

"I understand all that," Makirt said, "but if your strategy is to use the sarin as a deterrent, you'd do better to have us work on a less explosive delivery system. Or better yet, eliminate the explosives altogether."

"What would be the point of that?" Lon Kyth wondered.

"Explosives aren't needed to release the gas," Makirt explained. "There are other devices that can release it the same as if you were spraying aerosol, only the sarin would be in its most natural state, invisible, without smell."

"I think he has a good idea," said Dy Lii, who'd felt from the onset that Phyr's idea of arming the Stingers with G-agents had been nothing more than a ploy to diminish Lii's accomplishment in securing the weapons.

"Sarin has been used in conjunction with explosives before," Phyr insisted. "During the Vietnam War the Americans dropped it from planes in Laos when they were trying to track down deserters."

"That was never proved," Lii responded. "If I remem-

ber correctly, that news story was retracted nearly as fast
as it came out.''

Phyr held his ground. ''There are other instances.''

''Perhaps,'' Lon Kyth said, intervening, ''but let's give
the professor a chance to finish his thought. Go on, Dr.
Makirt. How would you suggest we put this sarin gas to
better use?''

The lab physicist thought it over a moment, then said,
''If you had some men capable of penetrating rebel strongholds, they could place these bombs strategically. Inside
barracks or headquarters. Have the gas unleashed in an enclosed place and men will drop like flies, seemingly without
reason. I guarantee you, *that* would strike fear into the enemy.''

The two younger generals began to speak in unison. Lon
Kyth held up a hand to silence them, then told the physicist,
''How quickly could you ready the bombs for the kind of
use you're describing?''

''They're ready now,'' Makirt said. ''I know we've been
calling them bombs, but they're designed to work more like
tear-gas grenades.''

''Do this, then,'' Lon Kyth said. ''Continue working
with the bomb you've already opened. If they can be made
to work with the Stingers, fine, we'll adapt several of the
missiles as General Phyr has suggested. As for the others,
have them readied so that we can send them out with a
commando force as soon as possible.''

Makirt nodded. ''That is not a problem.''

Lon Kyth turned to Phyr and Lii. ''Follow me. We need
to have a talk, the three of us....''

Phyr bristled as he and Lii followed Lon Kyth down the
hallway leading away from the laboratories. He was in for
a tongue-lashing; he was sure of it. But, much as he wanted
to defend himself, he also knew that Lon Kyth was in no
mood for argument. Like it or not, Phyr knew he had no

choice but to take whatever the senior general was about to dish out.

The laboratories were located underground. Once they'd taken two flights of steps up to the second floor, the generals stepped out onto a terrace overlooking the base's training ground. More than five hundred Tatmadaw troops were on the field performing drills with assault carbines. Lon Kyth watched them briefly, then guided Phyr and Lii over to a makeshift boxing ring set up at the far end of the terrace. There, two junior officers sparred gamely, working their way around the canvass, occasionally tying up on the ropes.

Watching the fighters, Lon Kyth asked his underlings, "Have you ever known of a boxer who became a champion without mastering the use of both fists? Without knowing when to feint with one, then punch with the other? When to hold up both fists before him to fend off the blows of an opponent?"

"No," Lii responded sullenly.

"More to the point," Lon Kyth went on, "have either of you ever heard of a one-armed champion?"

"Of course not," Phyr said.

Lon Kyth forced a smile. "I know what you're thinking. 'Enough with the metaphors.' Fine, let me speak plainly," he said. "As you are both aware, there is change in the wind, both within the SPDC and the Tatmadaw. The old— myself, We Nin, all the others—like it or not, we are on our way out.

"You two are the future. And there is room enough for both of you to have power and influence beyond your wildest dreams. You need to decide, however, which is more important to you—personal glory or the good of your country. Work together, and Myanmar will assume its rightful place in the world. Continue with your foolish rivalries, and as a nation we will continue to struggle, compromised by our own infighting. We will remain on the ropes. Do I make myself clear?"

Both Phyr and Lii nodded, though each made a point not to look the other's way. Lon Kyth scowled irritably. "You pretend to listen, but the words go in one ear and out the other. Well, so be it. I've had my say."

Disgusted, the senior general was prepared to head off when a young aide strode out onto the terrace and approached Lii. "We've received word from one of our agents in Nyaung-U—Bari Tu. He's infiltrated the NLD and learned their plans for observance of the Four Eights."

Phyr expected Lii to take the aide aside so he could hear the news first and decide how to control the information. Instead, however, his rival stayed put and told the aide, "Let's hear it."

"Someone is claiming it wasn't Ku-Syi who made the speech calling off any rallies," the aide said.

"What nonsense," Lon Kyth responded.

"Maybe so," the aide said, "but her followers are eager to grasp at any straw, it seems. They've taken a vote and decided, despite the speech, to carry out demonstrations."

"Fools!" Lon Kyth seethed. "They are slitting their own throats."

"What are their plans?" Lii asked his aide. "Where will they be demonstrating?"

"In the country, near shrine sites like Bagan and Inle Lake." The aide went on to explain how the demonstrators had been secretly gathering for days inside some of the larger shrines, including the caves of Kyaukgu Umin temple.

"This complicates matters," Lon Kyth stated once the aide had been dismissed and the generals were alone. "This is what we'd hoped to avoid."

Lii nodded. "If this rumor about the broadcast spreads, it could wind up backfiring on us," he said, casting a swift look Phyr's way. Phyr could see that the other general was secretly pleased by this latest development.

The exchange didn't go unnoticed by Lon Kyth. He decided this was as good a time as any to see if the men had heeded any of his advice.

"Tell me," he asked them, "how do you two suggest we deal with this?"

Phyr looked Lii's way. It was clear that his rival had a solution in mind, no doubt the same one Phyr had thought of the moment he heard that the demonstrators would be gathering prior to the rally in large, enclosed spaces. Much as it pained him, he nodded at the other general, gesturing for him to speak first. Lii offered the faintest of grins, then turned to Lon Kyth and said, "I think we've found the perfect use for our sarin bombs."

Colorado Springs, Colorado

THE APACHE HELICOPTER carrying Jack Grimaldi and Able Team had just cleared the mountain tree line and was bearing down on the suburban outskirts of Colorado Springs when a com link call came in from Stony Man Farm.

"Better use the headset," Grimaldi shouted over the reverberating howl of the chopper's engines.

Lyons, riding shotgun in the cockpit, took the call. It was Brognola. The Able Team leader quickly briefed him on the situation in Colorado Springs, then listened, incredulous, as Brognola proceeded to recount his meeting with General David Brooks. Lyons wasn't sure which news was more mind-boggling: the Myanmar military's likely recovery of hydrogen bombs from the belly of a long-sunken B-52 or the fact that the bomber's pilot had been Christopher Randolph.

Once off the call, Lyons relayed the news to Schwarz

and Blancanales. To them, Brooks's disclosure raised as many questions as answers.

"What about the rest of the crew?" Schwarz wondered aloud. "Those Strats usually flew with six men aboard, didn't they?"

Lyons nodded. "According to Brooks, when the fire broke out in the cockpit, Randolph had everyone else bail, saying he'd be right behind him once he dumped all the ordnance."

"Which we're saying never happened," Blancanales said.

"We won't know for sure until we get a report from James and Encizo," Lyons replied, "but you've got to figure the only reason the junta went salvaging there was that Randolph told them what they'd find."

"But why now?" Blancanales wanted to know. "That bomber went down, what, thirty-five years ago?"

"I didn't get an answer on that," Lyons confessed. "But if you look at all the trips Randolph made to that neck of the woods over the years, he was probably building up connections and trying to line up the best deal possible before he tipped his hand. Kind of like these Patriot shitheads with their sarin bombs."

"Wait, that's crazy!" Blancanales countered. "That's saying when the bomber caught fire Randolph instantly figured, 'Hey, I've got it! Maybe instead of dumping everything I'll lie to everybody, then put this baby down in the water and hope nobody double-checks so maybe I can peddle the ordnance thirty-five years from now.' I mean, c'mon, give me a break!"

"Seems to me the simpler explanation is that he just panicked and ejected without dumping the load," Grimaldi called out. "That or maybe the fire screwed up the release controls for the bay doors. Who knows? Either way, he could've left the bombs behind when he bailed, then gotten the idea about peddling them later on.''

"Good point, Jack," Lyons said. "For me, though, the only way it all fits is if you consider Randolph had everything planned out in advance, from where he was going to stash the plane on down to starting the fire in the cockpit.''

"Guys, guys," Blancanales interrupted. "We could go back and forth on this all day. I say we just forget about it for now. Once Rafe and Cal make it to Guna, I'm sure they'll check the plane out and we'll have more answers.''

"One problem with that," Lyons said. "Rafe and Cal haven't been heard from since they set out for the island. It's going on seven hours now.''

"Damn," Schwarz said.

"David and the others are heading out to look for them," Lyons went on. "And we're right behind. Once we've checked this storage place, Hal wants us to pull stakes.''

"Fine by me," Blancanales said. "I don't know if it's the altitude or just trying to keep track of everything this Randolph guy's been up to, but my head's starting to spin. I'm all for a change of scenery.''

"Same here," Schwarz said. "C'mon, Jack! Let's wrap this up!''

It took the men another five minutes to reach the industrial park where the storage facility was located. The place was easy enough to spot. Authorities had cordoned off an entire two-square-block area and were escorting employees from the other buildings. Meanwhile, at the end of a long row of cinder-block storage cubicles, a SWAT bomb squad and hazmat team milled around the opening to one of the units. With their gas masks and bulky protective gear, they looked like space aliens. Grimaldi radioed down and was given clearance to land in a parking area just beyond the farthest cubicle.

As the Apache set down, a tall, athletic-looking woman broke away from the ground crews and strode over. She wore a bulletproof vest under her jacket and had the initials AF-IA emblazoned across the front of her navy-colored baseball cap. She introduced herself to Lyons as Smitt Ripley, Evan Harris's replacement.

"We just finished checking the place from top to bottom," she explained. "No sarin bombs."

"Shit," Lyons said.

"It wasn't a complete bust, though," Ripley stated. "Come on, you've got to see this."

Lyons grinned at Schwarz and Blancanales as they followed the woman to Randolph's cubicle. "Cooperation. I like it."

Ripley overheard Lyons and told him, "Harris was an asshole. Don't judge the rest of us by him."

"No, ma'am, we sure won't."

Once they reached the storage area, Ripley waved away the hazmat crew, telling them, "We'll take it from here, guys."

Lyons had expected to see the usual assortment of stray junk and stacked boxes, but Randolph had transformed his cubicle into something more closely resembling an office. A large desk was set against one wall, flanked on either side by two sets of file cabinets. There was also a bookcase, a space heater and an old Army cot, upon which lay a down-filled sleeping bag.

"Cozy," Lyons said. "I take it he set up shop here so there wouldn't be anything incriminating at his condo."

"Pretty much," Ripley said. "But he knew we'd stumble onto his lair here sooner or later. Get a load of this."

Stacked on Randolph's desk were four thick, well-worn

notebooks. The woman picked up the top one and handed it to Lyons. There was a note taped to the cover.

If you're reading this, the odds are I've completed my mission but didn't live to tell the tale. This should explain things.

Lyons opened to the first page, then turned to the others, who'd closed in around him. "A diary," he told them. "Starts back in 1969."

CHAPTER TWENTY-SIX

Guna Island, Mergui Archipelago, Myanmar

The morning sun filtered warmly through the trees overhead, where a pair of gibbons scampered from branch to branch. A faint breeze blew across Calvin James, carrying with it the briny smell of the harbor. Slowly he sat up. His entire body was sore.

"Good morning," Pag Ti called out to him.

James glanced over his shoulder. His comrade was seated nearby on a large chunk of driftwood, picking apart what looked to be a mass of green cotton candy. Pag Ti took a bite of the substance and began to chew. "Dried seaweed," he told James. "A little salty, but not bad."

James's stomach was growling, but the seaweed didn't look any more appealing to him than the sea cucumbers, mollusks or urchins left behind by the Moken aboriginals who'd been slaughtered the day before, apparently before the Tatmadaw had laid seige to the longboat and taken Enciz prisoner. James and Pag Ti had discovered the bodies when they'd first come ashore. Men, women and children, all unarmed, had been gunned down in a spray of gunfire. Now they lay buried in graves a few yards into the jungle. James and Pag Ti had set up camp fifty yards away, near the jungle's edge, leaving themselves a clear view of the harbor. They'd been marooned nearly twelve hours now, and during that time they'd slept in shifts so that one of them would always be awake, on the lookout for another Moken longboat or some other means of getting off the island. So far the closest thing to a mode of transportation had been a whale that briefly surfaced far past the mouth of the harbor just before nightfall.

James noticed a large plastic container filled with water lying in the sand near Pag Ti's feet.

"Where'd you find that?" he asked.

"I took a walk." He gestured over his shoulder. "There's a campsite back in the brush the Tatmadaw must have been using during the salvage operation. They left behind some salvage gear and supplies. No food, though."

"Maybe in another couple hours that seaweed will start to look appetizing," James said without much conviction.

He hefted the water container and rinsed out his mouth, then waded into the harbor. The water was shallow, and James could see more mollusks and bits of driftwood poking up through the sand. Twenty yards out, the water still came up only to his shins. He splashed some on his face and rinsed a few cuts and scrapes along his arms. He saw a crab scuttle out from beneath a submerged log and was about to chase after it when he suddenly heard, off in the distance, a faint rumbling sound. There were no clouds in the sky, ruling out thunder. As the noise drew closer, James hurried back ashore. Pag Ti was on his feet, peering northward.

"You hear it, too?" James said.

Pag Ti nodded. "Helicopter."

James tracked down his MP-5, propped against a palm tree at the edge of the jungle. "We better take cover."

Pag Ti grabbed the water container, as well as the MP-5, then followed James into the foliage. Crouching in the brush, they stared out into the harbor. Soon a sleek Agusta A-129 Mongoose droned into view, skimming over the water as it approached the island. The Italian-made helicopter, powered by twin 825-horsepower turboshafts, was armed externally with four Hellfire antitank missiles and a 20 mm gun pod.

James and Pag Ti could see two soldiers in the cockpit, but the gunship was commonly used for medevac, as well as search and rescue, so there were likely more men in back.

"Tatmadaw," Pag Ti whispered.

The chopper slowly made its way along the perimeter of the harbor. As it drew close, James could see the gunner peering into the jungle through a pair of binoculars. He and Pag Ti ducked lower as the chopper hovered in place before them.

"They spotted our tracks in the sand," Pag Ti guessed.

"If they start strafing, we're dead meat," James said. He raised his MP-5 and flicked off the safety. "I don't think we should give them a chance."

Pag Ti placed a hand over the barrel of James's gun. "Wait," he said. "Let's try to keep it in one piece."

"Why?" James asked. "Can you fly it?"

Pag Ti nodded. "The Company has a couple of these back in Thailand. We use them along the border to provide cover during refugee crossings."

"Yeah, well, this time, we're the refugees," James said.

"We should spread out," Pag Ti suggested. "If they set down to come looking for us, maybe we'll have a chance."

"Sounds like a long shot to me," James said. "But let's give it a try."

Dropping to the jungle floor, the men crawled off in opposite directions, doing their best not to disturb the brush around them. James lost sight of the chopper, but he could hear it moving closer. Fortunately there was no clearing anywhere within a hundred yards of the beach. The Tatmadaw was either going to have to fire blindly into the jungle or set the Mongoose down in the shallow water and get out. Of course, they could fly off for reinforcements. If it came to that, James figured he'd have no choice but to break from cover and try to bring the chopper down with his MP-5.

Soon James heard a faint splashing and guessed it was the chopper's rotor wash stirring up the surf. He stopped crawling and elbowed his way to the jungle's edge. Fingering aside a few thick, coarse blades of saw grass, he saw the Mongoose come to a rest in the shallow water only a few yards from where he'd been standing when he'd first heard it. Moments later, the engines shut off and the rotors twirled to a stop. James was facing the pilot's side of the cockpit. His hopes stirred when he saw the man get up from his seat and head toward the rear of the cabin. The gunner followed suit.

"That's it, guys," James murmured. "Come and get me."

Moments later, a rear panel hissed opened and lowered into the surf, becoming a ramp down which the two Tatmadaw bounded, then waded away from the chopper, each man clutching an AK-47. James lined them in his sights. This was going to be easier than he thought.

Before he could pull the trigger, however, James saw a third man scrambling down the ramp, then a fourth. Cursing under his breath, he held his fire as, altogether, five men joined the pilot and gunner in the surf. The Phoenix Force commando had a bead on only three men, total. The others had circled around the other side of the Mongoose.

James was pondering his next move when a burst from Pag Ti's MP-5 sounded across the harbor and was quickly answered by a volley from the Tatmadaw.

"Okay, we'll do it that way, then," James said, rising to a crouch and unleashing his subgun's firepower. The pilot and gunner both went down with the first spray, dead before they could get off a shot. The third man, wounded, managed to stagger back behind the chopper. Cursing, James broke from cover and charged into the surf. Forty yards to his left, Pag Ti was doing the same thing, obviously with the same intent: to wrap things up before the Tatmadaw could bring the chopper's guns into play. Both men zigzagged in the shallow water, dodging fire from two soldiers who'd made it to cover back near the ramp. Pag Ti made it to a large stump of driftwood jutting from the surf and called out to James, "I've got them! Try the pilot's door!"

James nodded and charged the Mongoose head-on, placing himself out of view of the gunmen in back. Once he reached the copter, he grabbed hold of the handle to the pilot's door and pulled himself up, then yanked the door open. Bullets screamed out at him, one of them taking out the side window. James spotted the shooter in the rear of the cabin and returned fire. The other man screamed in pain and spun away from the crate he'd ducked behind. Down but not out, he brought up his AK-47 and was about to pull the trigger when James finished off his ammo, nailing the man with a burst to the chest.

Outside, James could still hear gunfire, so he charged past the man he'd just killed. The lone surviving Tatmadaw still fired at Pag Ti from the cover of the ramp. He glanced up and swung around his rifle, but before he could get a shot off, James dived forward and tackled him. Both men fell to the surf. James, a tae kwon do black belt, quickly overpowered the man and stripped him of his rifle. The man reeled backward but quickly recovered and was drawing an eight-inch combat knife from his ankle sheath when James turned the rifle on him and pulled the trigger.

The Phoenix Force commando waded away from the body and stared past the other corpses bobbing in the surf. Pag Ti stepped cautiously out from behind the driftwood, slamming a fresh magazine into his MP-5.

"Save it," James called out to him. "We got them all. I think the bird's still in one piece, too. I say we hop on out of here, pronto."

"We should do something with the bodies first," Pag Ti suggested. "In case there's a follow-up team."

"You're right."

The two men dragged their seven victims ashore and concealed the bodies in the foliage, then used palm fronds to sweep their tracks and the traces of blood on the beach. The surf was red around the chopper, as well, but the men knew that would dissipate.

On their way back to the Mongoose, James asked Pag Ti, "How's the comm gear on these things? Any chance we can spit out a message to the folks back home?"

"Maybe, but I doubt we'd be able to scramble the signal," Pag Ti cautioned. "We'd run the risk of tipping our hand."

James thought it over. "What the hell," he said, as they clambered aboard, "let's risk it. If we want to spring Rafe from that hellhole in Insein, we're gonna need some backup."

Insein Prison, Yangon, Myanmar

STRIPPED TO HIS boxer shorts, Rafael Encizo huddled, shivering, in one corner of the dog cell last used to imprison the late Soe Paing. Before tossing him into the cell, the guards had beat him with a section of PVC pipe, raising welts across his back and shoulders near his now infected shrapnel wound. His wrists and ankles, bound tightly with an electrical cord, were chafed and numb, and dried spit, another present from his tormentors, caked his hair and face.

Though he hadn't slept since his capture at Guna harbor, Encizo clung doggedly to consciousness, berating himself for the way he'd let himself be taken prisoner. The previous day, while waiting on the Moken longboat for Calvin James and Pag Ti to finish their underwater recon in Guna harbor, Encizo had let himself get so engrossed in trying to get the comm gear working that he'd failed to notice a pair of Tatmadaw soldiers emerging from the jungle. By the time he'd been alerted by the Moken in the boat with him, the soldiers had their guns trained on the women and children who had been left ashore.

When Encizo reached for his Beretta, one of the soldiers fired a bullet into the head of one of the children, then stared out into the harbor, shaking his head to warn Rafael that more would die if he didn't toss the gun overboard. After some hesitation, Encizo complied, hoping he might still be able to get to his MP-5, poking out of the gear bag across from him. But as soon as he dropped his Beretta, Encizo heard the sputter of a motorboat rounding the peninsula. One look at the armed men aboard the craft and he knew that resistance would be futile; all he could hope to do was protect James and Pag Ti.

Remembering Rick the Texan's notion about sunken treasure, Encizo waited for the other boat to pull up alongside him, then explained that he'd hired out the Moken to bring him here to case out the harbor. He had another boat moored at one of the other islands, he explained, and had planned to return with scuba equipment if he spotted anything worth diving for. The soldier he'd spoken to translated his explanation to the other soldiers, who proceeded to board the ship, seizing the communications equipment. When the Moken, sobbing, begged for the Tatmadaw to spare his family, his pleas were answered by five slugs from a Walther PPK.

While his body was being flung overboard, the soldiers on shore calmly gunned down the other aboriginals, then waded into the harbor. By the time they swam to the boat,

Encizo was transferred from the Moken's craft, which then was set afire. As the motorboat sped from the harbor, the Cuban was asked which of the other islands he had left his boat at. Having succeeded, at least for the moment, in buying James and Pag Ti some time, Encizo fell silent.

Now, more than twelve hours later, he had yet to say another word. Inwardly, though, he cursed himself for having let down his guard. He was convinced that if he'd spotted the two soldiers stealing from the jungle, he could have gunned them down and held the other boat at bay until James and Pag Ti had surfaced with their submachine guns. Instead, there'd been a massacre, his cohorts had been left stranded and here he was, a pawn the Tatmadaw clearly intended to exploit to full advantage before executing.

Once he tired of second-guessing his actions back at the island, Encizo turned his attention to the cramped cell around him. He could hear water running overhead. There was apparently a small leak in the plumbing, because he could also see a dime-sized bubble in the mortar seam separating one of the walls from the ceiling. The bubble grew larger, then popped, sending a trickle of water down the wall. There was a small puddle at the base of the wall, so Encizo figured the pipes had been leaking for some time. If that was the case, it was likely the mortar had been weakened. If he could somehow free his hands, there was a chance he could claw one of the bricks loose, providing himself with a weapon and, perhaps, an avenue of escape.

With difficulty, Encizo wriggled toward the leak. He was halfway to it when his cell door opened. A soldier appeared, carrying a tray with the same provisions Soe Paing had been offered the day before: two plastic plates, one holding water, the other fish paste. Encizo stared at the plates, wondering how easy they would be to break. The guard, in turn, stared back in his direction. Chagrined, Encizo realized the man was looking, not at him, but rather at the leak in the ceiling. The guard stooped low and crossed the cell, clucking his tongue with disapproval as he ran a finger across the wet mortar.

So much for that plan, Encizo figured. When his eyes fell on the guard's holstered service revolver, however, he saw another opportunity and went with it. Pitching himself sideways, Encizo knocked the guard off balance. He'd hoped the man might strike his head while going down, but it wasn't to be. With a curse, the guard quickly scrambled away from Encizo and drew his gun. Encizo kicked outward with both feet, but managed only a glancing blow to the guard's shins. The guard kicked back, slamming the steel toe of his boots into Encizo's thigh. A flash of pain shot through the Phoenix Force commando's leg and he was forced to go on the defensive, wriggling to one side as the guard swung at him with the butt on his revolver. In the cramped quarters, the guard couldn't put much heft behind the blow. Still, it was enough to stun Encizo. A second blow sent his head swimming. He felt himself being dragged across the floor and tried to resist, but the fight had been beaten out of him, at least for the moment. By the time he was hauled out of the cell, Encizo was unconscious.

Airspace over Prachuap Khiri Khan, Thailand

ACCORDING TO ITS flight manifest, the Thai Air Express Cessna coursing over the limestone peaks of Mirror Tunnel Mountain was making a routine service run along the narrow peninsula Thailand shared with Myanmar as far south as Ranong. After routine stops in Chumphon and Surat Thani, the freight plane was scheduled to refuel in Trang, then continue up the western coast, making deliveries in Phuket Bay and Ranong before crossing over into Myanmar airspace to drop off construction supplies in Kawthoung and Myeik. What the manifest neglected to mention, for obvious reasons, was that Thai Air Express was a shell company operated by the CIA as part of its long-standing covert operations in Myanmar. While its range was far more limited than that of sat-cams orbiting the heavens above, the plane's photographic surveillance equipment produced clearer images of designated ground activity. And, of course, cargo toting allowed for espionage opportunities unobtainable by satellites. Embedded in the Cessna's shipment of ergonomic swivel chairs, bound for a military installation in Myeik, were thumbtack-sized transmitters that would allow the Company to eavesdrop on conversations between Tatmadaw radar technicians.

The manifest had also failed to acknowledge the last-minute human cargo taken aboard before the CIA plane had set out from Bangkok. Gary Manning and T. J. Hawkins sat uncomfortably in the Cessna's parcel hold, having cleared space for themselves on the floor near the bay doors. David McCarter was up front in the flight cabin, copiloting the aircraft.

Over their camou fatigues, Manning and Hawkins wore lightweight hip packs and full MT-1X parachute gear. Packed alongside them was a small, hastily assembled arsenal. In addition to the assault rifles used in the seige at Gui Rahb's heroin distribution center in Bangkok, the men had brought along two AGS-17 30 mm grenade launchers, a Barrett .50-caliber sniper rifle, and enough ammunition for each weapon to last through a substantial firefight.

With the men aboard, the Cessna had reversed its itinerary and was now bound first for Myeik, after which it would sweep wide over the Mergui Archipelago on its way to Kawthoung. Somewhere along the way, the men from Phoenix Force hoped to spot some trace of their missing comrades—Calvin James, Rafael Encizo and CIA Agent U Pag Ti. Failing that, they would parachute into the harbor at Guna Island, taking with them a 150-pound NAVY SEAL combat rubber raiding craft outfitted with a forty-horsepower engine. The raft, resting on its side in the cargo hold, gave off a smell of fuel and fresh tires. Hawkins was less troubled by the odor than he was with the dead-eyed gaze of four life-size figurines that peered at him through the slats of a large straw-packed crate strapped to the walls across from him. Once unloaded in Myeik, the crate would be shipped by train to Taungbyon, where the coming full moon would mark the beginning of a seven-day festival honoring religious spirits represented by the figurines.

"*Nats,*" Manning told Hawkins.

"What?"

"They're called *nats,*" Manning said. "They're like the statues of saints in those fine churches of yours."

"I don't care what they're called," Hawkins groused. "I wish they'd quit staring at me. They give me the creeps."

"Try not looking at them," Manning suggested. The big Canadian's nerves were on edge, too. It was bad enough knowing the odds were against spotting James and Encizo in the eight hundred square miles of archipelago. To have to conduct the search in hostile territory where the enemy had apparently just armed itself with eight hydrogen bombs made their mission seem all the more futile. Stuck in the cramped, darkened confines of the cargo hold, Manning felt entombed. When, despite his own warning, he glanced at the unmoving faces of the crated *nats,* he shared Hawkins's sense of foreboding.

The plane had passed over the mountains and was nearing the border when McCarter opened the inner door to the cargo hold. "Change in plans," he told the others, his expression torn between relief and dread. "We're heading to Yangon."

"Yangon?" Manning said.

Hawkins jumped to the obvious conclusion. "Cal and Rafe turned up?"

"I guess you could say that." McCarter crouched with his partners, explaining that James had just been in touch with Akira Tokaido at the air base in U-Tapao. Before Manning and Hawkins could get too elated, the Briton quickly sobered them with the news that Encizo had been taken prisoner.

"Hell, I've heard about Insein," Hawkins said. "That place is harder to bust out of than Alcatraz."

McCarter nodded, adding, "And the thing is, we need to find a way to bust *in*..."

CHAPTER TWENTY-SEVEN

U-Tapao Royal Thai Navy Airfield, Thailand

After his twenty-minute long-distance conversation with Hal Brognola, Yakov Katzenelenbogen slowly hung up the phone. He'd barely spoken during the exchange, and he was equally succinct in summing up his reaction to the latest news from Stony Man Farm. "Unbelievable," he murmured.

Akira Tokaido, who'd just finished apprising David McCarter about Rafael Encizo's imprisonment in Yangon, glanced over at Katz. "You're going to have to do better than that," he said, swiveling away from the AFB computers. When the Farm's senior adviser stared at him questioningly, Tokaido went on, "From what I picked up, Able Team found some kind of journal Randolph left behind before he disappeared."

"Yes," Katz said. "A diary. It pretty much clears everything up."

"Must be a pretty thick diary."

"It turns out we were wrong about him," Katz said.

"What do you mean? About his being a double agent?"

Katz nodded. "Triple is more like it. Randolph's working with us after all."

"No way," Tokaido said.

"I know. I found it a little hard to swallow, too."

"You're gonna have to spell it out for me."

"I don't really know where to begin," Katz said.

"Try the beginning," Tokaido suggested. "Look, I read everything the chief managed to get out of General Brooks, so I'm good up to the point where Randolph's on his way here with a Stratofortress full of Mk-28s. And, obviously, I know he didn't make it."

"Fair enough." Katz sighed, hoping he could remember everything Brognola had just told him. He'd managed to jot a few notes, but they only covered the tip of what was a particularly large iceberg. "When the fire broke out in the cockpit," he began, "Randolph followed procedure and started dumping ordnance. The Hound Dogs dropped off without any problem, but there was a problem with the bomb bay. The crew tried helping, but there wasn't much they could do with the fire spreading, so Randolph told them to jump. He said he'd be right behind them after he tried a few more things. This was around the ninety-second parallel, just south of the Andaman Islands. We had a carrier in the area, and they sent out a search-and-rescue copter almost immediately.

"Randolph kept wrangling with the controls until he got a dash light confirming that the bay doors were operative. He made sure he was still over open water, then dumped the bombs...or so he thought."

"The dash reading was bogus?"

Katz nodded. "Some short from the fire or something, I'd guess. At any rate, Randolph had already radioed in a successful dump and bailed from the plane before he saw the bay doors were still jammed closed."

"And by then it was too late to radio back."

"Exactly," Katz said.

"What about when they picked him up?" Tokaido asked. "Why didn't he tell them then?"

"Well, that's just it," Katz said. "He didn't get picked up. Not by SAC, at least."

"Why not?"

"S&R was needling on empty by the time they reached the archipelago," Katz explained. "They looked as long as they could, then they had to get the chopper back to the carrier. A couple search planes made some quick follow-up passes, but they couldn't find Randolph, either. They figured his chute must've failed or else something had gone wrong after he'd radioed in and he'd gone down with the plane."

"But they still thought he'd dumped the bombs."

"Right." Katz nodded. "That whole part jibes with Brooks's story. Looking for the bombs on the ocean floor would have taken weeks, if not months, and they didn't want to nose around the plane because nobody else knew it had gone down."

"Fine, I follow all that," Tokaido said, "but let's just stick with Randolph. Search and rescue leaves him stranded out in the archipelago. I assume he's got on some kind of flotation collar. What next?"

"At some point he passed out and wound up washed up on one of the other islands," Katz said. "There were some researchers there from some oceanographic society based out of Yangon. One of them was a nurse, a woman named Dharni Loi."

"Ah. The plot thickens."

"It sure does. They had Randolph airlifted to a hospital in Yangon, but he had hypothermia and had been stung so many times by jellyfish nobody held out much hope for him. He rallied, though, and this Dharni woman wound up taking him into her home and nursing him back to health."

"They fell in love," Tokaido guessed.

Katz nodded. "Apparently there's some snapshots from then in some photo album that turned up at the storage facility. Kurtzman'll pass along the scans as soon as he can. But, to make a long story short, once Randolph was well enough, he proposed to Dharni. She didn't see it working out, though. She reminded him he had unfinished business, and he finally got back in touch with SAC and let them know what had happened.''

''Must've thrown them for a loop,'' Tokaido said.

''To put it mildly. They sent agents to debrief him, and—at least the way it's spelled out in his diary—they came on so strong he was afraid to admit the bombs hadn't been dumped before he bailed from the B-52.

''He figured he was looking at a court-martial for going AWOL, but the SAC honchos back in the States were more concerned about keeping a lid on things. They cut him a deal—a cushy desk in Colorado Springs provided he forget about the past six months. As far as anyone was concerned, that time frame would be classified. He went along, more or less.''

''But he stayed in touch with this Dahrni woman,'' Tokaido guessed.

''Yeah,'' Katz said, checking his notes. ''They traded letters for another six weeks, then she stopped writing. Not only that, his letters started coming back unopened.''

''She just sent them back?''

Katz shook his head. ''She moved. No forwarding address.''

Tokaido whistled. ''All those vacations he took out here,'' he recalled. ''He was looking for her.''

''Right again,'' Katz said. ''According to the diary, it took him four years. Lyons says he had file cabinets at the storage place filled with all the leads he followed up on.''

''And he finally found her?'' Tokaido asked.

''Her grave,'' Katz said. ''It turned out she'd died a little over a year after she stopped writing.''

''How'd she die?''

"She was murdered," Katz said. "Apparently she'd joined this group of women trying to stop sex-slave traffickers at a border crossing near Tachilek. If they saw anyone suspicious, they'd corner them and shout for the authorities to do something. Usually the smugglers would just ditch the girls they had with them and run for it. One time they didn't. They turned on the women and gunned them down. Randolph managed to track down witnesses, and apparently the guards stood by and let it happen because the smugglers had just bribed them."

"And these guards," Tokaido said. "They were Tatmadaw?"

"Correct," Katz said. "And the smugglers? Our friends the Gold Dragons."

Tokaido was incredulous. "So that's what all this is about? Randolph's carrying out some kind of vendetta?"

Katz nodded again. "That's why he kept taking his vacations out here. He'd made some contacts with the Tatmadaw and Gold Dragons and peddled himself as this disgruntled pencil pusher looking to switch sides, and they bought it. They figured him for their answer to Kim Philby."

"Only he was stringing them along the whole time, right?" Tokaido said. "He was looking for a way to make them pay for what they'd done to Dharni Loi."

"That's pretty much it," Katz agreed. "Back in the States, he crossed paths with Evan Harris while he was trying to score points with the Gold Dragons working the Colorado smack scene. He figured he could use the guy. Harris had the same idea, though, so they wound up using each other."

"Then Randolph's the one who ordered the hit on Harris?" Tokaido asked.

"No," Katz said. "That was the Dragons' idea. Not that Randolph didn't suspect something. His last entry in the diary came a day before the shooting. He said the Dragons were concerned Harris had too much information on them and couldn't be trusted.''

Tokaido was amazed. ''I swear, this Randolph guy's like Mack Bolan all over again. Goes off on a one-man war looking to wipe out everyone he figures has done him wrong.''

''One big difference for starters,'' Katz said. ''Mack never helped his enemies get their hands on eight hydrogen bombs.''

Dwiti Military Base, Myanmar

CHRISTOPHER RANDOLPH WAS overcome with emotion as he stood before the eight Mk-28 thermonuclear warheads stacked inside the Dwiti military base's R&D wing. He'd arrived at the facility by helicopter forty minutes earlier, two hours behind the two F-105 Thunderchiefs he'd procured for the Tatmadaw from Entai Lette's traveling aerocircus. It had taken some insistence—as well as General Phyr's intervention on his behalf—for Randolph to be allowed access to the bombs on his terms: alone, with special equipment placed at his disposal so that he could make the final inspection and determine whether, after all the effort put into their retrieval from the watery depths of Guna harbor, the Mk-28s were deployable.

From the onset, Randolph was stunned by the pristine condition of the bombs. Thirty-four years they'd lain in their underwater grave. From his years of research, Randolph knew the B-52s bomb bays were, by design, airtight, but he'd been concerned that the seals might have ruptured when his plane plunged into the sea, allowing the elements to seep in and act upon the bombs in a way that would have rendered them useless. But here they were, after only a few days of minor cleaning, looking for all the world as if they'd just come off the assembly line. It was nothing short of miraculous.

Or, as Randolph had come to believe, it was fate, the culmination of more than twenty years of obsessive determination to avenge the killing of Dharni Loi, a woman who in death had exerted an even greater influence on him than during their few fleeting months together. At first it had been the onetime pilot's hope merely to track down the individuals responsible for her murder, but as the years had dragged on and he'd learned more about the base nature of the Gold Dragons and Myanmar Tatmadaw, the more Randolph had come to despise them. Eventually there had come a time when he'd decided that revenge against a mere handful of perpetrators wouldn't be enough. The more he'd allowed his rage to foment, the wider the blame he'd cast, the broader the ranks of those he'd vowed to bring judgment against, until, finally, two months ago, he'd set his sights on a new plan: to kill them all.

As Randolph had set his plan into motion, fate had been his ally. He was sure of it. How else to explain the string of dramatic events, especially over the past few days, that had brought him here to the Tatmadaw's isolated stronghold, entrusted, without supervision, to make a final inspection of the hydrogen bombs he had so fortuitously laid to rest at Guna harbor all those years ago, as if in anticipation that there would come the day when he would need them to, at long last, carry out the mass extermination of those who had done him wrong.

Staring at the bombs, realizing that his moment of truth was finally at hand, Christopher Randolph began to weep. He let the tears spill freely down his face and turned to a steel cart, upon which rested a rack of precision tools and instruments that had been set out for him according to his painstaking specifications. Also on the cart was a small leather bag, no larger than a shaving kit. Of all the seemingly insurmountable tasks Randolph had under pursuit of his plan, getting his hands on the bag's contents had been the most difficult. It was also the closest he'd come to being discovered and having his plan turn to dust. Inside the bag, carefully wrapped in individual compartments, were eight wallet-sized triggering mechanisms nearly identical to those that had been installed, more than thirty-four years ago, in each of the long-lost hydrogen bombs. The one difference was that while the Mk-28s had been originally configured to be detonated by a remote signal, Randolph's replacement triggers worked off built-in altimeters. Once reaching an altitude one hundred feet higher than their presets, the altimeters would trigger the fusion reaction necessary to unleash the bombs' thermonuclear capacity.

In short, after the eight warheads were loaded into the two F-105s, all that would be necessary for fate to play out its hand would be for the jets to take off from the runway. The moment they'd risen a hundred feet off the tarmac, all eight bombs would go off simultaneously. The entire military base would be obliterated in a matter of seconds. All Tatmadaw personnel within a ten-mile radius of the explosions would be either vaporized or brought to death's door by a nuclear firestorm of the likes humankind had never witnessed.

"They'll pay," Randolph murmured as he began the slow task of replacing the bomb's triggers. "At last they will pay."

CHAPTER TWENTY-EIGHT

Airspace over Micronesia, Pacific Ocean

"I should've held out for that B-1," Jack Grimaldi said with a yawn, trying to keep himself awake at the controls of the Lockheed C-130 Hercules cruising westward at thirty thousand feet over the Pacific Ocean. "Or at least something faster than this bolt heap."

Grimaldi had been goosing the Hercules since takeoff, hoping to reach Southeast Asia in time to help defuse the growing crisis in Myanmar. He'd originally planned to reconnoiter with Katz and Tokaido at U-Tapao, but a few minutes ago he'd received orders from Stony Man Farm to proceed on to Imchar Plains, a remote Indian air base set in the mountains bordering India and Myanmar. There, they would be in closer range to the Tatmadaw's key northern military bases, leaving Phoenix Force to handle matters in the south.

Able Team was in the back cabin of the Hercules, resting, knowing all too well that once the plane landed they'd be going full bore until the dust settled. Grimaldi had managed an hour catnap while the plane was being prepped for takeoff back in Colorado. It would have to do.

Peering out of the cockpit's windows, the Stony Man pilot saw a sprinkling of islands scattered across the blue waters below. How ironic, he thought. Somewhere among those specks of land was Bikini Atoll, where, almost fifty years ago, the U.S. had set off the most powerful hydrogen bomb ever detonated. They'd called the test Castle Bravo. The bomb, a Teller-Ulam configuration fueled with lithium deuteride, was only supposed to yield 6 megatons' worth of thermonuclear kick, but abnormally high tritium levels brought on by fast fission of Li-7 had magnified the blast by a staggering 250 percent. The detonation site, along with some 150 million tons of coral reef just off Nam/Charlie Island, had disintegrated in a fireball that left behind a mile-wide crater deep as a football field. The mushroom cloud had risen swiftly to 114,000 feet, three times the altitude Grimaldi was flying at. Fallout readings had turned up more than four hundred miles away, and the overall blanket of contamination had been measured at 570,000 square miles, equal to one percent of Earth's entire landmass. Most experts agreed the destructive force was a thousand times more powerful than the combined blasts that had razed Hiroshima and Nagasaki. A few analysts claimed even that figure was conservative.

And now these Tatmadaw psychos had eight bombs, each one four times as potent as those that had humbled the Japanese into surrender. How much of Myanmar's population would wind up fried if those bombs went off like a string of firecrackers? Grimaldi didn't even want to hazard a guess. And, of course, the damage wouldn't be confined to Myanmar's borders. Fallout would drift into neighboring countries, including China and India, who had their own nuclear arsenals and would likely be under pressure to retaliate. The possible chain reactions were endless, all but guaranteeing death and destruction across the entire width and breadth of the continent. Grimaldi stared straight ahead and tried to imagine what it'd look like, seeing one blooming, top-heavy cloud after another rise up against the horizon.

"Mushroom salad," Grimaldi murmured.

They had to be stopped. Impatient, Grimaldi checked over the controls, looking for a way to coax more speed out of the Hercules. "Faster, dammit!" he cursed.

Dwiti Military Base, Myanmar

THE FIRST THING Bien Phyr noticed when he returned to the hangar was the smell of solvents and paint fumes. They hung thickly in the enclosed space, sweet and cloying, strong enough to make him feel light-headed. One of the painters rushed over, holding out a protective mask. Phyr grabbed it eagerly and pressed it to his face. Still, the odor weighed on him. He wouldn't stay here any longer than he had to.

The F-105s from Entai Lette's aero-circus now occupied the same hangar space where the MiGs had been the day before. Their cargo of harvested opium from the Golden Triangle had been removed while en route to the base and was being stored at a warehouse near the railyards in Bago. The opium was of little interest to Phyr. Right now he was more concerned with the jets' transformation into replicas of similar aircraft flown by India and the Chinese. Things seemed to be going well on that front. Two detail crews, each one composed of more than a dozen men—all wearing masks similar to Phyr's—roamed about both planes. One jet had already been scrubbed clean and was taking on its first coat of primer coat. Stencils were being positioned on the other for the application of decals that would identify it as belonging to the Chinese air force. Phyr was impressed with the speed of the operation.

"By afternoon tomorrow," one of the workers told him when he asked when the exteriors might be finished.

Phyr tracked down the design schematics for both MiGs and started a walk-around inspection of the would-be Chinese "Thud." Comparing the schematics against the work being done, he pointed out a few cosmetic touches that were slightly off. Two days earlier he might have considered the discrepancies minor and not worth trifling over. But now, given the ever-growing public suspicion regarding Semba Hru's performance as Maw Saung Ku-Syi, Phyr felt it was important to be a stickler for details. He told the workers both jets would need to stand up to the scrutiny of sat-cams, recon planes and any other witnesses who might spot them if they were pressed into action.

The general was inspecting the decals for the Chinese jet when one of the men climbed down from the bomb bay and headed toward him. The man had to lower his mask momentarily for Phyr to see that it was Christopher Randolph.

"The bombs are in place," Randolph explained as he followed Phyr out of the hangar.

"And you're sure they're deployable?" Phyr asked.

Randolph nodded. "The bombs, yes. But I'm concerned about the carriage mounts and bay doors on both jets. Entai Lette was lax with his maintenance."

"I'll have our crew go over them," Phyr said.

"Good idea," Randolph said. "And once the jets have been repainted, I think they should both be taken up for a test flight, just to make sure the bay doors are functioning."

"Of course." Phyr shed his mask the moment they were outside the hangar. "The jets are only a contingency at this point, but with all that's going on, we need to be prepared."

"Absolutely," Randolph said.

"What did you think of Entai Lette?" Phyr said. "Quite a character, hmm?"

Randolph nodded. "Quite a showman, too," he said. "I think he was P. T. Barnum in a previous life."

Phyr chuckled. He'd known Randolph for a few years now and liked the American's sense of humor. It was one of the things that had first assured him that the American was worth luring into the junta's camp. To be easygoing and gregarious—these were good traits in a spy, Phyr felt. It was a way to win people over and earn their confidence. And apparently Randolph had done a good job of charming his counterparts back in the States. How else to explain the steady supply of classified information he always brought with him whenever he flew in to Thailand for his biannual vacations?

As the men headed for Phyr's jeep, parked at the far end of the hangar, Randolph said, "I noticed the sarin bombs were moved from R&D this morning."

"Yes. Something came up," Phyr said. He gestured out at the airfield, where one of the Tatmadaw's MiGs rested near the main runway next to the helicopter that had brought Randolph to base during the night. Phyr told Randolph of the intelligence coming in about the dissidents' plans to rally at Bagan on the anniversary of the Four Eights. "Obviously we can't allow that," the general said.

"You're going to gas the demonstrators?" Randolph seemed surprised. "I thought the bombs were for use on rebel strongholds."

"That was the plan, but we've had to change our strategy." Phyr glanced at Randolph. "Is there a problem with that?"

"No, of course not." Randolph stared at the jet a moment, then changed the subject. "I was wondering…you have a senior general by the name of Lon Kyth. He's headquartered here, isn't he?"

"Yes," Phyr said. "You've heard of him?"

Randolph nodded. "His name is always coming up in intel back in Colorado. The Myanmar Patton, they call him."

Phyr laughed. "He would like that. He's getting on in years, but he's a good man."

"Maybe I'll get a chance to meet him."

"Actually, he's reviewing the troops right now," Phyr said as they reached his jeep. "Come, I'll introduce you to him."

"Thank you. I'd like that."

Once they were both in the jeep, Phyr drove along the runway toward the exercise field. On the way, Randolph glanced once more at his helicopter and the MiG carrying the sarin bombs. He was about to say something, but changed his mind and remained silent. Before they'd cleared the runway, the men had also passed by two of the stolen U.S. Y-25 LAV antiaircraft vehicles. Phyr saw Randolph eyeing the weapons and told him, "We have the others deployed to the north, for use against the rebels."

"Good," Randolph said absently.

From the airfield it was a short drive to the training grounds. Senior General Lon Kyth was standing at the edge of the field, a portable phone to his ear as he watched soldiers go through their drills. He set down the receiver when Phyr pulled up in the jeep. "There you are," he said. "I've called the other generals for a meeting in my office in twenty minutes."

"More problems?" Phyr asked.

"Yes." Lon Kyth seemed reluctant to go into detail. He eyed Randolph suspiciously.

"General, this is Christopher Randolph," Phyr said.

Lon Kyth's expression lightened. "Of course." He shook the American's hand. "A pleasure to finally meet you. You've been very helpful to us."

"The pleasure's mine," Randolph said. "I was hoping we could have a moment to talk, but I see it's a bad time."

"Yes, I'm afraid so."

Randolph got out of the jeep and motioned for Lon Kyth to take his place. "I'll leave you two to your meeting. I was wondering, though," he asked Phyr, "do you know where I might find the woman who gave the speech yesterday?"

Phyr and Lon Kyth exchanged a glance, then Phyr told Randolph, "Maw Saung Ku-Syi is still under house arrest. She's not allowed visitors."

Randolph smiled knowingly. "I watched the telecast yesterday with Entai Lette. He said it wasn't Ku-Syi, but rather a woman he knows from Bangkok. Semba Hru."

Phyr's neck reddened. He would need to have a talk with Lette about being more circumspect. "Why do you want to see her?" he asked Randolph.

Randolph offered a sly grin. "Entai has spent time with her and he said I owed it to myself to… Well, I don't think I need to spell it out."

Phyr smiled faintly. If Randolph was the type to be ruled by his libido, maybe Lette had done the right thing after all. Forthcoming as the American had been regarding U.S. secrets, perhaps he might open up even more under the influence of Semba Hru. He certainly wouldn't be the first man whose tongue she'd loosened after a dalliance between the sheets.

"She's in a room at the officers' quarters," Phyr said, gesturing toward a two-story building adjacent to the research-and-development complex. "We can count on your discretion about her identity, though, I trust."

"Of course," Randolph assured him.

Randolph excused himself and headed off. Phyr waited until the American was out of earshot, then quickly told Lon Kyth what he had in mind. "I just need to call Swarng Bancha so he can brief Semba Hru on what we want from her."

Lon Kyth let Phyr make the call on his portable phone. Once Phyr had finished speaking with Bancha, he put the jeep in gear and drove Lon Kyth across the tarmac toward base headquarters. On the way, the senior general briefed Phyr on the reason for the emergency meeting.

"We have word the Karen and Shan rebels are both massing forces to the north," Lon Kyth explained. "It seems they've decided to ally themselves against us."

Phyr was stunned. The two factions had long been at each other's throats, a situation the junta had done everything in their power to encourage. The idea of them forging an alliance was unsettling. United, Phyr knew they could give the Tatmadaw a run for its money.

"They were prompted by the Four Eights," Phyr speculated. "They think we'll be too distracted to hold them in check."

Lon Kyth nodded. "We need to figure out a way to deal with them. Something decisive, and I'm not talking about sarin bombs or a handful of antiaircraft guns."

Phyr realized what Lon Kyth was getting at. "You want to use the H-bombs on them?"

Lon Kyth stared at Phyr. "If it comes to that, why not? This business of turning China and India against each other is all well and good, but if it turns out that we have to clean up our own backyard first, so be it."

Phyr didn't know what to say.

"There's another matter, as well," Lon Kyth said as Phyr pulled into Lon Kyth's parking spot in front of headquarters. "We've captured an enemy soldier at Guna Island. A Westerner."

Phyr cursed to himself. What else could go wrong?

"Where's this prisoner now?" he asked Lon Kyth as they headed up the walk.

"Insein," Lon Kyth responded. "I've sent Dy Lii down to question him."

"Dy Lii?"

CHAPTER TWENTY-NINE

Stony Man Farm, Virginia

After two hours of prowling cyberspace for up-to-date intel on the layout and operations at Insein Prison, Carmen Delahunt merged the most reliable information into an encrypted file and sent it out. The CIA's Cessna carrying David McCarter, Gary Manning, and T. J. Hawkins to Yangon was computer equipped. She could only hope McCarter would be able to download the files and make use of its contents.

Her task finished, Delahunt crossed the Computer Room to where Hal Brognola—just back from his second trip to the White House in as many days—was briefing the others on the latest developments in Myanmar. She took a seat next to Barbara Price. Huntington Wethers and Aaron Kurtzman were still at their computer stations but had turned their chairs so that they could partake in the briefing while staying on top of the steady flow of intel coming in over their monitors.

Things were happening fast, at least for the moment, and the focus had abruptly shifted away from the intrigue surrounding Christopher Randolph. Brognola reported that Shan and Karen rebel forces, initially thought to be on a collision course in the mountains eighty miles east of Taunggyi, had instead drawn together and were now advancing on one of the Tatamadaw's key northern military installations in Eichyi Valley. "It's got *civil war* written all over it," he told the group. "Normally we'd stand back and play wait-and-see, but that's not an option now. Not with the Tatmadaw sitting on those damn bombs. We need to assume they have nuclear-strike capacity and act accordingly."

"That accounts for the naval movements I'm picking up," Kurtzman called out, eyeing his computer. "I've got both the Fifth and Seventh Fleets headed for the Bay of Bengal."

"The Air Force and SAC are on the move, too," Brognola said. "Every base in a thousand-mile radius is on high alert. I just got off the phone with Katz and U-Tapao's gone DefCon 1. The other bases will follow suit soon enough."

"None of this is on the sly, I take it," Price said. "We want them to see us coming, right?"

"Affirmative," Brognola said. "Whoever's got their finger on the button over there, we want them to know we're ready to come at them full bore."

"Sounding a little interventionist," Delahunt stated.

"We have more grounds for intervention than you can shake a stick at," Brognola countered, "but I know what you're getting at. As far as the world stage goes, all these maneuvers are routine. If people choose to read between the lines, that's something we have no control over."

"Of course, we're making sure the lines are wide enough you can't help but read between them."

"Precisely," Brognola said.

"Where does all this leave us?" Price wanted to know.

"It leaves us with twelve hours," the big Fed replied.

"Twelve hours?"

Brognola nodded. "That's our window. If we can't put the fire out by then, it's out of our hands."

"Good Lord," Delahunt complained, "'Our hands' are

practically tied behind our backs right now, in case no one noticed. I mean, Phoenix Force is out trying to spring Rafe from prison and Able Team won't even be landing for another two hours.''

"I realize that, but this deadline is firm," Brognola said. "I had to fight to get us twelve hours. The President wanted it to be three."

"I know the boys respond well under pressure," Kurtzman said, sighing, "but this might be stretching things."

"It is what it is. Let's move on."

Brognola turned to Price. "What do we have lined up for Able Team once they land?"

Price glanced down at the notes she'd scribbled over the past hour while conferring with the Farm's contacts in India. "They're offering something called a Shivagi 4-H."

"Never heard of it," Brognola said.

"It's a prototype assault chopper," Price said. "Racks six TOW missiles on the side along with a 20 mm pod gun. Range is about seven hundred miles and they say it can outrace anything short of a PaveHawk."

"But can Grimaldi fly it?"

"He won't have to," Price said. "They're throwing in a pilot. Which means we can put Jack in a fighter."

"You've lined up a jet?"

Price nodded. "An F-117A."

"A Nighthawk? Outstanding!" Brognola said. "If we can pinpoint where they're keeping those bombs, Jack can come in for a strike."

"That was my thinking," Price said.

Brognola grinned at the mission controller. "I'd promote you, but that would leave me without a job."

"I'll take the compliment."

Brognola clapped his hands. "All right, then, everyone, back to your stations." On his way out, he added, "With any luck, we just might pull this off!"

While Wethers and Kurtzman swiveled their chairs and resumed work at their computers, Price followed Delahunt back across the room.

"What did you come up with on Insein?"

"A decent package. Some diagrams, a couple sat-com shots and… Hell, I'll just show you."

When Delahunt sat down at her computer, she saw that two e-mails had come in over the past few minutes. One was from McCarter. He'd gotten her file on Insein and would be going over it with the others once they'd rendezvoused with Calvin James and U Pag Ti. The second message was from Smitt Ripley, the AF-IA agent overseeing the search through Christopher Randolph's storage cubicle. As she skimmed over the note and began to download an attached file, Delahunt whistled, shaking her head. "That poor bastard," she murmured.

"Randolph?"

"Yeah. They were going through the file cabinets to corroborate everything in his diary and came up with a bombshell. They found a file that spelled out why Randolph stopped getting letters from that woman friend of his."

"Dharni Loi?" Price said. "We already know that. She moved."

"Yeah, she moved, all right," Delahunt said, highlighting part of the dispatch from Colorado Springs. "She moved because Randolph'd gotten her pregnant."

"What!" Price glanced at the display, in which Smitt Ripley had explained that Dharni Loi had given birth six months before she was gunned down at the border in Tachilek. "Why wasn't this in his diary?"

"Beats me," Delahunt said. "Maybe he wanted to keep it separate from this vendetta of his. Here, let's see what else it says here." She opened the file attachment and quickly scanned its contents. "I take it back," she said, drawing Price's attention to the second paragraph. "Look, it says here she had the baby with her when she was gunned down. Not only that, but there are witnesses who say the Gold Dragons took her.''

"Her?"

"The baby," Delahunt said. "It was a girl."

The women fell silent, stunned. Delahunt scrolled down the screen and together they read the rest of the file, which referred to a whole separate set of notes Randolph had kept dealing exclusively with his attempts over the years to track down the missing child.

"Poor bastard is right," Price said. "My God, can you imagine? The same day he finds out the love of his life was murdered, he learns he has a daughter he never knew about."

"Hold on," Delahunt said, directing her cursor to the scroll bar, "I'm going to jump down to the end of this and see if he ever managed to find her."

Dwiti Military Base, Myanmar

SEMBA HRU LOOKED UP from the drink she was pouring herself and glared at Swarng Bancha. "And what if I don't want to see this Mr. Randolph?"

Swarng Bancha smiled indulgently. "You'll be well compensated, as always."

"You didn't answer my question."

They were in an officer's suite where Semba Hru had been staying since her masquerade as Maw Saung Ku-Syi the day before. A guard had been posted outside her door to make sure she stayed put until it was decided when she should next appear as the imprisoned Nobel laureate. The forced isolation, however brief, hadn't sat well with her, and she wanted to make sure Bancha knew it. When he strode forward and reached out to stroke her cheek, she swatted his hand away.

"I said what if I don't want to see him?" she repeated.

Bancha sighed and lit a cigarette, then poured himself a shot of bourbon from a decanter resting on the wet bar. "It's not as if you have a choice," he reminded her. "This is what you would call another command performance."

Furious, Semba Hru turned her back on Bancha and took her drink to the living-room window. Her suite was on the second story, overlooking one of the observation towers rising up from the garrison walls. She could see a sentry posted inside the tower, pacing restlessly with an AK-47. The sight depressed her even further. How fitting, she realized, that she should pose as Maw Saung Ku-Syi. They had so much more in common than just their looks. Just as Ku-Syi had been a prisoner of the Tatmadaw, so was she a prisoner of the Gold Dragons. Queen of the Royal Peacock indeed, she mused bitterly. Bancha had called her his pet back in Bangkok. he was right—she *was* his pet, like all the other whores. And like he'd just told her, she had no choice but to go along with whatever he asked of her.

Bitter tears began to well in her eyes. She fought them back and turned to Bancha. "Who is it this Mr. Randolph is coming to see?" she asked. "Semba Hru, the prized whore? Or do I put back on my makeup so he can have an audience with Maw Saung Ku-Syi?"

"He knows who you are," Bancha responded. "And you know what's expected of you."

Semba Hru nodded. "I'm to make him feel so smitten he'll spill all his deepest secrets without my having to ask." She made no attempt to hide her sarcasm.

Bancha crushed out his cigarette and carried his drink over to her. "I know this has not been easy for you," he said, his tone softening. "When it's over, I'll make it up to you. A week in Monaco. Or Paris, maybe. You decide."

She wanted to slap him, tell him she saw through his

smooth talk and cheap promises. She held herself back, though.

"It would seem to me it's already over," she said instead. She gestured at the television set in the corner. "I saw the news earlier. The uncensored news on CNN. Everyone suspects it was an imposter who gave that speech yesterday."

"Yes, people are suspicious," Bancha admitted. "But we will deal with it. We have a plan."

"A plan?"

Bancha nodded. "It will come out that Ku-Syi is dying of cancer," he said. "That will explain why she seemed so unlike herself during the broadcast. It will also explain why she wanted to call off the demonstrations. A dying woman's last wish, to see an end to divisiveness in her country."

Semba Hru laughed contemptuously. "It will never work. Cancer? People will see through it in a second."

"We shall see. But we can concern ourselves with that later. Right now, I need to make some calls and check on things in Bangkok. And you need to prepare yourself for Mr. Randolph."

Bancha finished his drink, then pursed his lips and blew Semba Hru a kiss as he headed for the door. Once she was alone, she went back to the window, opening it to let in a faint breeze. Two floors down, a sidewalk ran past the quarters. She stared at the clean-swept concrete. There was a faint crack in one of the slabs, as if something had fallen on it. As she continued to stare, an idea slowly took form in her head. Perhaps, like Maw Saung Ku-Syi, she had finally found an answer to her dilemma, a way to end her pain.

Semba Hru's reverie was cut short by a knock on the door. She ignored it and opened the window wider, then leaned out, breathing in the afternoon air. Behind her there was another knock, harder this time, more persistent. Semba Hru stared down at the concrete, then closed her eyes. But, try as she may, she couldn't will herself to lean out any farther. When she heard yet another knock on the door, she slowly pulled herself back inside the suite and closed the window.

"One minute," she called out. There was a mirror over the hearth. She wiped away her tears and brushed back her hair, then pinched her cheeks to redden them; it was something the men seemed to like.

Semba Hru went to the door and opened it. To her surprise, she recognized the man standing before her. She'd seen him the morning before back in Bangkok at the Royal Peacock. He'd been loitering in the bar when she'd dropped off Entai Lette for his meeting with Swarng Bancha.

"May I come in?" the man asked. Behind him, the guard, no doubt on Bancha's orders, continued to stare across the hall, making a point not to intrude on the rendezvous.

"Of course," Semba Hru said. She gestured for him to enter, then sashayed her way to the wet bar, certain that he would be watching her every step. "Would you like a drink?"

"No, thank you."

Semba Hru glanced back at the man. Sure enough, he was staring at her intently. There was no trace of lust in his expression, however. He seemed stunned.

"Are you all right?" she asked him, puzzled.

Randolph continued to stare at her. Finally he said, "You look just like her."

Semba Hru put on as sweet a smile as she could manage. So he was one of *those*. "Yes, I've been told that," she replied. "If you'd like, I could put up my hair and—"

"No, no," Randolph interrupted. "Not Ku-Syi. Your mother."

It was Semba Hru's turn to stare with disbelief. "What are you talking about?" she said.

Randolph told her, "You look just like your mother."

CHAPTER THIRTY

Taukkyan, north of Yangon, Myanmar

As the CIA's Thai Air Express Cessna began its descent toward Yangon International Airport, T. J. Hawkins and David McCarter braced themselves and tugged open the cargo door. Wind howled into the cavity and grabbed hold of the men, trying to yank them from the plane. They resisted momentarily, then McCarter gave in first and plunged outward, spread-eagling in the air to stabilize himself. Before joining him, Hawkins glanced back at the crated *nats* and shouted, "Adios, creeps."

Gary Manning was the last one out. Once clear of the Cessna's wings, he tore at his rip cord. McCarter and Hawkins had already deployed their chutes and soon all three of them were drifting earthward. Below them, scattered across the manicured landscape of Taukkyan War Cemetery, were the graves of twenty-seven thousand Allied soldiers killed during the Burmese and Assam campaigns of World War II.

The men had been directed to Taukkyan after Aaron Kurtzman had run a quick check on all available intel and determined it was the closest thing to a safe drop point within a ten-mile radius of Yangon. The cemetery was maintained by the Commonwealth Graves Commission and was rarely frequented by the Tatmadaw military. The greatest risk of being spotted came from the memorial's proximity to the main highway leading from the capitol to both Pyay and Bagon. Manning could see traffic out on the road and hoped that anyone looking their way wouldn't be unduly alarmed by the sight of three parachutists dropping from the heavens.

Tugging at his shroud lines, Manning steered clear of the graves, as well as the massive, columned edifice of the memorial itself. There was plenty of open ground to set down on, and once he'd landed on a grassy sward, he tumbled expertly and cut loose from his chute. Hawkins and McCarter were already on their feet, having touched down fifty yards away on a wide strip of lawn running from the memorial to the grave sites.

"So far, so good," Manning called out as he rejoined them. "Now we just need to commandeer a set of wheels."

"We better make it quick, too," Hawkins said. "The natives are getting restless."

Manning tracked Hawkins's gaze to a family huddled over one of the graves on the far side of the cemetery. An older man stared back at them as he raised a cell phone to his ear. There were perhaps another dozen mourners elsewhere on the grounds. They all seemed equally unnerved by the sudden presence of commandos.

"On the way down I saw a truck behind the memorial," McCarter said. "Looked like the rear bed was covered."

"Sounds like a winner," Hawkins said.

The men had divvied out their arsenal before the jump. In addition to their side arms and machine guns, Hawkins and McCarter carried the AGS-17 30 mm grenade launchers. Manning, the marksman of the group, had the weighty Barrett .50-caliber rifle slung across his shoulders. Thus armed, they mounted the steps leading up to the monument, then crossed to the rear. The truck McCarter had mentioned was backed up to a walkway leading from the parking lot.

The tailgate was down and the rear bed, covered by a rib-walled canvas shell, was filled with plants.

"We get to bring Rafe some flowers," Hawkins said.

The trio was heading to the truck when a sudden spray of gunfire hurtled their way, pocking the columns on either side of them. Hawkins and McCarter scrambled quickly behind the nearest posts, while Manning, already on his way down the steps, flattened himself near the staircase railing. Peering through the uprights, he saw an open-bed military personnel truck rumble into the parking lot. Six men were in back, one of them cradling the M-4 A-1 carbine that had fired the opening salvo. It was too quick for them to have responded to the call from the old man at the grave site. Manning figured the truck had to have detoured from the highway after someone spotted the air drop.

"Dammit." Manning unslung the Barrett and set it to one side in favor of his MP-5. Poking the barrel through a gap in the railing, he squeezed off a quick burst, dropping two of the soldiers clambering out of the truck. Return fire slammed into the railing, showering Manning with concrete dust. Meanwhile, two more soldiers piled out of the truck's cab, both armed with assault rifles. Using the truck for cover, they directed their fire past Manning, keeping McCarter and Hawkins pinned behind the columns. As they did so, a second vehicle rolled onto the scene—four more soldiers in a military jeep armed with a rear-mounted 7.62 mm machine gun.

"JUST WHAT we didn't need," Hawkins muttered over the thunder of his subgun. Taking out the jeep's driver drained what was left in his clip. As he was reloading, a stream of 7.62 mm slugs pelted the column and pinged off Hawkins's grenade launcher. One column away, McCarter stayed out of the line of fire and hastily assembled his ASG, then fed it a high-explosive 60 mm round.

"Give me some cover, T.J.!" he called out as he prepared to nudge the mortar out into the open.

"Will do." Hawkins let fly with his MP-5, raking the hood of the convoy truck. Down on the steps, Manning chipped in, directing his fire at the jeep's gunner.

The mortar's base plate scraped noisily across the concrete as McCarter slid the ASG into position. He eyed the sights and drew a quick bead on the jeep, then fired. The launcher danced backward as it sent its round whooshing toward the parking lot. McCarter's aim proved off by a good ten yards, but the shell kicked up enough shrapnel and asphalt to force one of the soldiers to his knees, screaming as he clawed at his riddled face. A follow-up round from Manning's MP-5 put the man out of his misery.

"Next time I'm packing a bazooka," McCarter grumbled, shoving the mortar aside. He grabbed his submachine gun and bolted to the next column away from Hawkins, wanting to put more distance between them. Bullets chased him all the way, one of them glancing off his calf. McCarter ignored the red stain that began to soak through his fatigues. He surveyed the parking lot and did a quick head count. They were still outnumbered, more than two to one.

As if those odds weren't enough, the scrambled drone of rotors announced the approach of a helicopter. It swooped into view from behind a tree line marking the east perimeter of the cemetery. It was a gunship, missile pods extending outward on either side of the fuselage like a pair of small wings. And it was coming straight toward McCarter.

"Not bloody fair!" he muttered.

THE MOMENT HE SPOTTED the chopper, Gary Manning grabbed the Barrett and straddled it on the staircase railing. He was pestered by ground fire as he peered through the rifle's scope, but he wasn't about to duck for cover.

Training his crosshairs on the chopper's cockpit, the Canadian waited for it to pass out of the glare of the sunlight so he could put his first shot through the pilot's skull. When the gunship suddenly banked, he got the visibility he wanted and tugged at the trigger. At the same instant, however, he jerked the barrel to the left, botching the shot. The .50-caliber round punched a hole in the fuselage well wide of the pilot. Manning lowered the rifle, grateful his instincts had prevailed.

"It's Cal and Pag Ti!" he called over his shoulder.

"HOT SPAM WITH okra on it!" Hawkins shouted.

As he watched, the Mongoose suddenly veered and turned its armament on the puzzled Tatmadaw, who, like Manning, assumed the air support was for them. Dumbfounded, the soldiers gaped as two HOT missiles, one fired from each side of the chopper, bore down on them. One detonated two feet in front of the truck, flipping the vehicle backward as if it were no heavier than a morning flapjack. The other caught the jeep squarely, engulfing it in a fireball. Six Tatmadaw soldiers died on the spot. The others were bowled over by shrapnel and the concussive force of the two explosions, which also managed to tip the groundskeeper's truck on its side. Hawkins and McCarter sprang from cover and joined Manning in the charge down the staircase to the parking lot. By the time they'd finished off the surviving gunners, U Pag Ti had set the Mongoose down on the asphalt.

"Come on!" Calvin James yelled from the gunner's perch. "They've got more backup on the way!"

With no time to lower the rear ramp, McCarter, Manning and Hawkins had to squeeze their way past James to reach the rear cabin. As they did so, they each palmed James a high-five.

"Never thought I'd be this happy to see that ugly mug

of yours, Chi-boy,'' Hawkins told James. "When'd you learn how to fire one of this floating popguns?''

"Got a quick crash course from Pag Ti.'' James quickly introduced the others to the Myanmar operative.

"Nice to meet you all,'' he said. "We can get acquainted later.''

"Good idea,'' Hawkins said. "Let's bail.''

Pag Ti took the chopper back up, guiding it past the smoldering carnage of the bombed-out vehicles and out over the cemetery, heading away from the access road where he and James had seen Tatmadaw reinforcements racing to the scene.

"We're low on fuel,'' he told the others, "but Insein's only a few miles.''

"We'll keep our fingers crossed,'' Manning said.

"Meanwhile,'' McCarter told them, "we'd best put on our thinking caps and start figuring how we're going to bust Rafe out of the clink. I couldn't print out the info Carmen sent on the layout, but from what I remember, we have a couple options.''

"Pag Ti knows a few guys who did time in Insein,'' James interjected. "He'll be able to fill in the blanks.''

"Decent,'' McCarter said.

"I've got a couple ideas, too, if you don't mind,'' Pag Ti said.

"Mind? Are you nuts?'' Hawkins said. "Lay them on us.''

CHAPTER THIRTY-ONE

Bagan and Nyaung-U, Myanmar

Thatbyinnyu Temple was one of the more prominent of Old Bagan's legendary Buddhist shrines. Lying just outside the crumbling city walls of the ancient city, the monument had been fashioned out of quarried limestone in the twelfth century on orders of King Alanugsithu. There were three inner levels, each brightly illuminated by sunlight pouring in through a series of widely spaced tiers. Although the vast enclosure seemed deserted, more than eighty Burmese loyalists had made the temple their hiding place as they awaited the anniversary of the Four Eights. Most were concealed in hard-to-reach corridors in the east portico, but a few had encamped outdoors on the parapets. Daw Bodta Paing and Lon Mar had spoken to a few of the people, telling them of the woman who'd passed herself off as Maw Saung Ku-Syi in hopes of calling off demonstrations. As hoped, the news only hardened the others' resolve to remain for the rally.

But Daw Bodta Paing and Lon Mar had come to Thatbyinnyu for another reason besides touching base with other demonstrators. They'd come to see if Lon Mar's camcorder would indeed enable them to broadcast the rally as it was taking place. As they made their way to the uppermost level, Daw Bodta paused before a regal-looking Bud-

dha enthroned on a masonry dais. With her she'd brought
a small, thin sheet of gold leaf. There was no time to tap
it into place over the countless other layers that already
adorned the image. Instead, she set the offering at the Buddha's feet and whispered a quick, silent prayer, then turned
and joined Lon Mar, who crouched before a narrow staircase carved out of the thick stone walls. The young man
fished through his knapsack for his camcorder, as well as
an AN/PRC-126 two-way radio.

"Okay, I'm ready," he said.

In single file, the two dissidents climbed up to an opening
that led out to a narrow ledge encircling the temple's lone,
tapering spire. They were nearly two hundred feet up, and
in every direction they looked, they saw the thousands upon
thousands of other ancient monuments studding the green
plain like colossal chess pieces on a long forgotten game
board. Most were small stupas, brick structures no more
than a dozen feet high, but that left hundreds of larger temples, many of them as vast as Thatbyinnyu, some newly
white washed, others earthen colored, all topped with
spires. It was a site of breathtaking beauty and grandeur
unlike any other in the world, and yet, despite all efforts
by the revenue-hungry SPDC to sell the place as a tourist
destination, the plains remained tranquilly—almost eerily—
deserted. Daw Bodta could see only a handful of tourists
and even fewer villagers.

"It's hard to imagine there are people hiding in nearly
every temple," Daw Bodta said.

"That's the idea," Lon Mar said, adjusting the frequency
on his transceiver. "What's even more amazing is that
we've brought so many people in without the Tatmadaw
catching on."

"I wonder how many there are of us altogether?"

"Here in Bagan? Thousands easily. Hopefully more. We
won't know for sure until the day of the rally."

"I can hardly wait."

"Here." Lon Mar handed Daw Bodta the radio. He'd made contact with the woman's brother back in Nyaung-U. Aung Paing's voice crackled through the headset.

"Can you hear me?"

"Yes." Daw Bodta quickly told Aung where they were, adding, "Lon Mar's just getting the camera ready. Do they have the other relay antenna in place?"

"Yes, they set it up atop Htilominlo," Aung said, referring to a temple nearly as tall as Thatbyinnyu, situated just off one of the two roadways linking Bagan with Nyaung-U. If all went well, Lon Mar's camera images would bound from Thatbyinnyu to Kyaukgu Umin and then on to the chain of other relay stations that, come the anniversary of the Four Eights, would broadcast the actual rally to the world on both television and the Internet.

Lon Mar set aside his camcorder long enough to retrieve his laptop. Once he'd connected the two devices with a feed line, he picked the camcorder back up and peered through the viewfinder. Instead of focusing on one of the temples, he panned the camera and zoomed in on the distant hillock where, the day before, he'd seen the military's Y-25 anti-aircraft vehicle. The LAV was still there, still being watched over by a handful of soldiers. Lon Mar was relieved to see that none of them seemed interested in the temples. As near as he could tell, most of the men were playing cards while a lone sentry kept his eye on the airport three miles to the north.

Daw Bodta stared intently at the camcorder propped on Lon Mar's shoulder. Once the recording light flashed on, she closed her eyes and mouthed yet another silent prayer. Please, she thought to herself. This has to work.

FOUR MILES AWAY, Daw Bodta's brother knelt before the small portable television set Lon Mar had linked up to the relay antenna before setting out for Bagan. Unlike his sister, Aung wasn't praying; he was trying to keep the sun's glare off the screen so that he could better see the image being transmitted from Lon Mar's camcorder. When nothing appeared but the same snowy blur he'd seen when he'd first turned the set on, Aung began to despair. Had all this work been in vain?

Then, almost instantaneously, the screen filled with the image of four Tatmadaw soldiers stationed around the Y-25 armored vehicle. Aung grabbed the radio from the ground beside him. "It's working!" he told his sister, barely able to contain himself. "I see the LAV, as clear as day! It's working!"

Aung heard his sister let out a small cry, then Lon Mar's voice crackled over the radio. "We're all set, then. Come the Four Eights, we will be ready to broadcast!"

Aung closed his eyes a moment, overjoyed.

Lon Mar said that he and Daw Bodta would be back at Nyaung-Il shortly. First they were going to stop by the bus terminal to pick up more demonstrators.

"Be careful," Aung warned him. "We don't want the Tatmadaw getting their hands on your equipment."

"That won't happen," Lon Mar assured him.

"And remember to pass along word that no one is to head for the temples until after nightfall," Aung said. "We'll keep a lookout posted to make sure the Tatmadaw aren't watching the temples from the LAV."

After exchanging a few quick words with his sister, Aung shut off both the radio and the television set. Disconnecting the antenna line, he wished the others down in the temple could have witnessed the test, especially those who'd expressed doubts about going on with the rally. Surely one glimpse of the sample broadcast would have been enough to change their minds.

Aung was about to leave the terrace level when he heard a commotion behind him. Turning, he saw five of his associates clear the uppermost steps and head toward him. Two of the men stood on either side of Bari Tu, grasping the monk's arms and forcing him, clearly against his will, to keep walking in step with them. From the looks on the men's faces, Aung knew that something was terribly wrong. His euphoria dissipated, replaced by concern. "What is it?" he asked.

One of the men showed him a small handgun.

"My daughter was playing in the caves and found this among his things," he said, indicating Bari Tu. "A cell phone, too. Not the sort of things true monks carry around."

"I can explain," Bari Tu pleaded.

"Before you try," another of the men said, pulling up the orange sleeve of Bari Tu's robe, "first explain *this!*"

Aung's spirits sank as he stared at the tattoo on the pseudo monk's forearm. "A Gold Dragon," he murmured.

"From years ago," Bari Tu insisted, "when I was a teenager. I did it as a lark, to impress my friends!"

"Quiet!" Aung ordered. Now over his shock, he felt a stirring rage inside him. He grabbed Bari Tu's wrist. "I know the difference between an old and new tattoo. This is new."

"No, I'm telling you—!"

"Quiet!" one of the others interjected, shaking Bari Tu.

Aung eyed the man hatefully. "You're a spy," he said slowly, "sent by the Tatmadaw."

Bari Tu shook his head. "No!"

"Liar!" The men on either side of him shook him again.

"We want answers," Aung demanded.

Bari Tu stared back. This time he said nothing. The fear slowly left his eyes, and a faint, defiant smile worked its way across his lips. Let them question me all they want, he'd decided. He would tell them no more. After all, what could they do to him? For all their grand talk and dreams, he knew these people for what they were—peaceful sheep with no taste for violence. The man holding his gun had clearly never fired one before. He clutched the weapon fearfully, as if it were a scorpion about to bite him. And the others, as rough as they'd been with him, were trembling now, as well, cringing no doubt at the mere thought they might have to lean more strongly on him in hopes of making him talk.

"You and your Gold Dragons are nothing but lackeys for the Tatmadaw!" Aung's voice rose in ire. "When they snapped their fingers, your goons stormed the university and hauled my father off to Insein. You sell heroin to children and steal girls from the north country for your sex shops in Bangkok."

Bari Tu remained silent.

One of the other men ventured, "I wonder now if maybe Hahrn-Li Jym's death was more than an accident. Maybe he didn't fall from the terrace here. Maybe he was pushed."

Bari Tu swallowed hard. He glanced at the ground, suddenly struggling with his resolve. Aung took a step closer, then reached out and grabbed the man's robe with both hands, shaking him with so much unexpected fury Bari Tu lost his balance and nearly tumbled backward over the same railing from which he'd sent Hahrn-Li Jym to his death.

"You killed him!" Aung accused.

Bari Tu bit his lower lip but refused to answer.

"Somehow he found out who you were, so you killed him."

Bari Tu remained silent, refusing to meet Aung's gaze.

Aung glared at the spy a moment. Then, without warning, he thrust an arm forward, shoving Bari Tu squarely in the chest and sending him reeling once more against the railing. In the same motion, Aung grabbed the lower hem of the man's robe and shouted, "Let him go!"

The men flanking Bari Tu released their grip. A howl sprang from the spy's lips as he tumbled backward over the railing. Aung braced himself, both hands now clutching the bottom of Bari Tu's robe. One of the other men reached over and took hold, as well. The fabric held under the downward pull of Bari Tu's weight, leaving the spy dangling upside down on the far side of the railing. A hundred feet below, several dissidents glanced up, then moved away from the spot where Bari Tu would most likely fall if he were let go. For the first time, the Gold Dragon was beginning to realize that perhaps he'd misjudged his captors' capacity for violence.

"You have five seconds!" Aung shouted down to him. "Talk…or die!"

Bari Tu needed less than one second to make his decision. "I'll talk!" he wailed. "I'll talk!"

U-Tapao Royal Thai Navy Airfield, Thailand

"THE BOTTOM LINE IS, if things go their way, David figures they'll have Rafe sprung from Insein within the hour," Yakov Katzenelenbogen told Akira Tokaido. Both men were still in the communications room at AFB headquarters.

"And if things don't go their way?" Tokaido asked.

"I don't even want to go there," Katz said.

Tokaido checked his watch and shook his head grimly. "Even if they pull it off, they'll be down to less than three hours before the President sends in the heavy guns," he said. "There's no way they can make it to Dwiti and still have time to track down those nukes, much less take them out."

"I couldn't agree with you more," Katz said. "As a matter of fact, I told them that regardless of how things play out in Insein, they're to head out afterward to the Bay of Bengal. We'll have a carrier in place by then for them to land on."

"I bet that went over well with David," Tokaido said.

"He didn't like it," Katz replied, "but at this point I'm more interested in making sure they live to fight another day."

"Which means it's up to Able Team now."

"Exactly," Katz said. "They're due in at Imchar Plains any minute. We need to help level the playing field for them."

Tokaido quickly sized up the situation and turned to the computer he'd all but appropriated over the past seventy-two hours. "We've already got three more satellites repositioning to boost our sig-intel all over Myanmar. That'll help some, but I'll see if I can get even more coverage."

"Good," said Katz. "Now, as far as deploying Able Team, I think their first option should be Raitiph."

"Agreed," Tokaido said. "It's just north of Bagan, which means they can get there in less than an hour. And if we're wrong about the H-bombs being in Dwiti, Raitiph's definitely another candidate. There or Eichyi Valley."

"Eichyi Valley's too far away for them," Katz said.

"I know. Besides, last I checked the Shan and Karen are closing in on the base there like a plague of locusts. No way do we want to get tangled up in that."

"Then Raitiph it is." Katz quickly radioed through to the Hercules transport plane carrying Able Team to its drop in India. Grimaldi told him they were in sight of the desolate airstrip and would be setting down in less than ten minutes.

"Provided the runway's long enough," Grimaldi added. "Looks like a tight squeeze for this damn Hercules."

Katz reminded the pilot, "If they could set down an

F-117 there, they sure as hell can accommodate a transport plane.''

Katz passed along the revised game plan. Grimaldi said, "Okay, fine, so Able Team goes to Raitiph. What about me?''

"We're working on that," Katz responded. "For now, I think your best shot is to make a recon pass over Raitiph, then swing south for Meiktila. That'll put you dead center in the middle of the country. Hopefully by then we'll have pulled in enough intel to steer you to these goddamn bombs of theirs.''

"Bombs of ours, you mean.''

"Of course.''

Katz was signing off with Grimaldi when he heard Tokaido mutter, "What the hell...?''

Katz joined the young man, who'd sectioned off his computer screen so that he could simultaneously monitor satellite feeds from four different sources. He was in the process of closing down all but one screen, which carried a handheld video image Katz quickly recognized. "A Frog Tongue.''

"Yep," Tokaido said. "It's gotta be one of those stolen Y-25s you were sniffing around for back in Tokyo.''

"Where's this footage from?" Katz asked.

"Quick geography quiz," Tokaido said, advancing the screen image to a point where the camera simultaneously panned and pulled out its zoom, revealing a cluster of old temples and stupas in the foreground.

"Bagan?" Katz said.

"What the hell's an LAV doing there?''

"Beats me," Tokaido said. "I'm still trying to figure out who sent out this footage. Not to mention why.''

"How are you going to figure that out?" Katz asked.

"Same way I figure everything out," Tokaido answered with a grin. "I just trust things to my instincts and wing it.''

CHAPTER THIRTY-TWO

Insein Prison, Yangon, Myanmar

As he slowly regained consciousness, Rafael Encizo's first sensation was that of pain. His skull and right thigh both throbbed, reminders of his failed attempt to overpower the prison guard. His chafed wrists and ankles burned as if they were on fire. When he tried to move them and realized he couldn't, he came to with a sudden start. He was tied to a wooden chair in the middle of a room far larger than the dog cell but no less squalid. His hands were bound tightly behind the back of the chair, and his ankles had been secured to the chair's front legs. Encizo had no idea of the time. The cell's only light came from a dim incandescent bulb dangling from a cord overhead. His stomach rumbled noisily, but he'd felt hunger pangs back in the other cell. How long had he been out? A few minutes? Several hours? He was still puzzling over the matter when the cell door opened. The guard who'd beaten him earlier strode in, carrying a thick bamboo shaft. Behind him was another guard and a man in a uniform. The latter introduced himself as General Dy Lii.

"How are you enjoying our fine accommodations?" he asked.

Encizo wasn't about to respond.

"Let me guess." Lii circled Encizo, eyeing him. "You

are one of the soldiers sent to look for your precious anti-aircraft vehicles. Only you heard there was something more intriguing to be found on the islands.''

Encizo stared coldly at the general. He said nothing.

"Ah, the strong, silent type.'' Lii glanced at the first guard and held his hand out for the bamboo shaft. Moving to the right side of Encizo's chair, the general assumed a batting stance, setting his feet apart and clutching the bamboo as if he'd just stepped to the plate with the World Series on the line.

Lii swung hard, striking his prisoner across the chest with so much force the chair wobbled. Encizo had hunched his shoulders to absorb the blow, but a fresh jolt of pain still raced through him. He stared at the general, breathing in slowly through his nose, trying to block out the pain. He reminded himself how, a lifetime ago, he'd survived tortures far worse than this at Cuba's dreaded Principe Prison. He still bore scars from that ordeal, but he'd withstood the abuse and eventually fought his way to freedom. With the Tatmadaw he was determined to do the same.

"Well?'' the general asked.

Encizo remained silent.

Lii took two more swings in quick succession, striking Encizo first across the kneecaps, then the ribs. Each time, Encizo winced and gritted his teeth, muting his involuntary groans.

With a harsh shove, the general sent the prisoner reeling backward in the chair. Encizo landed hard on the concrete floor. The air had been knocked from his lungs, and as he gasped for breath, he saw Lii stride over to him, unwrapping a candy bar taken from his pocket. The general pinched off bits of the chocolate and let them rain down on Encizo.

"Have some breakfast,'' Lii said. "If you're not hungry, feel free to share with your guests.''

The general turned and strode from the cell. The guards followed him, clanging the door shut behind them. Encizo slowly regained his breath. He pondered Lii's parting words. Share with his guests? What guests?

With great difficulty, Encizo wriggled about on the floor, craning his neck to see if there was someone else in the cell he hadn't noticed. There was no one.

Encizo tried next to right himself, lunging upward with all his strength, but his constraints prevented any sort of momentum. All he managed to do was tip the chair onto its side. Landing on his infected shoulder, he let out a brief cry. Then, gasping, he rested his head on the concrete floor and closed his eyes, trying to block out the pain.

It was then that he heard it—a light scuffling sound far across the cell. Turning, he peered into the shadows. The scuffling grew louder. Soon he saw a handful of small, furry creatures scurrying toward him. Rats.

CHIEF WARDEN BOESAN steeled himself, then left his office. Two guards fell alongside him as he left the main compound and crossed the prison yard toward the front entrance. With each step, the clamor on the far side of the outer walls grew louder: hundreds of voices, all shouting the same slogan.

"Bring us Ku-Syi! Bring us Ku-Syi!"

The chant had begun earlier in the morning in response to growing rumors that an impostor had given the speech calling off demonstrations to mark the anniversary of the Four Eights. Boesan had tried at first to ignore the cries, assuming the people would weary soon enough and leave the prison without incident. He'd assumed wrong. As the morning progressed, the crowd outside the prison had only grown larger, their cries more persistent. "Bring us Ku-Syi! Bring us Ku-Syi!"

Now the mob numbered in the thousands. Boesan had

been forced to draw guards away from their regular posts to fortify the entrance. The maneuver had backfired. Instead of being intimidated, the crowd's rancor had only increased. Though the anniversary was still two days off, some of the demonstrators had begun to add a new cry to the fray. "Remember the Four Eights!" they shouted.

When General Dy Lii had arrived to question the prisoner, Boesan had put in a request for reinforcements. The general had refused; barring a riot, no troops would be deployed to Insein. Further, Boesan had been ordered to address the crowd, advancing the official strategy for dealing with Ku-Syi's death. Boesan had tried to get his brother-in-law to intercede, but from his hospital room in Yangon—which he'd been confined to for months as his health continued its slow decline—SPDC leader We Nin had responded that he wasn't about to rescind the power he'd bestowed upon his other generals during his illness.

By the time he reached the entrance, the warden had surrounded himself with a dozen more guards. One of them handed Boesan a megaphone. He took it warily, then fumbled through his shirt pocket for his bifocals and the folded paper containing the statement General Dy Lii had brought him to read. His stomach knotted as he climbed up the makeshift scaffolding that would allow him to address the crowd from behind the security of the prison walls.

Once he saw the crowd, Boesan was stunned. There were even more of them than he'd anticipated. Packed close, they spilled back all the way to the main road, a sea of angry faces, a din of angry voices that grew louder at the sight of him.

"Bring us Ku-Syi! Remember the Four Eights!"

Boesan had his orders, but he knew there would be no convincing these people. He raised an arm, gesturing for quiet. When his plea went ignored, he unfolded his speech and began to read, anxious to be done with it so that he could tell We Nin and Dy Lii that at least he'd tried.

"If it were possible, we would allow Maw Saung Ku-Syi to address you personally," he shouted into the megaphone, "but as you all could well see during her speech yesterday, Maw Saung Ku-Syi is gravely ill. She has been diagnosed with cancer."

"WHATEVER HE SAID, they're not buying it," Manning called down to T. J. Hawkins, lowering his binoculars.

"That would be my guess, too," Hawkins said.

The two men were five hundred yards from the prison entrance, crouched near the mouth of a four-foot-wide concrete pipe that emptied raw sewage into the Hlaing branch of the Yangon River. The river, brown and flecked with bubbly wisps of foam, gurgled noisily past the open pipe. Louder than the current, however, were the distant cries of the demonstrators. Manning had been monitoring the situation through his field glasses while Hawkins directed the flame of an acetylene torch at two of the vertical steel bars blocking access to the sewer line. Pag Ti had procured the torch at a supply yard before the men had split off shortly after their arrival in Yangon.

"Almost there," Hawkins called out. "Give me a hand."

Manning slung the binoculars over his shoulder and scrambled down the embankment. Together the two men grabbed one of the weakened bars and pulled. The bar resisted at first, then slowly gave way with a dull snap. The second bar offered even less resistance, and soon there was a gap the men would be able to squeeze past. Halfway through the opening, Hawkins quickly pulled back, gagging.

"I take it that means we better use these after all," Manning said, handing Hawkins a painter's mask, one of three Pag Ti had purchased along with the torch.

Hawkins nodded, donning his mask. "Smells like my Uncle Pete's outhouse that time the family got hit with diarrhea."

Once again Hawkins braved the opening. Once he was inside the pipe, Manning passed him a backpack, then hauled himself into the culvert, as well. Though both men wore gloves, neither one of them wanted to touch the curved walls, which were lined with a slick, greenish film. As they began wading toward the prison, the chunky flow of sewage sloshed at their ankles. Hawkins trained his flashlight upward. He didn't want to know what it was they were trudging through. "Rafe is going to owe us big time after this," he muttered.

ON THE FAR SIDE of the prison, Bahl Mel, one of the Insein grave diggers, shoveled dirt from a fresh hole in the ground, humming to himself to drown out chants that carried eerily through the afternoon air. He was in good spirits, having only one body to dispose of, that of a longtime prisoner who'd died in the infirmary of complications from malnutrition. Bahl Mel hadn't even bothered with the horse cart. The dead man had been light enough to transport in a wooden wheelbarrow.

Once he'd scooped out a shallow grave, Bahl Mel stabbed his shovel into the ground and returned for the body. The dead man was bundled in the same dirty linen that had served as a burial shroud for Soe Paing and Maw Saung Ku-Syi. He was light enough to carry, but Bahl Mel figured it would be easier just to wheel the body to the grave and dump it in. Grasping the handles of the wheelbarrow, he was about to head back for the graves when he suddenly stopped.

Directly in front of him stood a man who'd appeared as if out of nowhere. In his right hand was a knife.

"What do you want?" the grave digger demanded.

"Your wheelbarrow," Pag Ti said. Before Bahl Mel could react, the Myanmar operative lunged forward, plunging his knife into the grave digger's chest. Bahl Mel's fingers went limp and the wheelbarrow pitched onto its side as he collapsed to the ground, the knife sheathed in his heart. Pag Ti glanced around him to make sure no one had seen the altercation, then quickly stripped to his shorts, replacing his clothes with those of the grave digger. He dragged Bhal Mel into the grave, then laid the other corpse on top of him. Grabbing the spade, he quickly pitched a layer of dirt over the bodies, then retrieved a knapsack he'd left behind the shrubs that had earlier served as his hiding place. He placed the pack in the wheelbarrow, opening it just enough to allow easy access to his MP-5 submachine gun. After concealing the pack with the grimy shroud, Pag Ti pushed his load back toward the prison.

Once in view of the rear gateway, he made a point of keeping his head down to hide his features. As Pag Ti had hoped, the sentry posted above the gate eyed him only fleetingly before signaling for the guards to let him in. The gate door swung open. Pushing the wheelbarrow ahead of him, Pag Ti soon found himself inside the prison walls.

STRETCHING AWAY from the east wall of Insein Prison was a flat, desolate plain. The land had been leveled off three years ago in anticipation of expanding the prison, but the plan had been scrapped soon after when funds were diverted elsewhere. All that remained of the proposed project was a paved road extending in a straight line all the way from the prison's east gate to the Ywama Railway Station. After forty yards, however, the road pitched sharply down a steep incline, where it dead-ended into a gravel-strewn wash paralleling the train tracks. A thick stand of acacias rose up along the wash, providing a protective canopy under which drifters and transients were known to set up camp. That afternoon, however, the shielded area was being used for another purpose altogether.

At the base of the incline, Calvin James crouched before the front grille of a vendor's truck he'd stolen less then ten minutes earlier from the Ywama Railway Station parking lot. James had already secured two blocks of C-4 plastique to the truck's front bumper. Once the impact detonators were in place, James circled to the driver's seat. He'd already tampered with the locking mechanism built into the steering column, rigging it so the vehicle could travel in only one direction: straight forward. Once he'd started the engine, James slightly depressed the accelerator, then wedged a coin into the hinge connecting the heel plate to the floorboard. The engine's roar loudened.

Shifting the truck's automatic transmission into Drive, James bounded out of the cab. The truck lurched forward, gamely tackling the incline that led up to the straightaway that, in turn, led directly to the prison's east gate. Crouched low, James climbed up the rise, checking the truck's course. To his dismay, he saw the vehicle drift to the right as it picked up speed. He debated racing after it to correct its course but decided against it; after all, the truck was only a diversion. If it struck the prison walls rather than the gate, it would still serve its purpose.

Scrambling back down to the wash, James crouched over the mortar launcher Hawkins had brought from Thailand. A 60 mm round was already loaded in the muzzle, and James had already scoped out his target. Once he heard the drone of helicopter rotors and saw David McCarter swooping down toward him in the commandeered Tatmadaw war chopper, James triggered the launcher and sent its charge hurtling toward the prison.

"Fly true, baby," he urged the shell. "Make Daddy proud."

PAG TI MADE IT as far as the infirmary before one of the guards spotted the bloodstains on the front of his shirt.

"Bahl Mel! It looks like you cut yourself…"

The guard's voice trailed off once he realized he wasn't speaking to the grave digger. Pag Ti, taking advantage of the man's surprise, veered the wheelbarrow, ramming him in the shins before he could level his assault rifle. The man let out a howl as he went down. Pag Ti hurriedly reached under the shroud, yanking his MP-5 from his backpack. He killed the guard, then whirled to face three more soldiers charging toward him. He sprayed a volley their way, taking out two of the men. The third, however, managed to reach cover and returned fire, forcing Pag Ti to drop to a crouch behind the wheelbarrow.

The sentry who'd first mistaken Pag Ti for Bahl Mel had scrambled around the upper rampart and positioned himself for a clear shot at the intruder. Before he could get a shot off, however, James's mortar round detonated twenty yards away, ravaging one of the observation towers. The sentry was distracted by the blast, giving Pag Ti time to spot him and take him out with a round from his subgun. Even as the guard was tumbling from the rampart, there was yet another explosion, this one across the prison yard. The plastique-rigged truck had just exploded against the east wall with so much force that bits of debris began to rain into the prison yard.

The overall effect, as Pag Ti and the others had hoped, was that of a full-scale seige. The prison guards, already skittish in the face of the demonstrations outside the main gates, were now frantic. To add to their woes, more than fifty of Insein's more hardened prisoners—out lolling in the exercise yard when the commotion began—saw a golden opportunity to revolt and were soon grabbing free weights and anything else resembling a weapon they could use on the guards.

Amid all the chaos, Pag Ti slipped into the infirmary. Three men and a woman were in the process of jockeying for cover behind the furniture. "The Westerner!" Pag Ti bellowed, giving them a clear view of his MP-5. "Where is he?"

For a moment the infirmary workers froze uncertainly. Then one of them, a young man, slowly stood, keeping his hands raised above his head. "There's a back way that leads to the prison cells," he told Pag Ti. "I'll show you."

"You'll all show me together," Pag Ti told the group, not wanting to leave anyone behind to sound the alarm. He quickly frisked them to make sure they weren't armed, then motioned for the younger man to lead the way. They passed through a set of double doors into the main corridor, passing a number of treatment rooms where patients cried out, wondering about the disturbance out in the prison yard. Pag Ti ignored them and followed his prisoners past two small operating rooms and around the corner to another hallway.

"How much farther?" Pag Ti demanded.

"The end of the hall." The young worker pointed. "That gate leads to the first cell block."

Pag Ti glanced at his watch. He was running out of time and at this point the workers were only slowing him.

"Down on the floor and put your hands on your head!" he told them. The three workers responded, trembling. He started to back away from them, warning, "If anyone moves before I'm through that gate, I start shooting."

Halfway to the gate, Pag Ti passed another set of doors, one leading to the morgue, the other to a dental clinic. As he passed the clinic, a soldier suddenly sprang from the doorway, broadsiding him. Knocked off balance, Pag Ti heard his subgun clatter to the floor. He was grappling for it when a second soldier charged out of the clinic and kicked the weapon away, then directed the toe of his combat boot into Pag Ti's midsection. Pag Ti groaned in pain. He was struggling to his feet when the two soldiers overpowered him and heaved him into the wall. Stunned, he sagged into the men's arms. It was only then that a third man, General Dy Lii, stepped out of the clinic. He shouted to the infirmary workers, telling them to get up, then directed the soldiers to drag Pag Ti into the morgue.

"Maybe his tongue can be loosened quicker than his comrade's," Lii said, raising his voice to be heard above the unfolding bedlam out in the prison yard.

The soldiers dragged Pag Ti over to one of the autopsy tables. Pag Ti was already coming to, but the soldiers easily kept him pinned him to the table. Lii, meanwhile, glanced over the row of surgical tools laid out on a nearby cart. First he picked up a scalpel, then set it back in favor of the gleaming saw morticians used to cut through breastbone in order to facilitate the removal of a corpse's internal organs.

"Tell us who you are working for!" he demanded. "How many of you are there?"

Pag Ti glared at Lii, his eyes burning with contempt. "Do we count political prisoners being held against their will?"

Enraged, Lii lashed out, striking Pag Ti across the face with the flat of the saw. "Mock me again and I'll carve your heart from your chest!"

Pag Ti cried out defiantly, "Remember the Four Eights!"

The general, his face red with anger, drew his arm back and was about to thrust the tip of the saw into Pag Ti's chest when something hard slammed against his ankle. Crying out, Lii glanced down at his feet, amazed to see that he'd been struck by a large rectangular section of floor grating. Even more dumbfounding, when his gaze passed along the floor, he saw a pair of eyes peering up at him from the wide opening into which the morgue wastes were flushed. He was about to warn the other two soldiers when a burst of gunfire flew out from the sewer. Slugs from Hawkins's submachine ripped through the general's groin and lower torso, bringing him to his knees.

Before the other two soldiers could react, Hawkins—hoisted by an unseen Manning—rose into the morgue, cradling his MP-5 close to his chest. He stitched the two soldiers with a series of short bursts, then put a final round through Lii's head before setting the gun aside and pulling himself all the way out of the drain shaft.

"Good to see you," Pag Ti said, wincing slightly as he climbed from the autopsy table. A trail of blood ran down his face where the saw's teeth had bit through his skin.

"Glad to be out of that freaking sewer," Hawkins responded. "Give me a hand here, would you?"

Pag Ti came over, shaking off his injuries for the moment. He helped pull Manning up through the opening.

"We're close to the cell blocks," Pag Ti said.

"Good," Hawkins replied, glancing at his watch. "We better haul ass or we're gonna miss the bus."

WRITHING ON THE GROUND and shouting epithets at the top of his lungs, Rafael Encizo had thus far managed to keep the rats at bay, but the effort was exhausting and he didn't know how much longer he could keep it up. Each time he paused to catch his breath, the rodents inched closer. Fortunately he'd shaken most of the chocolate off his body and some of the rats contented themselves with fighting over the pieces. Others, however, merely congregated around Encizo, seemingly ready to swarm over him the moment he stopped moving.

"Beat it, you little bastards!" he seethed at them.

Encizo was making so much racket he didn't hear any

of the clamor outside his cell. At one point he thought he heard someone call his name, but when he cast a glance at the small window of his cell door, he couldn't see anyone.

"Great," he muttered to himself, "now I'm hearing things."

Seconds later, gunfire echoed in the hall. Encizo's cell door rattled on its hinges, then swung inward. The rats scrambled for the shadows as Hawkins rushed in, followed by Pag Ti. Manning remained in the doorway, trading gunshots with prison guards at the far end of the hall.

"Laying down on the job, I see," Hawkins said with a grin as he leaned over Encizo. Pag Ti helped right the chair, then used his knife to sever Encizo's binds.

"Goddamn, it's good to see you guys," Encizo said. "I was starting to feel like the world's biggest hunk of cheese."

"Well, we've still got our share of vermin to deal with before we're outta here," Hawkins said.

Once he was free, Encizo staggered away from the chair, rubbing his wrists. Hawkins handed him a Beretta as they fled from the cell. Between gunshots, Manning grinned Encizo's way and shouted, "Hey, Rafe! Ready to blow this pop stand?"

"And how!"

Manning had managed to drop all three guards in the hallway. He led the way to a nearby staircase, calling over his shoulder, "Let's hope this leads to the roof!"

Encizo's legs felt like jelly, but he willed himself to keep up with the others as they made their way up the steps. They'd reached the landing and were headed for the next floor when the upper doorway burst open and a handful of guards poured into view. A deafening roar filled the stairwell as Pag Ti and the Stony Man warriors fired in unison. The Tatmadaw soldiers went down easy, littering the steps.

"I'm nearly out of ammo," Manning said.

Hawkins tossed the Canadian one of the fallen guard's AK-47s, calling out, "Not anymore you aren't."

The men continued up to yet another corridor, this one swarming with seven more guards.

"This is ridiculous!" Hawkins shouted over the roar of his borrowed AK-47. "Where's our Get Out of Jail Free card?"

AFTER PICKING UP Calvin James, David McCarter flew parallel to the rail tracks a few hundred yards, then pulled the A-129 Mongoose up and banked toward the prison. A tendril of smoke rose from the flaming remains of the truck James had booby-trapped. The explosion had brought down a chunk of the east wall, drawing a dozen prison guards away from the cell blocks. The other guards had their hands full trying to put down the insurrection by the other prisoners. Far off, outside the main entrance to the facility, McCarter and James could see some of the protesters fleeing from the disruption.

"I'd say we did a good job of poking a stick into this hornet's nest," McCarter said. "Any sign of the lads?"

"No," James said, peering through binoculars at the mayhem. "They're gonna have company on the helipad, though."

As they drew closer, McCarter saw that ten prison guards had staked out a perimeter atop the flat roof of the tallest building. Most of them were firing down at the prison yard. Several of the men had spotted the Mongoose, however, and were waving it in for a landing.

"They must not have gotten word this bird was stolen," McCarter said. "They think we're the bloody cavalry."

"Lucky us. We could use a break."

"Go ahead and thin the herd," McCarter said. "And don't feel like you need to wait to see the whites of their eyes."

James grasped the controls for the chopper's pod-mounted 20 mm machine guns. He peered through the gunnery sights, then let loose, directing fire at the thickest concentration of enemy gunmen. Three snipers were cut down without ever knowing what hit them, and another took rounds in the chest as he turned to face the oncoming chopper. The guards standing near the helipad, meanwhile, quickly raised their rifles once they realized the Mongoose was in enemy hands. They managed to spray the chopper's fuselage with a desperate—and ultimately harmless—volley before James raked them with the 20 mm guns.

McCarter was setting the Mongoose down on the landing pad when Manning appeared, charging out of the doorway leading to the roof. The others were right behind him, and they made quick work of the remaining soldiers. Encizo was limping badly but Hawkins stuck close to him, propping him up as they made their way to the chopper. By the time they reached the rear door, James had scrambled from his seat to help them aboard. He gave Encizo a meaningful nudge. "Looks like they put you through the wringer, amigo."

Encizo grinned painfully as he plopped down in the cargo hold, drained. "Hell, nothing a week at Club Med won't cure."

As he was about to close the door, James saw a wounded guard on the helipad drawing a bead on the chopper with his gun.

"I don't think so," he stated, beating the man to the trigger with his Beretta. The guard's AK-47 fell from his limp hands as he crumpled back to the asphalt.

"All aboard?" McCarter shouted over his shoulder.

"Yes!" James called out. "Get us out of his hellhole!"

By now, the rest of the prison guards had figured out that the Mongoose hadn't come to provide backup. Those few who could divert their attention from the revolting pris-

CHAPTER THIRTY-THREE

Dwiti Military Base, Myanmar

Leaving the officers' quarters, Christopher Randolph was almost in a daze. After all these years, to have finally met his daughter had moved him profoundly. His joy, however, had been tempered greatly by the realization of the hell Semba Hru had gone through during her years in the clutches of the Gold Dragons. The experience had scarred her, so much so that he knew it would take years for her to recover, and even then he doubted she would ever be able to fully put the torment behind her. But at least now he could offer her some kind of hope, some kind of future beyond the one she'd resigned herself to.

First, though, he would have to get her away from these animals that had enslaved her. Toward that end, he'd already formulated a plan. Semba Hru had told him that her masquerade as Maw Saung Ku-Syi was more than a ploy to convince the people of Myanmar not to rally in observance of the Four Eights. Ku-Syi was dead. Further, Semba Hru told her father of the strategy to have her pose as the Nobel laureate awhile longer in hopes of fooling the world into thinking that Ku-Syi was dying of cancer. Like his daughter, Randolph thought the scheme would never succeed. It did, however, provide him with the means by which to help Semba Hru escape, once and for all, from the Gold Dragons and the Tatmadaw.

As he strode toward the base headquarters, Randolph finalized his own plan. He would convince the Tatmadaw to allow him to personally escort Semba Hru from the base. He could pose as a UN representative, he'd tell them he was sent to verify whether it was indeed Ku-Syi who'd given the speech the day before. If someone from the West were to step forward and back the cancer story, it would surely hold more credence and have a greater chance of being believed by the people of Myanmar. He'd hold an impromptu press conference, then put his daughter on the same helicopter that had brought him to Dwiti. Together, they would leave the base behind. With any luck, he could persuade the Tatmadaw to allow him to take Semba Hru out of the country, maybe to a cancer clinic in Thailand or India. If they balked at that, well, he would find a way to deal with their counterproposal. The important thing was to get his daughter as far from the base as possible before the Tatmadaw sent up their newly acquired F-105s with their altimeter-rigged hydrogen bombs.

There were two guards posted outside the entrance to the base headquarters. When Randolph approached, they lowered their assault rifles into firing position, blocking his way. Randolph calmly addressed them in their native tongue while pointing to the photo ID tag pinned to his shirt. He'd received the tag, on Bien Phyr's orders, the moment he'd arrived at the base. The badge identified Randolph as having the same top-level security clearance as ranking generals, with guaranteed freedom to move about the base unquestioned. Though taken aback, once the guards eyed the badge, they stepped aside and let Randolph enter the building.

Randolph told the sergeant manning the front desk that he wanted to see Senior General Lon Kyth. After inspecting his badge and realizing this was the American spy he'd been hearing so much about, the sergeant told Randolph that all the generals were still sequestered in the war room with orders not to be disturbed. Noticing the authorization stamp on Randolph's badge, the sergeant added, "Are you sure it isn't General Phyr who you wish to see?"

Randolph shook his head. No, he insisted, it was Lon Kyth he wanted to see. Beyond the plan to spirit his daughter away from Dwiti, Randolph had another matter he wanted to discuss with Lon Kyth and Lon Kyth alone.

"The reason I asked," the sergeant said, "is that General Phyr left the meeting early."

Randolph was intrigued. "Why?"

"He's flying up north to Bagan, then to our base in Raitiph," the sergeant said. "He's been put in charge of our forces up there while we deal with some rebel uprisings."

Randolph's intrigue turned to alarm, but he tried not to show it. "You said he's going to Bagan first?"

"It's on the way," the sergeant said with a shrug.

"Did he say why?"

The sergeant shook his head.

"Did he say how he was getting there?" Randolph asked.

The sergeant responded, "He said he'd be taking one of the jets. You know, years ago he used to be a fighter pilot."

Randolph nodded impatiently. "How much longer will the generals be meeting?" he asked.

Again the sergeant shrugged. "From what I understand, they have a lot to discuss."

"I'll come back," Randolph said. He told the sergeant to pass along word to Lon Kyth that it was imperative he see him after the meeting with regards to Maw Saung Ku-Syi, then strode back out of the headquarters. He was halfway to the airfield when he heard a roar and saw a MiG rise up into view from behind the hangars. Cursing, Randolph broke into a run, rounding the hangar, then slowing to a stop. As he'd feared, the MiG that had been parked next to his helicopter was gone. Randolph's stomach dropped as he glanced skyward and saw the jet retreating in the distance. It had to be Phyr; he was taking the sarin bombs to Bagan for use on the demonstrators.

The American cursed himself. He'd procured the bombs for the Tatmadaw with the clear understanding they, like the Y-25 LAV-ADs, would be used only against the Shan and Karen rebels, and even then he'd had misgivings. The thought that the poisonous gas would now be unleashed on innocent civilians filled him with shame and recrimination. How could he have been so blinded by his thirst for revenge? Yes, Bien Phyr had mentioned some last-minute change in plans, but he could have just as easily been lying. Perhaps they'd planned to use the gas on demonstrators all along, and had merely duped Randolph with the talk about neutralizing guerrilla forces.

"Fool!" he chided himself angrily.

Randolph's chagrin, severe as it was, paled to the sudden horror that overcame him as he glanced to his right and saw, for the first time, that the two F-105 Thunderchiefs had been hauled out to the runway and were being fueled by crews standing alongside a large tanker truck. The masking on both jets was nowhere close to being finished. One Thud was spotted with primer coats of paint, and the other had stencils still taped to its fuselage. Neither would pass, by any stretch of the imagination, as fighter jets flying the colors of India or Chinese. What was going on? Randolph strode over to the jets, but his way was blocked by a handful of soldiers. Even when he flashed his badge, they refused to let him past. They held him in place while a middle-aged colonel ventured over.

"Why are they fueling the jets?" Randolph asked the

officer. "I told General Phyr he could wait a couple days before putting them through test flights."

"No time to wait," the colonel said. "Our base in Eichyi Valley is under seige by the Shan and Karen. They've thrown their forces together, thinking it will give them a better chance against us. We, however, will use the situation to destroy their ranks while they're huddled together."

"You can't!" Randolph blurted out. "You can't send those jets off! Not now!"

The colonel eyed Randolph suspiciously. "Why not?"

"I told General Phyr there might be a problem with the bay doors and the bomb racks," Randolph said.

The colonel nodded. "He told me that, but he said we need to turn the situation to the north to our advantage. There is no time for delays. He said we should take the risk."

Randolph thought fast. If the jets took off before he and his daughter could leave, they'd be incinerated along with everyone on the base by the jets' deadly cargo of Mk-28s. At this point, he had no care whether he lived or died. In fact, he'd set out on this mission fully expecting it to cost him his life. But Semba Hru? Had he come this far, gone through so much pain and effort to find her and offer her some hope of a life, only to see her sacrificed on the altar of his revenge?

"Let me inspect the bombs," he told the colonel, thinking perhaps he could disable the altimeters. It would render the bombs useless against the rebels, but that did not concern him.

"There is no time," the colonel said, shaking his head.

"I insist."

"There is no time. I have my orders."

"And I have clearance to inspect those bombs!" Randolph stated, indicating his badge.

"My rank outweighs your clearance," the colonel responded coolly. "Once the jets are fueled, they will take off for Eichyi Valley. That is final!"

Randolph was crestfallen. There was no point in trying to muscle his way past the guards. They would only over-power him, or worse. He stared past them at the jets. "When did they start fueling?" he asked.

"The jets will take off within the hour," the colonel answered indirectly. "Forty-five minutes, perhaps fifty."

Randolph turned his attention from the jets to his heli-copter. He knew the aircraft was ready for takeoff at a moment's notice. He'd seen to it earlier, even before he'd tracked down his daughter. But even if he carried out ev-erything he intended to do and got Semba Hru aboard the chopper inside of thirty minutes, it was unlikely they could fly fast enough to be clear of the inferno unleashed by the hydrogen bombs.

Randolph realized there was only one course of action left for him. And even that option was a long shot. But he had to go with it. He turned to the colonel and asked, "Where is the communications center?"

Stony Man Farm, Virginia

"THEY MADE IT!" Hal Brognola called out to the others in the Annex Computer Room. He'd just heard from David McCarter.

Aaron Kurtzman glanced up from his computer. "With Rafe?"

Brognola nodded. "With Rafe. They didn't have enough fuel to make it to the carrier, but they set down on a frigate just north of the Andaman Islands."

The news was greeted by a chorus of jubilant cries, and for a fleeting moment the other business at hand was put aside as the Stony Man brain trust celebrated Encizo's safe return to the fold. Brognola told the group that nearly every member of Phoenix Force had sustained injuries in the rescue effort, but none was deemed serious. "Rafe took the worst of it, obviously," he reported. "He might have a concussion and he has some kind of infection in a shoulder wound, but he's already badgering to be let back into action. David wants a crack at Dwiti, too, but I told them to stay put."

Huntington Wethers eyed one of the wall clocks. "We're down to an hour before deadline, anyway," he said. "Let's just hope the others can manage something."

Brognola turned to Carmen Delahunt. "Anything new on that feed out of Bagan?" The woman had been working in tandem with Akira Tokaido, attempting to trace the routers that had relayed the video image of the Y-25 LAV perched in the hills overlooking the ancient temples.

"As we speak," Delahunt responded, scrolling through the latest info coming in from U-Tapao. "Jackpot."

Brognola headed over to Delahunt's station, followed by Barbara Price, who'd just finished speaking with Carl Lyons aboard the Shivagi gunship carrying Able Team across the Chin Hills toward Bagan and the Tatmadaw base in Raitiph. She told Brognola the team had yet to encounter any interference.

"I'm not surprised," Brognola said. "The Tatmadaw have their hands full elsewhere."

By the time they joined Delahunt, she'd finished scanning Tokaido's message. She quickly passed along the highlights. "Akira fixed a position at a university in Mae Hong Son in Thailand," she said. "It's just across the border. The CIA had a field team three miles away trying to track down that opium shipment headed for Bangkok. They raided the installation and talked to the professor manning the relay station. He said the footage was a test run by some cameraman who's going to film a huge rally in Bagan in a couple days to observe the Four Eights. They want to make sure there's not a repeat of what happened fifteen years ago when—''

"Hold on," Wethers called out from his station. "Are you sure about that rally being in a couple days?"

"That's what it says here," Carmen said, checking back over Tokaido's cyber communiqué.

"Well. I'm looking at a sat-cam feed trained on Bagan, and from the looks of it, there are people already beginning to gather around all those old temples."

"Maybe the schedule got pushed up," Brognola ventured, moving over to glance at Wethers's screen. The sat-cam image was amazingly detailed, focused tight on one group of demonstrators piling out of one of the larger temples.

"Can you pull back?" Price asked Hunt as she glanced over Brognola's shoulder.

"Of course." Wethers entered the appropriate commands. The screen blinked several times as its viewing range widened until it took in the entire plain, as well as the surrounding area. The demonstrators now looked like drones swarming around so many anthills.

"Look up to the north there," Price said, pointing at the screen. "It looks like a whole group of them heading down from the hills near the airport."

"I think that's Nyaung-U," Wethers said. "They have a few temples of their own up there."

Carmen Delahunt, still at her own computer, called out, "Akira says these people have apparently been hiding in the temples waiting for the rally. There're supposed to be thousands of them."

"Wait a second," Brognola said. "What about that Frog Tongue? Aren't these people from Nyaung-U going to be passing right by it on the way to Bagan?"

Wethers shifted the image on the screen, then tightened the focus and nodded. "Looks that way to me."

"Any sign the LAV's going to fire on them?" Brognola said.

"Checking..." Wethers zoomed in on the Tatmadaw position. Behind him, Brognola and Price could see the soldiers standing around the antiaircraft vehicle, assault rifles in hand.

"I don't think they can use the missiles on them," Wethers said, "but they can still throw down enough firepower to rack up some serious losses."

Price stepped back and called across the room to Kurtzman, "Try to raise Able Team and tell them to divert south to Bagan! They need to take out that LAV position or we're going to have a massacre on our hands!"

U-Tapao Royal Navy Airfield, Thailand

YAKOV KATZENELENBOGEN stared out at the flurry of activity on the airstrip. It was a stirring sight. Every available fighter jet and B-52 was being readied for liftoff. If Stony Man's deadline ran out, Katz felt confident that the airborne power from this base alone would be enough to neutralize the Tatmadaw...provided the Myanmar force didn't play its newfound nuclear card. If that happened, of course, all bets would be off. The latter prospect troubled Katz. If the bombs went off, besides the obvious—and immediate—destruction and loss of life, there would be long-felt ramifications. America's allies and foes alike would no doubt second-guess the way things had been played out, and there would be those who claimed that by forcing the Tatmadaw's hand, the U.S. was every bit as responsible for any thermonuclear catastrophe as the SPDC. The stain on America's image worldwide would be hard to overcome, no matter how deft the President's spin doctors might be at defending what had happened. Somehow, Able Team needed to resolve matters before the clock ran out.

Weighed down by his forebodings, Katz walked slowly back to the AFB communications center, hoping that during his brief absence Akira Tokaido might have received some sort of encouraging news. In his heart, however, he felt that Stony Man had used up all its luck rescuing Rafael Encizo from Insein.

Katz found Tokaido hunched before the computers, jaws working furiously at his bubble gum. "Anything new?"

"Our spy's come in from the cold," Tokaido replied, eyes glued to his screen.

"Randolph?"

Tokaido nodded. "He just radioed out an SOS from the communications base in Dwiti."

"How did he manage that?"

"I don't know," Tokaido interjected, "but he says the bombs are there. That's the good news, but hold off the victory dance, because there's bad news, too. Real bad…"

CHAPTER THIRTY-FOUR

Bagan, Myanmar

"As long as they don't spot us and fire first, this'll be a piece of cake," Gadgets Schwarz said, peering through the gunnery sights of the Shivagi 4-H war chopper streaking low over the barren desert west of Bagan. He had a clear bead on the Y-25 LAV-AD, which had yet to move from its position atop the hillock overlooking both the civilian airfield and the temple-strewed plains to the east. He counted two Tatmadaw soldiers but figured there were more, either on the other side of the armored vehicle or inside it. The men he could see seemed agitated and were pointing, Schwarz assumed, at the throng of demonstrators marching en masse from Nyaung-U to Bagan.

"Hold her steady," he told the pilot, a young Indian intelligence officer with a narrow black mustache and thick eyebrows that merged over the bridge of his nose. Carl Lyons and Pol Blancanales were back in the cabin, readying for battle. Lyons was also in touch with Akira Tokaido by way of radio headset.

As they were passing over the brown, slow-churning waters of the Irrawaddy River, Lyons suddenly called out to Schwarz, "Hold your fire, Gadgets!"

Schwarz, mere seconds from releasing a TOW missile from the chopper's weapon pods, frowned and glanced over his shoulder. "Come on! I've got the bastards dead to rights!"

"Tough, we're going to have to do things the hard way," Lyons said, snapping off his headset and grabbing his carbine. "Akira says we might need that Frog Tongue for ourselves."

"For what?" Schwarz said. "Hell, none of us even know how to operate it!"

"I'll explain later," Lyons said. "Just hold off on the TOW and switch to the 20 mms."

"Yeah, sure," Schwarz groused. "Only I'm not supposed to hit the LAV, right?"

"Nicks and scratches don't count," Lyons said.

Blancanales scrambled to the rear door and took down a length of drop rope. "I take it we're gonna crawl down on them," he said.

Lyons nodded, then told the pilot, "Get us as close as you can, then put her on pause."

"If that means 'hover in place,' I can do that," the pilot replied.

"Good," Lyons said. "One other thing. Does this twirly come with any kind of tear-gas charges?"

"Try the top cabinet next to the rescue platform."

Blancanales was already there. He opened the cabinet. Along with four tear-gas canisters were some flares and two concussion grenades, all prepacked into two web belts. He grabbed them both, muttering, "These should come in handy."

The Shivagi cleared the river near Wetkyi-in and passed over the two roads linking Nyaung-U with Bagan. They were within a hundred yards of their target when Schwarz saw the two Tatmadaw soldiers raise their rifles and take aim, not at the approaching chopper, but rather at the first handful of dissidents wading across a shallow stretch of the Wetkyi-in Chaung River.

"Here goes..." Schwarz triggered the Shivagi's 20 mm pod gun. With deadly precision, a steady stream of rounds charged up the hillock. The soldiers, hearing the shots over the roar of their own rifles, turned in time to greet the fusillade face-on. Both men staggered under the impact, then went down, dropping their rifles to the wayside. Another soldier, crouching low on the far side of the LAV, aimed his AK-47 and fired back. His volley was less accurate but still managed to dent the Shivagi's fuselage and create a spiderweb in the windshield just to Schwarz's right. Meanwhile, the Y-25's turret began to swivel about, giving Able Team its first glimpse of the LAV's 25 mm GAU-121 Gatling gun.

"Don't worry," the pilot told the others. "I can outmaneuver it, at least for a few passes."

"Good." Schwarz abandoned his gunnery post to join Lyons and Blancanales in the rear cabin. The two men had already yanked open the door and begun feeding out the drop line.

"Here's the deal," Lyons said quickly. He quickly passed along Tokaido's message about Christopher Randolph reporting in with the location of the hydrogen bombs, adding, "Of course, that's Jack's problem, not ours. We need to keep that LAV intact because there's a MiG on the way here looking to take out the demonstrators with some old friends of ours."

"The sarin bombs?" Schwarz said.

Lyons nodded. "Randolph's not sure how the MiG's carrying the bombs, but unless they're stashed in the equipment bay they've got to be mounted somehow on the missile pylons."

"For a dumb drop?" Schwarz wondered, "or are they strapped to the missiles."

"Don't know," Lyons said. "In any event, one of us is gonna have to stay on board while this bird plays interceptor. That means being on the wrong end of a one-sided dogfight.''

Schwarz looked at Blancanales. ''What he's trying to say is that whoever stays on board here is dead meat.''

Blancanales thought it over. ''The LAV launcher's got to be tougher to operate than the one here,'' he told Schwarz, handing him one of the weapon-laden web belts, ''You're the tech wizard around here, so you go. I'll stay.''

''Hey! What about me?'' Lyons said.

Blancanales handed Lyons the other belt. ''We need Gadgets inside that Frog Tongue as fast as possible, right? A psychotic'll stand a better chance of making that happen.''

''You think I'm psychotic?'' Lyons said.

''They don't call you Ironman because you get the wrinkles out of shirts,'' Pol said. ''Now, go on, get out of here.''

For a fleeting, somber moment, the three men eyed one another, then Schwarz grabbed hold of the rope and lowered himself from the chopper. Lyons was about to follow suit when he spotted a bundle of inch-thick rebar stacked alongside what looked to be some construction supplies. He grabbed two of the foot-long rods, shouting to the pilot, ''Stay tight overhead as long as you can. I wanna make sure that friggin' LAV can't shoot you in the back once you head out!''

''I can do that,'' the pilot repeated.

Lyons snapped Blancanales a quick salute, then followed Schwarz down the dangling rope. Blancanales moved to the opening and covered their descent, firing carbine rounds at the Tatmadaw crouched on the far side of the LAV. Once his partners had climbed down far enough to jump clear, he pulled the rope back in while calling out to the pilot, ''All right, let's go kick the Shivagi out of that MiG!''

ON THE WAY DOWN the rope, Lyons shouted out a quick battle plan to Schwarz. The moment they hit the ground, they began putting the plan into motion. In unison, both men hurled concussion grenades, making certain they landed on the far side of the LAV. The blasts sounded in quick succession, jostling not only the armored vehicle but also the entire hillside. More than likely, Lyons figured, the Tatmadaw gunman had been stunned enough to give them a few seconds to make their move. Scrambling up the hill, Schwarz charged around the front end of the Y-25 while Lyons made for the side.

As Lyons had suspected, the turret was beginning to pivot, not only toward him but also the Shivagi 4-H overhead. He knew the turret's gun could riddle the helicopter to shreds without any need for the four surface-to-air missiles housed on a separate swivel mount at the rear of the vehicle. To do that, however, those inside the turret would first have to get the chopper in their sights. Lyons wasn't about to let that happen. Cocking his arm, a length of rebar clutched in his hand like a miniaturized javelin, Lyons scanned the seam between the turret and the main frame of the vehicle. The gap was smaller than he'd expected—less than the width of a pencil in most places—but up front near the hatches, there were two wider openings. Lyons shoved the rebar into one of the gaps and held it in place. At first it seemed to have been a pointless maneuver, as the turret continued to swing about. Then, with the groaning, nerve-racking sound of metal scraping against metal, the pivoting chamber ground to a stop. At that same instant, there was a brief exchange of gunfire off to Lyons's right. Freeing one hand, he grabbed his pistol.

"Got him," Schwarz called out, bounding atop the LAV. He saw the rebar poking out from the turret and shook his head. "I thought we were supposed to keep this bastard operable."

"It's just jammed," Lyons said.

"You hope," Schwarz taunted.

Lyons held out the other steel bar. "Go jam that missile pod while I get these folks to open up."

Schwarz took the rebar and climbed over the turret, passing the huge radar screen on his way to the missile pod. Lyons, meanwhile, tracked down the ventilator and used the web belt to strap two of the tear-gas canisters into place so that, when activated, both sent their aerosol in through the vent ducts. Lyons jumped clear of the LAV and readied his carbine. He didn't have long to wait. Within ten seconds, the hatch door flew open and, like a human jack-in-the-box, one of the turret gunners sprang into view. He had an Uzi cradled tightly to his chest and he fired blindly in a wide swath, his eyes closed, gagging. Lyons ducked the gunfire, then out took the gunner with a single burst to the man's face. The gunner pitched sideways, dangling halfway out of the hatch. Lyons leaped back up to the same spot where he'd been only moments before. Schwarz joined him, having jammed the missile launcher.

"You pull, I'll clean up," he told Lyons, readying his M-16.

Lyons nodded and grabbed the dead gunner by the armpits and yanked him out of the hatch. Schwarz was already in place beside him, and he fired into the turret the moment he saw the second gunner. Together, he and Lyons pulled out the second body and shoved it onto the ground. By now the Shivagi 4-H was gone from view, having vanished into the hills south of Bagan. Staring down the hill, the two men saw the steady stream of demonstrators making their way through the fields toward the ancient temples, where hundreds of others could be seen gathering out in the open. Some of the people looked up toward them, apprehensive. Lyons set down his carbine and waved, hoping somebody had binoculars and would be able to figure out the LAV had been overtaken.

"What now?" Schwarz asked.

"Go ahead and yank out the rebar while I open all the hatches so this baby can air out," Lyons said. "Then we'll hop in and start looking around for an instructions manual."

CHAPTER THIRTY-FIVE

Dwiti Military Base, Myanmar

Lon Kyth set down his phone and rose from his desk.

"There," he told Christopher Randolph impatiently. "Everything's in order. You can take her and leave anytime."

Randolph had just run by his proposal to take Semba Hru from the military base in the guise of a UN official insuring that Maw Saung Ku-Syi would receive the best possible care for her "cancer" at an undisclosed treatment center. Lon Kyth, distracted by other, more pressing matters, had agreed to the plan and passed along the particulars to an aide, who was now seeing to it that Randolph's helicopter was ready to take them to Yangon. Randolph would give his press conference there. Lon Kyth had balked at letting the American take Semba Hru out of the country, but the American figured that once the chopper was aloft, he'd merely have to put a gun to the pilot's head to change their itinerary.

"I hate to rush you out of here," Lon Kyth told Randolph, "but I have other business to attend to."

"War with the Shan and Karen," Randolph said, making no move to leave. "You plan to drop all eight bombs on them?"

"It won't take more than one or two is my thinking,"

Lon Kyth said. "We'll hold the rest in reserve. If your country's troops make a move against us, we'll use some of the bombs on them and the rest on India and China. Let things turn into a free-for-all, and I am sure we'll become a low priority."

Randolph smiled. "Very decisive, General. And shrewd."

"Practical is more like it." Lon Kyth turned his back on Randolph and strode to the door. "Now, if you'll excuse me…"

"Practical. Of course," Randolph said. "But then, that's always been your way, hasn't it? Practical. No concern for mundane things like morality or conscience."

Lon Kyth whirled, alerted by the change in Randolph's tone of voice. As he did so, he let out a cry and grabbed at his shoulder, having just felt the sting of a needle. He stared wildly at Randolph, who stepped back from him, holding a half-emptied syringe.

"Sarin," Randolph told him. "I saved some, just for you."

Already the toxin was racing through Lon Kyth's system, shutting down everything in its path. The general's knees buckled and he fell to the floor even as he was trying to grab for Randolph. The American took another step back and watched the older man flounder meekly on the carpet.

"Think back, Lon Kyth," Randolph told the general, "because I want these to be your dying thoughts. Thirty-three years ago. The border at Tachilek. You were just starting to make a name for yourself as head of the unit stationed there. Of course, as the man in charge, you were also the first in line for bribes. When the Gold Dragons passed through, looking to smuggle young girls into Bangkok, they always took good care of you, didn't they?"

Lon Kyth stared up at Randolph, his fury, like his very life, draining from his eyes.

"One day, some women tried to intervene with the smuggling and the Gold Dragons shot them down," Randolph went on. "Shot them down without a care in the world. They didn't have to worry about the Tatmadaw, because you'd told your men to turn a deaf ear to the women's cries. You let the Dragons get away with their butchery, and this time they not only took young girls with them to Bangkok, they also took an infant. A baby less than a year old. My daughter, Lon Kyth. Semba Hru. Now, thanks to you, I will take her to freedom, all these years later. I just wanted to show you my gratitude."

The elder general's lips fluttered, trying to form a word.

"Bassssst…"

Lon Kyth fell silent. Even in death, his gaze held a look of incredulity at Randolph's disclosure.

Randolph pocketed the syringe and rushed to the door, tearing it open with great urgency. "Help!" he called out, "I think the general has had a heart attack!"

A dozen people rushed into the room and gathered around the fallen general. Though he was desperate to flee, Randolph stayed with the group, voicing his concern, even helping with CPR for a time before he was shooed away by arriving medics. It was only then that he took his leave, expressing his condolences to the general's staff. "What a tragedy," he told them. "He seemed like such a good man."

SEMBA HRU STARED in the mirror as she applied the last touches of makeup, enhancing her resemblance to the late Maw Saung Ku-Syi. Her father would be by soon to take her away from here. It'd been his idea to have her don the disguise.

My father.

Semba Hru was still reeling from the news. After all these years of wondering about her heritage, speculating what might have happened to her parents, now she knew the truth. It was incredible. Recalling Randolph's visit and the revelation about what had happened to her mother, she began to tremble. Tears came to her eyes. She fought them back and started out of the bathroom, then froze in the doorway.

Swarng Bancha had just entered the suite. Taking in her makeup and pulled-back hair, the Gold Dragon chuckled. "So, our American friend was into celebrity worship after all."

Semba Hru nodded faintly, trembling again, this time with suppressed rage.

"Are you all right?" Bancha said.

"I'm fine," Semba Hru said stiffly. "Just tired."

"Of course." Bancha eased himself onto the sofa and unslung his shoulder holster, tossing it onto the coffee table. "You should see it out there," he said. "Everyone running around like chickens with their heads cut off. Once things have quieted down, I'll arrange for us to leave."

"I'm glad," Semba Hru said. "In the meantime, I'd like to sleep a little."

"Come," he called out, patting the cushion beside him. "You can lie down here."

"Another time, maybe," Semba Hru told. "I'd rather just be alone. You can come by and pick me later."

Bancha stared at Semba Hru, sensing something was amiss. "What is it?" he asked her.

"I...I have a headache."

Bancha's expression hardened. "I don't think so."

"I'm sorry," she said, "but this has all been hard on me."

"You're lying. I can see it in your eyes."

"No, I—"

Bancha rose to his feet. "I'll ask you again. What's the matter? What are you up to?"

"Nothing," Semba Hru shot back. "Can't I just have some time to myself? Is that asking too much?"

Bancha grabbed the woman by the shoulders and shook her. "I can tell when you're lying!" he shouted. "Now, tell me what are you up to? Why are you trying to get me out of here?"

"Let go of me!" Semba Hru shouted back at him.

"Not until I have some answers!" He shook her again, harder this time. "Now!"

Semba Hru broke free of Bancha's grasp and spit in his face. Bancha quickly overcame his shock and grabbed the woman as she was about to break for the door. Forcefully he swung her about and shoved her toward the sofa. She toppled over the coffee table and landed hard on the floor. "I think you've let this makeup go to your head," he seethed, advancing toward her. "I think you need to be reminded of your place!"

"Get out!" Semba Hru shouted, scrambling away from him.

"I'm not going anywhere!" The Gold Dragon yanked off his belt and doubled it up, slapping it down hard on the coffee table. "And neither are you! Not before I've—"

Bancha suddenly fell silent. Semba Hru had managed to grab his Glock pistol from his holster. He was now staring down the weapon's bore.

"You should've left when I told you to," Semba Hru said.

"Put it back."

"So you can force yourself on me?" Semba Hru said. "I don't think so."

"Put it back," Bancha repeated calmly. He took a slow step toward the woman. "You know you aren't going to hurt me."

Semba Hru lowered the gun slightly and fired a 9 mm

round into Bancha's groin. Howling, Bancha dropped to his knees.

"A present for you, from my mother."

"You little bitch!" Bancha screamed.

Semba Hru adjusted her aim, drawing bead on the Gold Dragon's face. She pulled the trigger. Bancha's head snapped back as a bullet plowed through his cheek. Semba Hru continued to fire, drilling several more shots into the flesh peddler's body. It was only when she heard a pounding on the door that she stopped firing. She turned just as the guard was charging in with his AK-47. She fired at him twice, putting one bullet through his throat, the other through his heart. The man crumpled to the floor without firing a shot.

Hearing a commotion in the hall, Semba Hru rose to her feet, racing toward the fallen assault rifle. She was halfway to it when a man appeared in the open doorway, clutching a Smith & Wesson Sigma Compact. It was her father. He glanced past the fallen guard, taking in the carnage she'd reaped on Swarng Bancha. There was no need for any explanations.

"Let's get out of here," he told his daughter.

CHAPTER THIRTY-SIX

Airspace over southern Myanmar

After pushing Mach 2 over the Myanmar heartland, Jack Grimaldi dropped altitude and cut back his speed. He'd just sighted the northern range of the Dartyne Mountains. Soon the Nighthawk's IRAD sensors would be locking in on the Dwiti military base. Thanks to Akira Tokaido, however, he already had a pretty good idea of what he was getting himself into, and he didn't like the sounds of it.

"Randolph did what?" Jack Grimaldi cried out into his helmet mike.

"You heard me," Tokaido told him. "He's got all eight bombs set to blow as soon as those Thuds lift off. You need to nail them while they're still on the ground."

"The bombs won't go off when I hit them?" Grimaldi said.

"Come on, Jack, you know how triggering mechanisms work," Tokaido told him. "The way Randolph's got those bombs tricked up, it doesn't matter how hard you pound them as long as they stay grounded. That's the key. You can't let those F-105s get off the tarmac or it's curtains."

"I got that part," Grimaldi said.

"The good news is we've already got a lock on them."

"Come again?"

"Satellite bead," Tokaido explained. "Cue up your display and we'll send a feed."

"I'm on it." Grimaldi turned his attention to the eight-inch screen on the control panel to his left. As promised, the satellite tracking image was picked up by the FLIR turret and soon Grimaldi found himself staring at a laser glint representing his target. "Okay, we're in business."

"Good."

"What kind of reception can I expect?" Grimaldi asked.

There was a moment's hesitation, then Tokaido said, "Looks like they've got two of our LAVs up and running."

"Frog Tongues?"

"Yep," Tokaido confirmed. "But they can't be familiar enough with the equipment to pick you out, especially if you stay in stealth mode."

"My stealth mode goes out the window the minute I open my bomb bay," Grimaldi reminded Tokaido. "With those doors flapping I've got the RCS of the goddamn Goodyear blimp!"

"Maybe so," Tokaido countered, "but by then what are they going to be able to do about it? Hell, by the time they acquisition you, they're gonna be reeling from your GBUs."

"If you say so," Grimaldi muttered. By now he'd locked his aim point onto the screen's blip and was toggling the targeting basket into place. "Look, I'd love to stay and chat, but it's getting close to show time."

"One more thing," Tokaido said. "If you ace the Thuds and feel up to it, Randolph says the main ammo depot is in the large depot sitting at eleven o'clock from the jets."

"I'll see what I can do," Grimaldi said. "What's with Randolph, anyway? Is he still down there?"

"Negative," Tokaido told him. "He and his daughter hopped a chopper out about ten minutes ago. He commandeered it once it cleared the base and is headed for one of our carriers.''

"Good for them," Grimaldi said. "Got to run. I've got a hot date with the Thud sisters."

"Good luck."

"Thanks," Grimaldi said. "I'm going to need it."

The Stony Man pilot let out a breath to steady his nerves, then took one last glance at the display screen, confirming his aim before activating the Nighthawk's weapon system. The jet shuddered faintly as the bay doors snapped open.

"Special delivery," Grimaldi called out to the distant base as he released the first GBU-27A/B smart bomb.

TATMADAW Lieutenant Hayr Win grinned inside the turret as he eyed the targeting screen on the Y-25 LAV-AD. He'd just locked on an incoming jet and readied one of the Stinger surface-to-air missiles. He wasn't sure if it was the Shan or Karen, but he didn't much care. As soon as the intruder was within range, he'd let loose and teach the rebels better than to think they could strike the Dwiti base unnoticed.

"There's a medal in this, for sure," he boasted to the officer sitting beside him in the cramped confines of the armored vehicle.

"A medal and a promotion, I hope," the other man said.

Hayr Win was two seconds away from setting off the Stinger when the Dwiti airfield was rocked by a sudden explosion. The LAV lurched violently back and forth, slamming the men into each other. Once the vehicle came to a rest, the lieutenant, cursing, stared out the observation window at the fireball engulfing the fuel truck and two F-105s outside the nearest hangar. He was about to say something to the other officer when a second bomb from Jack Grimaldi's Nighthawk bored into the munitions depot directly behind them. This time they were caught up in the explosion, struck with so much concussive force the armored vehicle tumbled sideways across the tarmac as if it were some child's Tonka truck being kicked across a sandbox. Hurtled about inside the turret, Hayr Win struck the hatch door, snapping his neck. The other officer was already dead, his skull crushed as the turret roof caved in on him. Finally the LAV came to a rest, lying upside down on the runway, six of its eight tires ruptured. The remaining two spun lazily.

Forty yards away, the other antiaircraft vehicle lay in flames on its side. It, too, had never had a chance to fire at Grimaldi. Elsewhere, the munitions depot continued to be rocked by violent explosions, spewing debris and shrapnel like an erupting volcano. There were screams of agony amid the rubble, and bodies lay strewed about the runway and out on the training field. There would be survivors, but there could be no mistaking that the base and the Tatmadaw had been dealt a blown from which they wouldn't soon recover.

JACK GRIMALDI DROPPED the Nighthawk to a thousand feet and stared out his window at the clouds of smoke rising from the base. Much as they billowed, none of the clouds mushroomed outward. He had to make two passes before he confirmed that he'd taken out both of the F-105s. There was little left of them but fiery clumps of metal smouldering on the runway. Yet, amazingly, somewhere amid the debris, Grimaldi knew that were eight hydrogen bombs that, as promised by Akira Tokaido, had failed to detonate. Grimaldi was still eyeing his handiwork when his headset radio crackled to life. It was Tokaido.

"Looks good from where we're sitting, Jack."

"Affirmative," Grimaldi replied. "Those Thuds make Humpty-Dumpty look like an uncracked egg."

Yakov Katzenelenbogen's voice sounded next in Gri-

CHAPTER THIRTY-SEVEN

Airspace over Kyauk Padaung, Myanmar

Bien Phyr smiled to himself as he guided his MiG-29 Fulcrum through the cloud cover. It had been months since he'd been in the cockpit of a fighter jet, and the vibrant turbohum of the aircraft's Klimov RD-33 power plant was like music to his ears. His euphoria was in part due also to the way things were shaping up for him in his quest to gain more power in the ranks of the Tatmadaw. As he'd told Lon Kyth, he'd felt honored at being chosen to head the northern forces in their retaliatory strike against the Shan and Karen rebels. Hopefully by the time he'd dispensed with the miscreants gathering in Bagan and flown on to the Tatmadaw's air base in Raitiph, there would be news that the F-105s' nuclear strike had succeeded in crushing the rebel force marching on the military's base in Eichyi Valley. The blow would surely take the fight out of the rebels, and when Phyr continued the offensive by sending more troops after any remaining strongholds, the Shan and Karen would be bludgeoned into surrender. The Tatmadaw would emerge triumphant, their dominion over the entire country unquestioned. Phyr would no doubt find another star on his collar, and, in time, when We Nin and the senior generals were ready to pass the torch, he would be positioned to take control, not only of the military, but also the SPDC.

"All mine," he gloated as he changed course and directed the MiG toward the distant temples of Bagan. "All mine…"

Bagan, Myanmar

ROSARIO BLANCANALES finished strapping on his parachute, then turned his focus to the Shivagi 4-H's radar display. The chopper was hovering low in a deep valley near the Yeosin Chaung River, three miles south of Bagan. Akira Tokaido had just passed along coordinates giving the approach path of the MiG-29 he'd been tracking since its takeoff from the military base in Dwiti—a base, according to Tokaido, now crippled thanks to Jack Grimaldi's tactical air strike with the F-117A.

"Now it's our turn," Blancanales said.

Less than a minute later, a telltale blip appeared on the outer periphery of the radar screen. Blancanales turned to the pilot and told him, "Bring her up and let's cross our fingers."

The pilot nodded, sweeping along the river, then rising up out of the valley. Blancanales kept his eyes trained on the radar, at the same time laying his right hand on the weapons control panel. Once the MiG was in range, he'd lock in and flick the trigger to one of the TOW missiles mounted on the Shivagi's outer pod. They wanted the MiG down before it could come within firing distance of the temples, where he assumed the crowd of demonstrators was continuing to grow.

Suddenly, a second, smaller blip raced out ahead of the larger one. Blancanales gauged the trajectory and cursed, "Dammit, he's got us!"

Both men knew that they only had a few seconds before the Shivagi took a hit. "Out!" the pilot shouted.

Blancanales hesitated long enough to engage one of the TOWs, then bolted from his seat. "Come on!" he told the pilot as he jerked open the side door.

"Right behind you!" the pilot said.

"Now!" Blancanales shouted over the wind rushing past the cabin opening. "This bird's gonna be toast!"

"I'm coming!" the pilot shouted back at him. "Jump!"

Blancanales crouched slightly, then lunged outward, tumbling through the air. He contorted his body and swung around, glancing back at the Shivagi's cabin. There was no sign of the pilot.

"Come on, damn you!" Blancanales shouted, grabbing at his rip cord. But it was clear the pilot had remained in the cockpit. The Shivagi banked sharply to the left, then dipped away from Blancanales in a desperate attempt to maneuver clear of the MiG's incoming R-27R1 air-to-air missile. The ploy failed, however.

As Blancanale's chute deployed, tugging him upward, he saw the missile plow into the Shivagi's fuselage. The resulting explosion showered the air with the fiery shrapnel, some of which hurtled Blancanales's way. He felt the sting of metal slapping against his boot, then looked up and saw that more bits of the disintegrated chopper had ripped through the canopy of his parachute. Suddenly he pitched sharply to one side and began falling with precipitous speed. He yanked hard on his shroud lines to compensate, but was unable to slow the rate of his descent. The best he could do was to shift his body and continue pulling at the chute reins, veering away from a rocky, sharp-edged escarpment. With a loud, violent splash, he landed in the Yeosin Chaung River.

The water was deep, breaking his fall well before he

touched bottom. Blancanales held his breath, wrestling free
of the harness and untangling himself from the shroud lines
as he fought his way back to the surface. The current was
slight, and he treaded water as he looked around him. He
could hear the MiG racing overhead above the cloudline,
but there was only a ragged, dissipated puff of black smoke
where the Shivagi had been hit. Down on the ground, more
smoke rose in small tendrils from fallen bits of debris.

Blancanales slapped the water angrily. He'd failed.

PASSING OVER the fiery remains of the Shivagi, Bien Phyr
ignored the survivor who'd landed in the river below. He
had more important business to attend to than picking off
strays. He lost radio contact with the soldiers in Bagan but
figured they were busy laying into the demonstrators with
the Y-25. He would help them wrap things up before moving on to Raitiph. Phyr had used only one of his R-27R1s.
There were three more cradled on the wing pylons.
Strapped tight to the underside of each missile's fuselage
were two of the sarin bombs taken from the R&D laboratory back at Dwiti. From what he'd been told while en route
to Bagan, there were thousands gathering outside the temples. If he had to, Phyr would make three passes over the
site, each time bombarding the plain. Yes, as Dr. Makirt
had explained, he knew the sarin wouldn't be as effective
as if they'd been able to trap the dissidents inside the temples, but between the missiles and the three sarin death
clouds they would unleash upon detonation, Phyr was certain there would be enough casualties to break the spirit of
the protesters. Perhaps, in the years to come, the surviving
fools would speak of what was about to happen in Bagan
with the same fearful awe as they spoke of the Four Eights.
He might even help them out, giving them a catchy slogan
by which to remember his part in their undoing.

"Phyr rains," he muttered, turning his attention to the heads-up display targeting the distant ruins. "Phyr rains on Bagan."

"I CAN'T GET OVER IT!" Daw Bodta Paing exclaimed to her brother, her eyes red from crying. Her tears, however, were tears of joy. "I just can't get over it!"

"I know," Aung said. "It's like a miracle."

Standing alongside Lon Mar beneath the uppermost spire of Thatbyinnyu Temple, the son and daughter of Soe Paing stared down at the ever-growing crowd of demonstrators gathered amid the ancient monuments of Bagan. Several times Aung and Daw Bodta had thought the last of the ralliers had finally come forward to join those who'd made the march from Nyaung-U, only to see yet another group materialize out of the darkness of yet another temple entrance. Now, instead of a few hundred souls dwarfed by the immensity of the surrounding structures, the vast green plain was a roiling sea of more than a hundred thousand— men, women and children of all ages joined together, their colorful *longyis* blending into one large, collective fabric, like a flag. And of all the colors, one predominated: emerald green, symbolizing the cause of freedom that had brought them all here.

"Remember the Four Eights!" the masses cried out. "Freedom now, freedom forever!"

And all of it—from the arrival of the marchers to the brief skirmish atop the hillock in which two Americans had seized control of the antiaircraft vehicle—had been captured by the roving eye of Lon Mar's camcorder and, as planned, successfully passed along the makeshift patchwork of relay routers to transmitters reaching far beyond the country's troubled borders. This day wouldn't be a repeat of the Four Eights. This day, the media hadn't been blacked out. The whole world was watching.

"It's not *like* a miracle," Lon Mar said without taking his eye from the viewfinder. "It *is* a miracle!"

"If only Father could be here to see this," Daw Bodta told her brother. "He would be so happy and—"

Aung silenced his sister, placing a finger over her lips. Daw Bodta was puzzled at first, but then, for the first time, she heard, above the clamor of the throng below, the echo of a distant explosion miles to the south. The sound soon faded, only to be replaced by an ominous roar high up in the heavens.

"Thunder?" Daw Bodta whispered hopefully.

Aung shook his head. She saw him looking southward and tracked his gaze, then felt a sudden shiver snake its way down her spine. Dropping out of a bank of thin clouds and headed directly toward them was a fighter jet.

"No," Daw Bodta murmured. "No…"

Aung drew his sister close to him and started to lead her inside the temple. "Come," he called out to Lon Mar.

"No!" Lon Mar responded. Already he had turned his camera and pointed it at the approaching jet, continuing to keep his finger on the recording button. "Everyone must know what the Tatmadaw have stooped to."

Down below, others saw the jet and the chanting broke off, replaced by screams and cries. The crowd scattered in all directions, some fleeing back inside the temples, others racing farther out into the plains. Then, out of the corner of his eye, Lon Mar saw a puff of smoke. Glancing over his shoulder, he saw that the cloud was drifting up from the launch pod of the Y-25 LAV-AD perched on the far hillock. He could see the missile streaking toward the oncoming jet and hurried to capture the moment on camera. He was just bringing the jet back into focus when there was a blinding flash in the air, following almost immediately by a fierce explosion. Through the viewfinder, he tracked the blazing MiG-29 as it plummeted earthward like a fallen meteor, landing with a deafening crash in a field more than two miles away.

"It's all right!" he shouted to Aung and Daw Bodta. "It's all right! You can come out!"

The brother and sister reemerged from the temple and watched the quickly dying fire in the distance, then looked once more to the heavens, straining to hear if any more jets were on the way. They heard nothing, however, save for the cries of the people below. Over their shock, they were slowly drawing back together. Soon they had resumed their chant. "Freedom now, freedom forever! Freedom now, freedom forever!"

GADGETS SCHWARZ PEERED UP through the turret hatch of the Y-25 LAV-AD and asked Lyons, "How'd we do?"

"We did great. Stopped that bastard in his tracks!"

Schwarz let out a whoop, then keyed his headset, passing along the news to Buck Greene, whose long-distance coaching had enabled Schwarz to launch the Stinger that had put an end, once and for all, to General Bien Phyr's dreams of glory.

"Bucky, my boy!" Schwarz told the security chief, "You just took over the league lead in assists!"

Schwarz wrapped up with Greene, then climbed up out of the hatch, joining Lyons atop the turret.

"I guess we ought to fire up this minitank and go fetch Pol," he said. The men had already received word from Akira Tokaido that sat-cams had witnessed Blancanales's watery landing in the Yeosin Chaung River after his leap from the doomed Shivagi 4-H.

"In a minute," Lyons said quietly. He was staring down at the throng gathered around the temples of Bagan, determined to finish their rally. Their cries carried all the way up to the hillock, a hundred thousand voices speaking on behalf of an entire nation.

"Freedom now, freedom forever!"

"Who knows," Lyons murmured. "Maybe this time it'll be more than just talk."

THE Destroyer®

UNNATURAL SELECTION

Sexy scientist Dr. Judith White, who first attempted to repopulate the earth with mutant, man-eating tiger people, is back with a new plan for world domination. She's putting her formula into a brand of bottled water that's become all the rage in Manhattan's boardrooms and cocktail parties. Remo and Chiun hit the Big Apple and find that it literally is a jungle—even the cops have gone carnivorous! And when one of CURE's own falls prey to Dr. White's diabolical scheme, his top secrets may give the insane doctor the extra bite she needs to eat The Destroyer for lunch!

Available in April 2003 at your favorite retail outlet.

Or order your copy now by sending your name, address, zip or postal code, along with a check or money order (please do not send cash) for $6.50 for each book ordered ($7.99 in Canada), plus 75¢ postage and handling ($1.00 in Canada), payable to Gold Eagle Books, to:

In the U.S.	In Canada
Gold Eagle Books	Gold Eagle Books
3010 Walden Avenue	P.O. Box 636
P.O. Box 9077	Fort Erie, Ontario
Buffalo, NY 14269-9077	L2A 5X3

GOLD EAGLE®

Please specify book title with your order.
Canadian residents add applicable federal and provincial taxes.

GDEST131

James Axler
Outlanders

TALON AND FANG

Kane finds himself thrown twenty-five years into a parallel future, a world where the mysterious Imperator has seemingly restored civilization to America. In this alternate reality, only Kane and Grant have survived, and the spilled blood has left them estranged. Yet Kane is certain that somewhere in time lies a different path to tomorrow's reality—and his obsession may give humanity their last chance to battle past and future as a sinister madman controls the secret heart of the world.

In the Outlands, the shocking truth is humanity's last hope.

Or order your copy now by sending your name, address, zip or postal code, along with a check or money order (please do not send cash) for $6.50 for each book ordered ($7.99 in Canada), plus 75¢ postage and handling ($1.00 in Canada), payable to Gold Eagle Books, to:

In the U.S.	In Canada
Gold Eagle Books	Gold Eagle Books
3010 Walden Avenue	P.O. Box 636
P.O. Box 9077	Fort Erie, Ontario
Buffalo, NY 14269-9077	L2A 5X3

Please specify book title with your order.
Canadian residents add applicable federal and provincial taxes.

GOUT25

DEATH LANDS®

Damnation Road Show

*Available in June 2003
at your favorite retail outlet.*

Eerie remnants of preDark times linger a century after the nuclear blowout. But a traveling road show gives new meaning to the word *chilling.* Ryan and his warrior group have witnessed this carny's handiwork in the ruins and victims of unsuspecting villes. Even facing tremendous odds does nothing to deter the companions from challenging this wandering death merchant and an army of circus freaks. And no one is aware that a steel-eyed monster from the past is preparing a private act that would give Ryan star billing....